say no more

Also by N. Gemini Sasson:

Say That Again (A Faderville Novel)

Say Something (A Faderville Novel)

Memories and Matchsticks (Sam McNamee Mystery #1)

Lies and Letters (Sam McNamee Mystery #2)

The Crown in the Heather (The Bruce Trilogy: Book I)

Worth Dying For (The Bruce Trilogy: Book II)

The Honor Due a King (The Bruce Trilogy: Book III)

*Isabeau: A Novel of Queen Isabella
and Sir Roger Mortimer*

*The King Must Die:
A Novel of Edward III*

*Uneasy Lies the Crown:
A Novel of Owain Glyndwr*

In the Time of Kings

say no more

N. GEMINI SASSON

SAY NO MORE

ISBN 978-1-9393440-4-5 (paperback)

Library of Congress Control No. 2014903143

For more details about N. Gemini Sasson and her books, go to:
www.ngeminisasson.com

Or become a 'fan' at:
www.facebook.com/NGeminiSasson

You can also sign up to learn about new releases via e-mail at:
http://eepurl.com/vSA6z

Cover art: Ebook Launch

This book is dedicated to all the old dogs,
good dogs, and misunderstood dogs.

And to all the loved ones watching over us,
waiting to see us again.

SAY NO MORE

A dog's love is forever.

A story of love, hope, and never-ending loyalty — as told by the dog.

Cam McHugh died in a tragic farming accident. He has a message for his son, Hunter, and only his dog can hear him.

Halo is no ordinary dog. Not only can she see ghosts, she can talk to them, too. If only she could tell Hunter that death doesn't mean an end to being around the ones we love, maybe she could help him find his voice again. Unfortunately, she may never have the chance.

Dognapped by the man who threatens to destroy the only family she has ever known, Halo must escape and find her way home — hundreds of miles away.

Halo's story is for those who want to believe there are places such as Heaven and the Rainbow Bridge, and that angels are always watching over us.

(This book is intended for adults and young adults. Some elements may not be suitable for young children.)

prologue

A thousand scents surround me: honeysuckle and hyacinth, grubs burrowing through damp earth, stagnant water mingling with black muck at pond's edge … and bacon frying. I lick my lips and swallow. It's all I can do to not put my nose to the air and explore until I discover their source.

But I have to stay here. It's almost time.

I have something very important to do. I'm waiting. For him. And I'll be here when he comes. The first one he'll see.

It seems like it's been forever, yet I can remember every detail about him, as if I left him only minutes ago.

Tender shoots of spring grass tickle my feet. I lower my head until my chin rests on the ground and nibble at them while I wait. After all, I don't know how long it will be.

To my right, a beetle scampers down a blade of grass before disappearing into the dense carpet of green. My ears perk. I swear I hear its tiny feet rustling. Or maybe that's the sound of its jaws sawing away on moist stems?

The barest of breezes tugs at my hair. There is a fluttering inside my nostrils. I lift my head, inhale. It'll rain soon. I know it before I hear the low rumble in the sky or see the clouds darkening on the horizon. I'm not scared of the thunder here. I became that way when I was old. In The Time Before This. But now I'm young again. Here, there is excitement in everything, wonder in the familiar.

Rising, I look toward the top of the hill where the great oak stands. Its boughs are twice as thick around as my middle. Its crown spreads far, every branch densely cloaked in leaves of green. In sunlight, it shields me from the heat. In rain, it keeps me dry. When the wind kicks up and the air cools, there is a little pocket in the earth between the sprawling roots where I have dug a hole and can curl up. Here, no one cares if I dig. It is expected.

The walk is long and steep, but my bones do not weary. I am young again. And I would climb a hill ten times as high, ten times over, ten days straight, just to see him one more time. My heart leaps at the thought.

He'll come. I know he will.

As I reach the top, a squirrel darts forth and stares me straight in the eye. My heart quickens. Her gray tail stiffens above her back like a bottle brush, then flicks to the side. Whiskers twitch nervously. I crouch in the tall grass, watching, patient. Boldly, she races forward and plucks an acorn from the ground. She clutches it to her chest, as if to say, "Mine, mine, mine."

Stupid beady-eyed creature. I don't want the acorn. I can think of tastier things. Squirrel, for one.

I lift a foot, creep forward, pause, step again. Her tail quivers. My head low, I move through the grass. So close now I can smell the wood scent on her fur and —

"Halo! Haaalooooooo!"

In a blur, the squirrel whips around and scrabbles up the furrowed bark of the oak, the knobby acorn stuffed in her tiny mouth. She stops above the first bough, gazes down at me, and huffs her cheeks in triumph. Then with another arrogant flick of her tail, she ascends in a spiral, and I lose her form in the tangle of branches and scattering of leaves. Far above, baby squirrels chatter in greeting.

"Halo?" the Old Man calls. "What're you doing up there, girl?"

At the base of the hill, the Old Man stands, gripping a shepherd's crook. It's merely for show. I suppose it makes him feel important, like he's in charge of things, but I don't really need him to tell me what to do. At least not as much as he thinks.

He walks partway up, tapping the bottom of the crook along the ground as he goes. Here, he doesn't need it to lean on. His steps are slow but sure. His spine, once bent, is now straight and strong. He reaches the top of the hill, his breath barely audible, but a sheen of sweat glistens above his brow.

My belly low, I slink to him, then sit and wait obediently. Gone from his face is the mapwork of blue veins beneath papery skin, although there are still creases around his eyes from squinting into the sun for so many years. He reaches his hand out, lets it hover above my head. I sniff his fingers. They're still spotted with age, but they're no longer gnarled. He scratches gently behind my ears.

I lean against his knee as his fingernails tickle my neck and then my back.

"Come on, Halo. We have to move the sheep before the storm blows in."

Silly man. There are no coyotes here. They have their own heaven, separate from ours.

He steps away and pats his leg, but I don't move. Doesn't he understand? I'm waiting for someone. What if he finally shows up and I'm not here? I can't leave my post. This is my job, my responsibility, my duty. Mine alone. My honor depends on it.

The Old Man frowns sympathetically at me. His shoulders lift in a shrug, emphasizing the wrinkles in that same old tatty shirt he always wears. I've always loved the smell of it and hated whenever he washed it. I hate the smell of soap. And shampoo. Things should

3

smell as they're meant to, not like almonds or coconut milk or baby powder.

"We were quite a team, weren't we, girl?" His mouth curves into a grin. Crinkles form at the corners of his eyes.

"All the ribbons, the belt buckles . . ." His voice softens as he reminisces. "All those titles . . . But they don't really mean a thing, do they?"

No, they don't. They're only things: colored scraps of cloth, metal discs, letters on a piece of paper. What matters were the many hours we spent in the field gathering the sheep, the cold mornings when we tiptoed into the barn to check on the new lambs, the times he let me ride in the cab of the pick-up next to him. I worked hard then, but I was happy. So was he. There was pride in a good day's work.

"You were always there when I needed you, Halo. Always. That's what matters."

"It is," I say. "And you were there for me."

Nodding, he turns to go, the wooden staff trailing behind him. The grass ripples in a rising wind and the bleating of sheep carries across the valley. Do the simple creatures ever tire of being afraid?

I gaze across the river, over the arc of many colors that is the bridge to here: the Other Side. There's no one there. Yet. If I hurry, I can help the Old Man and be back before the boy comes.

And he will. Because I'm waiting. Like any good dog would.

chapter 1

Warm hands encircled my ribs and lifted me up. Too sleepy yet to open my eyes, I sniffed the air. I knew the scent. She was the one who cared for my mother. The one who filled her water dish and brought her bones to gnaw on. The one who piled us in the basket and laid down clean blankets in our box, then put us back one at a time, as she kissed us each softly on the head and said our names.

Next to my mother, I loved Lise best. More than playing with my brothers and sisters. Just slightly more than the warm, yummy slop she put on the plates for us to lap up. Even more than naps — although right now, I was very, *very* tired.

I'd had a hard day, you see. I climbed on top of my brother Scout and fell out of the box. Then I wandered around for a long, long time on the cool, slippery floor, searching for my mother. My legs, not being very strong yet, slid in all directions until they splayed out from my body and my chest hit the floor. I tried to get up, but the same thing happened the next time. I tried again and again, with the same results. I grew more frustrated with each attempt, and yet more determined, even though my coordination was poor and my legs were wobbly. I decided to give it one last try, wiggling my body and bracing my front feet before me.

I was sitting. This was good. I tucked my hind feet beneath me and pushed my rear end up. I was standing!

But only for a second. My front legs careened from beneath me. My chin whacked the floor. That was when I started to wail. It seemed like forever before my mother came. She nuzzled me, licked me from end to end, and finally lay down beside me. Somehow, I squirmed my way to her belly and ate my fill. My tummy full, I dozed off. Later I awoke, aware of the soft, fuzzy blanket beneath me and my brothers and sisters pressed to either side of me. I was too big by now for my mother to carry in her mouth, so it must have been Lise who put me back.

It was Lise's arms in which I was now cradled. Her fingertips stroked my bare tummy. She stopped. I kicked my legs and groaned to let her know I didn't like it when she quit.

Ever so slightly, she squeezed me. "Oh, Halo. You're so demanding." She caressed my belly, my ribs, the insides of my legs. It felt so good. How wonderful to have a human who could do these things for you.

She let out a long sigh. "And why are you the one who always gets in trouble, huh? Nobody else has been out of the whelping box and yet you've managed it five times in just the past two days. I thought for sure it was a fluke, a lucky accident, but no, I think you've gone and figured it out. I'll be keeping an eye on you, Miss Halo. You're giving me gray hairs already, and I'm not even thirty."

She was praising me. I could tell by her voice. It meant I was a good puppy. Better than good. The best. And she loved me more than the others. That was easy to see. That's why I kept getting out. So she'd come and praise me for being so smart. The others were lazy and fat and dumb. But not me. I was different. Better. Clearly, I was her favorite.

Lise hooked her thumbs under my front legs and held me up. I turned my head to the side and yawned to let her know I needed to finish my nap. Later, when I wanted her to hold me and talk to me, I'd cry out. But right now I needed to rest. Ignoring my signal, she twisted my body sideways and touched her nose to mine.

"Hey, sleepy head," she said, her breath stirring my whiskers. "I have a special feeling about you."

I blinked, forced my eyes open. Her face swam fuzzily before me. Pulling her head back, she tilted it thoughtfully and stared at me for a long time. So long my eyes almost drifted shut again before her voice startled me into alertness.

"At least you're quiet." She swung my pudgy back legs from side to side. "Most of the time. Well ... for now."

On cue, one of the other puppies let out a loud, shrill bark. Lise shook her head. It was Tar, the big nearly solid black girl. She was always barking. I found it annoying. Sometimes I bit her in the haunch to make her stop.

Grunting, I squirmed in Lise's hold, then went stiff. She took the hint — finally — and set me back down, close to my mother's front paws. I crawled up next to Mother's ruff and curled into the softness of her fur.

"You're a good mama, Bit," Lise said to my mother. "I have a hard enough time running after one, let alone seven. I don't know how you do it."

What a wonderful, glorious world it was. We had each other to play with, Mother to clean us and feed us, Lise to give us kisses and tummy rubs. What more could we ever need or want? What more could there possibly be?

—o00o—

I hung with my front paws hooked over the edge of the box. What was this ... this *thing* in front of me? I looked up, and up, and up. It was tall, whatever it was. I wedged my nose between the cold wire bars and pushed. Nothing. I pushed harder. It wouldn't yield.

Did Lise put this here? And why? How was I supposed to explore when I couldn't get out?

My legs growing tired, I let go and fell on my rump. Where was Scout? I had used him to climb up only a minute ago.

Sharp teeth pierced one of my back feet. I whipped around to see Scout bowing before me, his front lowered to the ground and his butt raised in the air. His little stumpy tail wagged back and forth. The bobtail was a trait of our breed, the Australian Shepherd. He scooted back, growled at me, then charged.

I raised my chin and let out the biggest, meanest bark I could muster. Oblivious to my warning, Scout barreled into me. I toppled over backward. His weight pinned me to the floor, crushing the air from my chest.

Enough of this! I rolled to one side, dumping him on his back so that his fat legs stuck up in the air. He couldn't keep attacking me when my back was turned. It was going to stop *now*.

So I pounced on him, planting my front feet on his round, heaving chest. His legs stiffened. He tried to twist sideways, but I had him trapped. I lowered my face, bared my teeth, and barked relentlessly.

Yawning and stretching, Cooper and Tar sat up, then tottered toward us, curious, yet not bold enough to join in. Mickey, Jet, and Ruby slept on, unaware of the brawl unfolding.

Scout quivered. His legs relaxed and folded. He turned his head away and I took this as a sign of submission, although I stood there a few moments longer, glaring at him menacingly. I was superior. Next to Mother, I was the boss of everyone.

My hackles raised, I barked again, elated at my triumph. Suddenly, my other brother Cooper looked up from the puppy pile next to Mother, his bum wagging back and forth. He focused his gaze on something above me. *What the —?*

A hand clamped on the loose skin at the back of my neck, hoisting me up. I stared into Lise's eyes. They narrowed in anger. She shook me once, firmly.

"What am I going to do with you, little one? Escaping the whelping box, causing fights . . . Maybe you just have too much energy?" She blew out a breath, stirring the yellow bangs from her forehead. "Come on. Time for new adventures."

She tucked me in the crook of her elbow and we walked past the two big boxes that made noise. Washer and dryer, she called them. Yesterday, she dropped a sock when taking a load out. I found it and when she didn't come to get me right away, I chewed a hole right through it. I hadn't meant to. Chomping on it felt good to my achy gums. She wasn't happy, but if she doesn't want to share, she should take her things with her and guard them more closely.

The door squeaked as Lise shouldered it open. Gently, she lowered me to the floor. It was slippery, like in the other room, but this room was much, *much* bigger. I stood unsteadily, wary of moving too fast, as I took everything in. The walls were lined with wooden boxes with built-in doors. Curtains fluttered around an open window.

I sniffed the air. Smells curled inside my nose. Glorious smells. My tummy grumbled. *Food!*

I took off toward the tall, shiny box — source of all the wonderful smells — trying to dig my nails in, but the floor was slick. A tangle of chair and table legs loomed before me like a forest of ancient trees. I veered left, but another column of wood blocked my way. A quick spin to the right and I avoided it, only to have a third appear out of nowhere. I planted my front feet to stop myself, but just kept sliding, sliding —

Bam!

I lay sprawled on the tile floor. My head was ringing. And I'd jammed a toe. My foot started to throb. I let out a long, pitiful howl to let Lise know I needed attention — *now!*

"Oh, Halo." She stooped before me. "If you can't manage not to hurt yourself in the kitchen, how am I ever going to let you outside?"

Outside? I sprang to my feet, wagging my nub. Suddenly, my foot didn't hurt so much. *Yes, outside!* I gave a short, excited bark. Because that's what my mother did when Lise said the word 'outside'. I had no idea what it was. But it must have been a fabulous, super-exciting thing. Maybe a special toy. Or food. Or a magical place.

Outside! Outside! I barked.

"Yes, yes. I get the idea." She reached out to scoop me up. I began to toddle toward her, limping for dramatic purposes so she didn't forget to carry me, when another puppy appeared next to Lise — a very strange-looking puppy. Bigger than me, but not nearly as big as Mother. With pointy ears, wiry whiskers, and a long, fluffy gray tail. Most unbecoming. Downright ugly, in fact.

Twitching a pink triangular nose, it studied me in an oddly disturbing way. I took a step and woofed. It arched its back, hair standing on end, and drew its lips up to show pointy teeth. From deep in its throat, a low growl emanated, and then a demonic hiss issued forth.

Every hair on my body stood on end. A shiver of fear zinged down my backbone, urging me to run for my life, but I was frozen, couldn't move.

What was that ... that *thing?*

Its eyes glowed green, little slatted pupils reflecting the darkness within. Yes, I knew what it was now. All dogs knew. *That* was Evil Incarnate. Cause of all chaos. Enemy of all dogs.

And it must be killed before it hurt Lise or my littermates.

My muscles coiled tight. I bared my teeth. I wasn't afraid to bite. To kill even, if lives depended on it. The creature lifted a paw, drew back. I exploded forward, my nails scrabbling over the slick floor.

This will be a fight to the death!

I slammed the pads of my feet before me to take my stance. The devil flicked a tiny paw and —

A single, razor-sharp claw sliced the air. I jerked my head sideways, but not quickly enough. Its hook connected with the leather of my nose. It stung like a knife to my flesh. I yowled.

I've been cut! I've been cut! Help me, I'm bleeding!

My rump slammed into the devil's side, knocking him across the floor. We collided against the wall. But before he could strike again, I gathered myself and ran to Lise's feet. To protect her, of course.

"Shhh, shhh, little one." She gathered me in her arms and rocked me. "It's just a scratch. Trust me, that cat is more afraid of you than you are of him. Isn't that so, Trouble?" She looked past me toward where the cat had landed, but he was long gone. Apparently, I had made my point.

"What's going on here?" A deep voice sounded from behind her.

I squirmed against her chest to look over her shoulder. Lise's mate, Cameron, stepped through the door from outside. Scents, begging to be discovered, wafted in around him. I lifted my nose and inhaled.

"Barely a drop of blood." Laughing, he swiped a calloused thumb at my nose. "Poor little puppy. Sounded like you were going to die."

"Hey, Cam." Lise juggled me over to her hip and smacked her lips against Cam's. "How's the baling going?"

"Good. Just praying the rain holds off."

She frowned at him. "So you're not sitting down to dinner? Again?"

"Just helping Dad out, honey."

"I understand, but you're at the farm almost every day. Can't he get someone else to help, like one of the teenage boys around here?"

"Most are either too young or have other jobs. Jobs that don't break your back. It was easier on Dad when Ben and Drew were still around."

11

"Yeah, well, your brothers shouldn't have moved out of state after he paid for their college. You didn't."

"Because you were here." He slid an arm around her waist and nuzzled between her neck and shoulder. He pulled her closer, trailing little kisses from her chin to her collarbone.

I couldn't ... breathe. I was being crushed between them. It was worse than having my brothers and sisters piled on top of me. I grunted to let them know I was short on air. When that didn't work, I kicked my feet, trying to push them apart.

"Cam ..." Lise murmured, "the puppy."

Laughter rumbled from his chest. I loved the sound. It meant he was happy. If I could laugh, I would. I sneezed instead. It was the closest I could manage. He lifted me from Lise's arms and touched his forehead to the top of my skull, so that his face was close to mine. "You *are* keeping this one, right?"

"Oh, Cam, you know it's too early to decide. Besides, I kind of had my eye on that flashy red tri boy — Scout."

"Trust me, Lise, this red merle girl — she's the one. There's something special about her. Something ... different." He handed me back to her. "What do you call her?"

"Halo. But why do you like her so much? She's the runt, you know."

"Just a feeling. Don't ask why." He ruffled the fur on my neck, then patted me once hard on top of the head. "Someone has to look after you and Hunter if anything ever happens to me. This one's fierce."

"Don't talk that way, Cam. Anyway, I'm trying to build a breeding program. I can't go on 'feelings'. I have to pick the one with the best structure and type and —"

He silenced her with a long kiss. This time she was careful to hold me off to the side. Her eyes drifted shut. She took a deep breath, shivered. Was she cold? Afraid? Humans made very little sense sometimes.

"Maybe you could take pipsqueak here back to her mother?" Cam looked into her eyes, grinned. "I have forty-five minutes before I need to be back out in the field. You can stand here and talk — or join me in the shower. So, what d'you wanna do?"

Her eyelids fluttered. She glanced dreamily down at Cam's hand as she squeezed it. "The usual place?"

"Meet you there." He dashed from the room, tugging his shirt over his head. "Just let me rinse the dust off first."

Lise spun around to shout over her shoulder, "Not too hot!"

"Lukewarm! Got it!" he yelled back.

I bounced in her arms as she jogged down the short hallway to the laundry room. Then she plopped me down on the other side of the baby gate, not even bothering to put me in the nest. Mother lifted her head lazily from inside the box to look at me, blew out a breath, and laid her head back down. Scout was slurping away at her teat, his belly already plumped up like an engorged tick.

When I looked back up, Lise was no longer there. Whatever happened to 'outside'? I had to pee. Now. So I did. Lise or Mother would clean it up later. When that was done, I waited for Mother to come out, but she was locked inside that cage around the box.

I was alone. And hungry. My stomach twisted in pain. I might *die* if I didn't eat soon.

So I cried awhile, ramping up my volume as time went on. Desperate for a response, I hooked my front feet in the latticework of the baby gate, howling as loud as I could so Lise would hear me. But there were strange noises coming from the other end of the house — laughter, squealing, pipes clanging as water rushed through them, then muffled voices — drowning out my pleas. I shoved a back foot into one of the holes, pushed myself up, and reached with a front paw. Soon, I was hanging at the top. Carefully, I lifted a back foot again, my toes swinging through the air until they landed on another foothold. I pushed myself over and —

Thump!

Momentarily dazed, I lay beside the gate, waiting for someone to rescue me. But no one came. No one cared if I was okay or had just broken every bone in my body.

I shook myself off and trotted across the floor, more sure-footed this time. I could still smell the Devil-Cat, but I didn't see him. I slowed my pace, casting looks from side to side, behind me, pausing when I reached the edge of the big room to stare down the long narrow space where Cam had disappeared. There were doors on both sides of the wall. All closed.

I stood there, listening. But it was quiet now. I couldn't tell which door they were behind. I looked around. It was a long way back to the laundry room. A yawn pushed up from my chest. I was tired. Needed a nap. After that, I'd go back to Mother. Climb over the gate. The Devil wouldn't dare go in there with Mother around to guard me.

Again, I looked down the long narrow room lined with doors. That was when I saw Cam's shirt crumpled in a wad halfway down. The outside smells on it called to me. I went to it, sniffed, let the scent of crushed green stems and earth fill my lungs. Lay down. Stretched my legs. Closed my eyes. Just for a minute.

In my dreams, strong, protective arms cradled me. A kiss alighted on my brow. Scruff whisked across my cheek.

"You're the one," Cam's voice whispered. "Watch over my family, okay? They're going to need you."

chapter 2

The door creaked as Cam pushed it open. He put me down in the front seat of his truck, closed it, and got in on the other side.

Lise stepped up on the running board to lean in through the open window on my side. Clutched at her hip, their little boy Hunter tugged at his lower lip.

"Are you sure you want to take Halo with you?" Lise said. "She's barely twelve weeks old. She'll probably throw up. You won't even let me eat carry-out in here. Besides, you really should have her in a crate. What if she climbs onto your lap while you're driving? Puppies are distracting. You could crash, you know."

"Seriously, Lise, don't worry. I'm just going a few miles down the road. I doubt she'll get sick in the amount of time it takes us to get to Dad's house. Besides, if she's going to be my dog, you said it was okay for her to ride shotgun with me when I went to do chores."

"Yeah, but —"

He poked a finger in her direction. "You said she could, remember? At least I'm letting her ride in the cab. My dad used to make the dogs sit in the bed."

Lise opened the rear door of the cab and buckled Hunter in his car seat. After shutting the door, she reclaimed her spot on the running board.

I dug at my new collar with the nails of my back foot. *Itchy, itchy!* It hung around my neck like a yoke of stone, a supposed symbol of my inferior status to humankind. I scratched furiously at it, waiting for her to realize how uncomfortable it was and take it off, but she simply hissed 'Stop it!' at me.

Lise's nose crinkled as her gaze returned to Cam. "Okay, okay." Subtly, she extended her hand over my head and dropped something beside me. It had a shiny metal clip on one end and a loop on the other. "You'll keep a leash on her while you're there, won't you?"

What? And drag me around like a circus monkey? I don't think so!

A barely audible sigh escaped Cam.

"Please?" Lise added, gripping the inside edge of the door.

"All right, all right. I won't let her out of my sight." He hooked the snap of the leash onto a link in my collar. I didn't like it there. It was heavy. I bit at his hands to make him stop, but he pinched my mouth shut and gave me a firm 'No!'

When he let go, I sneezed. Hunter laughed. I sneezed again, which sent him into a fit of delight. He had just turned five, so not quite old enough to go to school himself, which meant Cam's mother, Estelle, would be taking care of him today while Lise went to work. Estelle and Lise had a tenuous relationship at best. It was easy to see Lise's irritation every time she got off the phone with her.

"Don't let her near the cows," Lise said over Hunter's laughter.

"Well, that's kind of impossible, seeing as how I'm going there to help take care of them."

"Cameron Scott McHugh, don't you dare —"

"I got it, I got it. Don't let her near the cows, right." He slipped the key into the ignition and twisted it. The engine coughed, sputtered, and then roared to life. He yanked the shifter into reverse, but his foot was still locked against the brake. "I'll be back by supper tonight. Mom and Dad have a dinner date with the DeLeons at 5:00."

Lise stared at the side of Cam's face until he turned his head.

"What?" Cam said. "Did I forget something?"

"No, just …" — she stepped down from the running board so I couldn't see her anymore and patted the outside of the door twice — "just be careful today, okay? And tell Estelle to keep an eye on Hunter. His asthma's been acting up lately."

"I will, hun. See you at 4:30." He blew her a kiss. Lise's open hand appeared briefly through the window. Her fingers snapped shut, then disappeared.

"You can have your kiss back," she said, "when you get home later."

"Okay. Promise not to keep you waiting. Have fun at school today."

"Yeah, right. We're talking about second graders. The first rule is always survival."

"See you later, then."

"Bye now."

"Bye, Mommy!" Hunter yelled. "Byyyyyyye!"

Chuckling, Cam eased off the brake. The truck rolled backward, jerked to a brief stop, then lurched forward. Through the open window, I saw the clouds spinning. I hopped over to the door and planted my paws on the armrest to raise myself up and look out. Trees whizzed by, low branches slapping the sides and top of Cam's big black truck as we rumbled down the lane.

In the little mirror next to the window, Lise stood before the house, its crisp white clapboard siding a stark contrast to the flaking green shutters. A minute ago she was very big. Now she was tiny. And how did she get inside the mirror? This confused me. Next to her sat my mother, Bit, looking very unimpressed with the fact that I was flying as fast as a bird down the lane in the big wheeled monster Cam called 'The Ram'.

Bit and Lise got smaller and smaller and smaller. I looked toward the rear of the truck. There, I saw them only a moment longer before they disappeared beyond the cloud of dust billowing out behind the truck's big rear wheels. We turned a corner and the house, too, vanished.

I leaned out further, wind beating against my face, my ears flapping back. I smelled clover, freshly cut grass, manure from those stupid creatures, or sheep, that Lise called 'The Girls', which she said were for training and keeping the grass down. That was when I saw them on the far side of a pasture as we drove by — ten big puffs of wool on skinny stick legs. Eating, like they constantly did. Around them were about a dozen miniature versions, the lambs, bouncing and bucking through the tall grass. They did this every day. Sometimes they stopped, looked up, and bleated franticly when they realized they'd lost their mothers. The ewes bleated back to give their location and the lambs leaped to them, suckled a bit, and then got lost again. They were even dumber than their mothers. No wonder Bit had to help Lise put them away in the barn every night so the coyotes didn't get them.

Cam snagged my collar and yanked me back down to the seat. He flicked a switch on his side of the truck and the glass in my window slid upward, so I couldn't stick my head out anymore. I stood on the armrest and pressed my nose to the glass, watching new sights appear with every passing second. Who knew the world was so big? That there was so much to be discovered and explored?

A few weeks ago, most of my brothers and sisters had disappeared one by one, until only Scout and I were left. It always began the same. The dogs outside would erupt into a chorus of barks, alerting everyone to visitors. Lise or Cam would poke their head out the back door and shout, "Knock it off!", which was our cue to be silent so that they could assess whether or not there was any threat of danger. In my opinion, they often made those decisions too quickly. Humans were shifty creatures. They could open doors with their long, nimble fingers, and they apparently communicated with one another through small devices held to their heads or stuck right inside their ears. With those capabilities, who knew what they might try to steal from us? Any one of them could snatch a bag of our kibble, toss it inside a car, and be gone in seconds.

Now they were stealing puppies. I'd be darned if they took me away from Lise and Cam. I wasn't going anywhere.

Cam turned the radio on and fiddled with the knob until he got to a certain song. "Ah, my man Keith. Lise loves it when I sing Keith Urban songs to her." He peered into the rearview mirror at Hunter. "Wanna sing with me, Hunter?"

He cranked the volume up and began to croon. Hunter waved his hands above his head and joined in, but the words came out a little differently than Cam's.

"Take yo' wreckers, take yo' feet home,
Take yo' mommies, I don't eat 'em ..."

I was about to howl along with them when we pulled onto a bigger road and gained speed. The world blurred past. Suddenly, I saw a hundred things that needed investigating: buildings of different sizes and shapes, endless fields of hay, rows of wheat and corn and soybeans, thick patches of woodland, and then more houses, crowded close together. Cam slowed to a stop at a flashing red light where two roads crossed. He flipped a bar beside the steering wheel and an odd 'click-clack, click-clack' came from somewhere up front. I cocked my head sideways, listening, then tilted it the other way, trying to zero in on the sound. Cam laughed at me and ruffled the fur on top of my head.

A car pulled up beside us. In the front were two full-grown humans, but in the back I saw a little face peering up at me. A boy-child. Younger than Hunter. His mouth opened in an 'O', and he pointed a chubby finger at me. He had an honest face. Plump cheeks and a small nose. His smile matched the joy in his eyes. I would trust

19

him. We could be friends. I barked a hello. The boy flapped a hand at me and smiled. But soon the car pulled ahead, and the boy disappeared from view.

I was jerked back down onto the seat when Cam turned the truck onto another road. The houses became more spread out, the people fewer, and again the land opened up to far-reaching fields and expanses of rolling pasture. Beasts, bigger than the sheep but less shaggy, clustered near a muddy stream. Their great black eyes were vacant and lacking in intelligence, but one glance told me they were sturdy creatures who could shatter a dog's ribs with one well-timed kick of their hooves.

The truck slowed, turned down a bumpy lane like ours at home. A tall white house sat atop a hill at the end of the lane, framed by two enormous trees. Cam's dad — or Ray, as Lise called him — was standing on the front porch, one hand gripping the handle of his cane, the other clutching an old smoking pipe at his hip.

We rolled to a stop in the generous shade of one of the trees. A haze of dust drifted around us, lit golden by the morning sun. Cam tapped at the switch, and my window lowered.

"Hey, Dad," he called. "Like my new sidekick?"

Ray emerged through the brown veil of dust and peered into the truck. He was tall and lean like Cam, but with a gaunt face, sunken below his cheekbones, and eyes squinty from years in the sun. The pipe was pinched loosely between his teeth. It bobbed as he twisted his lips in thought. "The two-legged or the four-legged one?"

"The pup, Dad."

He pulled out the pipe, spit into the dirt, and put the pipe back in. "Kinda scrawny, ain't she?"

"She'll grow." Cam grabbed my collar before I could dodge his reach. He gathered me up, slid out his side, and put me on the ground before wrestling Hunter from his car seat. As soon as Hunter was out of the truck, he raced across the yard to the front door. His

20

grandmother, Estelle, let him in. Ducking my head, I searched beneath the truck.

Beside Ray sat a hulk of mottled gray and black fur. Another dog. He dipped his muzzle to glare at me. Black lips curled in a snarl, and a low growl vibrated deep in his throat. I lowered my belly to the ground and flattened my ears to show my submission. His growl grew louder, until finally Ray tapped him with his wooden cane and told him to hush.

"Well, if'n she don't," Ray said, "them small dogs are good in the loading chutes, 'cause they can get down low and snap at hocks to get 'em moving. Big dogs ain't quick enough to get outta the way. But she's gotta have the attitude to make up for it. Her daddy, Slick here, is the toughest cowdog east of the Rockies. Sure hope she don't take after her momma. Them show dogs don't have the sense God gave a —"

"Bit's a good chore dog, Dad. She does what we need her to." Cam tugged on my leash until I stood. I considered resisting — I was utterly humiliated by having that rope slung about my neck and had meant to make a point of letting everyone know — but I decided I was better off going where Cam did for now.

Cam gave another pull and I trotted beside him, staying close to his leg for safety. I snuck glances behind me as Ray walked around the truck with Slick just a pace behind. As far as I could tell, the old dog didn't seem to be watching me. Still, I was wary of him. I was even more wary of Ray's cane.

Cam's shin smacked me in the side of the head. I jumped forward, but it was in the wrong direction. Cam stumbled sideways. His foot came down on my paw. I let out a big yelp and he immediately jerked his leg away.

"Sorry, pal." Stooping over, he looked me sternly in the eye. "I was walking a straight line. Guess you'll pay better attention now."

"Say, when're you starting that new job?" Ray asked as he

hobbled by. Slick barely glanced at me as he slunk along in Ray's shadow.

"Next week. I'm looking forward to it. The commute on the last one was a killer. This one's just fifteen minutes down the highway. Pay's the same, but the vacation time and benefits are better."

"Why didn't you start this week?"

"Guess I figured you could use some help around here."

Ray halted in front of the barn, slipped the pipe into his pocket. "I've been thinking ... I can't hold down this place forever. Some days it's just too much. Been trying to talk Estelle into buying a little house in town, then maybe you and Lise, you know, you could —"

"Dad, that's generous of you. Really, it is. But it's just not the life Lise and I want. After all, I've seen you struggle in the hard years. I know how a drought can crush all your dreams into dust, or a flash flood can destroy years' worth of hard work."

"It's an honest life, Cameron. God's work. This country don't run without farmers and ranchers to feed everybody."

"I know, Dad. I know. It's just not for me. I like my work and taking care of a farm is more than a full time job. Plus, Lise and I want to be able to travel someday and —"

"Ain't nothing stopping you from going places now."

Cam studied the dirt at his feet. He had a look on his face like there was something stuck in his throat. "Well ... there *could* be, soon. We're trying for another."

Wherever this conversation was going they were both uncomfortable with it. The silence that dropped between them was more awkward than the argument they were having only moments ago. Whatever the deal was, Cam needed comforting. I jumped up and braced my front paws against his leg. He reached down as if to brush me away, but I licked at his fingers to let him know I was there. He smoothed the hair on top of my head, tweaked my nose, then glanced around. His eyes seemed to hone in on a large piece of machinery with two great big wheels in the back and two smaller ones up front.

"Now why in blazes would you take the roll-over bar off the old John Deere, Dad?"

"Wouldn't fit in the shed if I didn't. Doorway's too low. Nearly ripped the gutter off trying and decided that was the easiest way to fix the problem."

"Why not just store it in the big barn?"

"That's where the good combine goes — you know that, Cameron. 'Sides, this ol' rust bucket don't got many years left. No sense babying it."

Cam shook his head, opened his mouth as if to say something, then snapped it shut. Some arguments were better not had.

—o0Oo—

He'd forgotten about me. That's the only explanation there was. Said he'd 'be right back'. And yet there I sat, tied to that post. Growing hungrier, thirstier, hotter. An eternity.

Or at least it seemed like it.

Really, it had been a matter of minutes. Well, less than an hour. I was never sure about time. But the sun hadn't slipped any lower. Instead, it just hung there up there in the sky, blazing down on me. Singeing my fur. Making my tongue dry out and stick to the roof of my mouth.

I'd spent the day trailing along behind Cam as he cleaned out troughs and refilled them, letting me bite at the spray of the hose before he lowered it in. After that, we made a trip to the feed store and loaded up the bed of the truck. Hunter didn't go with us. He was busy 'making macaroons' with his grandmother, whatever those were. Back at the farm, Cam toted the big floppy sacks on his shoulders, two at a time, and piled them in a corner of the hog barn. He scraped manure from pens and stall floors with a broad shovel and tossed it into a wheelbarrow, then dumped it all in a pile outside the barn door. When he pushed the wheelbarrow back into the barn, I dashed over to the pile and helped myself to a treat.

He peeked around the door's edge. "Get out of there!"

I froze with the tasty, dried out patty in my mouth. Then I crunched down on it, gulping the little bits down as fast I could, because I knew what was going to happen next.

Two seconds later he had his fingers in my mouth, prying the manure out of it. That was when he'd clipped the leash back on me and tied me to this post. Then he left me here while he tromped out into the hayfield with Ray and Slick to round up a bull that had gotten out of his pasture. Unfortunately, a tall water tank stood between me and the view of them doing their work. That alone was cause for protest.

I lowered my chin between my paws and whimpered pathetically for dramatic purpose. But Cam was too far away to notice. Much longer and I'd have to start barking. Which never went over well.

The leash that tethered me to the fence post was thin, yet strong, made of three braided strips. I sniffed it, let the molecules stir my memory. Ah, leather. Now this I could do something about. When I was younger, I found one of Lise's leather sandals under the bed. Since it was on the floor, I figured it was fair game. So I eased my aching gums on it. Lise had been very unhappy when she discovered me beneath the bed, the straps worked loose from the sole, which I'd chewed in two. I learned then not to eat things that had Lise's scent on them. Or Cam's. Although Hunter didn't seem to care if I ate his plastic toys or shredded his coloring papers. My situation, however, was getting desperate now … I really shouldn't … I should wait …

But this was an exception.

Sneaking a look around to make sure Cam or Ray hadn't reappeared, I sank my teeth into the stiff leather and worked it back and forth between my jaws, until what little saliva I had softened it.

Off in the distance, the bull snorted and bellowed. Ray and Cam clapped their hands as they shouted back and forth. Slick barked once, twice. Why didn't *he* get in trouble for barking, huh?

Almost at once, two of the braids on the leash separated. I pinched and sawed at the remaining strip as fast as I could.

"Dad, Dad!" Cam's voice rose sharply. "Get back!"

Leaping to my feet, I bolted to the end of the leash. Ray and Cam were now in the corner of the pasture.

Then, I saw it. The bull rushing at Ray.

Ray swiped his cane sideways, then back, trying to fend off the raging beast. But it kept coming. Hooves slapped at the ground, flicked up chunks of earth. A great black mass hurtled toward an old, brittle-boned man.

The bull lowered his head, the gleaming tips of his horns pointed squarely at Ray's chest.

Desperate, Ray flung the cane in the bull's direction, but it fell harmlessly, lost in a sea of grass. He sucked his torso backward, dodged to the side. But his feet were unsteady, the movement too quick. Ray went down, covered his head. Fifty feet away still, Cam shouted.

A gray blur exploded around the side of the bull. Slick slammed his paws into the ground, no more than a few feet from the bull. He went in low, teeth flashing and clicking. Grabbed onto the bull's nose. Let go. Snapped again.

The bull threw his head back, nostrils flaring wide. Great sprays of snot flew from his nose. He lifted a hoof, stomped it. Lowered his head once more in challenge.

While Slick was having a standoff with an angry monster ten times his size, Ray had crawled further away. Cam snatched up the cane and rushed toward his father.

Slick needed no direction from Ray or Cam. He *knew* what to do. Like some foreknowledge that had been ingrained into his brain before birth. A genetic map waiting to instantly unfold when duty called for it. Millennia of instinct, shaped by selection, to a distinct purpose.

To protect. To control. To command.

Awed, I watched as Slick ducked low, timed his bites to perfection, burst beyond reach, went in again. In snatches, it looked like a stalemate — the bull's mass and might versus Slick's blinding speed and deadly accuracy. Gradually, though, Slick was edging the bull back, turning the beast's line of view away from Ray.

As the feud raged, Cam helped Ray to his feet. It seemed like hours that it took them to cross to the nearest gate, Ray's arm slung over Cam's taller shoulder.

His chest heaving, Ray grabbed onto the gate post and steadied himself. "Slick, that'll do!"

Instantly, Slick froze in his spot. He pulled his lips back, growled fiercely once more, and barked three times. The bull shook his shoulders, stepped back, stilled. Blood dripped from his nose. The battle had been decided.

Being the obedient cowdog he was, Slick turned to go to Ray.

The war, however, was not over.

The bull was right behind him. He came at Slick like a lead ball shot from a cannon.

"Slick!" Ray shouted. "Look back!"

At the sound of his name, Slick hesitated, unaware of the danger bearing down on him. It took just the tiniest of moments for the implication to register in Slick's keen mind. He flipped to his left, spinning with deft speed.

It was a moment too late. And in the wrong direction.

Because he had turned directly into the bull's path.

A black, muddied hoof smashed down on Slick's front leg, pulling him beneath the raging beast. Slick's curdling yelp was cut short as his body crumpled, rolled, disappeared beneath the shadow of the bull.

The bull circled around, bucking madly, his curved horns twisting through the air. The dappled mess of fur that was Slick lay trampled and defeated in his wake. The murderous beast pawed at the ground, bellowed his intent.

My heart seized. If there was still life left in old Slick, it wasn't much. Maybe just enough to yet pump blood through his veins, to draw a final breath. His chest was stone-still, his limbs unmoving.

I was sure he was dead.

"Goddamn you, Slick, you old buzzard!" Ray shouted through cupped hands, his voice cracking as he choked back a sob. "Get your lame ass up off the ground and back that sonofabitch steer down like you were taught to!"

And then ... Slick popped up. Well, not 'up' exactly. He was listing to one side, his left front leg dangling low from his shoulder. Ever so slightly, he swayed. Then steadied. Gingerly, he put his paw down. Limped a step. Then another. Until finally, he was trotting. Right at the bull.

I think the bull was just as shocked as the rest of us were. He stepped back, visibly fazed by Slick's miraculous resurrection. His tail swished at his rump as he dipped his head briefly. Sort of like a nod. Then he turned his bulk to one side, presenting his massive flank to Slick, and began back toward the barn.

Which was roughly in my direction.

It took a moment to sink in. The gate that stood between him and me was shut, but not latched. It was a sticky latch and had been a problem before, until Cam fixed it. But rain and rust had taken their toll. When Ray walked through the gate earlier, he had pushed the gate shut behind him like always, trusting that the latch would snap down on its own. Except it hadn't.

A gap, no more than a few inches wide, beckoned the bull onward. I may have mentioned that cattle are not always the smartest creatures. But one thing they are good at is finding a way out of wherever they are. Even if by accident. Like now.

See, I don't know that the bull looked around and saw the gate was partly open, but Slick had turned him that way and the gate was where he was used to going. What I figure Cam and Ray had meant to do was have Slick direct him to the far gate that led into a series of chutes, where they either loaded the stock into trailers or vaccinated them.

Something funny happened to me in the moment that I realized the bull was going to blast through that gate. And by 'funny' I mean odd, because even I didn't expect it of myself. What happened is that I got mad. Like fuming, steam-coming-out-of-your-ears kind of mad. No way was I going to let that snot-nosed knucklehead run over me.

Our eyes locked. He was bearing straight down on me. Like he thought he'd just pound me into the dust on his way to freedom. Did he really think I'd let him?

So I lunged at the gate. Barked with all my might. A string of ferocious, authoritative barks. Even though my collar was crushing my windpipe.

The leash snapped. I lurched forward. Caught myself.

I bounded to the gate. Hackles raised. Up on my toes.

Time seems to change pace sometimes. So it took me a second to realize he was actually slowing. And turning. Away from the gate.

I stayed where I was. Barked a few more times, just to make my point.

By then, Cam had darted across the field and flung the gate to the chute wide open. The bull trotted over that way, as compliantly as a hog zeroing in on a feeding trough full of slop.

As soon as the bull was secured in the chute, Cam came to me, patted me on the head.

"Brave girl, Halo." Pride beamed from his smile. "That was a *very* good dog."

On the way home that day, we stopped at the corner ice cream cone stand. Cam got two cones. One for Hunter, one for me.

Somehow, I doubted that Ray ever bought Slick an ice cream cone. Too bad. He deserved one.

Instead, Slick got a cast on his front leg. Estelle did let him stay in the kitchen while he healed. She put a blanket down on the floor for him, too. If he was lucky, he might have gotten some of the scraps that accidentally fell on the floor. Knowing Estelle though, that probably never happened.

But sleeping on a blanket inside ... Old Slick probably thought he'd died and gone to heaven.

chapter 3

Steam curled upward from the mug of coffee Lise cupped between her hands. She crossed the kitchen and slid onto the chair across from Cam. "On a Sunday?"

It was barely light out. She was still in the old sweats she always wore to bed, her hair all rumpled and falling out of her lopsided ponytail. Cam was already dressed in his jeans, a clean white T-shirt, and a freshly washed hoodie.

After I crunched away on the last piece of kibble in my bowl, I trotted to the table and flopped down underneath it. Cam's leg was stretched out there, so I rested my chin on his foot and closed one eye, keeping the other eye trained on the floor next to Hunter's chair.

A wave of bile pushed up my throat. I swallowed it back. I'd eaten too fast — a habit developed from competing with my brother for food. Lise had learned to separate us because of it. Today was my turn inside. I reminded myself to take it more slowly the next time. Still, a heavy, sour feeling sucked at my gut, filling me with a strange unease. Maybe it was the way Lise was forcing her breath out through pinched nostrils or the fact that Cam seemed anxious to be on his way, but a cloud of dread hung suspended in the room.

Nauseous and drenched, my day had not started well. My fur was still damp from sitting out in the rain. An hour ago, Cam had taken me out of the crate where I slept at night and ushered me out the door to potty while he went to take his shower. By the time he finally came to get me, I had been soaked in a downpour. I didn't mind being wet, but Lise had fussed about my muddy paws and rubbed me all over with a towel while Cam held me at arm's length.

Hunter was seated next to his dad, with his feet tucked under him. In between spoonfuls of cereal, he hummed to himself. I was tempted to join in, but Hunter was the only one who liked my howling. He was also the only one who seemed to be in a good mood that morning.

"Hunter, you're going to choke if you keep singing," Lise said tersely. "Eat."

"Oookay, Mommy," Hunter replied. A moment later, he peeked under the table and grinned at me. He held his hand out. In his palm lay three glistening nuggets of sugary cereal. I snarfed them down as fast as I could. This was Hunter's gift to me every morning: a few bits of cereal, a corner of toast, a piece of bacon fat. Sometimes when he had pancakes, he'd dip his fingers in the syrup, then dangle them beside his chair for me to lick clean.

"Hunter!" Lise scolded. Usually he was good about making sure she wasn't watching, but sometimes, I think, he just plain forgot.

Hunter dropped the edge of the tablecloth. "Just saying hi to Halo."

"Halo's fine. You go get ready to go to Grandma's. It's supposed to stop raining soon, so she said she's going to take you to the zoo today so Mommy can get some work done around here, okay? If you're good, she might even let you pick out a stuffed animal."

"Can I have the kangaroo?"

"It's up to her. And you *have* to be good. No wandering off. Now go."

Hunter jumped to the floor and hopped out of the kitchen, his hands folded over at the wrists at chest height. It was tempting to follow him, but I figured Lise wouldn't appreciate me running through the house as wet as I was. Humans were unreasonably obsessed about cleanliness.

Lise tapped her foot on the floor, then stomped it abruptly. "Really, Cam? Couldn't you take today off? I was thinking after you dropped Hunter off, you could come back here and we could … you know, spend some time alone together? You start your new job tomorrow and —"

"All the more reason for me to be there today," Cam said. "Look, maybe if I can help him get through this harvest, he and Mom will realize it's time to retire. He even said it's getting to be too much for him to handle by himself."

Again, bile splashed at the back of my throat. I laid as still as I could, hoping my stomach would settle.

Lise set her cup down so hard it jarred the table. "You haven't told him yet, have you?"

Cam's foot slid from underneath my chin. As he stood, I clamped my teeth on to his pants leg. I didn't want him to go.

He shook me loose. "Stop it, Halo."

I balked at the sternness in his tone. Confusion tore at my conscience. Yes, we dogs know right from wrong, although our ideas of such often differ from those of the human species. Obedience wars with instinct constantly. If we are hungry, the trash can is fair game. To eat is to survive. A scolding is small punishment for a full belly. In this case, however I couldn't explain my need to deter him. Cam went to work every weekday, at least until recently. He went to his parents' farm frequently, as well. Why should his leaving now be any different? Flattening myself to the floor, I acquiesced.

Cam walked over to the sink, rinsed his cup and set it on the counter. "Told him what?"

"Cameron Scott McHugh, you know what I mean. About the

transfer to Florence if the new company's contract gets renewed. We talked about this. You better not be having second thoughts. We'll be closer to my mom then. Ever since Dad went into the nursing home it's been rough on her. She needs me there. And we won't be so far away that we can't visit your parents on weekends."

Cam didn't reply right away. He gripped the edge of the sink, his eyes fixed on the gray gloom outside the window. "You're right. She does need you. I'll tell him today. It's just … it's not easy, you know? There are so many things I like about working on the farm with him. But it *is* time to move on. Working the land is hard. It's never ending. You're never off duty. And the benefits, well, there aren't any. No paid vacations, no sick hours, no company matched retirement fund … I want to be able to provide for my family, give you everything you need."

She was so quiet in her terry cloth slippers that I didn't notice her moving from her chair until I heard her voice from further away. She slipped her arms around Cam's middle, laid her head against his back. "I know it's hard, sweetie. He probably won't take it well. But there's never going to be a good time. It's just one of those things you have to do. He'll make adjustments."

Cam turned around and drew her close, kissed the top of her hair where it parted. "Thanks."

She leaned back to look into his eyes. "For what?"

"Understanding."

He tilted his head. Their lips met. Cam's hands slipped lower on her back, stroking. Soon, he was cleaning the inside of her mouth with his tongue. *Here they go again.* I grunted a sigh, stretched my long legs, and yawned.

Lise grabbed Cam's hand to tug him toward the hallway. "Ten minutes?"

He stood his ground firmly. "God, I wish, but I'm late already. Besides, Hunter will throw a fit if I'm not ready to go out the door in less than two. He's got kangaroos on the brain."

Lise grinned mischievously. "If you're home on time, I just might have a surprise for you."

"Cheesecake?"

"Nope."

He arched an eyebrow. "Did you buy that little black dress? The one with the —"

"Nope. Just come home on time. And ask your mom if she could watch Hunter for an extra hour or two. I thought we could go to Leonardo's. Order that sinful lasagna and some tiramisu, maybe. Maybe a couple of cocktails to wash it all down with." She pulled up the half-zipper on the front of his hoodie for him, held onto the collar of it like she didn't want to let him go, either. "Hey, be *extra* careful today, okay?"

"You tell me that every time, Lise. I'm always careful, you know that." He gave her a quick smooch on the cheek and snatched his raincoat off the hook next to the backdoor. "See you later."

Just as he grabbed the doorknob, Lise blurted out, "Wait!"

"What?"

"Aren't you forgetting something?"

"Oh, yeah." He smacked a palm to his forehead. "Hunter!"

Hunter sped through the kitchen with his raincoat flaring out behind him. On the back of it was a picture of an elephant holding an umbrella in its trunk. Cam zipped it up, then inspected the inside of Hunter's mouth to make sure he had brushed his teeth.

"Something else, Cam?" Lise said.

He dug his hands in his front pockets, jangled his keys, and patted his back pocket where he kept his wallet. "Naw, I'm good."

She tipped her head in my direction, her long blonde hair sweeping across her shoulder as she did so. "What about Halo?"

"Can't. I'll be on the tractor all day. She'd just end up parked in the outside pen, looking like a drowned rat."

"Oh, all right. Go. But don't forget to tell —"

"I will, promise. And I'll be back before 6:00. Go ahead and make reservations. Can't wait to spend the evening with you, sweetie. Love you." Nudging Hunter out the door, he blew her an air kiss.

She caught it in her hand, brought her fist to her heart. "Love you, too, Cam."

It was my last chance to stop him. I rushed forward to stand in front of him, swayed over the doormat, and regurgitated every last bit of that morning's kibble in a sloppy steaming heap at Cam's feet.

"Eeewww!" Hunter pointed at my offering.

Cam flipped his hood over his head. "You have fun cleaning that up."

The door banged shut behind them. Outside, rain came down in sheets. Lise went to the door, stepped carefully around my pile, and pressed a palm to the glass. In the first puff of air from her lips, her breath fogged the window. She watched as he got in the truck and drove away.

—o00o—

Rain pattered on the metal roof of the house again later that day as Lise slipped her feet into a pair of high heels. Sitting on the edge of the bed next to me, she studied her red painted toenails a moment, then kicked her shoes off.

"Who am I kidding?" she said. "What I need are duck boots on a day like today."

She rifled around in the closet for a minute, before plucking up the dust ruffle of the bed and poking her head underneath. With a disgruntled sigh, she sat back on her haunches. "Dang it, must have given those boots to Goodwill. Now I'm going to have to change my entire outfit."

After flipping through her blouses and skirts again, she pulled out a pair of tan fitted slacks and a white silk shirt. From the bottom drawer of her dresser, she dug out a yellow sweater. Holding it up to her front, she twirled around to me. "What do you think, Halo? Will he be suspicious if he sees me in his favorite outfit?"

I understood humans needed clothes because they had no fur, but why so many of them? And what did it matter what they wore, aside from having protection from the sun or enough layers to keep them warm?

"I want to save the news until the waiter brings him his Long Island Iced Tea, not just blurt it out when he walks in the kitchen door and sees me all dolled up. It's not every day that a woman makes an important announcement like this to her husband. You don't know how hard it's been to hold it in since Friday. That's two whole days! Oh, Halo," — she knelt before me, the clothes draped over one arm, and scratched beneath my chin — "everything is turning out just perfect: Cam has a new job, by next summer we'll have a new house, bigger and nicer than this one, and soon after that —"

She flipped her wrist over to look at her watch. "Crap! I don't have time to change."

Flinging the clothes on the bed, she grabbed her strappy heels and raced down the hallway. "I'll just wear the ugly duck boots until I get in the car. Cam can drop me off at the front door of the restaurant. They have an awning out over the sidewalk. Or do they? Yes, I'm sure they do. Shouldn't be a problem. Tonight's going to be perfect. Absolutely perfect. Except for the pouring rain. And the horrendous hair day I'm having. Otherwise, perfect."

I trailed after her. Humans think we follow them everywhere out of loyalty, but the truth is we do it because we're bored. They may be complicated and senseless sometimes, but they do the most interesting things. I was always trying to understand what the purpose was of some of their rituals, though. Like now. Lise popped into the bathroom and studied her face close up in the mirror. Why the constant fascination with appearances?

"Sloppy job with the mascara, chick. Who did your makeup? A chimpanzee? And look at that hair. My God, did you just walk through a wind tunnel?"

As she snatched the hairbrush off the counter, the phone downstairs rang. I barely dodged her feet as she spun around and stomped down the hallway again. "Probably those stupid survey people again. Do they ever give up?"

In the kitchen, she looked at the caller ID. "Oh, it's Cam's mom. Seems to think her cell phone is only for emergencies. Probably telling me he's running late. Well, I'm going to give him grief if he is. He knew tonight was important."

Lise tucked her hair behind her ear and put the receiver to it. "Hi, Estelle. Are the guys almost done? I was expecting Cam home by —" She paused, shook her head. "Excuse me? Who is this again?"

A muffled voice buzzed through the phone. It wasn't Estelle or Ray, that much I could tell.

Lise clasped her forehead. She took a step back, her shoulders collapsing with an invisible blow. She stumbled to the nearest chair.

"Oh, God. Are you sure?" Elbows planted on the table, she cradled her head between her hands, crushing the phone to her ear so I couldn't hear the voice anymore. "No. That can't be right. It can't be. Let me talk to Estelle."

Lise sucked in a ragged breath, squeezed her eyes shut. Her knees were bouncing up and down beneath the table. She started to rock back and forth in the chair. Its frame creaked in time with her motions. She stopped abruptly, exhaled loudly. Her words had a hollow tone to them. "She won't come to the phone? No, I ... This is horrible. So, *so* horrible. I can't even fathom ... Is Hunter —?" Another pause. "Oh, thank God. Tell her I'll be there as soon as I can. Thank you, Officer Diehl."

There was a long pause and then a resounding 'thunk' as the

phone fell from her hand onto the table.

Sitting near the sink, watching her, I wasn't sure whether I should go to her, stay put, or flee into another room. Her head folded down against her forearm. A tiny wail leaked from her mouth, hidden in the bend of her elbow. The sound rose to a howl, broke as she gulped in air, then rose again. Her shoulders shook uncontrollably with each sob that gripped her.

On soft paws, I crept to her. I sat for a minute at her knee, waiting patiently while she continued to cry. Finally, I lifted a paw and tapped her on the foot. Then I pushed my muzzle against her shin and whimpered in sympathy. She sobbed twice more, sniffed, lifted her head to look down at me. Her eyes were puffy, ringed in red. Tears streaked down her cheeks. Her hand drifted down to touch the top of my head.

"Halo, what are we going to do?"

Do about what?

The chair groaned as she scooted it back. She settled down on the floor and wrapped her arms tight around me.

"Cam is never coming home," she whispered into my ruff.

Reaching my front paws onto her shoulders, I hugged Lise and licked away the trail of sadness on her cheeks as her tears wet my fur.

I will always come home, I wanted to tell her. *I will always, always come home.*

chapter 4

A whimper rose in my throat. The cold had settled deep in my bones. I stretched my paws to reach upward, but I was too short to see through the kitchen door window to inside. Scout was probably warm and asleep in his dog house in the kennels, which was inside the garage. I hadn't seen him or the other dogs since Lise shoved me out into the backyard an hour ago. I wished I was curled up with Scout, muzzle to muzzle. I'd even put up with him chewing on my ear just to be out of this cold.

Another frigid wind blasted around me. Shivering, I let out a few woofs, but still Lise didn't come to let me in. It was the first really cold day I could remember. The wind was brisk and biting, the clouds gray and low. Gently, I scratched at the door, my nails scraping away the paint to leave tiny parallel marks.

In the distance, a car rolled down the gravel lane, tires crunching over rock. I ran to the gate to see who it was, barking to alert everyone of a visitor. Even the dogs in the kennels joined in with me. I heard Scout's high yip and Chase's deep, long bellow, mixed with Cricket's and Bit's rapid woofs. Still, no Lise.

A dark blue Buick stopped just outside the yard. Estelle got out of the driver's side, blew her nose on a tissue, and wiped at her eyes with gloved fingers. As she walked toward the gate, my barks became a greeting. I kept my eyes on the car, waiting for Ray to step out and walk with her, but he didn't. He just sat there in the passenger seat, gazing blankly at her through the car window. His face was an odd shade of pale, almost transparent. He raised a hand, waved at her, then leaned closer to the window, his breath fogging it until I could no longer see him.

Why didn't he get out and come in with her? Was he sick? Hurt, maybe?

Something was wrong. Very wrong.

As Estelle swung the gate open, I backed up, resisting the urge to jump up on her. Unlike Cam or Lise, Estelle and Ray never let their dogs in the house. They never so much as patted me on the head, either. Even though Cam took me to their place many times, I was never allowed inside. If I wasn't with him while he worked in the barns or the fields, Cam would lock me inside Slick's pen so I wouldn't 'get into trouble', as he put it. I couldn't see how my exploring meant I was getting into trouble, but he wasn't always pleased with what I did to occupy my time, so that was where I went when he was busy. Slick was seldom inside the pen himself. Whenever he was not at work with Ray bossing the cows, he would lie on the front porch, his chin and paws draped over the top step as he surveyed his domain. I was not given such freedom. Yet. Cam had told me I'd have to earn it.

Today, Estelle was dressed differently. Her stretchy jeans and loose sweatshirt had been replaced by a fitted black skirt and jacket, tan stockings covering her lower legs. Instead of her white sneakers, she was wearing a pair of black leather shoes, dull and stiff from years of infrequent use. Now that she was closer, I could see that her nose and cheeks were chapped from crying, her eyes rubbed red. She nearly tripped over me as she fumbled to put the key in the lock and open the door.

I glanced back at the car, still expecting Ray to step out and follow her, only … he wasn't there anymore. Gone. Like he'd never been there at all. The window was free of fog, drops of water sliding down the pane like rivers of tears.

"Did someone forget you?" Estelle said as she nudged the door open with her hip, her hands held above her rounded stomach so as not to contaminate them with dog germs should she accidentally brush against me.

It wasn't like her to willingly let me in the house, but I rushed through anyway, glad to be inside. After lapping up some water, I plunked down on top of the register to let the waft of heated air warm my tummy. Her eyes unfocused, Estelle peeled off her gloves and hung up her coat. She lifted the teapot from the stove and ran water into it from the sink faucet.

"I don't know why she lets you smelly creatures inside," she mumbled, her back to me. "It's hard enough to keep a house clean … clean with just …"

Her words broke apart. She snuffled back tears. "No, none of that, Estelle Ruth Skidmore McHugh. You're going to be strong today. It's just that … Damn you, Ray. You can't just up and die on me like that. I can't run that farm by myself. You left two hundred acres of wheat in the field. What am I supposed to do with it? And the corn! I don't even know how to drive that stupid combine. And Ned Hanson can only take care of those cows and hogs for so long. Damn you for not thinking of me and —"

A rustle sounded from behind. Lise hovered in the entryway to the kitchen, one hand resting against the doorjamb.

"Estelle?" Lise said softly.

The teapot nearly dropped from Estelle's grasp. She clutched a hand against her mouth, as if ashamed of what she'd said.

"It's okay, Estelle." Lise's voice was husky, like she'd been out in the cold for hours, even though I knew she hadn't. She took the

41

teapot from Estelle and set it on the burner. She twisted a knob and a tiny blue flame leapt up beneath it. A tight black dress clung to her gentle curves. Glimmering pearls hung from her slender neck to brush the low neckline. I'd seen this dress before. It was the one she wore a couple months ago when Cam took her out for their anniversary. He told her she looked 'hot' in it. Which made me wonder why she didn't take it off and put on something cooler. Humans are such slaves to fashion. They took Hunter to his grandparents then and went to dinner. Within minutes of them coming home, the dress was on the floor and they were on the couch, touching and kissing each other, making happy sounds. It seemed so long ago now.

"I get mad, too." Lise fished two teabags out of the ceramic snowman and dropped them into a couple of mugs. "Mad that it happened. Mad they weren't more careful. Mad that Cam won't be here when I need him most."

"It's my fault, Lise, dear." Estelle touched her shoulder, but quickly drew her hand back before the gesture became something more. "I should've insisted Ray put that roll bar back on the tractor. Even if I had, though, he probably would've ignored me. He could be so stubborn sometimes."

"That's absurd. It's not your fault." But she didn't say the rest — that Ray had removed the roll bar that at least would have saved Cam's life. The whistle on the teapot shrieked. Lise poured the hot water into the cups and set them on the table. She sank into her chair and bobbed her tea bag up and down, before scooping a teaspoon of sugar into the cup.

"I saw it happen from my sewing room window."

Lise dropped the teabag into the cup. Her head snapped up. "What?"

Eyes lowered, Estelle joined her at the table. "I saw Cam drive the tractor over the silage pile. They were trying to tamp it down so they could pull a tarp over it. Keep the rain from ruining it." She took her handkerchief from her pocket and twisted it between her hands. "Ray ran up beside the pile to tell Cam to back up. And when, when he did, it ... the tractor, I guess it hit a pocket of air. One of the tires spun. The tractor slipped sideways and, and I screamed at them from inside the house. Screamed. But it rolled. Cam was thrown. Ray couldn't get out of the way in time."

Her mouth twisted into an ugly shape. She clenched her fists until her knuckles whitened. "I rushed outside, but all I could see at first was the mangled underside of the tractor. When I moved around to the other side and saw, saw ... I knew. There was nothing I could do." Estelle's gray eyes took on a distant look, as if she were reliving the day. "They found them right next to each other."

"It wasn't your fault." Lise lifted her cup, her mouth tight. They were words spoken out of civility, not compassion. "They couldn't have heard you that far away. Not with the tractor running."

"I screamed at them because Hunter had run after his grandpa." Her voice diminished to a scratchy whisper. Like autumn leaves skittering over concrete on a windy day. "I was afraid for Hunter."

Lise's hand froze in mid air. "He saw it happen?"

Estelle nodded dully, her jaw trembling as she dissolved into muted sobs.

Half-standing, Lise reached across the table suddenly, her cup tumbling onto the floor. Hot tea splashed everywhere. The ceramic mug shattered into a dozen pieces. A shard skittered across the linoleum, nicking my back paw. I jumped, as much because of the anger I saw in Lise's face as from the sound of a mug breaking.

"How close was he?" When Estelle didn't answer right away, Lise smacked the table with her palm. She repeated herself, more loudly, more accusingly. "I said how close was he?!"

Estelle's shoulders hunched forward. Tear stains dotted her blouse. She unwadded the tissue, blew her nose. It took a few seconds for her to find her voice. "I don't know. Ten feet, maybe?"

"You mean, he could've —?" Lise collapsed onto her chair like she'd been struck. "Oh my God."

Whatever trust there was between them broke at that moment. Just like the cup hitting the floor. Even if you glued it back together, it would never be as strong again, never be whole.

The clock on the wall ticked loudly. Each pulse of the second hand sounded like the drum beat of a death march. I had never noticed that sound before. Never realized how time actually *could* change pace. But it did. It plodded.

Finally, Lise pushed her chair back and got up. She turned away, one hand covering her mouth, as if to dam back words better left unsaid. The other hand drifted downward to touch her stomach. It was something she'd been doing a lot this past week. I didn't understand why until she spoke again.

"Thank God this baby will still have a big brother to look up to." There was a steeliness to her voice. She was trying to be strong, even though inside she was dissolving like a chalk drawing in a downpour. By the way Estelle's mouth drooped heavily, I could tell there was also an edge of blame in Lise's words.

"You mean you're —?"

"I am. Just two months." Lise lifted her chin, shoring up her resolve. "So you know, my mom invited me to come live with her. I told her 'no' at first, but I think maybe I should. Hunter doesn't need to be reminded of what happened. He needs to stay safe, where someone can keep an eye on him." Lise glanced at Estelle, who was still staring at the snotty tissue balled up in her fist. "You don't know how hard a decision this is for me. My mom needs me. Hunter ... and the baby, they'll be looked after there."

Estelle raised her face. "I can look after them."

"Obviously you can't. You *knew* Hunter wasn't supposed to be around running machinery after what happened to the Hiddleson's little girl last year. We discussed it. You both promised Cam that you —"

"So you're going to take Hunter away from his home? From me? Because of something that didn't happen."

Lise didn't answer right away. She let that silence stretch between them, making it all the more potent. "Because of something that very nearly did."

Estelle turned her face away. Fury brewed beneath her shroud of grief. "And the dogs? The sheep? What about them?"

"You know I can't ..." Lise expelled a weighty sigh, then twitched her shoulders in a shrug. "I'll figure it out."

That was when I noticed Hunter standing in the doorway to the kitchen, the fingers of one hand covering his heart, his favorite stuffed animal clutched in the other arm. Bernard the Bear is what he named it after Cam brought it home from a trip to San Diego once. Hunter had slept with it every night since. Today Hunter had on a dark gray suit, complete with a little black tie. He looked like a tiny adult — except for the bare feet.

In the four days since his daddy had died in the accident, Hunter hadn't said a single word. Not even so much as a grunt. In fact, he didn't respond at all when people spoke to him. As if he didn't hear them. I'd often noticed him rubbing a hand over his chest, like he was soothing an ache in his heart.

Hunter drifted across the kitchen, which seemed a vast distance, it took him so long. He sank down next to me, wrapped his spindly arms around my neck, and hugged me hard, crushing Bernard between us. I licked his face once, then tucked my muzzle against his shoulder.

It turned out it was the day of Cam and Ray's funeral. I was not allowed to go, which made me sad, because Lise had said something about saying goodbye to Cam, right before she dissolved in tears. I had wanted to see him one more time, too. Now, all I had left of him was his scent. I stole an old T-shirt of his from behind the laundry hamper, ran out the door with it later that week, and buried it behind

45

the bushes in the dog yard. Just so I'd always have something to remember him by.

I used to think Cam would always be with us. Never assumed my world would be anything different than what it was those first few months.

How quickly everything can change.

chapter 5

Everything started off like normal that day. Although 'normal' wasn't really normal anymore. Nothing had been the same in the weeks since Cam died.

Lise floated through life as if she were a body without a spirit, trapped in a place she couldn't get out of. She didn't go back to her teaching job. Told her mother, Becky, over the phone that she couldn't sit in front of all those kids every day and pretend there was nothing wrong.

More than that, though, she didn't want to leave Hunter with Estelle, who'd been responsible for watching him while Lise went off to work since he was six weeks old. In a single day, years' worth of trust had been destroyed. Snapped like a fishing line yanked into the deep by a whale. That's what Lise said, anyway.

Every day she sat watching Hunter, never letting him get more than ten feet from her before she launched into a state of panic. If he wandered into the next room, she darted in after him to see what he was doing. When he went to bed at night, she checked on him half a dozen times before going off to her own bed, where she lay awake for hours.

If Lise showed her emotions to an extreme, Hunter kept them

zipped up inside him. She asked him a hundred questions every day, but all he did was shrug or shake his head. Most of the time, he just sat in front of the TV or lay on the floor with a book about animals propped open in front of him.

"Platypus." Lise pointed to the picture. "Can you say platypus, Hunter?"

He traced his finger around the outline of the animal. Remained silent.

Lise tapped on the page. "'P', platypus starts with a 'p'. Do you want to practice your letters today?"

Nothing.

"Would you rather go to the park? We can even invite your friend Max along. If we bundle up, it's not too bad outside. Should get even warmer if we go after lunch." She squatted beside him and tilted his chin up with her hand, but he wouldn't meet her eyes. "Hunter, I know you can hear me. I know you're very sad about Daddy. I am, too. I miss him every day. And I wish there was something I could do to bring him back. But I … I can't."

Her words trailed away, overlain with that same vapor of sorrow that seemed to pervade everything about her these days. It had been two months and still not a day went by that she didn't fall apart. Sometimes she'd lie in bed for hours after putting Hunter down and cry herself to sleep. Other times she'd be sitting there watching TV and all of a sudden a reminder of him would leap out at her from the flickering screen: Adam Levine in a crisp white T-shirt, a commercial for Ram trucks, a movie about a rancher, a Keith Urban song …

Cam was everywhere. And yet … he was nowhere.

Hunter punched up the volume button on the remote control to drown out any further interruption from his mom. It was a program about prairie dogs, but they didn't look much like dogs to me. Then he rolled onto his side and pulled himself into a ball. Snagging the corner of the blanket next to him, he covered his head with it. I sniffed at the lump where his head was. When he was very small, he used to play 'turtle'. I'd nudge him and he'd poke his head out and erupt in laughter. But today he just wrapped the blanket tighter around him.

Looking up at the ceiling, Lise said, "Oh, Cam, I don't know how to do this without you. I'm trying. I'm *really* trying. But I need help."

She tromped into the kitchen and rattled some pans as she put them away in the cupboards. Part of the routine that she'd fallen into after Cam died was finding ways to fill up her day whenever she wasn't hovering over Hunter. She rarely let more than a few dishes pile up on the counter before scouring them clean. Crumbs on the table were banished with a vengeance. Closets were purged, filing cabinets reorganized, and shelves dusted. More than filling up the hours, I think it was a way of refusing to acknowledge the emptiness that Cam's absence had left in her life.

She slammed a cupboard door and collapsed onto a kitchen chair. She let out a sigh so long and heavy it sounded like all the air was rushing out of her lungs at once. Then the tears started — tiny sniffles at first, building until they were full-blown sobs, broken only by gasps for air and muffled nose blowing.

I nudged at Hunter until he lifted a corner of the blanket to peer at me. He glanced toward the kitchen, the corners of his mouth weighed down with a frown.

"It's my fault, Halo," he whispered. "I yelled … but Daddy didn't hear me."

Before I could position myself beside him for a hug, he had rolled back up in his little woolen cocoon to shut out the world.

Several taps sounded against the kitchen window. I got to my feet, padded the few steps to the hallway, and looked. It was only the branches of a crabapple tree planted too close to the house slapping against the pane there. Outside, the wind blew hard, leaking around the old windows so that it began to make a howling sound. The soffits rattled something fierce and the front storm door suddenly started

49

banging against its frame every time a gust came along.

It didn't look like a good day for going to the park to me.

"We're probably going to lose shingles again," Lise complained as she rose and went to the front door. When she opened it to pull the storm door shut and latch it, a frigid draft of air rolled through the room. She tossed herself on the couch with a loud *oomph*. "After gutting the kitchen and having it eat up all our spare weekends, you didn't want to fix anything else. And I get that, Cam. I do. But you also promised me we'd be out of here by the end of the year. And now ..."

For a painfully long time, she stared into space, her gaze finally settling on the buffet table where the family pictures were arranged. On one end was a photo of Cam showing his prize steer at the Adair County Fair. Chin held high, his right hand gripping the braided halter on the steer, he looked back at the camera from beneath the brim of his white hat with an almost arrogant pride. He was younger then, not quite as tall, not nearly as muscular. But Lise had often told him how dashing he looked in that navy blue checkered shirt with the mother-of-pearl buttons and his calf-high cowboy boots. Although Hunter was barely five now, he was already starting to look a lot like his father, with the same straight, sandy blond locks, dark eyelashes, and deeply carved dimples.

Sniffing, Lise tugged the hem of her shirt up and stroked her bare tummy. "Your daddy was a handsome guy, Baby Girl. Oh, I know you're a girl, all right. I just know."

Then she put her shirt back down and covered herself with the throw blanket that had been wadded up at the end of the couch. I expected more tears, but maybe she was too exhausted for another round. Instead, she tugged her phone out of her pocket, tapped out a text message, then laid it on the floor and went to sleep.

—o0Oo—

Find him, Halo, Cam's voice whispered. *Find him.*

I drifted on the verge between dreaming and waking, as I tried to focus on Cam's words. But the harder I tried, the less I could hear him.

The phone rang.

Lise sat up straight as a rod, blinking hard. We must have all fallen asleep. Even with the TV blaring and the wind beating at the house like it was going to lift it off its foundations and carry it away to Oz.

Cool air swirled around me, so I crawled my way over to the register and stretched out over it. The heat wasn't on, but the metal was still hot. Any moment now, I'd hear the familiar 'clunk' of the old furnace down in the cellar and its warmth would tickle my stomach.

"Hey, Grace." Scrunching up her face, Lise rubbed at the back of her neck. "Naw, where would I go, anyway? ... Yeah, sure. This afternoon is perfect. Bring as many boxes as you can fit in your car. I haven't gotten much of a start — just thinking of it is like ... I don't know. Frightening. Painful. Like packing up my heart. This place isn't much, but it was ... *ours.*" She forced the last word out in a raspy whisper, like she was going to fall apart one more time after the hundreds of times she'd already lost it. But never in front of Hunter.

I looked toward the heap of blankets he'd burrowed beneath earlier, but he wasn't there. While Lise talked on the phone with her friend Grace, I sniffed around. There were traces of him everywhere. But the strongest scent was in the direction of the front door.

Which wasn't completely closed.

Maybe Lise hadn't properly latched it? I glanced at her, but she was too absorbed with pouring out her heart to a sympathetic ear. I scratched at the door. Her back was now to me, one hand pressing the phone firmly to her head, the other covering her other ear so she could hear over the still blaring TV. The Lawrence Welk show was on now. A man in a red jacket was playing the accordion and Bobby and Sissy were dancing to The Beer Barrel Polka. Why didn't she just get the remote control and turn it down? I stared at her awhile, hoping she'd figure it out. Or look my way. Or realize Hunter wasn't in the room. Something.

But she just went on and on. My agitation was increasing by the second. I retrieved the remote from beside where Hunter had been and sat in front of her. By then, she had a hand over her eyes. I woofed once, softly. As I did so, the remote fell from my mouth. Onto her foot.

"Ow!" Lise straightened. When she saw what I'd brought her, she glared at me. She picked the remote up, wiped my saliva from it, and slapped it on the end table. "Halo, no! Bad dog!"

Rats, I should have brought the blanket over. Then she would've noticed Hunter wasn't asleep there.

In one smooth movement, she scooped me up and marched across the room. I was almost too big for her to carry anymore. My back legs swung against her hip. I felt myself slipping as she hugged me to her side. I squirmed when I saw where she was headed — the back door — but she just held me tighter.

"My friend Katherine suggested I take him to a counselor, but I don't know that it'd be worth it, Grace. I mean, if he won't talk, what's the point? I'd be paying someone a hundred and fifty bucks an hour to babysit him while he stares off into space... Sure, I understand. I really do... Well, I think he just needs time. And I certainly can't let him go over there again. Talk about trauma. Besides, who knows what could happen if she takes her eyes off of him, even for a minute? With his asthma, I can't leave him with someone who's going to just let him wander off like that."

We had passed through the hallway and were headed into the kitchen. I couldn't let her do this. Hunter was in trouble. I sensed it. Every second mattered.

So I bit her. Not enough to draw blood, mind you. Just a pinch of my front teeth on the tender flesh between her thumb and fore-finger.

She gasped. Then through tight lips, she growled, "You little turd!"

The hand that was holding me latched onto my collar. She swung me down, slamming me onto my side on the linoleum. The air whooshed out of my lungs. I drew in one quick breath and held it, bracing myself.

"Hold on a sec, Grace. Someone's being a brat… No, not him. The puppy. Be right back."

Lise set her phone on the floor and clamped down on my muzzle with a death grip. She brought her face close to mine and stared me down.

I didn't like what I saw in her eyes. Deep down in my soul, it scared me. It was a glimpse of what we're all capable of when life has exploded around us and we're desperate to survive. So I looked away. She was angry. *Very* angry. Not just at me. At the world.

Instead of alerting her to a possible crisis, I'd pricked her last nerve.

Every muscle in my body stiffened. I kept my eyes averted, my ears pinned against my head. Lifting my front and back leg of the side nearest Lise, I exposed my belly. Had I been upright, I would have urinated. At times, it is necessary to display total, utter submission. I had terrorized my littermates until they exhibited these very same signals. Because it was important that they understood who was boss. I had learned this from my mother. There was no mistaking the message that I was trying to send to Lise right then: that she was supreme leader, master of all, and even if she was wrong, dead wrong, I would cede to her.

Her hands relaxed just enough so I could breathe through my mouth. Still, I didn't look at her. It wasn't safe to do so yet. Gruffly, she lifted me up and attempted to scoot me toward the back door with her foot as she reached for the knob. But I was quicker than her.

I ran.

Past her legs and across the kitchen. I skidded into a turn as I headed toward the living room.

"Halo!" Lise screeched. "Get back here — now!"

A sliver of daylight flashed from around the edge of the screen door. Churning my gangly legs, I bounded across the room, my nails digging into the area rug for added traction, and dove for it. I slammed my nose between the metal frame and the door, the force of my weight propelling it open. I burst through, to the outside, and leapt from the top step onto the concrete of the sidewalk.

Four more strides and I was racing over the front lawn. Papery red and gold leaves crunched beneath my feet as I ran. Ran, and ran, and ran.

Lise's voice behind me got further and further away, then faded to nothing.

chapter 6

The sheep lifted their heads as I sped past, no doubt jealous that they were stuck behind a fence and I was not. A noisy cloud of blackbirds lifted from a stubbled field on the other side of the driveway. I didn't stop to chase them, either. Ahead, the great woods loomed — dense and dark beneath a leaden sky.

Nose to the air, I searched for Hunter. But the wind had dissipated his scent, wherever he was. I smelled only damp earth and decaying leaves, bruised stems of grass, and wood still green and growing.

I slowed, looked behind me. The house was far away now. Lise had stopped following me, probably gone back inside. My heart thumped against my ribs. My lungs heaved for air. Every breath tasted of water. The rain was coming. A lot of it. My skin prickled. Soon, thunder rolled down from the sky, shaking the ground. I felt it in my bones. In every sinew and hair follicle. In every tooth and nerve.

The first drops of rain followed, cool and gentle at first, then colder and harder, more and more. The wind gained force to drive it across the land like a horizontal waterfall. Until it was hard to see at all.

Knives of rain stabbed at my face. I forced my eyes to stay open, but all I wanted to do was fold to the ground and wait for the storm to pass. I knew, though, that I'd never find Hunter if I did that.

Glancing around, I looked for shelter — for a barn in which to hide or a car beneath which to crawl. Nothing but a gray bleariness surrounded me. An unwelcoming, watery world. I saw no sign of Hunter. Couldn't smell him. Couldn't hear anything above the percussive roar of the rain as it hammered at every surface.

To my left, a slash of yellowish-brown moved amongst the woods at the edge of the field. I started that way, but upon coming closer, I could see it was only the leaves of a yet-fully leafed bush waving in the wind. My spirits plunged. The urgency that had gripped me only minutes ago was giving way to panic. The longer Hunter was gone, the harder it would be to find him.

Perhaps, I thought, I should return to Lise and get her to help. I turned back. Trotted awhile. Down a slope. Waded through a swale that had turned into a belly-deep stream. Over clods of upturned earth and channels deep with mud.

Where was the driveway? The sheep field? The house? I couldn't see any of them. Didn't know in which direction they lay. But if I went back now, Lise might not be there. Or if she was she would be angry at me for having bolted out the door, only to come back a drenched and dirty mess.

There was no alternative. I had to find Hunter.

And when I did, even if we didn't know the way home, at least we would be lost together.

I forced myself onward, while rain fell hard and cold around me.

—o00o—

It was desperation that sent me into the woods. That or stupidity.

Youth is bold, you see. It is also quick to hope, for life's realities have not yet tempered it with the caution that follows experience. Youth believes what is possible; it does not dwell on the many ways we can fail.

It was a blessing that day that I was so young. Because it meant I believed I could do anything, without knowing what I could not. In my own mind, I was invincible. It was all I needed to keep going.

I wouldn't go home without Hunter. Lise depended on me, whether she knew it or not. She had simply misunderstood me when she tried to usher me out into the backyard. She had not known what I knew.

By now, she did.

When the rain finally began to abate, rifts of blue were showing at the sky's rim. Low black clouds had given way to gauzy blankets of gray. The wind that had been so fierce and unforgiving not so long ago had diminished to a soothing breeze, whispering in my ears, *Find him, Halo. Find him.*

I wandered until the pads of my feet were cracked and raw. Thorns tugged at my fur. Cockleburs tangled themselves in my britches and feathers. I sniffed and sniffed and sniffed. I smelled a hundred smells. None of them were Hunter.

Often, I stopped to listen. For a cow bellowing. For the plaintive bah of a ewe. For the familiar rasp of truck tires crunching on a limestone road. Anything that might clue me in on where home was, for Hunter couldn't have gone far. But I heard only the hushed remnants of the wind and the caw of blackbirds scattering from the trees as they arose in a black tornado of wings to blot out the bleary autumn sky.

Tired to the bone, I stopped at a ditch that ran between two fields and drank some water. It was gritty with soil, but I was thirsty from my running. And growing hungry, too. I climbed up the embankment and sank to my belly, mist falling gently on my face. I wanted so badly to rest, to sleep until morning. But this was not a time to think of my own needs. Duty called. As long as I had breath and a heartbeat and strength enough to walk one more step, I would go on searching.

But which way?

From somewhere, I thought I heard a human voice calling my name. A familiar voice, a man's voice. I held my breath, turned my head to listen. Nothing.

An amber beam of sunlight stretched from below the last of the clouds, just above the nearly bare treetops. It would soon be dark. My energy may have waned with the hours, but my determination had not. There was still hope. Always hope.

The hum of an engine sounded in the distance. Tires whirred over asphalt. For a few seconds, I thought it was coming closer, but the sound was muffled by countless trees, their branches clattering as a gust of wind rattled them.

I sat there minutes longer, barely breathing, just listening. Another vehicle whooshed along the unseen road, then another. If I went toward the sounds, I would find people, but racing by in their cars, I wasn't sure they would bother to stop for me and if they did, how would they ever know I belonged to Lise and that Hunter was lost?

No, I had to keep searching. No matter how long it took. So I put my nose down and cast in sweeping arcs — left, right, left, right — until I found a thin path of trampled grass. The downpour had washed away any traces of scent, but still I followed it. Down a gentle slope, across a gulley, through a patch of bramble.

Halo! This way!

There it was again. It was Cam's voice. I swear it!

I took off blindly in the direction I thought it had come from.

In a clearing, I raised my face and looked about. The sun had bowed behind the treetops. Shadows filled my vision, black edging columns of gray along the wood's edge. There, a man stood. He hooked an arm in the air, beckoning to me. I tried hard to focus, but the light was dim. The silhouette was familiar. It could have been Cam.

Between here and there stretched a pasture where cows had been not long ago. I could smell their waste. Piles of it. Their scent was strong, overpowering. So I let my eyes do the work, while I was still able to see. Barely.

It was nearly dark now. There wasn't much time left. When I looked again toward the edge of the woods, the man was gone.

In a depression in the field glimmered the surface of a pond where the cows would come to drink. They had left deep hoof prints in the mud around it. My eyes followed the pond's edge around to the other side.

My heart vaulted. I knew this place. Cam had brought me here once with Bit. We had stayed for hours while he cast his line into the water and sat with his pole propped between his knees, gazing at the sky. He said he was fishing, but he only caught two fish and those were very small, so he threw them back. A ripple at the surface caught my eye and I looked past it, up the slope —

And there, I saw him.

Hunter was sitting, hugging his knees, halfway up a hill on the far side. His head was bent, resting on his forearms. My boy!

I barked, a small bark of excitement, happy to have found Hunter, to be in a place I had been before.

Except, I didn't know the way back from here. Cam had brought me here in his truck on the way home from Ray's and I had fallen asleep on the seat between him and my mother.

But like I said before, what mattered was that I'd found Hunter.

I barked again, louder, more clearly. Hunter raised his head, then stood. I wasn't sure he could see me, so I ran.

He began to run, too. Toward the pond.

As fast as my feet could fly without twisting around each other, I raced to him. My toes, as quick as lightning, clipped the ground. I plowed through the tall grass, holding my head tall, bounding high every few strides to try to catch a glimpse of him. But it was hard to see him in the failing light. His head bobbed above the reeds rimming the pond's edge. The water was deep there. I had discovered it that time with Cam when I thought I'd go wading to snap at tadpoles. Instead, I'd found myself in water over my head. My feet had hit the murky bottom then and I'd burst upward, desperate for air. When I surfaced, I paddled my way back to Cam, who laughed at me. But as with so many things, dogs were born with the memory of how to swim. I was not so sure it was true for humans. If Hunter fell in —

So I barked my warning as I curved around the pond. Until finally Hunter saw me and turned. Barely in time.

I gathered myself in mid-stride, sprang from my haunches, and sailed at him. My feet hit his chest squarely, knocking him back, away from the water. He landed in the tall, wet grass with a soft *oomph*, me on top of him. I kept him pinned there to make sure he didn't move just yet. Then I licked his face all over, a wet and thorough washing, rapidly lapping him from chin to forehead.

He flung his arms around me. "Halo!" he cried, his small voice breaking into sobs of relief. It was the most joyous sound I had ever heard.

Exhaustion flooded through me. I collapsed beside him. We lay like that awhile, his arms hugging my chest, my snout tucked in the crook between his neck and shoulder.

"I saw him," Hunter whispered in my ear. "I saw Daddy."

I did, too.

Salty tears slid down his cheeks. I licked his face clean and pressed myself closer to his shivering body.

—o00o—

I don't remember hearing Lise and Grace tromp down the hill and come to us. I only knew that they did. I was aware of it. Yet I never looked up, never left Hunter. They were just there all of a sudden, standing over us, squealing with relief as tubes of light from Grace's

60

flashlight bounced around us.

Lise scooped Hunter up and crushed him to her chest. I sat at her feet, waiting for some acknowledgment of what I had done. For the longest time, she didn't look down at me. When she finally did, it was in response to a comment Grace made.

"Do you think he followed the dog out the door?" Grace cocked her head sideways, staring at me with suspicion through her narrow glasses. She had two little yappy dogs herself — toy poodles named Henri and Sophia. I didn't like either of them and I wasn't sure I liked her. She spoke nonsense to them in a baby voice, fed them canned gourmet food on crystal plates, and dressed them in little coats speckled with sequins. I was from a working lineage, farm-bred Australian Shepherds, and I took immense pride in it. My kind guarded the homestead with the ferocity of lions and watched over the children like the mastiffs of the ancient Roman army. We kept predators at bay, hunted vermin, and herded bulls twenty times our size, sometimes risking our own lives in the process. We weren't afraid to get dirty or work beyond the point of exhaustion. Warming laps, having my toenails painted, and getting carried around in a faux alligator purse, had I been small enough, would be beyond disgraceful. It would be mortifying.

"I think," Lise began, setting Hunter on his feet, "that maybe it was the other way around."

Scooting closer, I leaned against her leg. She stroked the top of my head. After awhile, her fingers wandered to rub the crease of my ear.

"Good girl, Halo." Her voice was hoarse. She'd been hollering for Hunter a long, long time. "That was a very, *very* good girl."

I leaned into her more heavily and closed my eyes. I was only doing what I was supposed to. What dog worth his kibble wouldn't have?

And yet, I needed to hear those words from Lise. I needed them more than I needed food or sleep or water. I needed her. And Hunter. What she didn't know was how much they needed me.

chapter 7

My skull rattled against the cool glass of the window as we bumped down the road in Lise's Subaru. I just realized it had only been late morning when Hunter disappeared. It was fully dark now. We'd been gone a long time. I should've been tired, except when Lise found us a new surge of energy had filled me. I hadn't come down from the thrill of it yet. I'd found Hunter and Lise had found us. Everything in the world was as good as it could be again.

Only it wasn't. I sensed it.

An exhausted Hunter was piled beneath blankets in the back seat. I peered from the storage area in the rear over the top of the seat at him. Wet hair still clung to his forehead. Mud was streaked across his cheek and at his temple was a fresh scab, the blood barely dry.

In the front, the glow of the dashboard illuminated Lise's pale face like moonlight on still waters. She gripped the steering wheel so tightly the veins on the back of her hands bulged. Every once in awhile she'd steal a glance at Grace, but the moment Grace looked her way, Lise's eyes would dart back to the flickering yellow line in the middle of the road.

At the edge of the tunnel of light cast by the car's headlights, a pair of green eyes flashed, then disappeared into the darkness of the ditch. Lise jerked her arms to the left, overcorrecting, and my shoulder slammed into the wheel well with a thump. She straightened the steering wheel and glanced at me in the rearview mirror. "Sorry, girl."

Grace burned a stare into the side of Lise's head, but Lise was purposefully ignoring her now.

"Look, I know you're mad at me," Grace finally blurted out, "but I still think you should have called the sheriff. Or the neighbors. They could have helped search for him. At the very least you should have given Estelle a head's up. He was probably headed that way and —"

Lise punched the brake. The tires skidded on asphalt for a heart-clenching moment, then crunched over gravel as we slowed to a stop on the shoulder of the road. She locked her arms straight on the wheel and swiveled her head to glare at Grace. "Are you crazy? I want nothing to do with that woman. Nothing!" She shot a glance at Hunter, but there was no sign he'd been awakened. She lowered her voice to a growl. "Hunter slipped out of her house and could have died because she couldn't watch him for one minute and you think I should —"

"Hunter left the house right under *your* nose, Lise. Does that make you a bad person?"

As suddenly as if she'd been slapped, Lise's head snapped forward. Angry tension melted from her shoulders. Gradually, her hands slid from the steering wheel and into her lap. "It's just that … God, I don't even know where to start. My life is such a mess. In more ways than one." Her cheeks puffed with an exhaled sigh. "I didn't just call you over to help me pack, Grace."

Her friend shifted sideways in her seat and placed a hand on Lise's arm. "Whatever it is, you can tell me. You know that. Hey, who rescued you on the first day of school from Tyler McRory, huh? I did. I swooped in and threatened to call his mother. He never gave you a hard time again, did he? Who taught you how to deal with Mr. Penright? I did. Told you all the magic words, like learning module and core curriculum, that would make him happy enough to stop pestering you for a few days. Yeah, that was me. And who flattened the mouse that took up residence in your desk drawer? Me, again."

Lise cracked a smile. "Tyler McRory put it there."

"Whatever." Shrugging, Grace flipped her long black hair behind her shoulders. "Look, I'm just saying, if there's something on your mind, you need to talk to someone. Looks like that someone is me. So, what is it?"

Lise reached for the gearshift. "Let's go back to the house so I can put him to bed. I'll tell you then."

"Sure, honey. I'll make some of my special Irish coffee for you to spill your guts over. I even brought a couple of dark chocolate chunk raspberry muffins with me. If you're going to pack up memories, you need to medicate, heavily."

"Muffins would be great, but I'll pass on the coffee."

"Don't worry, girlfriend. It's decaf."

"No, not that. It's the whiskey. Can't have it."

"Ah, see, I *knew* you were keeping secrets. Didn't tell me you were a recovering alcoholic. And here I am offering you poison."

"Not that, either."

Grace's eyes drew to slits. It took a moment before an understanding dawned on her. Her eyes slipped to Lise's stomach. "Ohhhh." She covered her mouth. "Does anyone know? I mean, besides me."

"Just Estelle. It kind of slipped out."

A beam of light bounced off the rearview mirror as a horn blasted behind us. A car had rounded the corner and swerved around us.

"I'd hug you," Grace said, as she flipped her middle finger at the receding tail lights of the passing car, "but I think we need to get off the side of the road."

Okay, maybe Grace was a decent person after all. She just treated her dogs like living Barbie dolls. I ate the head off one of those once.

A Barbie doll, I mean, not a dog. Well, the face, at least. Hunter's pre-school friend Olivia left it under the kitchen table, which is where I preferred to keep my own toys (except Lise insisted on collecting them at the end of every day and putting them in a basket behind the couch). So, I figured that anything I found there was now mine, a gift. Turned out it wasn't, maybe … I don't know — the whole thing was confusing. Anyway, I chewed the face off — my gums had never felt so good — leaving chunks of it on the floor beneath the table. I had started nibbling on the hands when Lise pounced on me and gave me a good shake. I could only deduce that I had partaken of my gift in the wrong place. If I couldn't destroy the evidence, then I needed to take it elsewhere so that humans wouldn't be bothered by the mess. After that, I learned to be more discreet when I chewed on things. As far as I knew, nobody ever discovered the gouge out of the wood on the backside of the TV stand.

The rest of the ride home was quiet. Not talking was a hard thing for Grace to do, just like some dogs have a hard time not barking or whining. Or chewing. We need to express ourselves, too.

Bit locked her legs, her whole body stiff and unmoving in the doorway, blocking my entrance. Lise shooed her back with a foot and I scurried in, clumps of mud falling from my belly as I scrabbled forth. I was careful to avert my gaze and not look at Bit. She was a show dog by breeding. She didn't like to get messy, although she would work in the fields when Lise needed her to. She just made a point of going wide around the puddles.

"Wait," Lise told me. I stood over the door mat, water dripping from my chest and belly. The rain had started up again just as we'd pulled into the driveway. The moment Lise opened the back hatch, I'd sprung from it and across the soggy lawn to the back door. I wanted to empty the water bowl, then collapse over the register. Some of yesterday's leftover chicken wings would have been a bonus for all my hard work, but I'd settle for a stale dog biscuit.

Shivering, I watched Lise go down the hallway and deposit Hunter in his bedroom.

"Don't you dare!" Lise warned as she came down the hallway, then ducked into the laundry room.

Don't what? And who was she talking to? Bit? Bit was lying under the table now, not doing a thing.

I shook myself. Water flew from my coat, speckling the linoleum with drops of runny brown. Ah, the relief! I felt drier and warmer already.

Lise appeared in the doorway, an old towel stretched between her hands. "You didn't."

"She did." Chuckling, Grace tugged on the fridge door and searched inside. She took out two bottles of root beer, popped open the caps, and poured them into mugs. Foam bubbled over the rims. She haphazardly mopped it up with a dishrag. "Told you I'd wait outside with her while you got the towels."

"Yeah, I heard you. The problem is I didn't really *hear* you. My mind was on Hunter, the funeral, this crazy day … anywhere but here." Lise threw the towel on the floor and trudged into the living room. Grace followed, a mug in each hand, kicking the baby gate shut behind her.

Bit and I sat next to each other behind the gate, our noses pressed between the vertical bars.

"Spill," Grace said. "Your guts, not the root beer, please."

"Pffft …" Lise's bangs lifted off her forehead with the puff of air. "I don't know, Grace. You've already done more than enough. I don't want to drag you down into this cesspool that is my life right now. I mean, I'm twenty-eight and a widow with a five-year old son who won't talk or stay put and …" — she set her mug on the end table and laid both hands over her belly — "and another on the way. What a mess. And today, just as I'm dealing with every-thing that's happened, more gets thrown at me."

Bit sniffed my head all over, my ears, my neck. I twitched a lip at her. I didn't need to be cleaned up right now. She took the hint and lay down, stretching her paws out and placing her head between them. Bit was an attentive mother, but not obsessive. I was almost six months old now and she was quick to let me have my independence.

"Hunter's just upset, Lise. He misses his daddy. Maybe he went looking for him?"

"No, he knows what happened. He saw it, remember? I know exactly why he ran."

"Okay. Why?"

"Because I told him we were moving up north, to be near Grandma Becky."

"And?"

Lise's shoulders sagged. She chugged the root beer and set the mug between her feet. "I told him we couldn't take the animals."

"Of course you can't have sheep at a condo. He'll get over it. Take him to the Cincinnati Zoo up there a few times. Zebras and giraffes are much more interesting than sheep."

"It's not just the sheep, Grace. We can't have dogs at Mom's condo."

Grace swung her mug over to the end table so fast the froth sloshed over the top of the glass and onto her hand. She flicked some of it off, then wiped the remainder on her pants leg. "Not even Bit and" — she glanced furtively in my direction, her voice plummeting to a whisper — "the puppy?"

"No. The condo management almost went to court last year over a guy who brought in a service dog after he lost some motor function following a stroke. They caved eventually, but still —"

"Shut. Up. What a bunch of ... I won't say it. But what are you going to do with all of them?"

"I already have a home lined up for Scout with a breeder out in Oregon. Janice referred a family to me that's looking for an adult or two, so I'm hopeful they take Cricket and Chase. As for Bit and Halo, well, I had to call Estelle and tell her we were moving soon and she agreed to take them. For now. I'm hoping that by the time the baby is born, things will have stabilized with Mom, and I'll be back to work full time and can find a place of my own close to her, because there aren't even supposed to be children in the condos, but they made an exception because of my circumstances. Then I can take the dogs back. Except …"

"Except what? There's something else, isn't there? Is the … Oh my God, is the baby okay?"

"What? Oh, no, no. Everything's fine on that account as far as I know. I go for my first real OB visit next week. It has to do with Cam. He, um … he wasn't completely honest with me about a few things."

Grace slapped a hand over her mouth. "He had a mistress?"

"God, no."

"Drug habit?" Grace's brows drew down to hood her eyes. "Street or prescription?"

"No!"

"Okay, Lise, you're freaking me out. What could Cam possibly have done? He was as vanilla as they get."

"I thought that, too. But his lawyer called yesterday afternoon and —" She inched closer to Grace, then glanced into the hallway to make sure Hunter wasn't nearby. "You remember I told you a few years back, when Cam was just out of grad school, how he tried to start up a consulting business with a friend, but the friend bailed on him and then the business went belly up just a few months after he'd started it?"

"Not the details, but I remember the gist of it. No shame in that. Don't most of all small businesses fail?"

69

"Yeah, but turns out Cam omitted some details when he explained it all to me. There were bank loans. Big ones. Much bigger than he'd ever let on."

"And you knew this when you married him? Did you know how much they were for?"

"No, I didn't. I know, I know. That sort of thing should all be up front when you marry someone, but Cam just seemed so responsible about everything. Not to mention the fact that I found the whole environmental risk assessment thing too far over my head to be of interest. Plus, he stayed close to home just so he could help his aging parents with their farm, all when he could have had much more lucrative jobs in Louisville or Cincinnati or Nashville. I was the one who pressed him for the move and the new job. His parents were doing fine and I had finally convinced my mom that my dad needed to be in a facility where they could care for him 24/7, but she was having health issues of her own. So moving north just seemed like the right thing to do. Cam resisted. He stalled. He even suggested I take a leave from my job to go help my mom. I should have known there was something up. It wasn't like Cam to be so … uncooperative. Maybe that's not the right word, but he was, in his own subtle way, avoiding making any big moves."

Grace tugged a crocheted throw, one of Estelle's creations, from the back of the couch and spread it over her lap, tucking her feet neatly beneath her. "He defaulted on the business loan, right? Or was about to."

"Yes, but that's not the worst of it. After the funeral, his lawyer got in touch with me. Asked if Cam had life insurance, something that would cover any debts we might have. He did, but it was barely enough to cover funeral expenses. That's when everything really started to unravel. This house …" Lise's eyes swept around the room, taking in the carved mantel over the seldom used fireplace, the high ceilings, the doorways with their glass transoms. "This old, *old* house that we worked so hard on — I'm going to lose it to the bank. There's no way I can swing it. The debts are too much and even with the money we were saving up to get us a new house up north, it wouldn't even come close to covering it. Cam had taken out a second mortgage to pay on his loan, because he was getting behind. He never told me any of this, Grace. I feel so stupid for trusting him and not having more of a hand in our finances. He could have asked his parents for help. God knows they owed him *something* for all the time he's put in on that farm."

"You could still ask Estelle." Grace tilted her head. "Couldn't you?"

"I can't, Grace. The amount is astronomical. She'd have to give up her retirement, sell the farm ... No, it's just too much. Besides, I can only blame myself for not having been more aware of things. It's going to take awhile to get it all sorted out. I meet with the lawyer on Tuesday. Then I have to take Hunter to a specialist Thursday and for tests on Friday. Somewhere in there I have my own doctor's appointment. Meanwhile, I need to streamline my life, even if that means giving up some things I truly love. This house is the least of it. I'm going to miss seeing the lambs in springtime. Most of all, I'm going to miss the dogs." Her head sank down to meet her shoulders as the weight of everything bore down on her. "What happened today ... I'm grateful for what Halo did, believe me. I'll never forget it. But it only makes it harder."

"I wish I had room, Lise. I'd take you in, kids, dogs, and all, but ..."

Lise clenched her eyes shut for a moment, fighting back the tears that she kept to herself so much, but one leaked out of the corner of her eye. She swiped it away with her fist, then punched the pillow in her lap. "I'm going to survive this. I will. I'll be okay. I have to be. For my mom. For Hunter... The baby."

Scooting across the couch, Grace wrapped her arms around Lise

71

and hugged her hard. "Don't forget yourself, honey. You have to get through this for *you*. Or else there won't be anything left for anyone else."

"I've been telling myself that, but it's just so damn hard." Lise sat back, her fingers teasing at a loose thread on the hem of her sweatshirt. She grabbed a handful of tissues from the end table and blew her nose. "There are times I wake up and I don't think I can get through the day without losing my shit. Yesterday I burned the grilled cheese and I almost went postal on Hunter for spilling his orange juice. Then I had to tell him about the move and not being able to take the dogs with us … No wonder he took off."

"I can only imagine how tough this is for you. You call me anytime, you hear? I don't care if it's 3 a.m."

Lise's head bobbed in a nod, but her lip was quivering again. "Why didn't he tell me? We could've figured something out. Now I've not only lost him — I've lost everything."

"Hey, girl." Tapping a finger on Lise's still slim abdomen, Grace gave her friend an admonishing look. "You still have the two most important things in your life and a good mom who's going to help you get back on your feet. I know things are pretty bad, but they could be a whole lot worse."

A weak smile flitted over Lise's lips. Still, she looked anything but optimistic. Grace rose, folded the throw hastily, and draped it over the arm of the couch. "I need to get to bed. I'll be over after work tomorrow with more boxes. I expect to see progress before I get here, though. Got it?"

"See you." Lise didn't get up to see her friend out the door. She just sat there, staring off into space, too exhausted for tears, as the door clicked shut behind Grace.

It saddened me to see Lise like that. I pawed at the baby gate, signaling her to let me out so I could crawl up onto the couch next to her to let her stroke my fur. But Lise didn't move. Not even when I let out a soft whine. I didn't want to make too much noise and wake Hunter, so I sank down next to the gate.

When Lise needed me, when she was ready, I'd be waiting. It's one of the things dogs do best. We are very, *very* patient. We can be foolishly hopeful that way. It's not that we *want* to wait for the things to come our way. It's that we usually have no other choice. Why torment yourself with what you can't control?

Patience, though, requires faith. And we always … *always* have faith in our humans. It's why our bond with them is so strong, what makes us indispensable.

—o00o—

A bellow of anger came from the office at the end of the hall. I popped up from my spot over the register and sped down the corridor, turning the corner by the window just tightly enough to avoid crashing into the mountain of boxes piled against the wall there. I slowed as I reached the doorway, cautious.

Seated in the tall-backed leather chair before the computer where Cam used to spend hours, Lise swept a stack of yellow papers onto the floor.

"My God, this is going to take weeks — no, *months* to sort out." Defeated, she plowed her hands through her hair and cradled her head, elbows planted on the desk. "And I thought this couldn't get any worse. What dream world was I living in? The Land of Make-Believe? Never-Never Land? Everything's Rosy in Faderville? Talk about naïve … Why didn't Cam just come clean? I mean, exactly when was he planning to tell me he owed so much money? When we found our dream house and the bank turned us down? How could I have been so —?"

The floor creaked beside me. Lise whipped her head up to see Hunter standing in the doorway. He looked down the moment their eyes met.

"Oh." She twisted her wrist to check her watch. "I promised you lunch half an hour ago. Sorry, sweetie. I just need to finish with this drawer of papers first. Then I promise I'll take a break. I'll make your favorite: grilled cheese."

He twisted his face in disapproval.

"Right. I burned it the last time, didn't I? Peanut butter?"

The same face.

"And grape jelly?"

His head swiveled back and forth.

"Chicken fingers?"

A light shrug, a faint nod.

"Okay, then. Chicken fingers it is. And corn. I know you like corn. You do like corn, right?" she asked, but she didn't sound very sure about it. She pushed the chair back on its rollers and stood, reaching her hand out. "Come on. I'll start lunch. The paperwork can wait. Meanwhile, we'll put your coat on and you and Halo can play ball in the yard."

She led him down the hallway and to the back door in the kitchen. A minute later she had him bundled up in his puffy blue coat and matching Spiderman hat and mittens. She flung open the laundry room closet, fished out an old tennis ball, and dropped it into Hunter's open palm. The yellow fuzz on one side of the ball was shredded so badly the rubbery insides were showing. She'd tried to give me new balls to play with, but I always abandoned them in favor of this one. Newer wasn't always better.

"Throw it until you're both too tired to play anymore, okay? Lunch should be done by then." With that, she spun him around and nudged him out the door. "You, too," she said to me.

I raced out into the sunshine, relieved to be out of the house. As much as I loved Lise, there was a cloud hovering over her lately that made it difficult to endure her company for long. I'd tried hard to offer comfort, to distract her with kisses and games of fetch, but she seemed mired in troubles that she didn't want to burden the rest of us with.

Time, I told myself. Just give her time.

Meanwhile, Hunter needed a friend. After a few laps around the yard, I did my business, then hurried to stand before Hunter, my nub wagging enthusiastically as he squeezed the tattered ball in his fist.

Bouncing on all fours, I barked. *Throw it! Throw it! Throw it!*

He cranked his arm back, swung it forward, and lobbed the ball in a high arc. The grungy yellow dot spun across a blue, blue sky. Bursting forward, I ran to the far corner of the yard, my eyes tracking its trajectory and speed. As the ball began to descend, my instincts told me I hadn't gone quite far enough. I launched myself skyward with the strength of my haunches, twisting in the air as I stretched my neck. The ball hurtled toward me, whirling on its axis. My teeth snapped together, sinking into the rubbery orb.

Gravity commanded me back to earth. The moment my feet hit the ground, I bounded forward, racing back toward Hunter. I dropped the prize at his feet.

He threw it again. And again and again and again. Until it was so coated in my slobber that he refused to touch it. So I picked it up in my mouth and ran in small circles around him. He laughed, spinning around to watch me. It was the first time he'd done that since before his daddy died.

Panting, I dropped the ball at his feet again and barked at him. When he reached for it, I grabbed it before his fingers could close around it and sped off. He ran after me, his short arms windmilling at his sides. On the other side of the leafless tulip tree, I pivoted and darted past him. He exploded in laughter. Back and forth we raced, until my legs began to tire and my breath became heavier. I slowed, turned around to face him, waiting for him to catch up with me.

"Halo," Hunter said, his small chest heaving, his jaw hanging open as he gulped in air, "come … here. Give —"

He swayed, went down on his knees. His eyes rolled up to disappear beneath fluttering lids. He hit the ground like a sack of kibble tossed from the truck bed.

I spat my ball out and hurried to him, first nudging him with my nose and then licking his cheek and neck vigorously when he didn't respond. I woofed softly in his ear, thinking maybe he was just playing turtle again, but he didn't move. I wasn't even sure he was breathing.

I ran to the back door and barked as loudly as I could. I didn't stop until Lise pushed open the door. She was about to scold me when she saw Hunter lying on the ground.

She flew to him, touched his back, said his name. Still, he didn't move. Carefully, she rolled him over and placed her ear against his chest, listening. With a nervous sigh of relief, she pulled her cell phone from her pocket and punched in a few numbers.

"Come on, come on, come on … Yes, I need an ambulance. It's my son. He's unconscious … Yes, he's breathing … He does, but it's faint. Very faint. And rapid. I don't know what that means, but please, please, *please* hurry."

By the time the ambulance arrived, Hunter was alert enough to respond to his mother, but when the EMTs asked him questions, he wouldn't speak, only nod or shake his head.

What it meant, I learned later when Lise spent an hour on the phone relaying the day's events to her mom, was that Hunter had a condition called hypertrophic cardiomyopathy, a thickening of the walls of the heart. He had inherited the condition from his father, it seemed, although it had never caused much of an issue for Cam. The only thing the doctors could tell Lise was that chances were that Hunter would lead a normal life. All that could be done for now was to watch him carefully. If the need ever arose, there were medications that could be administered, even surgery that could be done. In rare cases, however, the condition was fatal.

When Lise brought him home from the hospital that evening, she made him a bed on the couch, popped in his favorite animal video, one about giraffes, and watched him from the kitchen as he drifted off to sleep. Every time Hunter stirred, she abandoned her stacks of paper and went to stoop over him, watching his chest rise and fall in a slight but steady rhythm.

"I can't lose you, Hunter," she whispered, sitting on the arm of the couch as she stroked his sandy locks from his forehead. "You mean the world to me. You and this little one are all I have. I have to keep you safe. Nothing else matters."

I curled up in my crate, one eye cocked open as the light from the TV flickered, then went off.

chapter 8

He came a few days later, so early that Hunter wasn't even awake yet. His name was Ned Hanson, Ray and Estelle's next door neighbor — although when you live out in the country 'neighbor' means the person whose property abuts yours, even if their house is on the other side of the woods and across the bridge, three miles away.

I'd seen him a few times before at Ray's barn. Usually with a wrench or two hanging out of his front overalls pocket and an oily rag dangling from the back one. He always had scruff on his chin, never a full beard and never clean shaven. Then there was that baseball cap. Always the same one, green with the threads on the logo on the front so worn and smudged you could no longer make out what it had once said. He wore it over a full mop of greasy blond hair, no matter whether it was a hundred degrees out or like an icebox.

Which was what it was the day he came for Bit and me. Cold. Bitterly, bone-biting cold.

The moment I saw him, the hair on the back of my neck bristled. He'd never paid us dogs much heed, not even Slick, but I didn't mind that. He left me alone and so I never had reason to fear or mistrust him. But that day, it was the first day he'd ever really looked at me. And I didn't like it, although I had no idea why. It was like I had a feeling deep down in my guts, like a tiny worm gnawing at my intestines, filling me with a queasiness. Maybe if I ate some grass right now, I could spew bile and get rid of the feeling.

I stared at him through the chain link, safe on my side of the fence, sizing him up.

His lip lifted in a sneer. "You sure that lil' one with the weird spots don't bite?"

Lise tossed a bag of kibble into the bed of his truck. "No! Why would you say that? Did Estelle say something?"

"Just the way he's looking at me." He rubbed at his nose with a dirty sleeve. "Not sure I like it."

The feeling was mutual. I slunk behind Bit, who was wagging her whole bum. Bit loved everyone. That trait would get her in trouble some day. Better to be cautious about people you didn't know. Take time to make sure they didn't mean you any harm. Lise was always encouraging me to let people pet me, but the older I got, the less sense that made to me. Why should I automatically trust *everyone?* Wouldn't it be safer not to? Bit climbed up the chain link fence to hang her paws over the top rail. Couldn't she see that this man's arrival was bad news for us? I nipped her hock and darted away before Lise could reprimand me for it. Bit just tossed me a look that said she was too busy to play right now. Stupid dog! I went and hid behind the broad trunk of the old tulip tree.

"You mean 'she'," Lise said.

Ned scratched at his neck, his dirty fingernails scraping over stubble. "Huh?"

"Halo is a girl." I heard the latch slide up, then ping as the metal clicked back into place. "Come here, Halo."

As stealthily as I could, I peeked around the tree. Lise was inside the fence now, crouching down, her hand outstretched. She already had a leash on Bit, who was sitting obediently beside her. I noticed Bit's ears were flattened, which meant even she knew now that something was up.

"Please, Halo," Lise said. "It's okay. Ned here's just going to take you to Estelle's to stay awhile. I'll come and get you as soon as I can."

I stayed put. Her words didn't match the tremor in her voice. I wasn't as gullible anymore as she might believe. I'd been lied to before. More than once, I'd come trotting when she offered a treat, only to find out that the biscuit she'd promised meant a soaking in the bathtub. Something in her voice had not been right then, and it wasn't right now. We weren't going on a walk or taking a car ride to the feed store. She was sending me away with this Ned.

I glanced at Bit and saw the tension in her muscles, but every time Lise took a step forward, Bit followed, the leash hanging slack. There was a fine line between obedience and sheer stupidity.

"Please, don't make this any harder on me than it has to be." Lise crept closer, tugging Bit along. I flattened myself against the backside of the tree, trying to make my point as obvious as possible. The moment I heard Lise's footsteps close in on me, I sped to the corner of the yard and hunkered down, but she was quicker than I'd counted on. She swooped in and hooked her hand into my collar. She snapped the leash onto the metal ring, then reeled me in close. My instinct was to bite her again, a sharp nip to let her know this was wrong, a hundred ways wrong, but if I did that in front of this man, that would give him even more reason to hate me. Lise might hate me, too, then.

She breathed into my fur. "I can't bear to do this."

Then why are you? I didn't understand. Lise and Hunter were my whole life. How could I not be theirs?

"Hey, if you don't mind," Ned said, "I need to get going. Gonna be all day out in the field, so ... if you could just throw 'em in the back ...?"

Lise shot to her feet. Her grip on my leash tightened. "No, they can't ride in the back. It's too dangerous."

"Listen, sweetheart, I rode in the bed of a pick-up my whole life as a kid. Didn't do me no harm. Couple of farms dogs like that'll be just fine. Ain't that far to Ray and … I mean to Estelle's place, anyway." He shoved the bag of dog food over to the side of the bed. "Now, do you want me to take 'em or not? Only got so much time."

"Okay, okay." When Lise stepped forward, I locked my legs in place. She dragged me a few steps, my pads scraping over the roots of the tree. Bit glared at me reproachfully. I hung my head, although I had no intention of giving in. Lise was ignoring every signal I could send. Somehow, though, I sensed I was only making things worse, that Lise was doing what she had to do, even though she didn't want to.

Finally, Lise picked me up. I tucked my head against her chest, pressing myself close. This didn't feel right. I couldn't let her do this.

Before I knew it, we were at the gate. I looked up in time to see Lise's fingers hover at the latch, hesitate.

Don't do it, Lise, I thought. *Don't.*

But the words I think never make sounds, even though I know their meaning. A dog's language is subtle, our gestures simple. And yet … humans are so blind to them.

Lise flipped the latch and swung the gate open. The tailgate of the truck gaped before me. In the bed of the truck a man sat on top of a short stack of feed sacks with his elbows resting on his knees. He wore a checkered flannel shirt, buttoned up halfway, and beneath it a plain white T-shirt. He patted the side of the bag on which he sat. My gaze wandered to his face. I knew those eyes, that strong chin, the broad shoulders, and sandy hair. Joy squeezed my heart. It was Cam!

It's okay, girl, he said softly, winking at me. His words were muted, like the sounds that came out of the TV when Lise had it turned down really low so it wouldn't wake Hunter up. And he looked all blurry, like a reflection in water. His lips curved into a smile. *Everything'll turn out fine. Trust me.*

I lurched toward the truck and let out a happy bark, almost pulling Lise off her feet. Ned scuttled aside and waved his hands in front of him. "Whoa, there."

Cam laughed softly, and I leaped up to put my front feet on the tailgate. It was too high, or else I would have jumped in on my own. He reached for me.

"Stop it, Halo! What are you doing?" Lise jerked back on the leash so suddenly it caught my windpipe. My head dipped as I coughed, waiting for the airflow to return to normal. "Calm down. Honestly, Ned, she's usually not like this. I think she knows something's up."

He clucked under his tongue. "Whatever you say. Just put her in the back."

Lise tapped on the tailgate. Bit sprang onto it and Ned tied her leash to a hook by the rear window. As Lise bent down to gather me up, I backed up to look into the bed. Cam wasn't there anymore. He was gone. It was as if Lise had never seen him. Slipping from Lise's grasp, I pulled to the end of the leash and scanned beneath the truck, beside it, behind me. I swung around, hoping he might be inside the fence or on the porch. Nowhere.

Lise's arms wrapped around me, lifted me up, just like when I was a little puppy. But there was none of the tender warmth, the little strokes of my fur, the scratches behind my ears. She slid me onto the rusty bed, shoved me as far as her arms would allow.

"I'll come back for you," she said flatly. "Soon."

Ned grabbed my leash and yanked me closer to the window as he clipped me in. Bit nuzzled my neck, then licked inside my ear to let me know it was okay.

But it wasn't.

Lise didn't wave goodbye or watch us go down the road. She just turned her back and walked inside.

And everyone thinks dogs have it easy. Try being one for a day.

—o0Oo—

I was sure that 'soon' meant tomorrow. Or at most, next week. But 'soon' turned out to be a lot longer than I thought.

Months passed and Lise didn't come to get us. The dumb thing was, I kept hoping that she would, even as mad as I was at her, because I knew my place was with her and Hunter and the little baby not yet born.

Instead of being with my family, I was tossed in an outdoor kennel next to Bit at Ray and Estelle's farm. Left forgotten in the cold, no children to play with, no home to protect, no job, no purpose.

Boredom, though, was the least of my problems.

Even though Estelle still lived in the big farm house, she never checked on us. Sometimes she'd come out the door, gaze our way for a few moments, then get in her car and drive away. When she returned, we weren't even afforded a glance. Ned took care of us. But I wouldn't even say he did that.

I dreaded his arrivals as much as I looked forward to them. Ned's rusted out Chevy truck bumping down the limestone drive meant food, when he remembered. Once a week we'd also get clean water, if he could be bothered to crack the ice in the buckets to replace it. Although a week could mean five days or ten, there was never any way to know.

The snow in my kennel had drifted up so high in the corner that Ned had to scoop out a path with the snow shovel to open the kennel door.

"Goddamn good-for-nothing dogs." His breath billowed outward in a fog of ice. He spat a glob of brown phlegm near me and I backed away. Whatever he kept tucked between his cheek and gum stank. He never swallowed it, but would spit it out when he'd chewed on it long enough. Then he'd take a crinkly pouch out of his front coat pocket, dig his fingers in, and draw a pinch of brown leaves out and stuff it in his mouth again. He was never without it. "Y'all don't do nothing but eat and shit. That's about the sum of it."

Bit stayed hidden in her dog house in the kennel next to mine. For weeks, she would come out to greet him, hopeful for a pat on the head or a biscuit, but he was never generous like that. We were a chore, an imposition, not his friends. I had no intention of pushing the matter. Even Bit finally gave up on him, keeping her distance ever since he'd whacked her in the ribs with the pooper scooper for putting a muddy paw on his already dirty jeans.

Ned slammed the shovel in the bank of snow, so that the handle stood upright, tugged his gloves off, and blew his nose, one nostril at a time. Then he wiped his upper lip with an oil-stained sleeve. "My hunting dogs are each worth ten of you. Buster treed three coons last Sunday alone. And what have you done?" He glared at me accusingly.

What was I supposed to do? I couldn't do the work I was bred for. Estelle had sent all the cows off to auction a month ago. Too much to take care of, she'd told Ned. She'd even sold Slick to some cattleman out in Missouri. Fetched a pretty penny for him, she boasted. The hogs and chickens were gone, too. The farm was not the same without them all. What had once been a place of endless fascination for me was now a wintery wasteland, Bit and I being the last two occupants.

The clatter of tree branches broke the silence as a fierce wind kicked up, carrying in its wake last night's dusting of snow to swirl in crystalline eddies. Beneath the fresh powder lay an icy crust. Two days ago, a wicked storm had blasted over the land, daggers of rain descending from steely skies as the north wind ripped away every shred of warmth within its reach. By the time the clouds broke and rolled away, every surface — the electrical wires hanging heavy from their poles, the leaning outdoor lamp post, the stubble of old flowers in Estelle's garden — was coated in a layer of ice an inch thick. The flimsy piece of metal siding that had served as a roof over our kennels had blown away within the first hour, exposing Bit and me to the

January misery. At least if we had been housed in the same kennel, Bit and I could have huddled together for warmth. As it was, we had only our cold dog houses and a compacted bed of straw. If not for the windbreak afforded us by the fact that our kennels sat on the east side of the barn's outer wall, we might have frozen to death.

In those two days since the storm, Estelle had emerged from her house only once, forgetting to feed us or bring us thawed water. We knew she was in there. We saw the lights — or *a* light, at least. A very dim light that floated from the kitchen, to the living room, and then to the upper bedroom as night came on fully.

Yesterday morning, we had heard the crack of ice as the kitchen door was hammered open. Bit and I stretched our frozen limbs and braved the cold to stare at the back porch. Estelle snatched three logs from the woodpile stacked against the house and went back inside, never once looking our way. I let out a bark as the door clicked shut, then several more. Bit gave me a cynical look. Yes, I knew my efforts were futile, that I was probably just wasting energy, but I had to try.

A minute later, Bit had walked stiffly back to her doghouse and crawled inside. I barked for an hour, pacing back and forth, jumping against the kennel door, anything to warm my blood, until my throat gave out from the strain and my muscles grew weak and shaky. And then I watched and waited for a long, long while, while my mouth went dry and my toes numb and my belly cramped with hunger.

Through it all, I kept wondering when Lise would come back to get us. Or if she ever would.

Ned smashed the shovel against the kennel door's bottom. The ice that had locked it in place chimed as it fell to the ground, shattering into a hundred glassy shards. He yanked the door open, grabbed the handle of the bucket sitting in the corner and grunted.

"Well, shit. Frozen solid." He hauled it out, then smacked a metal bowl down beside my dog house. Kibble rattled in the bottom.

I hung back, wary.

"What the hell's the matter with you?" he said. "Come here if you wanna eat. I ain't gonna hurt you." He nudged the food dish forward an inch with his foot.

Hunger overruled my sensibility. I dove for it. But before I could vacuum up the first piece, Ned swung his boot at the bowl. It skidded across the crusty ice, slammed into the door with a bang, and overturned. Half the kibble fell in a loose pile. The rest of it scattered beyond the outside of the kennel. Before I could react, he landed another kick between my ribs and stomach. Yelping, I scurried into the corner. He guffawed as he went out through the door and then swung it shut. Not until he was out of sight and I had my breath back did I go for the food. I gobbled up every nugget within reach, rooting with my nose beneath the bowl to flip it over and find a few more.

Returning, Ned removed Bit's bucket and placed her bowl down. She was wise enough to stay inside her dog house and wait for him to leave. I hid while he took mine. As he tromped away, blocks of ice swinging from each gloved hand, he made a point of grinding the food scattered on the ground outside into the snow. He disappeared into the barn.

I reached a paw through one of the kennel links nearest the bottom, but I could only get my leg through partway. In the end, I managed to pull just two nuggets inside. The rest were either too far away or had been crushed to dust beneath his heel.

A pale sun climbed high in a watery sky laced with pastel clouds. Its brightness, what little there was, was deceptive, for it shed no warmth on the frozen earth below. The snot had frozen at the edge of my nostrils. The leather of my nose was dry and cracked. My pads were split and bleeding. Pea-sized balls of ice clung to my feathers and britches on the backs of my legs and rear, making little clacking sounds whenever I moved about, which wasn't often anymore. My attempts to get someone's attention from inside the house had fallen on deaf ears and sapped all my strength.

In the next kennel, Bit groaned. We were both still hungry and might have been thirsty as well if we hadn't learned to bite at the ice and let it melt in our mouths.

Finally, I gave up watching and went inside my doghouse, rooting around in the straw until I had dug a deep nest. There I hunkered down, able to see most of Ned's comings and goings as he went from the barn, to the shed, to the house, and back out to the barn. He didn't return to our kennels with fresh water.

I must have dozed off, because the sun was sliding low when I heard the garage door go up and Estelle's big blue Buick back out. Rolls of white exhaust billowed from the tailpipe. It was Ned who got out of the car. He shut the door and went inside. A few minutes later he reappeared with two suitcases, which he tossed in the trunk. The moment he slammed the trunk closed, Estelle stepped out the kitchen door.

"You sure about this, ma'am?" Ned said, in a suspiciously polite tone.

"Never been more." Estelle hoisted her oversized purse on her shoulder and clung to the handrail as she descended the stairs. "I thought maybe if I unloaded the farm animals and just let you lease the land, I could handle things. But being here by myself ... the loneliness is just eating me up, Ned. This ice storm is what did me in. Going on three days now without power. Roads so bad I didn't dare go out on them. What if I fell and broke my hip? Nobody'd ever know. I'd just rot in the big old house until the mail piled up."

"I'd check on you, Mrs. McHugh. D'you need me to run some errands for you? Do some more chores around the house?"

Estelle put her hand out, and Ned laid the car keys in them. "I can't even get you to show up regularly, as it is. Your mama and me, we go way back, God bless her soul, but you got enough on your plate with your own place." She opened the passenger side door, tossed her purse inside and waddled around the back of the car. "I'll be back in the spring for the rest of my things — and to help Sheridan Bexley get the place ready for auction. Breaks my heart, leaving this place, but my sister has a great condo down in Naples, Florida and —"

"Ain't you gonna miss seeing your grandkids?" Ned stood before the driver's side door, blocking her path, like he didn't want to let her leave.

Her chin sank. She tugged at the lapel of her coat. "Haven't seen my dear little Hunter since Lise took off for Covington. My friend Marcella is a friend of Lise's friend Grace's mother, if you follow that. Said Lise was having some trouble with her pregnancy. Minor stuff, she swore, but the doctor told Lise to stick close to home — meaning up north, not here. Poor Hunter has his own problems. Her mother's not been well, either, I hear. Had one of those mini-strokes. And her father's in a home with Alzheimer's." She looked around, her eyes skipping past the kennels to the barn, then over the fields. "Lord, and here I am going south. Never thought I'd see the day. Tears my heart right out of my chest, it does."

Awkwardly, Estelle shifted to her right, trying to wedge past Ned, but he stood firm, his fists crammed deep in his coverall pockets.

"For crying out loud, Ned, I need to get in my car and go. Is there something you need?"

He drew his hands from his pockets, looked down at his palms. His gaze flitted my way. "Just that … the dogs need some more food and, well, I hafta come out here every day. They ain't like cows. Cows you can just throw down some hay and let 'em drink out of the creek and they'll be fine for days, or even weeks, but them dogs, they —"

"There's a check on the kitchen table. Should cover things for a while. In the meantime, I think Mr. Penewit is gonna come take a look at the girls this weekend. Ray had promised him a pup once for helping out when we had that big flood, but the timing was never right. I told him he might as well take those dogs off my hands. Heaven knows Lise hasn't taken enough interest in them to come and get them. I think that whole bit about not being able to have dogs where she is is a lot of nonsense, but what do I know?"

She shuffled past him, got in her car and backed into the turnaround. Ned barely scooted out of the way in time to avoid having his boots crushed beneath her tires — which would have served him right. Estelle wasn't fifty feet down the driveway when she threw the car into reverse, stopped next to Ned, and rolled down the window.

"Thanks for warming up the car for me, and bringing my suitcases down from the attic and all."

He shrugged. "Weren't nothin'."

She started to roll the window back up, then paused it halfway. "Almost forgot. I think there are mice or something in the garage. I moved an old bucket in there a week ago and found a pile of shredded newspaper. Ray always kept too much junk around. I warned him it would attract varmints."

"Yeah, I saw a hole in the drywall in there the size of my fist. Rats, more likely."

Even from a distance I could see her eyes get huge. "Rats, really? You think so?"

"I'd bet on it."

"You'll take care of them? I don't want any damage to the property before it goes up for auction."

"First thing tomorrow."

"Good. You have my number if anything comes up, right?"

"Sure do."

"And don't forget to water the dogs. I was just too afraid to go all the way out there with the ice, but I could see from the kitchen window that they were all right."

See us? Could she see us shivering and hungry? If she had noticed one of us frozen to the ground, would she have bothered to venture out even then?

At least wild coyotes could dig dens to wait out the winter. Our kennels were on a pad of concrete. The only way out was through the door. Why not bring us in before the storm ever came? Bit and I had been used to being in the house. Even the barn or the garage would have been better than being stuck out here.

"Don't worry," Ned reassured her. "I got it all under control here. Enjoy Florida."

"Too darn hot for me, but it'll be good to be with my sister. Haven't seen her since the reunion three years ago. Bye now, Ned."

As Estelle rolled away in her big car, on her way south, Bit came up and leaned against the kennel panel next to me. If I pressed myself really close, I could almost feel the heat from my mother's body. Almost.

chapter 9

Ned Hanson never brought our water buckets out that day. I might have been thankful for the snow, but the snow was cold and eating it only made me colder. Even when the wind died down and the sun came out, it became harder and harder to stay warm. I had almost forgotten what it felt like to lie over the register in Lise and Cam's old house, the hot air tickling my belly and heating me to the core. Those days seemed so long ago — even to me, a dog not yet a year old. But, a lot can happen in a year. Sometimes, even more can happen in a day.

Three more days went by again before Ned came back. By then, I could sense that my belly had shrunk, the skin pulling tight up into my ribs. I hadn't felt my toes for over a week. Sometimes I had to look down, just to check that they were still on the ends of my legs. The first day after Estelle left, I paced in circles, trying to warm my bones. But that only made me more tired. I'd barked and barked the first two days, hoping to alert a distant neighbor or passerby on the road, but now even that was too much effort.

When a truck clanged down the driveway, I emerged from my doghouse, hopeful it was the other man Estelle had spoken of. But it was only Ned. I almost went back inside my flimsy shelter, when it occurred to me I ought to pee while I was out. I hadn't peed in … I couldn't remember. I squatted, straining to empty my bladder, but only a few drops came out, staining the dirty snow a dark orange. Layers of my excrement were frozen beneath the ice. I was ashamed of the filth, my fur even smelled of urine and poop, but what could I do? If I had been allowed out, I would have done my business in a corner of the yard, like Lise had taught me. Ned could seldom be bothered to clean up after us, so it had piled up until there was hardly any place I could step that hadn't been soiled. At least in the last few days I hadn't had much inside me to get rid of. Like now.

Over Ned's shoulder flopped a sack of dog food. It wasn't our usual kind — the supply that Lise had sent with us had long since run out. The sacks Ned brought with him were often torn and taped. Remains, he called them. Sacks damaged in transit or by careless customers at the store. Sometimes chewed into by mice. So we got whatever was available. Once it had even been cat food. Tasty, but the diarrhea afterwards had almost made it not worth it.

He ducked into the barn. A minute later he came out and went back to his truck, where he fished out a plain brown sack. On his way back to the garage, he pulled a small bright yellow box from the sack. His grungy baseball cap turned backwards, he came out of the barn, rattling the kibble around in our metal bowls. Bit came out of her house, but I stayed inside. Even when he opened my door and slapped the pan down, I didn't come out. No sense risking getting kicked. Or having my food spilled again. I'd waited three days already. I could wait three more minutes.

Bit could hardly help herself, though. She danced on her toes and did a couple of little leaps, she was so happy to be fed. This time she was smart enough to keep her distance, at least. I cringed as the door creaked open and Ned stomped inside Bit's kennel.

Belching loudly, Ned dropped the bowl in the corner. "Yup, cheap beer and tacos. Breakfast of champions." He rubbed his stomach in a circle and belched again. Just as he stepped out of Bit's kennel and lifted his hand toward the latch, the sound of a donkey braying came out of his front pocket. He pulled his cell phone out. "Hey, Garth, you jackass! What's up? ... Naw, it's your turn to bring the case. Mine to bring the smokes. Marcus is bringing the food. Those girls still coming? ... Oh yeah, what *kind* of videos?" He turned in a circle, his pinkie stuffed in his free ear as he picked at some wax. His eyebrows waggled. "Yeah, man, that's what I'm talking about. Gonna get me some. Now you remember that I got my eye on the redhead. Keep your hands off her, you hear? Else you're gonna feel a rifle barrel jammed against your spine... Shut. Up. I ain't kidding, you dumb asshole. Try me."

He ambled away toward the house, his coat flapping open in front, the laces on his shoes loose and trailing over the muddy ground, as he rambled on about beer and girls.

Mud? Oh, the snow had melted. Funny, I didn't feel warmer.

In the time it took him to go into the house and come back out lugging buckets of fresh water, Bit had licked her bowl clean, but I still hadn't come out of my house. My brain was in a fog. It was like watching everything through a veil of cobwebs. I should have been excited about the food, but I could barely muster the energy to lift my head and watch as Ned put the buckets in our kennels, then went and got in his truck.

He left without incident. I had food and water. But somehow, it didn't seem like enough.

Yawning, I stretched my legs. I knew I needed to eat, but my stomach hurt. I forced myself to sit up, then stand. My heart was racing so fast, it felt like I'd just run down to the pond and back at breakneck speed. But all I was doing was standing there.

A wave of dizziness swept over me. I sat down until it passed, closed my eyes for a moment. When I opened them again, I saw three little yellow birds with tufted crests perched on the edge of my bowl.

I tried to bark at them, but it came out as nothing more than a breathy huff.

"You're losing it, girl," one of the birds spouted, puffing up her feathers. The other two flapped their wings in agreement.

I blinked, hard. *What the ...?* Their chirps morphed into clicks. No, they weren't birds anymore. They were three golden hamsters hanging over the edge of the bowel, crunching on my kibble. They chattered in squeaky voices, laughing, and pointed at me with their tiny claws. More hamsters squeezed beneath the bottom bar of the kennel and jumped into the bowl. *How dare they eat my food?!*

I lunged forward in attack mode. My paws slammed into the bowl. It flipped up in the air, twisting on its axis, a wobbling disc of silver against a broad blue sky. At its apex, it hovered, kibble raining everywhere. Then it plummeted straight down before landing with a bone-clattering clang. The sound rang and rang in my ears like a gong that wouldn't stop.

Furry lumps with red beady eyes scattered before me as I snapped and snapped and snapped, gobbling them up one by one. I swallowed without chewing or tasting. Until the ache in my stomach returned.

My guts twisted in agony. A cramp gripped my middle. Pushed up my throat. A heave rolled through me. I gagged. Moist nuggets spilled over my tongue in barely eaten blobs. I vomited again. And again. Piles of it. Kibble. Not hamsters or birds. No fur. No feathers. Just ... dog food.

I sat there awhile, staring at my dinner, a chunky puddle of bile spreading steadily outward. I didn't feel well. No longer hungry, I backed away from it.

Then I heard Bit's soft whimper. She was standing just outside my kennel, her black nose pressed to the links.

Outside? How did she get outside?

The latch. Ned had forgotten to flip down the latch on her door.

Bit pawed at my door, but it wouldn't give. She stared up at my latch for a long, long time, the wheels turning in her head. Finally, she backed up a step, then sprang upward, over and over. With each leap, she gained height. She bounced off the door with her front feet, reaching her paws as high as she could.

But it wasn't enough. The latch was too high. She quickly began to tire.

Go, Mother. Just go, I wanted to say. *Run as fast as you can, as far as you can.*

But of course, I couldn't. All I could do was wish myself on the outside with her, wish for Lise to come and take us home, wish for this misery, this limbo, to end.

I folded to the ground, the bottom of my rib cage sinking into a stinking puddle of melted snow and urine. There was nowhere I could sit that wasn't damp and dirty. I no longer cared.

The sun slid low, dipping behind the woods to the west of the small pasture. Shadows marched across the farmyard. Along with them, Bit retreated.

—o0Oo—

The silver light of dawn spilled over distant hills. On the bark of the broad oak that stood in the center of the big pasture, a pearlescent sheen of frost glimmered, each gnarled branch reaching outward likes the grasping fingers of an old man. A thin snow fog lingered above the ground, the air as breezeless as the inside of a house.

I remembered how it was, to be inside. Warm, dry, fed. I remembered being happy and loved, too. Belly rubs from Hunter. Playing ball. The way Lise used to dribble the warm, leftover gravy from dinner over my food. The quiet mornings spent with Cam by the fishing pond and all the times he took me to ride along in the truck.

Then Cam died. And everything changed.

On the top bar of my kennel, a robin sang a morning revelry, her rosy chest puffing with rapid breaths. Of course she was happy. She was free to come and go. All she had to do was spread her wings and fly.

A gray form emerged from the barely open barn door and floated through the breaking mist. It was Bit, looking far more energetic than I had felt in weeks. She paused before my kennel, gazed at me forlornly for a moment, then pawed at the links.

I lifted my head in greeting. It was all I could do. I was so, so cold. So very tired.

Whining, she trotted away toward the garage. Halfway there, she stopped, looked back at me as if I might suddenly be following her, then went inside the building. How careless of Ned to have left so many doors open and unlocked. There were valuable tools and machinery inside still. Ray would have been irate. I'd seen how he kept his wrenches lined up by size on the pegboard in the garage, the neatly ordered shelves with all their bottles, glass jars and boxes, and the garden tools hanging along the wall, grouped by purpose. Ray had taken pride in his home and his farm. And now Estelle had abandoned it all and left it in the care of Ned Hanson? He would have been so disappointed.

Inside, metal scraped over concrete. Bit was searching for something. Food? Or had she seen a rat dart beneath the wooden workbench? Metal rattled, clanged as it hit the floor. Then all went quiet.

A long time passed before Bit emerged. She walked slowly, licking her lips, her belly much fuller than it had been yesterday. She must have found the food.

But there was something off about her gait. Instead of coming straight to me, she veered to the left, staggered, then zagged right. She tripped over nothing, righted herself, and stood swaying, her head hanging low.

What's wrong with her?

She stopped midway, rested awhile, then went toward the barn, her movements still off, but less obvious as she went more slowly.

When she disappeared inside the barn, I dragged myself to my doghouse, although every muscle in my body begged me to lie down again right where I was. Inside, I curled up and shut my eyes, sleep calling.

Hours must have gone by, for when I awoke, the sun was on the other side of the property, suspended above the bare tree branches of the woods. A pair of buzzards circled the pasture, gliding on a gentle wind. Then they banked away, disappearing somewhere beyond the roof of the barn.

I surveyed the barnyard, looking for Bit. It was a long, long time before I saw her. She came around the house, across the driveway and headed toward me. Something long and furry dangled from her mouth — a squirrel!

How many hours had I sat on Lise's couch, with my front paws slung over the back of it, as I watched out the picture window at the squirrels taunting me from the maple trees in the front yard? I had studied them, dreamt of them, watched with nearly unbearable patience while they danced from limb to limb, flicking their tails teasingly. I was not allowed in the front yard, however, where Lise's flower beds were, with their pansies and primroses, petunias and daisies. And the dastardly squirrels never ventured into the backyard, where Bit and I lounged beneath the shade of the tulip tree.

I was always hopeful, however, and never gave up my vigil. One day, I was sure, a squirrel, being as scatter-brained as they were, would tempt fate and invade our territory.

Its long tail swung side to side as she veered around an overturned wheelbarrow. Saliva pooled beneath my tongue. I licked my lips, anticipating the taste of it. Bit stopped in front of the kennel, bobbed her head, then spit the squirrel on the ground. She coughed once, then nudged it forward with her nose. But the bottom bar was too tight against the concrete, the links too small to pull it through. I tried, even though my experience with the kibble spill had taught me that my legs were too big to manage the task, but we dogs are ever persistent.

I pulled my paw back through the links and sat. There would be no supper tonight.

Bit coughed again, this time retching. When her cough had calmed, she gathered up the squirrel in her mouth and trotted to the garage, her steps uneven, her path crooked.

Late afternoon slid into evening. Darkness came early as clouds thickened in the west. Somewhere in the woods, a pack of coyotes yipped. Bit poked her head out of the garage, her amber eyes scanning the property. The yipping came closer. They were just on the other side of the barn now. Bit withdrew to the safety of the garage. They would not go in there. Coyotes kept to the open. They must have remembered the animals that used to live here. More than once, Ray had loaded up his shotgun in the evening and gone to sit at the back edge of the pasture, waiting for them to come by.

Their yips rose in pitch to a chorus of cackles. A shiver of terror shot down my backbone. I tucked myself deep inside my doghouse, where I waited for morning.

Tomorrow, maybe, Lise would come. To take us home.

Stupid of me to hope, I know. But hope was all I had.

—o00o—

Head low, Bit swayed. It had taken several minutes for her to cross from the garage to the kennels. She would stagger, lie down, struggle to her feet, and stumble forward a few more meager steps, before stopping to rest. When she came close enough for me to see her more clearly in the dreary mist of morning, I noticed long globs of drool dripping from her mouth.

Although I had barely enough energy, I got to my feet and went to stand by my door, wagging my nub in encouragement. Instinct told me she was sick, terribly sick. Without someone to care for us, this might not end well.

Things got worse very quickly for my mother. She was there, mere feet outside my kennel, and all I could do was watch as she vomited up vivid yellow-green bile. In time, her trembling turned into violent tremors. She fell to the ground, stiffened, and gazed at me with her golden eyes, begging for help. Then her legs began to jerk in erratic spasms.

I had to look away. I wanted so badly to lie beside her, to lick her face and comfort her, but I was powerless to do anything.

It went on for the longest time. Finally, she lay there, her chest barely rising as her breaths slowed. A trace of blood trickled over her swollen tongue — that long, gentle tongue that had cleaned me at my birth, washed the mud from my face so many times in my puppyhood, and licked my chin in affection as we sat together in the back of Ned's truck and left the only home we had ever known.

She shut her eyes, blew out one last breath, and then … her body was still. Drops of rain pattered over her once glossy fur, slicking down the stray tufts of her wavy coat.

I sat in the cold rain, trying to blink away the stinging in my eyes. Dogs don't cry, I told myself. We can't.

A deep and heavy sadness sucked at my gut, tugging my soul into a chasm so deep and dark that I, too, wanted to lie down and die beside my mother and go to sleep forever. There was no one to comfort me, no lap to rest my head in, no gentle fingers to stroke my ears, no small arms to wrap about my neck and whisper that everything was going to be okay.

I lifted my head to the unseen moon and let out a howl so long and woeful that even the coyotes joined in my keening.

In some primeval way, we were kindred — dogs and coyotes. We both nurtured our young, hunted together, and mourned the loss of one of our pack. I had seen them in the distance, loping across a harvested field in the golden light of an autumn sunset, and mused at how alike they were to my own kind.

And yet they were not. They were free to roam.

Still, they had also never known the warmth of a couch on a cold and rainy day, or tasted the smooth goodness of gravy, or played chase with a little boy while he laughed with absolute glee.

My yowls fell away to a prolonged whine, then a broken whimper. The rain had stopped. A chilly breeze parted the clouds to let the light of the moon stream down over Bit's deflated form. Her hair was flattened against her wasted body, her spine prominent. Whatever she had eaten the past couple of days had been expelled in her bloody vomit.

I raised my face to the moon, embraced by a halo of silver. To its right, a star winked brightly. Hunter used to make wishes on stars. Maybe in this place called Covington, where he and Lise lived now, he could see the same star. Maybe he would wish for me to join him. Maybe.

My gaze drifted downward from the heavens. There stood Bit, her fur gleaming in the moonlight, her eyes as bright as that star. And yet, she looked as if she were made of air. She shook from head to tail, bowed her front playfully, and jumped up high. Her feet made no sound when she landed. She curled her body in circles and let out a soft, distant-sounding *woo-woo-woo*, her way of talking, Lise called it. She raced about, alternately leaping and bowing, her energy boundless.

I'd never seen Bit so happy, so uninhibited. I wanted to join her, to feel what she was feeling!

As she ran within the circle of light cast by the sole floodlight that stood between the garage and the barn, that's when I noticed — that wasn't Bit. It was her ghost. It was her soul set free.

Her body still lay where she had drawn her last breath.

As she crossed to the far side of the light's circle, she — my mother's ghost — dissolved into the darkness, leaving me alone.

If mere hours before I had wanted for Lise to save us, I no longer did. I was beyond hope, beyond caring. Cold and hunger and pain were all I knew and I'd had enough of suffering.

So I waited. For the end. For something better than the life I knew.

chapter 10

I didn't die that night. It didn't matter that I wanted to. That I was tired of fighting to survive. That life had lost its joy. That love had gone.

Death can be cruel like that. It comes when you don't expect it. Eludes you when you're ready for it. It can be sudden or slow. It takes both young and old. Strong and weak. The question is never 'Will I die?', but '*When* will I die?' and '*How?*'

I had a lot of time to think as I waited for the final sleep that never came. And one thing that I began to wonder was what happens when you die. Do you go someplace else? Do you simply stop ... being?

I had seen Ray, Cam, and Bit after they died and they were as real as the living. Ray sitting in Estelle's Buick the day of the funeral. Cam crouched in the back of Ned's truck. Bit frolicking around the barnyard in the moonlight. Had I just imagined them? I lay awake all night long, thinking about it, wondering how it was that I could see them at all. Maybe no one else could?

That night it turned bitterly cold. Pressed against the back inside of my doghouse, I shivered myself to utter exhaustion, sleep coming in snatches. I dreamt of Cam and Ray, tending to the cattle in the chutes. I dreamt of Bit, rolling in the grass, a Frisbee clamped in her mouth. I dreamt of my earliest days, nestled between my mother's forelegs, her breath tickling my whiskers. I dreamt of yellow tennis balls and squeaky stuffed squirrels. Of my brothers and sisters. Of Hunter and Lise. Of home. And family.

Then morning came. And Ned's rust-pocked truck backfired as it came down the driveway. I retreated deep within my plastic doghouse.

"Aw shhh—!" He slammed the truck door so hard his front bumper rattled. Muttering curses, he stormed into the garage and came out with a shovel. Then he turned the wheelbarrow over and rolled it over to Bit. He grabbed her stiff legs and slung her inside the wheelbarrow. "God dang, stupid dog. Musta got into the rat poison. Just cost me five hundred bucks. There goes my gambling weekend. Well then, I guess the price on the other'n just went up."

He wheeled her to the back corner of the barn, dug a shallow grave, tossed her in it, and covered it up with loose clods of soil and the remains of the manure pile. Then he went inside the house, but not before he gave me a heaping bowl of dog food and a fresh bucket of water. I waited until he was out of sight before venturing out and ate slowly, mindful to let my stomach settle before I ate more, remembering how I'd made myself sick the last time. I lapped at the water, letting its wetness refresh me from the inside out.

I still had my head in the bucket when I heard the smooth putter of another truck engine. A big white truck, gleaming in the faint winter sunlight, pulled up next to the house. A tall old man in a red fleece jacket knocked on the door. Ned stepped out and motioned him in my direction.

My first instinct was to hide. Strangers were bad news. I didn't trust them. But as he moved my way, I could see there was an unassuming ease to his stride, a gentleness in his movement.

"The other'n snuck past me and ran away not two days ago," Ned said as he hurried to catch up to the old man's long steps. "Spent half the day looking for her. Neighbor said he saw her out by the parkway. Sure 'nough, I found her flattened by the side of the road between here and there. Shame about her getting hit like that, ain't it? Good dog like that."

We sized each other up, the old man and I, while Ned blathered on.

"— know you was thinking of taking both of them, but, well, seein' as how there's only the one left, I figured I might keep her to myself. But maybe, y'know, if you really wanted her, I could part with her. For a price."

The old man turned around slowly. A smile spread over his mouth, folding the finer wrinkles on his face into deep crevices. "Now Mr. Hanson, I know that dog belongs to Mrs. McHugh, or more rightly her daughter-in-law. She was never yours to barter." At that, Ned's features hardened. The old man tilted his head, his twinkling blue eyes never wandering from Ned's face. His voice was so soft, his words so slow and measured, it forced Ned to pay attention. "Ray once told me he'd give me a pup for helping him out, but I never thought to take him up on it. That's just what we neighbors do. We help each other. And I'm helping the McHughs now by taking this dog with me."

A tic developed in Ned's jaw muscle. He jangled the keys in his pocket, one shoulder jerking in a half-shrug. "Umm, guess I could've misunderstood Mrs. McHugh, but it was my understanding the dogs were my payment for taking care of the place. Been here every day for months, sometimes two or three times a day, making sure everything —"

"I may be older than dirt, son, but I can see. This dog here, Halo is it?" — he glanced at me — "she hasn't been looked after properly. Poor thing's a good seven or eight pounds underweight, maybe ten. And for a dog her size, that's a heck of a lot. Had you taken better care of the dogs, not lost the one, if indeed that's what happened, I might've offered to pay you for their care."

The old man hunkered down before me, slipped his fingers through the links. I approached cautiously, sniffed him, then backed away. I wanted to trust him, but …

He pulled his fingers back, stood, then opened the kennel door and slipped inside.

"I, uh," Ned said, as he kicked broken bits of ice across the barnyard, "did pay for their dog food out of my own pocket."

"Were you saving it for a special occasion?" The old man's joints cracked as he knelt down, one knee sinking into a dirty puddle.

"Huh?"

"Doesn't look to me like she's been fed for days." His spotted hand slid into his pocket and brought out something long and skinny in a crinkly plastic wrapper. He tore the wrapper with his teeth, then tugged it down and broke off a piece. "'Sides, I talked to Estelle McHugh just this morning. Told me she left you a rather generous check."

Ned slapped his thigh. "Ohhh, yeah. That's right. Plumb forgot about it. Still in the pocket of my other jacket, I think."

My nose twitched as the scent of the food the old man offered wafted to me. It reminded me of the sausage links Lise used to make for Cam and Hunter on Sunday mornings.

"Here." The old man extended his hand. In the flat of his palm lay a small brown piece of sausage-like food. "Slim Jims. Had an old dog named Luke who used to love these."

I looked past his outstretched arm at his face, all creased like a wad of paper. His eyes were the same sky blue that plays off a bank of snow when the sun strikes it. His brows were winter white, each wiry strand going in a different direction. His head, fringed in the same white, was bald on top.

He reached his hand out one more inch. I looked at the treat, then at him, then at Ned, scowling at me with his hands stuffed in his pockets.

I still didn't trust strangers. But I was smart enough to know I'd be better off with the old man than with Ned Hanson, whose carelessness had killed my mother.

Cautiously, I took the treat. He gave me more and gently clipped a leash onto my loose collar.

Like I said, a lot can happen in a day. Sometimes, it doesn't seem like much at the time, but when you look back at it, your whole life can turn on one decision, one action.

And one person ... just one person can make your life heaven or hell.

—o0Oo—

His name was Cecil Penewit, but to me he was always the Old Man, because, well, that's what he was. He lived alone, you see, so there was never anyone to call him by name. The house he lived in was small, with only two bedrooms and a kitchen that also served as his dining room and office, and he didn't own much in the way of furniture or knickknacks. Cam and Lise's house was always cluttered with toys and family pictures. Ray and Estelle's home had been filled with old furniture, oiled to a shine monthly, and they even had a row of pictures with matching frames in the hallway. But the Old Man kept just one picture in a gold frame on his bedroom dresser. It was in black and white and it was of a woman much younger than him. She had a smile like Mona Lisa and a bob of dark waves that framed her strong face. I don't know if the woman had once been his wife, his girlfriend, or perhaps his sister, but every once in awhile as he passed the picture, he'd touch the glass over her face and speak to her as if she were there beside him.

"You'd like this one, Sarah," he said. "Bit shy, but she's a beaut, all right. Reminds me of our first one, Shadow. I'm hoping she takes an interest in the woolies. And, if she doesn't, well … it doesn't matter, does it? Sometimes an old man just needs a little company."

I looked around the corner of the doorframe at him, feeling unusually bold. It had been months since I'd been inside and I intended to find out where the registers were so I could keep warm.

"Ssscat," he hissed at me. "Back to the kitchen with you. You'll have to earn your keep here and the first day you come inside belly-deep in mud don't you dare think of stepping foot past that doorway again. Now get back there." He shooed me away with a flick of his pale long-fingered hand and I retreated to the kitchen.

Just as I curled beneath the table, where he had put down an old sheet, I heard him mumble, "Bath tomorrow for you. I suppose the outdoor hose is out of the question, seeing as how it's still winter and all."

I shuddered at the thought of standing in a tub, dripping wet, while he sudsed me with shampoo smelling of citrus fruit. And yet, the more I considered it, the more it seemed a small price to pay for being warm and clean and sleeping indoors.

That was the last thing he said to me that night. I soon learned he didn't say much most of the time. Not even to me. He didn't need to, really. He was so easy to understand.

chapter 11

From the beginning, our relationship was very clear and uncomplicated. I was his silent companion and soon to be his working partner — but he never rushed the point. The Old Man had limitless patience. That's the difference between youth and age. When you're young, you think everything has to be done now and that you have far too many things to do than you can ever get done. When you're old, you realize most things aren't as important as you'd like to think and that there's always tomorrow, until … until there just isn't, anymore.

While his house was small, the bank barn next to it was ten times the size. The barn had been built into a manmade hill, so a tractor or truck could be driven to the upper level and unloaded. In the barn's second story was a loft, stacked with sweet-smelling hay and golden straw, and below were rows and rows of sheep pens, some big, some small. He kept two kinds of sheep: Barbados Blackbelly and Suffolks. He never mixed the two and I quickly learned how different in behavior they were.

At first, he just let me follow along. Well, not quite 'follow', because I had to go wherever he did. He kept a leash on me, he told me, until he was certain I knew my place was beside him. I never balked when he snapped the leash on. I was well fed, warm and even clean — although I had never quite appreciated how good a bath could make me feel until I had lived in filth for far too long.

Days became weeks; weeks became months. There was a rhythm to our routine that brought with it a sense of peace and purpose. Every morning he rose before first light and made sure my bowl was full before he sat down to his cup of coffee and buttered toast. Sometimes, there was even a raw egg on my kibble. Then we did chores until lunchtime, which meant a ham sandwich for him and a heel of bread for me. After that, more chores and occasionally an errand into town. In the evenings, he let me lick his plate clean. My ribs filled out and my fur became full and glossy again. Every day, the ritual was the same, no matter what day of the week it was. Animals, he said, did not go on holiday. A farmer's work was never-ending. Cam had said the same thing more than once.

I trailed after him as he fed the sheep, cleaned their watering troughs, and scooped out manure. He did his chores without complaint and with a vigor that belied his years. Some of the sheep's bellies grew big and fat on the hay he fed them and before that first winter had retreated in full, we were greeted one morning to a pair of little black-faced twins standing on wobbly legs beside their mother. Curious, I pressed my nose between the wires of the fence. The ewe stomped an angry hoof at me in warning. I growled softly at her and stood my ground.

The Old Man nodded his head as he looked down at me. "You tell her who's boss. But mind you, she'll defend those babies with her life, so treat them kindly, y'hear?" Then we moved on to the next pen. "Remember, it's the black-faced ones you have to be careful of," he told me.

Three pens further down, we found a stillborn lamb. It was cold to the touch and long past saving, but in the weeks to come I saw him revive more than one lamb and bring it back from the brink of death. He had powers, I surmised, beyond that of ordinary humans.

Sometimes I wondered if he had been there when Bit was sick, could he have saved her, too?

Whenever I thought of my mother, I was often overcome with sadness. Simple memories filled me with an ache that rooted itself deep in my chest and would grow to clench my stomach. Even though I was fed and warmed and cared for, I missed her comforting presence.

I never stopped missing her, even though I knew she was all right, wherever it was that she had gone to — because she had come back to let me know.

—o00o—

He was sly about it. Luring me into the truck for a 'ride'. And not to the feed store, but to that most awful of places that any dog with sense learns to dread: the veterinarian's.

I could smell the disinfectant before he opened the truck door and had to drag me out. The Old Man pulled me over toward a patch of grass that reeked of the urine of hundreds of other dogs.

I stood defiantly on the asphalt, glaring at him.

He tugged on my leash. "Hurry up, girl. You won't have another chance for a while."

What was that supposed to mean?

A small black car pulled into the parking lot. Paws slammed against the window as the driver turned the engine off. A middle-aged man in a gray pinstriped suit got out, went to the back door and opened it. Out bounded an imposingly large German Shepherd. It charged to the end of its flexi-lead, barking furiously.

My first instinct was to run, save my skin. I was wise enough to know I wouldn't last long in a fight with that monster. But my second — and stronger — instinct was to protect the Old Man.

I planted myself firmly between him and the lunging dog, my

teeth snapping as I returned the threat.

"Be a good boy, Rex," Suit-Man said, glaring at me with disgust. Then to the Old Man, "He *just* wants to say 'hi'."

"Huh," the Old Man grunted. "Heck of a way to greet somebody."

Then the Old Man hurried to the building, giving the rabid dog and its oblivious owner wide berth. Inside, I was assaulted by more smells: fear, sickness … and death.

The Old Man gave his name at the desk and sat down on a wooden bench. A mother and two children sat on the adjacent bench, the little girl clutching a small, scrappy looking dog that shook with terror. Across from us, a thin woman sat reading a magazine. At her feet lay a Golden Retriever, his muzzle streaked with white, his tail thumping happily every time someone looked his way. And tucked in the far corner was another woman with a cardboard box cradled in her lap. A row of small holes lined the longer sides and from those holes I could make out white whiskers and an orange, triangular nose set in a black face. A cat. I watched the box carefully, prepared to defend myself, if needed.

My anxiety escalated when the German Shepherd and Suit-Man walked in the door. But suddenly, the dog that was all bluster and ferocity outside was reduced to a whimpering mess of fur and slobber once inside. His nails raked at the slick linoleum as his owner dragged him to the desk. The dog flattened himself on the mat there, refusing to budge when his owner started toward one of the benches.

So, he'd been here before?

"Halo Penewit?" a cheery brunette chirped from the hall doorway as she smiled at me. "This way, please."

I no more trusted her than I trusted that German Shepherd and his owner. But Cecil got up, started after her and, of course, I followed him.

I probably shouldn't have. If I had known that morning what was in store, I would have hightailed it. There were two injections. The first was a thick needle that pricked the loose skin above my shoulder blades. This, she told the Old Man, was my microchip. If I was ever lost or ran away, a scan would tell who my owner was and how to contact him. The second shot was in the tender muscle of my flank. I quickly grew sleepy after that, but I remember her saying something about 'no puppies'. All I know is that I woke up several hours later with a sore belly full of stitches and a plastic cone around my head.

The humiliation was more unbearable than the pain.

The Old Man took me home, where I ran into the table legs, the kitchen cabinets, and the doorframe more times than I could count. My head ached for hours.

—o00o—

The Old Man's farm was tucked in a steep-sided valley, cut deep by a fast-flowing creek that swelled over its banks every spring. On the hillsides, junipers gripped the soil tight with their roots and in April the woods were dotted with the deep purple-pink blooms of redbuds. The land had been cleared generations ago by Cecil Penewit's own ancestors and, while it had first been used to farm tobacco, Cecil had turned his hand to sheep farming — a dying trade, he called it, but one unto which he felt called. I understood completely. Being around the flock filled me with a sense of purpose that I longed to fill.

The grass sparkled with dew the first morning he took me in with the sheep. When I was a pup, I had watched Bit move sheep many times. But Lise's flock had been small, her pastures a mere fraction of the size of Cecil's, and there was not much variation in their routine. Thus, Lise's sheep were perhaps just as well trained as Bit herself. They knew the dog, they knew where to go, and they knew that sticking close to Lise ensured their safety.

The Old Man's sheep, though, weren't as compliant. And they

hadn't seen a dog for months, if not years.

"Been a long time since Luke was around to help me." The Old Man swung the gate open just far enough for the two of us to wiggle inside. "I'm getting too old to do this by myself, so you're going to have to earn your keep from here on, y'hear, girl?"

Halfway across the small pasture, a flock of about twenty Barbados Blackbelly Sheep clustered tightly together. They were not white and wooly like the Suffolks, but had shaggy brown hair with black markings on their legs, bellies and faces. They were also noticeably more nervous than the woollies. In some ways, they looked more like small deer or wild goats than sheep. As much as they seemed to want to go to the Old Man, they kept their eyes on me, every single one of them. The younger ewes and the wethers stood to the back of the flock, while the older ewes stood defiantly in the van, their heads high, their forelegs stiff.

Curious how they would react to me, I took a small step forward. The Old Man snapped my line back.

"Lie down," he commanded. I did so, as he had taught me to do. Although soft spoken, he was also clear and consistent. As we did our chores every day, he would tell me to lie down while he did what he had to do. He gave a command only once. Failure to obey resulted in a quick correction, firm, never heavy handed. Compliance meant reward. Praise, mostly, although carrots, strawberries, and sometimes Slim Jims were added incentives.

He had attached a rope to my collar that must have been ten times the length of my normal leash. He held the line close to my collar, while the rest lay coiled at his feet. Clutched in his left hand was a tall crook. He leaned on it, just a little, his thumb stroking the polished wood of the curved handle.

"Patience, girl. Booger those sheep, and you and I will have a serious talk."

There was just enough firmness in his voice, as soft as it was, to let me know that I needed to control my instincts. The real problem, though, was not my patience. It was my inability to know what to do with the urges that were scraping away at my nerves, shouting at me to make those sheep move, move, *move*!

"Get around," he said, as he let out a length of line.

Confused, I gazed up at him.

"Get around," he repeated, nodding toward the sheep.

An older ewe, her nose scarred, twitched her hide and pounded a hoof on the ground. I didn't like the looks of that one, so I took off straight for her. The second I did so, the Old Man stepped toward me and smacked the end of the crook on the ground.

"Ach! Get out."

The whoosh of the crook and the sternness in his voice startled me. I veered away from him, keeping my eyes on that one sheep, because I was sure that whatever she did, the rest would likewise do. If there was one thing I knew about sheep, it was that they always stuck close together. The rebel that strayed forfeited its own safety.

"Out."

He stepped into me again. I widened my course into an arc. The flock drew tighter, twisted their heads to watch as I cast outward. The older ewe turned toward me, lowered her head in challenge. Someone, I decided, needed to learn who the boss was here. So I beelined straight for her. The leader. The elected one.

That was when all hell broke loose.

Half the flock went one way, half another. They didn't stay in one neat group, as they had been before, but they scattered like wheat chaff cast to the wind. I zeroed in on one pair, only to catch site of three more to my right, then another bearing down on me, while yet more raced in the opposite direction. They were fast. So fast! Bounding like antelopes across the open plain.

I felt a firm tug on the line, but I lunged forward, yanking the line out of the Old Man's grasp.

The chaos of motion sent my brain into overdrive. Adrenaline flooded my veins. Rational thought was impossible. Patience was out of the question. I could only react. The thrill of it made me explode with energy.

Run! Chase! Bark! Run! Bark —

The crook came sailing out of the air like a missile. It ticked the ground, flipped sideways, and crashed through the tall grass, nicking my left foot smartly.

Surprised, I jumped back, shook my head, and stared over the heads of a jittery group of younger ewes that were clustered about the Old Man's knees.

"Out, I said," he insisted through gritted teeth.

While I backed away from him, he went and collected his crook again. The sheep followed him closely, their eyes locked on mine. I stayed far, far away the next time, swooping around in a broad circle.

The sheep, although still slightly frantic, began to clump more tightly, until all of them had drawn together. As I tired and slowed, they calmed. My brain calmed down, too. I became more aware of the Old Man and the words he would say to me, like 'Out', 'Steady', and 'Ach!' That last one meant I was not doing what he wanted. It was the first thing I figured out.

Every day, we repeated this in the small pasture. He would let go of my line and tell me to 'Get around'. I would cast in a wide arc, turn, and push the sheep toward him. Whenever he turned, I turned, too. If he stopped, I stopped. If I pushed them too hard, he reprimanded me with his voice or a wave of his crook.

When that became too easy, we worked in a bigger pasture. I moved big groups and small ones, and sometimes a single ram. I learned by their movements how close I could work and how quickly. I came to learn the difference between the stubborn Suffolks and the flighty Barbs, which individuals were prone to give me trouble, and which ones the others followed.

115

I learned commands by repetition. When I was right, he let me know. When I was wrong, he let me know that, too. His meaning, usually, was clear. But sometimes he'd say 'go-bye', which meant to circle to the left, when he obviously meant 'way-to-me', which was the opposite direction. At first I'd always do as he said, but his frustration would quickly surface and, with a muttered curse, he'd step in to push me in the direction he *really* wanted me to go. I learned to check his body language if there was any doubt on my part.

As our sessions went more smoothly, our trust in each other grew. But it was never my place to let him know when he was wrong. What was important was that the job was done right.

"Go-bye," he said one morning, as we were moving the sheep to another pasture.

If I could have spoken, that would have been the opportune time. Somehow, I had to let him know his error by just showing him. Go-bye would have sent them right back to where they'd come from. I paused on my feet, gazed at him, then took a step to the right and paused again.

The sheep shifted toward the gate where he'd meant to send them. "Yeah, that way. Just ..." — he lifted his crook in the direction I was pointed — "get around."

I swung to the right and the sheep calmly trotted through the gate and into a fresh pasture.

The Old Man called me to him and thumped me once on the head.

"Good girl," was all he said.

And it was enough.

We were a unit, the Old Man and I. He made the plans, orchestrated our sessions, and saw to it that our routine was adhered to with religious zeal. I did as he said — well, most of the time — and in turn I got to do my job every day. I had a purpose. I had value.

The pampered life of the lap dog, the monotony of being a pet relegated to the backyard waiting all day for my people to come home, the aimlessness of the stray — those were lives I would not have chosen.

To work with purpose was to live in each moment, imbued with joy and fed by passion. It was to lose all sense of time. Effort became forgotten in the quest to achieve the goal. And when the work was done, rest was nothing more than a necessity, a chance for my body to refuel and my mind to reflect on all that had been accomplishment between sunrise and sunset.

I pitied the dog who had no purpose, for they did not truly live, they merely existed.

chapter 12

The grass grew tall and thick, its roots fed by abundant spring thunderstorms. The creek that cut through the valley became a raging river, brown with silt. The woods surrounding the farm grew dense with foliage, a tangle of undergrowth winding beneath the dappled shade of locust and ash trees.

On summer evenings, when our work was done early, the Old Man and I would rest beneath the towering catalpas, with their big heart-shaped leaves and elegant blooms that resembled orchids. The crickets strummed their wistful ballads and the bullfrogs crooned discordantly. When autumn came, the Old Man gathered walnuts from the yard and put them in paper grocery bags. Sometimes I would help him clean up by bringing him sticks, which always earned me a smile. These he gathered in a small pile and lit on fire when he had enough bigger branches. For hours he sat atop an old stump, gazing into the flames, poking at the embers with a branch, while I lay beside him, my ears keened for the movement of small animals in the nearby trees.

I was ever vigilant. I swore that one day I would catch one of the squirrels that jeered at me from afar, and I would make Bit proud of me. Studying them became my second job. In return, they studied me. I knew which boughs their nests were in, knew when the young ones ventured forth, and from which trees they collected their nuts. Their chatter was an endless taunt that drove me to insanity's front door.

In my dreams, as I slumbered beneath the kitchen table, they would surround me, an army of them, the plume of their gray tails twitching behind them. Their greedy cheeks were stuffed with acorns, their beady eyes a murderous black. Still, they chattered, a high-pitched prattle emitted in fits and stops. The moment I moved toward them, they'd vault into the trees that had grown up through the roof, scrabbling up the rough bark with their tiny claws. Then from the branches they lobbed walnuts at me. Walnuts so big that I had to run away to save myself.

When I awoke, I swore they would not defeat me. Let them laugh now. One day, I would hunt them down, every single one, and triumph over my enemies.

The days grew cooler, and soon the woods rimming the valley were a patchwork of fiery scarlet and glowing amber. As the days shortened, the leaves fell from the trees to carpet the earth in a crisp blanket. The frost came, glimmering like diamond flecks upon an emerald sea, and soon the colors faded from the world, winter's muted shades replacing the Technicolor of summer and the kaleidoscope of fall.

The daily tedium of farm life was offset by the rhythm of the seasons, the changing weather, and the unpredictability of all those things combined. Lambs were born and died. Ewes thrived, gave birth and grew old.

One year passed into two, and then three ... until, if I thought hard enough about it, I could count six winters spent with the Old Man. I often wondered what became of Lise, Hunter, and the baby girl, but I was no longer angry with Lise. Whatever had kept her away didn't matter any longer. The Old Man needed me. This was my home now. This was where I was supposed to be.

Some years, the fields flooded, droughts choked the air with dust, crops failed, and ice froze the blooms off the fruit trees. Other years, though, the rains soaked the earth at interludes and the days warmed gradually from spring through summer, until fall came and the harvest was good and the market was strong. We lived for those years and endured the hardships, as we clung to each blessing, however rare.

Almost every day, the Old Man and I gathered the sheep from the pastures and put them in the paddocks close to the barn. On mornings when snow dusted the world, we would rise long before first light, eat our breakfast in silence, then head out to take the hay to the sheep. One of my jobs was to keep the sheep back from the feeders until the Old Man had filled them. Sheep are greedy creatures. It is their purpose to graze all day long and even that is not enough. They would think nothing of trampling the one who cared for them just to have that one mouthful.

On bitter winter days, we checked the watering troughs to make sure the heaters had not been pulled out or the cords become unplugged. Whenever that happened, the water turned to ice, and the Old Man had to haul buckets of hot water outside to melt them. I even helped him load a dozen sheep into his stock trailer during my first January with him, but he drove off without me and came back with no sheep. I quickly learned it was the way of things, that when there were too many or conditions were too harsh, some were sent away.

As the years piled up, I could see the toll the work took on him, especially in the winter. He moved more stiffly and developed a limp that became more and more prominent. Some days he was slow to rise from bed and early to retire. In the evenings, he would light a kerosene heater that sat on the floor of the living room, not far from the doorway to the kitchen, and sit in his reclining chair, a Sunday newspaper in hand, Sarah's picture propped on the end table beside him. Glasses perched on his nose, he read until he fell asleep, his lips fluttering with soft snores.

And I would lie there with the warmth of the kerosene heater wafting over me, content.

Life was once again good. I was in no hurry to leave it. As far as I was concerned, it could go on like this forever.

—o00o—

It was late spring of my sixth year with the Old Man, when I was almost seven, that Bernadette Kratz came to visit. She drove a pale blue Volkswagen Beetle that sputtered and coughed as it struggled up the steep, bumpy driveway. The Old Man watched from the field as she rolled to a stop by the gate.

I woofed a few times before he shushed me. It was my job to let him know when someone was here and my job to let the stranger know that I was always on guard. I was exceptionally good at that job. The mailman, in particular, never stayed long.

The woman swung the car door open and the hinges let out a plaintive groan. She stepped out, her short legs clad in a pair of tight red slacks. Her face was round, her cheeks rosy, and her lipsticked mouth wore a cheerful smile. Her denim shirt sparkled with sequins that reminded me vaguely of the little coats Grace used to put on her poodles. She even had her hair done up like one, with tight strawberry blonde curls piled high on her head.

She flapped a plump hand as she waddled over to the fence line, her beaded bracelet clacking with the motion. On the other arm, the handles of a paisley satchel were looped over her wrist. The Old Man waved back.

"Good afternoon, Mrs. Kratz." He removed his ball cap and stuck it in his back pocket.

"Actually, it's Bernadette Kratz-Mihalovich, but no one ever remembers the last part. Mr. Mihalovich and I were only married nine years before he passed away, but we had three fine children in that

121

time. Not to make myself sound any older, but I have two great grandkids. Can you believe that?"

"Hard to believe. Is there something I can do for you, ma'am?"

"Now Cecil, no need to be so formal. How many years have we known each other? Going on forty, is it? If you don't call me Bernadette, I'm just gonna pretend like I don't hear you, how's that?"

He nodded. "Fair enough, I s'pose."

"Fair enough what?" She readjusted her leopard print eyeglasses.

His mouth twisted in thought as he tried to gather her meaning. His eyebrows lifted. He looked down. "Bernadette."

"That sounds so magical when you say it, Cecil." She laid a hand on her left breast pocket. "My heart's all aflutter now."

I crept from behind the Old Man to get a better look at her. Something about her smelled unbelievably good. She reached into her pocket, bent over, and extended a hand. In her palm lay a dog biscuit, smelling of liver.

The Old Man's hand shot out. "You might not want to —"

I snarfed it down so fast I nearly inhaled it.

"Might not want to what?" she asked.

I licked my lips and sniffed at her hand. She produced a few more.

"Well, it's just that … she doesn't always take to strangers."

"Oh, now, what a sweet thing," Bernadette trilled. "Seems just fine to me. You must love her to bits."

Need me maybe, but love? I wasn't so sure he thought in those terms. Then again, he had slipped me a whole slice of buttered bread that morning. The Old Man didn't use any more words than he had to. Instead, he just let his gestures speak for him.

Bernadette quickly covered her mouth and nose with a handkerchief and sneezed three times. "Sorry about that. Seems I'm a tiny bit allergic to dogs. Nothing a little Benadryl won't cure, though."

He cleared his throat. "There, uh, there must be some reason for your visit."

Her eyelashes flapped. "Oh, of course, of course." She lifted up the satchel and opened it wide so he could see inside. "Cranberry walnut scones. Half a dozen. Day old, but good as fresh. Baked them myself just yesterday morning."

"And you brought them here because …?" He fished his hat from his pocket and twisted it between his hands. "I don't mean to seem ungrateful, but why bring them here?"

"They were leftovers from the church bake sale. That could be because I made six dozen. And I just thought how I hadn't seen you at church since Christmas and —"

"The animals don't take holidays, Mrs… Bernadette."

If it was even possible, her cheeks got even redder. "I was just being neighborly, Cecil. Anything wrong with that?"

"You live on the other side of the county, practically."

Her lips pinched shut a moment. Something sparked in her eyes. "I'm trying to tell you, Cecil, that every now and then I wonder how you're getting along out here all by yourself. These scones seemed like just as good an excuse as any to pay you a visit. It's been five years since my Robert passed away. It doesn't get any easier. You of all people should understand what it is to just want someone your own age to talk to."

A gaping silence opened up between them. For a while, they both looked off into the distance: him at the grazing sheep, her at the trio of catalpa trees beyond the house. Then, as if on cue, they both glanced up and started speaking at the same time.

"Maybe I should just —?" She gestured toward her car.

"I was thinking …" he said, as he stuffed his hat away again and took a kerchief out of his chest pocket to dab at his neck, "that, uh, you could, maybe …"

"Aw, for Pete's sake, Cecil," — she clutched her satchel to her front — "you gonna invite me in to have some iced tea with these scones, or not?"

The Old Man's thin lips tilted upward on one side. "Sounds like a fine idea."

—o00o—

Bernadette was on her third glass of tea when the Old Man leaned to his left to look past her at the clock on the wall. He'd sat in his usual chair where he had a clear view of the clock. Usually. But the kitchen table, like all the furniture in his house, was small, so they had to sit close together, and there was no way for him to check the time otherwise. He never wore a wristwatch. The only thing that mattered, he said, was starting the day on time. Work was done when it was done. There was no quitting time on the farm.

He was still nursing his first glass and had eaten just one scone to her three, during which time, amazingly, she'd managed to carry most of the conversation herself. At first he appeared mildly interested in the news she had to share about the locals: Jeff and Collette's new twin girls, how Nathanial Weber's barn had lost its roof in the last windstorm, and that Marley Rankin had just opened a clothing boutique downtown, even though the new super Wal-Mart was set to open in two weeks next town over. Every so often he'd nod, or say 'Uh-huh' or 'Is that so?' and she'd babble on cheerfully for another fifteen minutes. After a while, though, he grew restless and began to fidget in his chair.

It wasn't until he stretched his neck to glance at the clock and a little yawn escaped that Bernadette herself noticed the time.

She tapped on the face of her delicate gold watch. "My, my, looky there. Half past three already. Where did the time go? Well, you must have plenty to do around here, running this big place all by yourself. I shouldn't keep you any longer." Straightening her shirt, she stood to go, but a small pile of dishes next to the sink seemed to stop any forward motion. "You know, if you need a little housekeeping around here, Cecil, I could always swing by once or twice a week ..."

Quickly, he scooted his chair from the table, placed a hand on her back, and guided her toward the door. If there was one thing the Old Man was, it was neat. On Sundays and Thursdays, he swept the whole house. On Mondays and Fridays he dusted. On Wednesdays he did laundry and hung it out to dry when the weather was good. And every evening he washed his dishes — except last night, when he'd fallen asleep early after a long day putting up hay.

"I'll keep that in mind," he told her.

"No charge, I mean." She sniffed and wiped her nose with her handkerchief. "Goodness, didn't mean to make it sound like I was peddling my services. Just a neighbor helping another neighbor. Maybe give you someone to talk to every now and then. Lord knows I could use the company now that my grandkids have grown up and moved off to the city. Folks these days just don't stick close to home like they used to. It's all about the money. But people like you and me, we know what matters, don't we? Family, that's what matters."

He looked away, as if he didn't know how to reply to that, and just as quickly she seemed to sense her error.

"Well, family and friends, right? Neighbors, community, that sort of thing." She reached for the doorknob, then drew her hand back. "Say, my nephew Tucker is arranging a stock dog trial next month at the Adair County Fair. You used to do those, didn't you?"

"A long time ago."

"You should think about entering this one. I heard Becket Wilson say how well trained that dog there of yours is. Bet you'd do well. There's even a two thousand dollar prize to the winner. Five hundred for the runner-up."

His left eyebrow lifted ever so slightly. We dogs pay close attention to every little facial movement, even the ones humans don't know they're making. He tilted his head, like he was mulling it over. "That so?"

"Saturday the fifteenth of next month, although I think there's one near Louisville sooner. I have some work to do at the literacy center in town tomorrow, but how 'bout I bring him by the day after, so he can tell you all about it?"

"Maybe I could just call him? No need for you to come all the way back out here."

In as kind a way as he could, he was trying to avoid another lengthy visit from Bernadette. Why that was so, I wasn't sure. I normally don't take a shine to strangers, but she seemed really nice. She smiled at me often, told me what a pretty dog I was, and had fed me a few bits of scone and liver treats. I wouldn't have minded her coming by again. But then, the Old Man didn't ask me. All he wanted to do was work, which was fine for the most part, but sometimes, like today, well, it was nice to do something different for a change.

"It's no bother at all." She pressed her fingers to her nose, holding back a sneeze. When it passed, she pulled the door open and paused just beyond the threshold. "Noon all right?" He hadn't even answered yet when she told him, "Tell you what, if anything comes up, you just holler. Otherwise, we'll see you then. Bye now."

The door was barely shut when she opened it again just far enough to stick her head inside. She reached an arm around and laid a scone on the counter. "I'll bake up a batch of my famous dark chocolate double chunk brownies and bring them along. I'm thinking of entering them in the fair this year, but some of the girls down at the sandwich shop where we meet every Friday, they think I should enter my blueberry muffins instead. Maybe you can help me decide?"

"Maybe," was all he said as he pushed the door shut behind her.

After she left, the Old Man stood where he was until he heard the faint cough of her car engine and then the receding putt-putt-putt as she drove off into the distance. Letting out a sigh, he parted the lace

126

curtains and peered cautiously through the window. "At least Sarah knew when to stop talking and let a man have his peace and quiet."

He took the scone from the counter and ate it.

chapter 13

Bernadette set the pan on the kitchen counter. "Sorry, not this time."

I'd had to wait two whole days for her return. During that time, I'd perked at the sound of every car that came down the county road half a mile away. I'd even had my hopes dashed once when the meter reader came. I barked at the man until he left. He always did. I was good at keeping people I didn't want away. When Bernadette finally came back, I'd stood on my hind legs to look out the kitchen window, let out a soft 'woof' to let the Old Man know, and then spun in circles until he opened the door to let me out to greet her.

She bent over and scratched my neck with her long, manicured nails. I think she kept them that way just for me. I noticed her eyes were red. Every time she touched me it seemed to initiate a new round of violent sneezing. She couldn't control her urge to fuss over me and pet me, despite her allergy.

"They say chocolate's not good for dogs," she said. "Although it's supposed to be good for people. Doesn't make much sense, I know, but I read about it on the internet down at the literacy center awhile back and ..." Turning to the Old Man, she tapped at her glossy coral lips with a single finger. "Say, you ever thought of bringing that dog of yours down to the library for reading hour?"

I sniffed at the edge of the counter, sat back politely, and stared at the pan. She pushed it further back and wagged a finger at me.

"Naw, I don't think so." He reached into the refrigerator and pulled out two dark glass bottles. "Sarsaparilla?"

Eyelashes flapping, Bernadette waved a hand at her face. "Goodness gracious, Cecil Penewit. Is this a special occasion? At my house, we don't break out the sarsaparilla for just anyone."

"Tom Harper gave it to me for fixing his mower a couple weeks back. Almost forgot I had it."

Her mouth plunged. "Oh." She fiddled with the beaded necklace draped over her red blouse. "Why?"

He got out two glasses and poured their drinks. "I s'pose because I'd shoved a gallon of milk and a pitcher of orange juice in front of it. That and the light bulb is burnt out, so I can't see in the back without —"

"I mean why not bring the dog. I meet with a group of children Mondays after school. Elizabeth, the head librarian, used to bring a rabbit, but it ... well, it expired. The little ones loved that rabbit. When it stopped coming, so did some of them. You wouldn't think it, but those kids will do their darnedest to read a book to an animal, even the ones that struggle. Maybe because the animals don't judge their efforts."

"Halo doesn't always take to strangers."

"Halo. Such a pretty name. Like an angel's." She smiled at me again. Smudges of lipstick stained her teeth. "Doesn't look unfriendly to me. Besides, didn't Lise and Cam McHugh have a little boy? What was his name?"

"Can't say I recall." The Old Man settled down in his chair, this time with it angled so he had a clear view of the clock.

After downing an antihistamine with a glass of sarsaparilla, Bernadette pulled open three drawers before she found the one with the knives. She cut the brownies up and put them on plates, then brought them to the table and took her seat.

"Henry? No, too old fashioned. Youngsters these days don't name their children that." She rubbed at her temple. "Harvey? Howard? Holden? Hanson? I know it started with an 'H'. Good heavens, I'm no good at this. Help me out, Cecil."

"Humphrey?" He took a slurp of his sarsaparilla.

Hunter! I barked. *Hunter!*

"See there," she said. "Even the dog thinks that's ridiculous. Well, whatever his name was, she's been around children. Bring her. It'll give you something to do besides putter around here like a fusty old hermit. You don't have to do anything. Just sit there with the dog while they read out loud. Will you try it, just once? If the dog doesn't like it, or you don't, I won't ask again."

To me, it sounded like heaven. Kids were different than grown-up strangers. They threw balls and gave belly rubs and giggled while they rolled on the floor with you.

"When did you say your nephew will be by?"

Bernadette flicked her wrist over to check her watch, her bangled bracelet clacking. "Well, seeing as how I told him to be here fifteen minutes ago, he should arrive any minute now." She tapped her sparkly red fingernails against her mug. An amused grin crept over her mouth. "You're good at that, Cecil."

"Good at what?"

"Avoiding questions."

"I wasn't aware you asked any."

"About the reading program at the library."

"Oh, that."

She waited awhile as he drank and looked off through the kitchen window. "Well?" she finally prompted.

I went and laid my head on his knee, puffing out my cheeks with a loud breath. *Please, please, please?*

His hand drifted down from the table to alight on my head. He curled his thumb beneath the flap of my ear, placed his forefinger on top and rubbed lightly. "Mondays, you said? I don't know if —"

Her spine shot up straight. "I'll pick you up at three."

—o00o—

"Damn almighty, that is one fiiine working dog!" Tucker Kratz swung a leg over the top rail to straddle the fence. He pulled a pack of cigarettes out of his back pocket and lit one up. Pinching the cigarette between the circle of his thumb and forefinger, he inhaled, held his breath in for a few seconds, then blew out a ring of smoke. "Wild coloration for a red merle, too. Kinda pretty."

The Old Man glared at him from fifty feet away.

"Tucker!" Bernadette swatted at the haze that drifted her way. "How many times have I told you?"

"Sorry, Aunt Bernie." He tipped his cowboy hat back. "You don't mind, do you?"

"Actually, I do," the Old Man said flatly. "Thanks for asking, anyway."

Smirking, Tucker smashed the glowing end of the cigarette on top of the fence post, flicked the dead butt away and stuffed the pack back into his pocket.

The Old Man turned back to me. I was holding a flock of twenty older Barb lambs in the nearest corner of our working pasture, which he'd once told me was over two acres. Every time one stepped either way, I'd shift my position before it could bolt.

When Tucker had shown up, I'd helped the Old Man sort the ewes from the lambs in the pen next to the barn. Although the lambs had been weaned for weeks now, their mothers still remembered their babies and clamored to be reunited with them. That part was always rough, but we managed well enough, and only two ewes gave me any problem. I put that issue to rest with a quick nip to their noses.

Next, we'd taken the flock of lambs from the pen, across the open area between the old bank barn and the driveway, and then I pushed them through an eight foot gateway into the pasture, where I moved them in various patterns: squares and small arcs, diagonal lines and backward Zs. The Old Man stood off to the side, one elbow resting on the top rail, the brim of his ball cap down low to keep out the noonday sun. His crook was propped against the fence next to him. He seldom used it these days and, when he did, it was to shoo away a wayward sheep, not to force me further out, for I had long since learned the point at which the sheep would move and at what pace to push them. Boogered sheep, as the Old Man called the frightened ones, were panicked sheep, and panicked sheep did stupid things. I was pretty sure that each five sheep only had one brain between them.

"Sure does take commands well." Tucker swung a leg over and dropped into the pasture. He walked up to the Old Man. "But then, some dogs that are great at home plumb lose their brains in a trial."

The Old Man worked his jaw in a slow circle. "That so?"

"Yup. I see it all the time. Different sheep, different surroundings … An' sometimes the handlers get all nervous, like they can't remember their left from their right. Or which obstacles to put the stock through. Dogs pick up on that."

"Do they now?" The Old Man called me off.

I tossed one last look at the lambs, trotted to him, and sat by his left knee, just as I always did. A bothersome horse fly buzzed my ears. I twitched my hide and then shook my head, trying to dislodge it. The moment it flew past my nose, I snapped. Missed it!

"Sure do." Tucker rolled his short sleeves up over his shoulder to show a tattoo of a bald eagle with outspread wings. The bulging muscles of his tanned arms were hardened and defined, nothing like the Old Man's thin, pale arms, with their sagging skin, or Bernadette's soft, plump arms. When his aunt had introduced him, she made a point of mentioning the fact that he'd been stationed in Afghanistan until just last year. He still wore 'dog tags' around his neck, although he'd long since grown his hair out to the point where he could pull it into a ponytail. He hitched his thumbs in his belt. "Bill Clancy's coming from St. Louis. He's a professional. This trial is usually a bit below his standards, competition-wise, but sure would be nice to see a local put him in his place. Think you could do that?"

The fly landed on Tucker's pants leg. Tempting, but by the time I closed the space, the fly would be in flight again. I waited.

"I have no idea." Gazing thoughtfully at the lambs still quivering in the corner, the Old Man stroked his neck. "But I'm game to give it a go."

"I'll put the word out. Just might draw the biggest crowd we've seen since ol' Angus MacDonald came down from Vermont to challenge him. Course, that was way back in '98, or maybe it was '99. My pa used to trial his dogs, but they was just farm dogs, not fancy trained trial dogs. Ain't nobody come within 5 points of Clancy since. Some says he has an 'in' with the judges, but this year it's some young uptight chick named Jessica Zink, who couldn't care less about reputation — hers or anyone else's. Some hate her for that. I hear she's a looker, though." Tucker took a fresh cigarette out of his pack and tucked it in the corner of his mouth. Bernadette shot him a warning look. He threw his hands in the air. "What? Haven't lit it up now, have I? Geesh, you'd think I was committing a felony or something. Ain't against the law to do this, y'know."

The fly landed on my nose. I jerked my head sideways, then back, snapping at air. Missed again.

The Old Man patted his leg. That was my signal to follow. We went through the gate and escorted Tucker to his jacked up truck with the dual wheels in back and the chrome pipe stacks that belched black exhaust. The young man went through some papers on his front seat, then said, "Sorry, man. Thought I had an entry form here. Just go to the web site for the Central Kentucky Australian Shepherd Club and download the flyer. And don't wait. Deadline is next Wednesday. No day-of entries. Got it?"

The Old Man nodded. "I think so."

He pounded the Old Man on the arm and stepped up into the cab. Before he put the key in the ignition, he lit up his cigarette, took a puff, and blew a smoke-hazed kiss at his aunt. The truck roared to life. Instead of carefully backing out, he turned a donut through the yard and sped off.

Bernadette clutched both hands to her breast. "I apologize for his manners, Cecil. The boy had a poor upbringing. His mama likes the moonshine and his daddy ain't around no more."

"Oh. How long ago did he pass away?"

She smiled sadly and whispered, as if someone might overhear, "Oh, he's not dead. He's in jail. Gambling charges. Tried to run slot machines in the back of his convenience store. He'll be out by next Christmas. Not sure that's a good thing, though. Tucker's his only child, so I've always tried to keep an eye out for the boy. Even managed to get him a job with the county extension office through my friend Merle. Mostly, he takes care of the grounds, but he's trying to work his way up. Merle put him in charge of the trial, since he knows a few things about livestock. His daddy ran a small cattle farm before he lost the place to gambling debts. The Army seemed to have straightened Tucker up a bit, but he's not perfect. He's been doing so well the last few years — relatively speaking, of course. Shame he got discharged like he did. He still claims it was all a mistake."

"They usually do."

"Well, I suppose I should fetch my dessert pan and be on my way, unless ... Know what? I should just leave the brownies here for you." She patted her big stomach. "I always sample a little too much of my own baking."

He nodded toward the house. "Tell you what — I'll get them and you can take them to your ladies' lunch tomorrow. Let them all try one. Then you tell them I said those were the best brownies this side of the Ohio River."

"Why Cecil Penewit ..." Bernadette fingered her beaded necklace. "If I tell my girlfriends that, they just might think you're sweet on me."

He turned away and hurried into the house before I could see his expression. Usually, I'd have followed him, but I decided to stay with Bernadette. Just in case she had a biscuit crumb or two in her pocket. I stared at her, hoping, but she didn't seem to notice me. She just kept her eyes trained on the door. It took him a few minutes to come back out, but he'd taken the time to wrap the remaining brownies individually in Saran Wrap.

As he handed the pan to her, he stumbled over his words. "Say, um ... I gave it some thought and figured, maybe, you'd like to have dinner Monday at Harris's Outdoor Café?"

"After going to the literacy center, you mean? At that place with the cute little red and white umbrellas over the tables and the flowers out front?"

"An early dinner, if that's all right. I have evening chores to do."

She eyed him sideways, like she was trying to figure out the catch in his proposal. "Just the two of us?"

He removed his ball cap, mopped at his forehead with a sleeve, then put his cap back on. He gestured toward me. "The dog would have to come along. I can't leave her in the truck this time of year."

"Oh, yes, of course. I don't think that'll be a problem."

He nodded. "Maybe you can tell me some more about your family then. They sound like a colorful bunch."

"I could, but ... I'd rather hear about you."

"Not much to tell, really."

"Oh, I bet there's more to you than you let on."

He opened his mouth to say something, then thought better of it. Instead, he just tipped his head goodbye and turned to go inside. I

135

followed him this time.

I'm pretty sure Bernadette understood things about Cecil that he didn't even know about himself. She was a lot like a dog that way. Maybe that was why I liked her so much.

chapter 14

The Old Man gripped my leash as we stood before what looked like four small buildings crammed wall to wall. Faderville's library was born when the local historical society donated the log cabin of the area's original settler to the town in the 1950s. Unsure what to do with such a small space, the mayor stored his collection of antique books in orange crates along the back wall. With no movie cinema in the county and nothing better to do, the more literate residents would borrow books from the unlocked cabin and return them on the honor system. Sometimes that was a few days later, sometimes a few years if they forgot about them.

Ten years later, an annex was added: a slightly larger room big enough for two rows of shelves, a librarian's desk and filing cabinet for index cards. The library had been added onto twice more over the years, each addition reflecting the architectural style of the times, rather than aiming to achieve any sense of congruity or practicality. Turned out the 'Literacy Center' was the smallest of the wings, its purpose dedicated to housing children's books and a collection of bean bag chairs.

We learned this because Bernadette told us the entire story on the twenty minute drive over. She knew so much about Faderville's history that the Faderville Historical Society had elected her president over fifteen years ago. She'd been in the post ever since — an honor which might have held some weight if they met more than once a year and actually performed any functions in the community.

One thing I liked about Bernadette was that if no one else was around, she'd even tell me things, whether it was the tale of how Faderville's first pioneers lived off possum stew their first year, current gossip like whether Ginny Holiday kept hundred dollar bills stuffed in her mattress, or commentary on the weather. None of it was truly earth-shaking, but it was the animated tones of her speech that held me captive. The way she lowered her voice to a conspiratorial whisper in one sentence, then flailed her hands in the air the next. Her eyes alone told a story — lined in kohl, with her lids highlighted in shades of brilliant blue, glittery green or sometimes gold, it was hard not pay attention to them.

Where Cecil was all humility and minimalism, Bernadette was spontaneity and excess. They were like shadow and light, yin and yang, distinct entities, yet a perfect complement to each other.

Bernadette laid her hand on the Old Man's forearm. "You're going to strangle that poor dog, Cecil."

He looked down at my leash, coiled tight in his hand. He let out some slack. I went to the end of the leash, gazing inside through the double glass doors, scanning the rows of shelves for small people. He tugged me back. "I just don't know about this."

"Are you talking about yourself or the dog? Because the dog looks just fine to me."

When no one moved, I turned around to stare at him. One more minute of him standing there like a fence post and I'd have to bite *his* ankles to get him moving. I turned back around, pulled toward the door, and whined. Just a little whine. Their reflections in the window remained firmly planted. I whined again.

"See there," Bernadette said. "She wants to go in. You're the one who's being a chicken. They're just children, Cecil. They don't have cooties."

"No, but ..." He was looking down at the ground. His shoulders slouched. He had shrunk in height. "They read to the dog, you say?"

"They try. Sometimes I help them, but we usually have five or six of them. If you want to help them out, you can."

"That, uh ..." His head disappeared into his shoulders with a prolonged shrug. "That might be a bit of a problem."

"Why? Did you forget your reading glasses? I'd let you borrow mine, but unless you're blind as a bat like I am, they'd probably only make things worse. Besides, leopard print would clash with your plaid shirt."

"It's not that." He shifted from foot to foot.

"Then what? You don't like children. Is that why you and Sarah —?"

"No! If we could have ..." He began to turn away, as if he were about to leave.

"That was too personal. I'm sorry." Bernadette grabbed his arm to stop him, then quickly released him. "Why then? Why don't you want to go inside?"

His shoulders twitched. "I get my letters mixed up. It's been a problem long as I can remember."

Realization dawned on her. "Cecil, a lot of the children who come here are dyslexic, just like you. It's nothing to be ashamed of. Tell you what — I'll tell them your job is to make sure the dog minds and they're not to ask you any questions. If you want, you and I can work on the reading alone together later."

"I'm too old for that, Bernadette."

She planted a fist on her round hip. "You're never too old for anything, Cecil Penewit. Soon as you realize that, why the whole world opens up." She reached out to latch onto his arm, but pulled her hand away as something behind him caught her eye. Her eyes lit up. "Oh

139

look, there's little Russell Stevens. Hi there, Rusty!" She waved at a mother and little tawny-haired boy as they turned the corner of the sidewalk a block away. She scooted in close to the Old Man and whispered, "I don't know why they call him Rusty. He's not a redhead."

The little boy kept his head down as his mother pulled him along. From a distance, I might have mistaken him for Hunter. The hair was the same straight sandy blond, his frame slight. My heart bounded. He kicked at pebbles and leaped over the cracks in the sidewalk, as his mother swung his hand vigorously. But as he got closer and raised his face to take me in, I could see his cheeks were rounder than Hunter's, his eyes a dark brown and turned up slightly at the corners, his lower lip slack with a string of spittle hanging down. This was not Hunter. Not at all. Still, there was something special about him, something very pure and uncomplicated.

As Rusty and his mother came near, she stopped to wipe his chin. "Say hi to Mrs. Kratz and her friends, Rusty," she told him.

Lowering his eyes, Rusty scuffed his sneakers over the concrete. "Hiw." Without looking up, he pointed at me. "Who dat?"

"I think he wants to know the dog's name," his mother said.

The Old Man tried to pull me in close to his leg, but I resisted. Bernadette finally nudged him with her elbow.

"Halo," he said. "Her name is Halo, but she's not used to —"

Rusty rushed forward and flung his arms around my neck. "Hiw dere, Hay-O."

And just like that, I was smitten. The thing that had been missing in my life — it was a little boy's love.

I licked his face clean as he giggled in my ear.

"Um, okay, Rusty." His mom guided him toward the door. "Let's go inside. It's story time."

Rusty collapsed like a rag doll. He started to scream. An ear-splitting scream that could have drowned out fire truck sirens.

His mother threw her head back and rolled her eyes. "I'm so sorry. He does this sometimes when he doesn't get his way. I thought it would stop by the time he turned seven, but apparently not. Fortunately, he doesn't do it as often anymore, but when he does …"

"Poor thing. What's he upset about?" Bernadette asked.

"The dog, I think. He likes dogs. His room is full of stuffed dogs. My husband painted puppies on his walls. He named every single one of them."

"Bus-ther," Rusty piped, his screams ending abruptly, "Thunny, Bo, Daidy, Luthy, Tham, Oliber —"

"His older sister is highly allergic," his mom went on, pulling him to his feet, "so we can't have one of our own."

And the screams started again, this time with stomping feet as Rusty jumped up and down on the sidewalk.

"Oh, I hear you. I know all about allergies," Bernadette said over the noise. "I carry antihistamines everywhere. Have you ever tried those with her?"

"I wish that was enough," Rusty's mother said, growing visibly tense. She pulled her son close, clamped an arm across his chest to keep him still, and stroked the top of his head, trying to soothe him, to no avail. "But she has asthma really, *really* bad. Between the two of them, we've had enough trips to the hospital to last us ten lifetimes."

Rusty started bobbing his head as he wailed.

"Say there," Cecil said, stooping down to Rusty's eye level, which was a long way when you're almost six and a half feet tall and talking to a seven-year old, "what if I let you read to Halo here today? That could be your job. She likes stories."

Rusty stopped bobbing. He stuck his fingers in his mouth and nodded.

"You go on in with your mom and pick out a book. We'll be right behind you."

His mother mouthed a silent 'thank you' as Rusty darted inside.

141

When they were both gone, Bernadette laid a hand over her heart and said, "That was the nicest thing I've ever seen anyone do for that boy. He's a special needs child — Down syndrome — so he has his moments."

"Nice?" Cecil harrumphed. "I just couldn't stand to hear him scream for one more second, that's all."

—oO0o—

"You wead?" Rusty held the book above his head, as close to Cecil's face as he could get it.

Cecil fought a scowl. "Why don't we ask Mrs. Kratz to read that, so everyone can hear it?"

Still holding the book up high, Rusty pondered the suggestion. He didn't seem convinced. He waved the book back and forth. "You wead."

This time it was a direct command, not a request. Cecil craned his neck sideways to stare Bernadette down. When she finally looked his way, he raised his shaggy eyebrows in a plea for help. She bustled from behind her desk and wrenched the book from Rusty's grip.

"Ohhh, would you look there! *The Misadventures of Sam Beagle.*" She fanned through the pages, then clutched the book to her chest. "Brook and Olivia love this book. And your friend Alex told me it's his favorite, too."

Upon hearing the name, a little boy with curly brown hair waved at Rusty from where he sat on the floor in a circle with the other children. They had all been instructed by Bernadette to treat me like a new kid: they were to be polite, to remain quiet, and they were not to invade my personal space. If they could follow these rules, Bernadette would teach them how to make friends with me. If that went well, I would return next week.

They may have kept their distance and their voices low, but they stared at me relentlessly. As if they'd never seen a dog before. It was more than a bit unnerving.

Bernadette combed Rusty's hair with her fingers. "So, is it okay if I share this book with the others?"

He tugged at his lower lip and rocked on his feet. "Yaw, is okay."

With a brush of her hand, Bernadette indicated for Cecil to take a seat just beyond the circle. As he trudged over to the chair, Rusty followed a foot behind, staring at my bobtail.

"Wha' happen?" Rusty said, pointing to my nub.

His knees cracking as he sat, Cecil shrugged. "I s'pose she was born that way. You don't have a tail ..." He turned Rusty by the shoulder to check his britches. "Or do you?"

Rusty giggled, then plopped down beside me. "Is boy?"

"Girl," Cecil said, even though that fact had already been established.

"She pwitty."

"I think so, too." Cecil put a finger to his lips, then pointed at Bernadette. "Shhh."

The children all fell quiet and went unusually still as Bernadette began to read. It was like she'd cast some spell over them. She held the book before her so the kids could see the pictures, looking over the top of the page as she read the upside down words. Gradually, they stopped staring at me to focus on Bernadette, her expressive eyebrows lifting and folding at turns, her lips drawing tight with tension on one page, then as she flipped to the next her whole mouth going wide in an 'O' of surprise. A few feet away, Rusty clutched his hands to his own mouth, then scooted closer to me. By the time Bernadette reached the end of the story, his elbow was brushing my fur.

He walked his fingers across the floor tiles, then tickled one of my toes. "Fwiends?"

I slurped at Rusty's cheek, which elicited a giggle of delight. It reminded me of Hunter. Happiness exploded inside my chest like fireworks in the distance: bangles of color swirling against an expanse of sky, their booms reduced to muted echoes. Every time he laughed, smiled or touched me, however tentative, the same sheer joy filled me with that excitable, floaty feeling.

Later, Rusty 'read' the same story to Cecil and me. He didn't get very far on his own. Cecil had to help him sound things out, even though Cecil himself stumbled over some words. Sometimes Rusty made words up or embellished on the story. But every once in a while, he got a few words right all in a row. The pride that beamed from his eyes was priceless.

Cecil displayed the same patience with Rusty that he always had with me, but the effort of dealing with a child seemed to exhaust him more. That didn't matter to Rusty, though. As long as I was Cecil's dog, Rusty would be firmly attached to him.

When Rusty's mother gathered him up in her arms later and he flapped an arm to wave goodbye, I puffed my cheeks out in a sigh of contentment. This had been a good day. A very good day.

I was glad for that. Glad I had survived Ned Hanson's care. Glad I had been rescued by Cecil. And, most of all, glad that Bernadette had barged her way into our lives.

—o00o—

The scalloped edging of the umbrella fluttered in the summer breeze. For the fourth Monday in a row, Bernadette and Cecil (the more I heard her say his name, the more I thought of him that way) sat at the round table, sipping on their lemonades. Beneath the shade of Cecil's chair, I stretched my legs out and laid my head between my paws. Our table was tucked in the furthest corner of the garden area of the café, which was surrounded by a wrought iron fence topped with flowerboxes overflowing with sunny yellow marigolds and trailing pink petunias. Neither the waitress nor the other patrons had ever said anything about my presence. Perhaps it was my intense stare that warned them to mind their own business?

I could still feel the impression of Rusty's arms around my neck. Today his face had smelled of bubblegum and mint toothpaste, his knees of freshly cut grass and his shoes of damp play sand. At the start of the reading hour, Bernadette had read to the children a book called *Charlotte's Web*. Disappointed there was no dog in the story, I focused my attention on Rusty, who lay against the bean bag chair pulling at his lip while his fingers raked my fur.

I learned so many things in those treasured hours at the library: about tropical rain forests and the many-colored birds that inhabit them, about cowboys and their cattle and horses, about wizards and witches and the spells they cast, about the dinosaurs of long ago, and about space ships that slipped through wormholes and boats with pirates that sailed on rough seas. But what I liked most were the stories with talking animals. That, to me, was the most magical thing of all. It was all I ever dreamed of.

Today a new little girl named Marissa had been there. She shrieked when she saw me and hid behind Bernadette, who tried to coax her out in the open. Minutes later, she peeked around Bernadette's hip, and said, "I don't like dogs. They bite." Then she brought her forearms up to cover her face and began to sob.

"Not this dog," Bernadette tried to reassure her. "Halo loves children. See how good she is with Rusty?"

All dogs can bite, I wanted to say. But we won't, as long as no one gives us reason to.

Bernadette could do little to comfort her. The girl ended up sitting on top of the desk behind Bernadette as she read from the book.

The rest of the children had always been friendly, if not a little overzealous. I tolerated them all, but only Rusty interested me. Rusty with his gentle fingers, his soft lisp, his shyness. Every week when reading hour was over, his mother had to unlatch his arms from around my neck. "My fwiend," he declared. Then, "B-bye, Hay-O."

I liked the way he said my name.

Of course Bernadette did most of the talking while she and Cecil ate their dinner. But on this occasion, both of them, I noticed, forgot to slip me a single French fry. It was as if their attention was turning more and more to each other. I might have resented it if I weren't so amused by the whole scene.

"Down syndrome. Rusty can be a challenge when he's frustrated, but otherwise he's the sweetest little boy. He's really taken a shine to Halo. Have you noticed?" Bernadette sopped the gravy from her plate with a roll. "His parents do the best they can with him. I'll give them credit for that. Missy and Jack have ten children between them. Rusty is the youngest."

"Between them? She can't be more than twenty-five, if that."

"Missy got pregnant at fifteen and married a car dealer named Austin Watts from Richmond. He was ten years older than her. Why her parents agreed to the marriage, I'll never ... Anyway, he beat her silly. She finally had the sense to walk away — four kids later. Jack's first wife ran off with some man from —"

Cecil held up his spoon. "I get it."

"Sorry. We have a lot of downtime at the library. Gossip tends to fly."

"So I gather." He dumped a pile of salt on the side of his plate, then squirted a glob of ketchup next to it. "You like your work there?"

"I do. I like helping people, seeing all the locals, getting to know them. You can tell a lot about folks by the books they check out. But since ..." — her usually cherubic face morphed into a frown of distress and, looking over the top of her glasses, she lowered her voice — "since everyone started reading on their phones and those little mini computers ... What do they call them? ... Those tablets. Well, people don't come to the library like they used to. Sad, in a way. When

146

they're done reading, they just delete the book. Delete it. Like it was never there. Do you believe that?"

"Can't imagine it." Cecil raked a handful of fries through the salt and ketchup, then stuffed them in his mouth so he wouldn't have to say more.

I kept my eye on a bumblebee as it floated from flower to flower. I'd caught one of those in my mouth once and paid for it with a swollen face and bloated tongue. Cecil had hauled me to the vet for that, where they forced some bitter syrup down my throat with a syringe. Visits to the vet never ended well. The only other time I'd been there had been to get 'spayed'. I was still unclear what that was about, but I woke up feeling like my innards had been sucked out through a straw.

Bernadette tapped her knife on the table. "Cecil, can you tell me what I just said?"

His hand paused in midair, two golden crisp fries pinched between his thumb and forefinger. He looked at them, then at her. Squinting, he opened his mouth, shut it. Tilted his head. "Something about phones at the library?"

She burst out laughing. "Look at us, will ya? Acting like an old married couple. I'd be mad as a hornet if I didn't enjoy your company so much. I have to admit, when you proposed the first date, I spent three days planning what I'd wear." She pulled her chin back. "It *was* a date, wasn't it?"

He eyed her seriously. "Did you tell your lady friends that's what it was?"

The napkin in her lap suddenly absorbed all of Bernadette's attention. She smoothed it repeatedly before answering. It wasn't often she was at a loss for words, so this occasion was particularly memorable. "I might have."

"In those exact words: I have a date with Cecil Penewit?"

She nodded.

His hand crept across the table. He turned it palm up. When she stared at it blankly, he said, "Give me your hand, Bernadette Kratz." She put her hand in his, one long fingered blue-veined hand cradling her plump, bejeweled fingers. "Then that's what it was."

For once, Bernadette had nothing to say. It was a sure sign that their relationship had taken a serious turn.

"Cecil, what … I mean, when I dropped by that first day, it was almost as if you didn't want the company. Like you'd rather have been alone. What changed your mind?"

Squinting thoughtfully, he wiped at the corners of his mouth with a paper napkin. "It's been a few years since Sarah was around. More than a few, actually. Going on seventeen now. I'd gotten used to the silence, I s'pose. But then, then it occurred to me that maybe we aren't supposed to be alone all the time. There are a lot of hours to fill between breakfast and bedtime. The day goes by faster when you have someone to share it with." He reached beneath the table and scratched under my collar. "Isn't that so, Halo, ol' girl?"

I rubbed my snout against the inside of his wrist. His hand curved around my head, until he was rubbing my ears. Finally, he understood.

The waitress brought another basket of fries. Around us, spoons clinked in iced tea glasses, forks scraped at plates and the conversation hummed pleasantly. Cecil and Bernadette ate in silence, comfortable in their newfound familiarity, like two people who had known each other for a very long time.

Sometimes, there are no words that can convey what is between two people. How can there be, when even those two people do not yet fathom what it is they have?

chapter 15

Its smell was distinct: decay. But I could tell this was a place of reverence, of remembrance. A hallowed place from where souls ascended.

Cecil parked the truck beneath the shade of a maple, cut the engine, and rolled the windows down. We sat there awhile, taking in the serenity and beauty. Ribbons of asphalt cut across swaths of manicured lawn. In the gridwork of greenery, the stones were lined up as far as the eye could see, the regularity of it broken only by the occasional columnar juniper, sprawling oak, or bed of pink shrub roses. Beside some of the slabs sat bouquets of plastic flowers on small metal stands, their colors long since faded from the sun's relentless assault.

Across Cecil's lap lay a fresh bunch of daisies, plucked from the tiny garden beside his front door. He had wrapped their stems in newspaper, carefully broadening the protective cone so as not to crush the delicate, snowy petals. Pollen had tinged Cecil's fingers a luminous yellow and when he brought his fingertips up to brush at the corner of his eye, he left a golden smear there.

"Come on, girl." He sniffed and cleared his throat. The newspaper crinkled as he curled his fingers around it. "Time I introduced you to my special gal."

We got out of the truck and went a few rows down, where we turned right. I followed close behind him, keeping my distance from the granite columns. At the eighth stone, he stopped. Next to it, very close, was a much, much smaller stone. For several minutes, he stood in silence, head bent, the flowers clasped to his chest. His lips moved and every so often I caught a few whispered words: "Yea though I walk ... shadow of death ... no evil, for you are with me ... Amen."

He removed the flowers from their wrapping and laid them at the base of the bigger stone. Then he placed a single flower next to the smaller stone. All too soon, they would wilt and wither under the intensity of the June sun, but for now they were a colorful dash of vitality in an otherwise inert scene. His fingers traced the letters on the larger stone lovingly, as if each stroke and curve represented some long ago memory.

"This was my wife Sarah, Halo. We were together thirty-seven wonderful years. Never raised any children — not that we didn't want them — but it just wasn't in the cards for us. God has his own reasons for everything. Sometimes they don't make a lick of sense, but you abide by them, just like you abide by the speed limit and parking signs. And then He saw fit to take her from me one day, seventeen years ago. Cancer, the female kind. She was only fifty-six. Still spry as the nineteen-year old knockout I married at the little white chapel down in Foxtail Hollow, up until the very end. I suppose it was a blessing she didn't suffer long, but when she died ... I was the one who suffered, instead."

He braced a crooked hand against the top of the slab and sank to his knees, his joints cracking. His forehead touched the smooth surface of the stone. He drew in several slow breaths, as if somehow he could capture the words he sought in a random lungful of air. In the end, they came in staggered bits of thought, scattered memories resurrected.

"We met at the root beer stand just west of town. Well, that's not true, exactly. I was two years older than her and she was still a senior in high school. She knew who I was, but I'd never paid her no mind. That was the first time I ever talked to her. Took me an hour to work up the courage, though. There she was in her little red skirt, white button-up blouse, and that funny little cockeyed hat that said 'Big Bob's', skating from car to car, tray balanced above her bent arm. Truth is, I kept hoping she'd dump one of those trays in the parking lot so I could jump out and help her sweep up the glass. Never happened. My buddy Frank prodded me to introduce myself, but I was sure I'd seen her with Roland Pflaumer the week before at the bowling alley. A gal as fine as that, I figured, had to have a steady guy. Frank finally pushed me out the car door. And I mean *pushed* me out. Landed right at her feet. She hopped over me and still managed to hang onto her tray. That was the beginning of something special. I never needed anything more than her and that farm I call home. Children or no, we were happy. She told me she could tell what I was thinking just by the way my eyebrows twitched or my mouth slanted — and she was usually right.

"Sarah always wanted to go to Paris, but we never had much money. Then, there was always the farm to take care of. She never pressed it, though." He gazed at me, sighed. "I should have taken her. You can't keep putting things off, telling yourself you're gonna do them later. One day, there may not be a 'later' anymore."

I cocked my head to show him I was listening. It was the most he'd ever spoken out loud in one stretch. Quite out of character, but I was enjoying being the object of his confidence.

He ran his tongue over cracked lips and wiped the sweat from his forehead. "One time I came in from the hills after having rounded up some weanlings that had gone through a gap in the fence. My dog Luke had just died, so it was harder work than it ought to have been. When I finally got them rounded up, it was after dark. I'd had a rough

151

day of it and was as grumpy as a bear just woken up from hibernation. Came home hungrier than I'd ever been. I could smell dinner when I walked in the door: honeyed ham with pineapple, green beans sprinkled with bacon, and banana walnut bread." He touched a hand to his stomach and inhaled deeply, as if he could still smell it.

"Sarah had it all wrapped up in foil and warming in the oven. I sat down in my chair, too tired to grunt a conversation, and she piled up my plate and sat down with me to eat. She'd been waiting all that time. Never complained once. When she reached for the butter, I put my hand on hers and said, 'Sarah, do you know how much I love you? What would I ever do without you?' and she said, without thinking, just as serious as could be, 'When I'm gone, promise me you'll take that love and spread it around.' So I promised her. Never dreamed I'd actually be without her."

A thick breeze stirred the leaves into a chatter. He swept his fingers over the flower petals. "I sure haven't kept up my promise. Felt like if another woman ever caught my eye, I'd be betraying her somehow. Truth is, I just felt sorry for myself. Figured it was easier to stay married to the farm, so to speak, than take a chance on someone else who could never be as perfect as Sarah was to me." Gazing up at the tree limbs, he rubbed a blue-veined hand over snowy stubble. "But maybe ... maybe what I was really afraid of was that there was no one out there who could possibly love me — close-mouthed ol' coot that I am — as much as she did."

Gripping the edge of the stone, he pulled himself up. "I'm about to remedy that. If Bernadette will have me, that is."

She will.

I nuzzled the back of his knee until he reached down. He stroked my neck, smiled in that steady, gentle way of his, and said, "I've never admitted this, but there were times just after Sarah died when I could've sworn she was standing right behind me. I couldn't hear her speak, but I always got the sense she was trying to let me know she was doing just fine and I should stop moping." He laughed at himself, and then slapped the dust from his knees. "Crazy old man."

Not crazy, no. Not at all. In fact, we had more in common than he'd ever know.

—o0Oo—

Thunder shook the windowpanes. It had been like this most of the day: bursts of downpours, clouds so black it looked like midnight, flashes of lightning that danced across the sky in jagged tines of white. The sheep had stayed in the barn, and Cecil had remained glued in front of the TV. Every fifteen minutes, he'd flip to the weather station, then back to another station. Nothing held his interest for long. He never watched much television. There was always too much work to be done.

Finally, when Dr. Oz came on the TV, the phone rang.

Cecil flinched at the sound, and then stared at the phone as if trying to figure out what he was supposed to do. After five rings he got up from his recliner and shuffled toward the phone. He placed his hand on the receiver, gathered a breath, and picked it up. A couple more seconds passed before he spoke.

"Hello?" His breathing was audible. A soup bone braced between my front paws, I watched him from beneath the table. His face, pale as a drift of snow, was long with worry. "It is... Oh, I see. Well, that's too soon... No, I can't make it then, either... I understand, but there's something I can't miss that day... Sure, I'll talk to him." Cecil walked slowly over to the kitchen table, the cord stretched so long the curliness of it had disappeared. He pulled out a chair and sank into it. "Dr. Detwiler, hello... Fine. Never felt better, in fact... Uh huh... Uh huh... Ah, I didn't know... Yep, I understand. But can it wait another week?" A bolt of lightning flashed outside. His gaze jerked to the window over the sink. "I will. You have my word on it ... Thank you.

See you then."

He clicked the phone off and laid it on the table before him. His hand drifted to his chest, grazed his breast pocket briefly. Then he looked up at the ceiling. The whites of his eyes, riddled with veins, were more gray than white, but his irises were still as blue as the sky on a summer day.

"You gave me this long, long enough to find her, but I just need a few more days to make it right, y'hear?"

A few more days for what? And who, exactly, was he talking to — himself?

I pulled the bone in closer and went to work licking the marrow clean.

—o00o—

Four days later we put the sheep out to pasture before daylight. That alone was confusing, because we always ate first, but there were several things about today that were distinctly different. For one, Cecil ironed the new shirt that he'd bought at TSC the night before last when we picked up mineral blocks for the sheep. I wasn't even aware he owned an iron until then, although I'd seen Lise use hers many times. Then he draped the shirt on a hanger and hooked it on the bathroom doorknob. It was royal blue with white piping around the breast pockets and had faux mother-of-pearl buttons all down the front. It was the first time I could recall him wearing something other than plaid. Cam used to get new shirts for special occasions, but Cecil hadn't really had any special occasions since I'd known him. Except for winter when he wore his coat, Cecil's wardrobe had pretty much been the same every day for six years.

He stood in a clean white undershirt and his best jeans in front of the hall closet. From the top shelf, he took an overturned white hat. It was a cowboy hat, like the kind Cam wore in his show cattle pictures, with the brim neatly turned up and a black band studded with sterling silver medallions around the crown of it. Before he flipped it over, he dipped his hand inside and drew from it a small box covered in dark green velvet. He flicked the lid open. A beam of yellow sunlight played through the lace curtains at the end of the hallway and danced off a jeweled gold ring.

"You think she'll like it, Halo?"

Honestly, it looked a tad modest for her tastes, but she loved all things glittery. I wondered if it had some symbolic meaning? We dogs are simple creatures. We have our basic needs, but if we can't eat something, sleep on it or play with it, it might as well not exist.

On the shelf beside where he kept this hat that I'd never seen him wear before were half a dozen trophies. I couldn't read what they said — how I wish that I could — but he traced his fingers over the gold plaques on the front and said quietly, "Halo and I are going to make you proud today, Luke."

Something was definitely strange about today. As much as I liked knowing what to expect every day, it also bored me. Our trips to the library over the past month had given me something new to look forward to. I'd even sensed Cecil anticipating Mondays by the way he made sure his clothes were clean and that our chores were done extra early. After visiting with Rusty and the other children, we'd go to the outdoor café with Bernadette for dinner. Cecil always ordered the meatloaf, but Bernadette had something different almost every time. One day it was breaded catfish, the next it was a rib sandwich. The waitress, Amanda, became so used to seeing me that she kept a tin of dog biscuits in the back room and always brought me two — one for dinner and one for dessert.

Today, however, was not a Monday. Cecil stood in front of the bathroom mirror in his undershirt. He dispensed shaving cream into his palm and slathered it on his face, then shaved. After that, he put on his new shirt and slipped a braided lanyard beneath his collar. He'd

155

just finished combing his hair when I heard the whoosh of the back door.

"Morning, you two early birds," Bernadette chimed. She no longer knocked. Cecil had told her there was no need, that she might as well make herself at home.

He took the little box out of his pants pocket. He looked inside, then snapped it shut again and stuffed it into the side pocket of his jacket.

I raced down the hallway, turned the corner, and skidded across the kitchen linoleum, nearly plowing into the refrigerator door. Bernadette had the door wide open, digging for something inside.

"Careful there." Holding a carton of eggs, she emerged from the arctic depths. "You have a big day ahead."

Ohhh. Maybe we were going to breakfast at the outdoor café? But why would she be getting the eggs out then?

Cecil nodded a 'hello', pulled out his chair, and rifled through the morning paper that Bernadette had brought in for him.

"You, too," she said, as she put the iron skillet on the stove and laid strips of bacon side by side. Bacon? This was better than the café. In another skillet she cracked two eggs.

He flicked to another page. "I'm not expecting anything, really."

"That's the biggest boldfaced lie I've ever heard you tell, Cecil Penewit. I've seen you out there training your dog from daybreak to dusk. I hear tell the trial you did over in Rowan County went well. Got a few fancy rosettes, didn't you?"

He huffed a little snort of humility as she laid out two place settings. We'd been to two trials in the past two months: one just over the state line in Indiana and another up northeast. We had sailed through the Started and Open levels, taking first place all but once.

I stared at the stovetop, the tantalizing aroma of bacon fat filling my nose. I practiced my sad, hungry eyes, waiting for Bernadette to toss me a piece. Licked my lips. Groaned softly to convey the tightening hunger in my belly. The strips popped and sizzled, taunting me, as she grabbed each one with the tongs and turned them over. Still, she kept her back to me. I scooted closer. Whimpered.

"Why didn't you tell me, Cecil?"

He gazed at her over the top of the newspaper. "What was I supposed to tell you?"

"About the trials you used to do." A full plate of bacon and eggs in her hands, she waddled over to the table and sat down. I followed her and claimed my usual spot underneath. "I was going through the microfiche at the library, looking something up for a patron when I discovered one of the articles. You were good. *Really* good. A local legend. The pride of Adair County. You suppose that Clancy knows anything about how you were state champ three years in a row?"

Eyes lowered, Cecil folded the paper up and laid it aside. "That was over thirty years ago. He was probably still in diapers. Besides, a man forgets a lot in thirty years."

"Why did you stop going to trials? You've had other dogs since then to help you around the farm, haven't you?"

"Trophies don't mean much at the end of a long day of chores, Bernie. The dog either does the job or they don't." Shrugging, he set his paper on the table and loaded his plate with bacon. "And maybe I just haven't had a dog as good as ol' Luke since then. Until now."

The coffee maker beeped. As Bernadette got up to pour two cups, Cecil dropped not one, but two pieces of bacon next to me. I snapped them both up before she ever turned around.

Bernadette set Cecil's cup in front of him. "You're going to make that dog sick, Cecil."

He opened the paper, folded it in half, and sipped his coffee. "I don't know what you're talking about."

chapter 16

The Adair County Fair was just waking up when we arrived. Rows of crisply painted white buildings flanked a central paved area, where carnival rides and food vendors were arrayed. There were more smells in that one place than I have ever in my life smelled: popcorn and candy apples, barbecued ribs and crispy onion rings, pine shavings and straw, and so many new smells that I didn't yet know. In small aluminum trailers curtained by striped awnings, the workers were just arriving to begin cooking. Fishing a ten dollar bill from her purse, Bernadette went up to one of the trailers. "Two, please." A bearded black man drizzled batter into a vat of oil, humming to himself. A few minutes later, he pushed two enormous elephant ears dusted with powdery sugar at her.

"Best part of the fair," she chirped as she handed Cecil his. "That and the freshly squeezed lemonade."

No, the French fries were. And if someone didn't give me some soon, I was going to throw myself down on the ground and refuse to move. Heck, I'd settle for some squashed, day-old, grit-encrusted ones off the asphalt if Cecil would ever lighten up on the leash and let me dive after them.

Mindless of my agony, they strolled down the midway, stepping carefully over the many electrical cords crisscrossing the thoroughfare, close enough to brush elbows occasionally, but not holding hands. They weren't yet ready for that public declaration.

I kept my eyes on the ground, looking for stale hamburger buns or smashed fries, a kernel of popcorn or a forgotten Skittle. Humans are unbelievably wasteful creatures. Even though my stomach was satisfied from my morning meal, I would have gladly cleaned up the thoughtlessly tossed food remains, but Cecil kept my leash tightly looped at his hip, restraining me from the smorgasbord of my dreams. I did manage a few nachos, although they were slathered in a cheesy sauce with tiny chunks of peppers that made my nose and eyes burn.

At the tallest and biggest of the amusement rides, Cecil paused. The brim of his hat shading his eyes, he leaned back to gaze up at the giant wheel. A fresh coat of blue paint concealed a scattering of rusty pockmarks. Unlit bulbs dotted its outer framework. Bench seats swung precariously all the way up to the top, their red vinyl faded from the weathering of many years.

To me, the thing reeked of grease and gasoline. I failed to see its purpose. No dog in his right mind would go up in that thing. Humans, though, do very senseless things at times.

"This was always my favorite," Cecil said. "I was thinking — maybe later today, before we leave, we could take a ride? If you'd like to."

"I'd like that very much," she said, her sight also fixed on the apex of the tall wheel. They stood like that, transfixed, for a full minute before the sputter and hum of a generator sounded behind them. Bernadette touched Cecil on the arm and leaned her head toward the stands of the arena at the far end of the midway.

He nodded. "I s'pose we should head that way."

They turned and began walking. Halfway there, Bernadette's steps slowed. She glanced at him, then turned her gaze ahead. "Being here, with you … it makes me feel young again. Like, I don't know … like

159

nothing else matters but right now."

His foot skipped over a stone, sent it bouncing across the cracked asphalt and under the trailer of a cotton candy vendor. He caught her hand in his and swung it, his wrinkly cheeks pressed into a wide grin. "Know what you mean. I feel the same way."

—o00o—

We had drawn the second to last run of the day, and there had been more entries than in previous years, so the runs had started in the relative cool of morning, only to stretch endlessly into the sweltering heat of late afternoon. Most of the dogs trialing were Australian Shepherds, but there were also a smattering of other herding breeds: Border Collies, Shetland Sheepdogs, a German Shepherd and a low-slung shaggy thing that even Cecil didn't know the name of. For a while, Cecil paced nervously behind the stands while I slept in their shade, but eventually the waiting had worn on him, and he left me with Bernadette while he went off to rest somewhere quiet.

"Oh my. I think I've died and gone straight to heaven." Bernadette's friend Merle fanned her face with the trial program. Slight-framed, she was as lively as a hummingbird, even though she was probably a good ten years older than Bernadette. The frames of her glasses were huge and round, giving her the appearance of an owl. We were sitting at the bottom edge of the arena stands, close to the action, which meant we were constantly breathing in a cloud of dust. "That one looks *just* like George Strait, don't he?"

A man with a dog at his side leaned over the gate that led into the main arena. Something very subtle indicated he was different from the rest who had stood there in the hours past. Maybe it was the tilt of his hat or the casual, yet confident stance. More likely it was the gleaming silver buckle fastened at his waist, imprinted with the design of a dog in full stride trailing after a compliant flock, a clarion of his conquests. It was probably not the only silver buckle he owned. He was neither old, nor young, but that golden age in between, still possessing of youth's vitality, yet with enough experience under his belt to command respect from the life-ranchers and a fan-girl sort of admiration among the hobby trialers. Arms crossed, he drummed his fingers idly against his biceps. He didn't carry the carved crook of the more serious handlers or the rudimentary stock stick of the neophytes purchased from TSC. He didn't need such crude implements. In his world, they were a symbol at best, a crutch at worst.

In the pens by the announcer's stand, the stock handlers were putting out a new batch of sheep. The last run had been disastrous. The dog had gone into prey drive and heeled one of the ewes too hard, bringing the sheep to the ground as its canines pierced the tender flesh above the hock. The bright red of blood shone against ivory wool. Everyone in the stands gasped collectively. The judge's voice had boomed over the speakers with a reproachful 'Thank you'. A condemnation.

Next up was the clean cut man with piercing eyes who hung over the gate. The one to be watched, studied, revered perhaps. His dog was a lanky blue merle Aussie with one upright ear and one cocked sideways. Despite his god-like aura, there was nothing intimidating about the man. His dog looked even less impressive. He took an index card with a number on it and held it up toward the judge.

"Five sixteen," he said.

Plucking the program out of Merle's hand, Bernadette unfolded it. "That's *him*," she whispered.

"*That* is George Strait? Oh my word! Right here in Adair County? Who'd have ever thought he did stock trials? Well, I s'pose a man's gotta have a hobby o' some sort. Can't just stand up there on stage and sing all the time, can he?" She dug around in her purse and produced a pen. She grasped at the flyer. "Give that back to me, will ya? I want to see if he'll sign an autograph before he goes into the arena."

Bernadette rolled her eyes. "For Pete's sake, Merle. That is *not* George Strait. It's Bill Clancy."

"Oh." The excitement vanished from Merle's thin face. She stuffed the pen back in her purse. "Bill who?"

"Clancy. Bill Clancy. The fellow from St. Louis. National champion eight times over, last count."

"Ohhh. Well, at least we have good seats. Say, where did Cecil go?"

"Back to the truck to get his number. He didn't say as much, but I think he left it there on purpose. Probably doesn't want to watch the runs right before him — this one in particular."

"Getting nervous, is he?"

"He won't say so, but I suspect he is. Truth be told, he doesn't say much about how he feels about anything. But he's not so hard to figure out. This dog here" — she glanced down at me — "is something really special to him. He just wants to show everyone what they can do."

Merle squeezed her friend's wrist. "Say, have you two ... you know?"

"Kissed, you mean?"

Merle poked her in the ribs. "What century are you from, Bernie? No, I don't mean kissed. If you're going to lasso a man, the marrying kind — and God knows you don't have time to dawdle in that department — then you need to take him for a test ride, so to speak. I mean, what if he, you know, can't ..." — squinting, she pumped her fists toward her twice — "*you know?*"

Tight-lipped, Bernadette simply stared at Merle. "This isn't the place to be talking about that sort of thing. In case you hadn't noticed, there are people all around us, Merle."

Merle hitched a shoulder. "He *is* getting up there in years. I'd want to know if I were you."

This time Bernadette raised her voice enough so that everyone within a five row radius could hear her. "Say, is Jasper is still using that over the counter, all-natural male enhancer?"

Next to us, two very elderly ladies wearing nylons, floral skirts, and starched blouses turned to gawk at Merle and Bernadette.

"Did she say what I think she said?" the blue-haired one asked.

The other one tusked and repositioned her Vera Bradley handbag in her lap as she motioned her companion to scoot the other way, away from Bernadette and Merle. "No morals these days. Can't even watch the soap operas on TV anymore, it's all about who's sleeping with who. Ain't no different in a small town like this."

Merle snapped her jaw shut and faced forward.

"Wonder what's taking them so long?" Bernadette said.

"Wrong group," Tucker informed her from beside the stands. He dipped his head at his aunt and leaned forward to acknowledge Merle, but she was still miffed about Bernadette's remark and was ignoring them.

"Oh," Bernadette said. Then, "What do you mean 'wrong group'? Shouldn't it be some sort of random draw?"

"Naw." He worked his jaw back and forth and spit a brown glob onto the dirt. Tobacco, just like Ned Hanson used to chew. "They use more dog broke sheep for the lower level dogs, but for the advanced teams, like Clancy and his dog Brooks, they use some kind of Barbados crosses. Spooky critters. If a dog steps two inches too close, they'll rocket into the next county faster than you can sneeze."

Clancy turned halfway, just enough to catch Tucker out of the corner of his eye. It almost looked like Tucker grinned, or maybe I just imagined that. He always wore a smirk.

A lady with a long blonde braid pushed open the window to the judges' box and shouted, "Number again, sir?"

"Five sixteen."

"Come on in."

He flipped the latch on the gate, walked through, and then shut it behind him. His dog, eyelids heavy with boredom, sat obediently. Clancy's hand slid down the leash and unsnapped it. He draped the leash over the gate. They'd done this routine hundreds of times, it was apparent from their little rituals, Clancy's easy stride, Brooks' serenity. Side by side, they walked across the churned dirt of the arena to the judge's box, the second story of a compact building perched at the far end of the arena. From there, the judge had an unobstructed view of everything that went on down below.

Clancy tipped the brim of his hat to the judge. "How are you on this fine afternoon, Miss Zink?"

"I'm good, Mr...." — she rifled through the papers in front of her, then leaned out the window to glance toward the pens, where wide-eyed ewes tapped their hooves — "Mr. Clancy, is it?"

"That's right, ma'am." His voice was like liquid honey. If the judge was in the least bit charmed, she gave no indication of it.

She drummed at the desk impatiently with her pencil. "Any questions?"

"No, ma'am."

She withdrew from the window. "Whenever you're ready."

Clancy muttered something to his dog. Brooks dropped belly to the ground like a stone from his hand.

The clouds that had veiled the sun earlier that morning had been blown eastward by a dry, hot breeze. Rain hadn't fallen in almost two weeks. The Old Man had begun to lament that the crops were not getting much needed rain and the price of feed was going to skyrocket because of it.

Clancy opened the gate to the pen and Brooks darted in to gently scoop the flock out. Ten sleek-hided sheep raced out, wary of the wolf on their heels. A billowing cloud of dust rolled across the arena in their wake. Brooks lowered his head and trotted calmly after them. Two sharp whistles signaled a direction and Brooks swung to the left.

The sheep's heads went up, their ears twitching side to side. The one out front whipped around, her sights on the pen they'd just run from, while the nine behind her began to arc back around.

Again, Clancy whistled with his mouth and Brooks redirected his flock. They beelined for the first panel, a single section of fence ten feet from the outer perimeter fencing. The moment the first one daylighted, Brooks burst forward to check them. They pulled up, slowed, then continued along the far fence line. Their instinct had been to return to the pen, because in their collective mind, since it had been the gate to this new hell, it also must be the way out. Never mind that there were other dogs shuffling groups from the holding pens to the take pen, snapping at their heels in close quarters. Sheep have very short memories.

The second obstacle consisted of two panels, one abutting the outer fence and the other one in line with the first, so that there was an opening between the two. Sheep, I once figured out, see the box created by the corner of the outer fence and the attached panel as a trap. If they go in, they forfeit their route of escape. Always, the foremost thing on their minds is their own survival. If you are being pursued, there are two choices: run … or fight. Sheep are not known for their bravery. They are lean of leg, so they can bound up hills and run through tall grasses. Their eyes are set more to the sides of their heads, so they can see both in front of and behind them. Their teeth are flat and blunt, made for grinding tough stems. A dog's teeth are sharp, for piercing. Sheep learn this single difference early. They live an idle and carefree life, with no more purpose than to eat their fill and loll in sunny meadows. Yet I would not like to be one of them, ever living in fear of dogs and coyotes.

Brooks pushed the sheep through the second obstacle. Again, they tried to bolt for the take pen. Clancy, who stood unconcerned in the same spot some twenty feet from the take pen, sauntered toward the center Y-chute. One of the smaller sheep veered in his direction.

Half the flock did likewise. The rest were still traipsing along after the lead ewe.

The collective mind of the flock does not always make a unanimous decision. Such folly can be fatal. When the coyotes descend upon a flock, their sole aim is to worry the sheep, to scatter them, until that one unthinking sheep tears off in its own direction.

We dogs, however, are not coyotes. A stock dog's purpose is to gather the flock or herd and take it where the handler asks. The livestock that do not understand this, those that seek to escape, they create their own chaos. Like I said, sheep in particular are stupid.

Until then, Clancy's run had seemed as close to flawless as a dog-handler pair could look. But the teamwork was being tested by a rogue sheep. An underling that had not acknowledged the wisdom of the eldest ewe, the experienced one, the thinker among them.

Two whistle blasts rent the dust-choked air. As if yanked by an invisible rope, Brooks suddenly peeled in a clockwise direction, his copper-colored legs raking lightly over the sandy surface. He arced wide, speed increasing with each powerful stride. Until he reached a point where the ewe out front pulled her head back, slowed, and then faltered in her commitment to reach the pen. The gang behind her eased their pace to avoid colliding with her hind end.

A moment hung suspended in which dog eyed sheep, sheep eyed dog. Indecision, challenge, command. A second sheep moved to its left. The dog froze, waited until the others followed suit. They were going exactly where he wanted. He broke the stare, turned away, then cast out again, his gait less hurried, his presence less forceful. Compliance had been accomplished.

In a pinched huddle, the sheep trotted through the center chute. The rogue, again, thought to break away, but Clancy had anticipated this and positioned himself to the side of the group where that one sheep was. When it lurched his way, he brought up a hand in a quick, but intimidating wave. Realizing this man was the wolf's accomplice, the rebel tucked in behind the trailing end of the flock as they bustled through the narrow funnel and on out the other end.

The crowd erupted in applause. The old ladies beside us sang their praises. Clancy and Brooks were the first team that day to find success in the center chute. It had defeated no less then fourteen teams before them. The sheep, flighty in their new surroundings and unaccustomed to being worked by strange dogs, had been particularly difficult that day.

As Clancy and Brooks headed for the re-pen, I glanced around, looking for Cecil. He was nowhere to be seen. My leash, I noticed, had been only loosely looped around the metal bar beneath the corner of the stands. Bernadette and Merle were gabbing away, recapping every glorious moment of Clancy and Brook's miraculous run.

I hopped down off the floorboard of the stands and went down the stairs. My leash trailed after me. People were clustered off to the side, the crowd of onlookers having grown with the onset of Clancy's run. Apparently word had gotten around that this was the event to watch. I slipped between kneecaps and cowboy boots. Worked my way through to the parking lot, back toward the truck. Except for a little curly-haired girl, who I stopped for so she could pet my head, no one took notice of me, the diminutive stock dog meandering through the crowd.

I heard the clang of the gate as the prideful, upraised, velvety voice of Clancy sang, "Here, Brooks. That'll do."

The crowd erupted in banging applause and long whistles of admiration. Shouts of praise flowed down from the top tier of benches to the bottom row, spilling out among the overflow of onlookers gathered alongside the stands. Tucker Kratz parted from the throng, casting his squinty-eyed gaze over the confusion.

I ducked behind a rusty old truck, bits of hay dangling from its tailless bed, and slunk along a row of vehicles to where ours had been parked. I arrived to no one.

I sniffed the tires. The scent of familiar earth was embedded in its treads. Yes, this was ours. I raised myself up on my hind legs, trying to look inside. The window was too high, but it was closed and I knew Cecil would not be sitting inside a closed vehicle in this suffocating heat. I put my nose to the crushed grass, searching for his scent. It was everywhere. He had been here many times today. Several times, I circled, until I found on offshoot trace that led to a nearby barn. His scent seemed fresh, so I followed it.

Beneath the body of a bright green tractor, I glimpsed pair of denim clad legs and work boots — a man crouching in its shade. An old man.

chapter 17

Cecil's head was bent over, his right arm crossed over his chest, hand kneading at his opposite shoulder. His face, usually expressionless and relaxed, was twisted in pain. On the ground between his knees sat a half full bottle of water. He dug in his hip pocket, tossed something small and white in his mouth, and took a swig of water. He tipped his head back, clamped his eyes shut, swallowed.

For a moment, I observed him. A grimace contorted his features. Concern flared in my chest. Cecil was a soft-spoken, stoic man, but it was not like him to hide like this. On soft paws, I crept to him. Still, he didn't notice me. I snuffled at his hand and his eyes shot open in surprise.

"Halo?" He rocked back, the giant ring of rubber stopping him from falling backward. Perspiration dotted his forehead. He forced a smile, but his eyes were still tight. "You were supposed to be with Bernadette."

What's wrong? I woofed at him.

But of course he didn't understand my meaning.

His head drifted down again, tension plain in his jaw. He sucked in a thin breath, then let the air out slowly, as if savoring every molecule of oxygen.

Dogs have a sense that something is not right without knowing what or why that is so. If humans have this same ability, they don't act on it. It's why we sense earthquakes before they occur. We feel the ground shift deep in the earth's mantle, feel its layers slide one against the other, the whole globe groaning deep within its molten belly. We know the power of lightning, how it can strip the air of electrons and stab them through your body, or a tree, or a rooftop. We feel its tingle from miles away, the warning carried on the sonorous undulations of thunder. We smell the danger of fire and know that its smoke can rob you of breath and singe your lungs. We know these things without ever having been taught them.

And we know when our humans, the ones we follow and wait for and guard with our lives ... we know when they are hurting, whether or not they bleed or cry out in pain. The confession lies not in the obvious, but in the unspoken — in the grimace, in the furrowed brow, in the far-off stare. The mournful tilt of the head. The sigh. We dogs can do none of these things ourselves, but we read them so well in humans. It as if God made us specifically for that purpose. As if He gave us the knowledge, but forbade us the power of tongues.

Watch, observe, He said, just ... be there. But say nothing.

Worry gripped my heart. I nosed the back of his left hand, lying limply across his knee. With painstaking slowness, his fingers curled around the top of my muzzle, stroked it twice.

"Mr. Penewit?"

I whipped around. Tucker Kratz tossed a cigarette stub on the ground and smashed its orange embers beneath his worn boot.

"They've been looking for you. You were supposed to be up after Clancy, but they couldn't find you. Arden Ashbrook took your spot, but you still have time. Best hurry, though. His dog's wound tighter than a top and is about to get thank-you'd off the course."

"Be there in a minute," Cecil said. "I, uh, need to use the facilities."

With a nod, Tucker lit another cigarette and left, his trail of smoke weaving through the parked cars.

Carefully, Cecil set his hat on the trampled grass beside him and wiped the sweat from his brow and neck with his sleeve. A mother hauling two whiny young children walked by. The little girl with bouncy curls, the one who'd patted me on the head, started toward me, but her mother, upon seeing the pale-faced Cecil huddled beside the tractor, reeled her in with a correction. They stumbled on, the mother yanking, the little girl looking back, and the even littler boy crying because he was hungry.

Cecil grabbed the end of my leash and stood. Before he took his first step, he steadied himself with a hand against the giant tire. "You'll be fine, girl. But me? Well, let's just get through this and go on home. Chores don't do themselves, now, do they?"

If it were up to me, we wouldn't have come here in the first place. I didn't quite see the point. But then, I never got a vote, did I?

—o0Oo—

The group of sheep we drew was a motley conglomeration of half-breeds. One had the face of a Suffolk, but the honey coloring of a Katahdin, while two others were mottled like black and white Paint horses. The rest were a curious mixture of tawny and white shorn woolies. They stared at me through the bright orange bars of the gate panel where the tarp had slipped to the side. I yawned and looked away. No need to get them riled before our turn had even begun.

"Guess we got the leftovers, eh, girl?" Cecil looped my leash over his shoulder and clipped the ends together. His fingers curled around the top end of his crook, clenched, released. I gazed up at his blanched face, hoping he'd reach down and rub his calloused fingertips across my topskull for good luck, but his gaze strayed to the stands, eyes squinting against the long rays of afternoon sun.

171

To show him there was nothing to worry about, I sank to my belly in the loose dirt. Particles of gritty sand dug between my toes. I sneezed at the dust and put on the most bored faced I could arrange, which is an easy thing to do when your expressions are limited. It's all in the ears, you see. I kept them relaxed, not flattened against my head or perked at full attention. Then, I yawned for emphasis.

"Whenever you're ready," the judge announced from the shadows of her box.

Cecil flashed his number at the judge, then stuffed it partway back in his pocket. He ambled to the take pen, his steps more plodding than sure. I trotted alongside him, my head down so as not to threaten the sheep. They stomped nervously, sending up little puffs of dust with each slap of their hooves.

As Cecil reached for the latch and pulled back, his entry number fluttered from his pocket. The gate swung open. At his command, I took one step, one slow, measured step, toward the pen, my muzzle aimed squarely for the right side of the group where there was the most room. A second step — and they bolted from the pen like a rocket launched off its pad. Cecil threw himself against the fence just in time to avoid being trampled to death.

They had blasted the gate open with such force that it ricocheted back. Cecil caught the edge and slammed it shut.

I remained where I was. My job, I knew, was to gather the sheep in a bunch and take them where my handler commanded. Even though I had already watched a dozen runs and knew the course by heart, my place was to never assume a course of action. It was to execute the plan my handler chose. Sometimes that was hard to do. Very hard. Like now.

Every neuron in my body shouted at me to take off, seek out the furthest sheep, cast as wide as the confines would allow, and come just enough within that sheep's line of sight to cause a change in direction. Hopefully, a calm, collected change. That possibility, however, had been shattered in the first heartbeat.

There are times when it's best to let livestock discharge their fear and not play a part in it. It takes a wise handler to know that and a dog that trusts in that handler enough not to assume anything less. Over the years, Cecil and I had developed a oneness, that extra sensory ability to operate as a single unit, two parts of a whole.

To the onlookers in the stands, it must have looked like chaos unfolding. Like Cecil had taken the lid off Pandora's Box, and I was merely some befuddled dunce, a sidekick at his downfall.

Head high, the black-faced wether bounded to the far side of the arena. The shorn sheep clipped blindly after him, their shorter legs churning madly. But the others, the mutt-sheep, scattered like colliding marbles. One raced toward the center chute, another followed, then changed course, while the rest loitered near the take pen, hopeful that the scatter-brained among them would snap to their senses and return to the safety of home base.

Cecil studied the situation. This was not altogether unlike some days at home, when new flock members were assimilated with testy older mothers and frantic lambs. So Cecil did what was prudent in that situation. He turned his back and walked away from them, calling me to his side with a voice so soft that no one but me could have heard.

Murmurs drifted down from the stands. Had he given up before even starting? What was he doing? Why not just send the dog?

He planted his crook in the shifting dirt, pivoted slowly around it, and watched as the sheep looked at us, then at each other, then back at us. The black-faced sheep twitched his ears, hovered a moment in indecision, then cantered back toward the center chute to join the few there.

Cecil lifted his crook, shifted three feet to the left, and waited. The sheep loitering by the take pen were wedged together as tight as gobstoppers in a gumball machine. The one with sideways ears twitched her shoulders and the movement rippled through them like whitecaps on choppy water.

Until that moment, I had restrained myself admirably. I had waited for Cecil to assess the situation, to formulate his plan of attack, and issue the directive. But he had hesitated. And I could see so clearly what should come next.

Popping to my feet, I ducked behind the *Old* Man — let's face it, he was being slow — scurried to the right three steps and dropped. Aware of the shift in pressure, a single ewe moved away from the group a few feet. Only a few. It was enough.

I crept forward. Low like a Border Collie. And I eyed that single ewe with the realization that she had become the transient leader of this offshoot faction. She had assumed the power of decision. The rest would do as she did.

I was an Australian Shepherd. Usually, we worked upright, with a looser eye than our distant Scottish kin, the Border Collie. But like other working breeds, we also *think* independently. Had I moved toward them too quickly, used my physical presence alone, they would have reacted in the extreme. It would only take one crazed sheep careening headfirst into a fence panel and breaking her gracefully arched neck for us to not only be excused, but possibly banished from trials indefinitely.

Control is measured in minute increments and I displayed that to the utmost degree.

"Stay," Cecil uttered.

I froze where I stood. Time stalled. Perhaps it even moved backward. The crowd was mute.

The single ewe tucked back in with her group. I took one more step, and they turned their heads toward those at the far end. Still aware of the ones orbiting the center chute, I shifted to the left. They, too, trotted toward the black-faced one.

"Steady, girl," Cecil said, his voice low and even.

As one congruent unit, they marched through the first panel, no more than a few inches between any two. I balanced myself perfectly as they progressed to the second set of panels. There was a momentary spurt in their speed, so I dropped back, releasing the pressure, and they eased their pace. As the first few daylighted through the second obstacle opening, Cecil turned, stepped into me, and commanded, "Way to me."

He meant the other direction, so I ignored the command and went the opposite way. He didn't correct me. Like a boomerang, I reversed direction, sailing out in a clockwise crescent, facing away from them.

Sheep are fast, but there is always one among them that is not as fast as the rest, that hangs back in uncertainty. It is to this weakness in the group that we dogs play. The group, when it truly behaves as one, slows to compensate for this. That is our advantage.

I flew, as I had never flown before. Fleet, sure-footed, focused. And I met them halfway, before they had even passed the center line, parallel to the opening of the Y-chute. Black-Face led his frightened minions toward the yawning chute. Cecil, who knew enough of how sheep think to place himself properly, stood to the right of it. By now, they were figuring out that he was their safe haven, that he would not allow harm to befall them. Their instinct, however, was to race at him full speed, as if the moment they reached his feet all danger would cease. The problem, you see, was that Cecil was on the *other* side of the fence panel.

I may have mentioned before sheep are not the brightest creatures on Earth.

To sheep, it seems like I, the dog, am the wolf. However, dogs are vastly different from wolves. We may have sprung from the same ancestral tree, some of my species may even look like wolves, but the greatest difference lies in our thinking and our behaviors. We dogs do not need to hunt for our survival. We can. Some do. Most of us, however, fully understand that humans will feed us all we need, sometimes with very little work on our parts. Grace's poodles had to do nothing more than let her dress them up and ride around in her purse (the shame!). But I digress ...

The sheep were on a direct trajectory for the fence panel when it occurred to one of them that perhaps they could not go *through* said panel. This caused Black-Face to stop. Confusion ensued. The cohesion of the group began to dissolve.

"Awaaay to me," Cecil said.

This time he was right. I had anticipated this counter move. Having sat patiently all day, watching other dogs fail so miserably at this juncture, I recognized their error. To put the thread through the eye of the needle, you must first pull the thread away from it, then turn it into the tiny metal loop before slipping it through. The sheep had to overshoot the opening to a slight degree. If the dog then checked them on the other side, but far enough away to present pressure in the direction of the chute at precisely the right spot, they would go through that seemingly too narrow opening because it was the fastest and seemingly safest way to get away from the dog.

In the split second that Black-Face considered this, Cecil turned his body slightly and backed away from the chute's end, headed toward the re-pen. This was their invitation to sanctuary. They followed him as I walked calmly behind. All ten. Filed through that slim canyon of metal tubing like children lined up for a carnival ride.

Thus, I became the second dog of the day to succeed at the center chute.

As the sheep trotted tranquilly toward their haven, Cecil appraised me with a look that reminded me our work was far from done. It could all unravel in a single misstep, an ill-timed flank, a hesitation. He flicked his crook at them — a warning to respect his territory this time, for he had command of the wolf. They halted. He took hold of the latch, lifted it, slid it back, and carefully opened the gate.

When he was clear of their path, he told me, "Around", which meant I could go either left or right. It didn't matter which way, so long as the job was done.

They went in, tucked themselves against the backside of that little square prison, and turned to look at me. The wildness that had possessed them at the beginning was gone from their eyes. They were home. They would join more of their kind soon.

I lay down to let them know my task was done. I would not pursue them any longer. The gate floated shut as Cecil slid his hand along it. The 'clink' of the latch resounded like the chiming of a bell, signaling the end of an ordeal.

"Good girl, Halo," he said, as we walked side by side to the outer gate. "But then ..." — his voice went soft, cracked just the tiniest bit — "you always are."

chapter 18

Praise is a wondrous thing. Intoxicating and uplifting. The drink of the ears. The drug of the soul.

We were showered with it. The exhibitors who had gone earlier in the day clapped Cecil on the back. They shook his hand. They recapped the tense moments of our run, the obvious triumphs, commiserated with him over the difficulty of his lot of sheep, praised him again. He shrugged it all off as mere luck.

"Amazing run." A short red-haired man with freckles clasped Cecil's hand and shook it vigorously. "Just ... amazing."

"Thank you, Becket. Parts were a bit rough, but I s'pose we got the job done."

Bernadette kissed him on the cheek. Her pride was barely containable. She hooked her arm through his and leaned against him as they walked toward the truck to put his crook away and get me a drink of water. "They're saying you ought to win this thing, Cecil."

He puckered his face up, then rinsed his mouth with water from the bottle that she handed to him. "Naw. Clancy's run was smooth. He did his in half the time." He tucked his crook under his arm on the side by me as we walked along. "Besides, doesn't matter whether we win or lose. She's an honest dog. She did what I asked of her and then some. Can't wish for more."

"She's your favorite girl, isn't she?"

He stopped, looked her square in the eye. "*You're* my favorite girl."

A declaration. Not public, but unmistakable. He removed his hat, bent his head toward hers.

I looked away. I'd had my moment. This was theirs.

—o0Oo—

The exhibitors, along with an impressive number of observers, had collected at the back of the building that housed the judge's box. Dogs sat calmly at their handlers' knees. Fifteen minutes had passed since our closing run and tension mounted as the judge and her assistants tabulated scores, their pencils scratching furiously, fingers tapping away at calculator keys.

Finally, the door opened and Jessica Zink emerged. Right behind her were the two people who had added scores for her that day, handed her the proper score sheets, and run the clock. Over the hours, her long pale braid had loosened. She brushed a stray lock from her face and addressed the crowd with the usual platitudes about how many nice runs and promising young dogs she had seen. She read through the placements for the Started and Open classes, then handed out the score sheets to the remaining qualifiers.

Clancy stood off to the side, one shoulder propped against a young tree, as he emptied a can of soda down his gullet. Brooks was asleep at his feet.

"And now for our top four placements in the Advanced class." Zink flipped through the entire stack briefly, pulled out the bottom four, and placed them on top. "I'll announce the remaining qualifiers after this. As for the rest of you ..." — she gave a smile that was more polite than apologetic — "I'll be happy to discuss the scores and where I may have deducted points after the conclusion of awards."

Arms crossed, Cecil looked down at the ground. Whatever had caused him discomfort an hour ago had faded. The color was back in his cheeks, the tension gone from his face. He appeared more agitated by the constant stream of small talk from the other competitors than anything. Cecil was always cordial with others, but he could only take so much before he sought to retreat to solitude. Most people would have itched with boredom to rise every day, work alone on a remote farm, and go to bed with no one to talk to but a scrappy little working dog. But Cecil found a unique beauty in that peaceful setting, a fulfillment in the mundane. We were alike that way.

"In fourth, we have ... Dylan Walton and Spin."

A man standing next to the flagpole dipped his head in disappointment, then raised his hand to gentle applause. The pair wove through the crowd to accept their rosette.

"In third ... Maggie Kirton and her partner Cirrus."

A scream of elation broke above the soft clapping of hands. Everyone turned to the back of the crowd where a woman wearing a Cincinnati Reds cap and mirrored sunglasses jumped up and down. Her dog, a perfectly groomed blue merle male, leapt into the air and barked. Her friends hugged her. She bounced her way to the front, hugged the judge, and had her picture taken.

On the way back, Kirton pumped her fists above her, the streamers of the rosette twisting around her forearm. The judge raised the stack of papers in her hand to hush the crowd. The air crackled with anticipation.

"Today's runner-up was ... from St. Louis, Bill Clancy and his dog Brooks."

Shock flashed over Clancy's features. His fists clenched. He molded his face into a plastic smile to show off bleached teeth. As he passed through the crowd, his pace a tad sluggish as if he were reluctant to accept the consolation prize, he nodded in acknowledgment of their congratulations. When he passed by Tucker, however, his cordial glance became a brief glare.

Cecil, who had not witnessed the exchange between the two, expelled a breathy sigh, then checked his watch. "We'll have to rush home to get the girls put away before sunset, Halo."

His lips drawn tight, Clancy snatched the runner-up rosette from the judge a little too abruptly.

"Nice work, Mr. Clancy," the judge told him as she held up the envelope containing his prize money.

"Could've been nicer, apparently," he muttered, taking the envelope from her.

Bernadette wedged her way between a young couple and their children to give Cecil a pinch on the arm. "Do you know what that means?"

"Goodness gracious," Merle chirped beside her. "I haven't seen this much excitement since Jasper passed his kidney stone."

Cecil shook his head. "Means we didn't even make honorable mention. Come on, Halo, time to head home."

Just as he turned to go, Zink raised her voice. "I think today's winner was a surprise to us all."

Bernadette blocked his exit and jabbed a finger at his chest. "Just wait, will ya?"

"Even though this team didn't have the quickest time, and parts of the run looked, well, ugly, it was the best example of teamwork I've seen since the 2005 Nationals. Congratulations are in order for Cecil Penewit and Halo."

"I told you! I told you!" Bernadette screeched, her bosom heaving every time she bounced on the balls of her feet. Her bracelet and necklace clacked like a pair of maracas.

Cecil blinked at her. "Who did she say?"

Merle slapped him on the back. "You, you old goat. Now get up there!"

I nosed the back of his knee to prod him along.

Half the county, it turned out, already knew who Cecil was. There had been pictures in the local rag of the two of us attending story time at the literacy center. We were small town celebrities. The soft-spoken shepherd who owned the farm at the end of Sweet Potato Ridge Road, childless and widowed long ago, was engulfed by a sea of congratulations.

It seemed to overwhelm him as much as it uplifted him.

With a shy smile and twinkling eyes, he accepted his awards with humility. He shook the judge's hand and posed with her for the photographer, who was also the reporter of The Messenger, Faderville's only newspaper. But instead of mingling with his admirers or granting an interview, he ducked out the back way.

Cecil and I caught up with Clancy just as he was packing his pop-up canopy into the side door of his gooseneck trailer. The trailer was twice as long as his truck. Through the open door, I could see the inside of the place, decked out with velour benches, oak cabinets, and brass trim everywhere. A palace on wheels compared to Cecil's modest home.

"Mr. Clancy." Cecil raised his hand to his brow in a half-wave.

"Congratulations on your win, Mr. Penewit." They clasped hands. "You made the best of a bad situation and proved your dog's talents."

"Thank you, but I just wanted to tell you, before you go, what an impressive dog you have there. Finest I've seen in all my years — and that's quite a lot of years."

Clancy zipped up his canopy pack and slid it through the door. "He's done some winning here and there. Six national champions in the first four generations of his pedigree. Three all-around titles himself." He turned, searched out a small cooler, and set it inside the door. "How's your girl bred, by the way? Looks like she might have some Windy Knoll in there. Maybe some of Ted Kinnard's Boss

182

behind her?"

"I don't really know," Cecil said. "Never bothered to find out. Just the pup of an old neighbor's dog. Farm lines mostly. Does what she was bred for. That's all that ever mattered to me."

"That right?" Clancy piled a few more things inside his trailer. "You ever think of breeding her? 'Cause if you ever do, Brooks here is a top sire. I'd be interested in taking a pup from the litter in lieu of a stud fee. Can't say as I've ever done that before, but for one of hers, I would."

"I'm flattered, really am, but she's spayed."

"Kind of a shame, but I understand." Clancy locked the side door to his trailer, dug into his pocket for his keys. "Well, I'm headed up north to Michigan. Another big trial next weekend. Busy time of year. Usually spend most of the summer on the road." He climbed into the cab of his truck. Brooks sat up to peer past him at us. The key clicked in the ignition and the engine purred to life. "See you at Nationals in two months?"

"Naw, can't leave the farm." Cecil looked off into the crowd that was still filtering from the stands toward the barns and the midway.

A smile alighted briefly on Clancy's face, then vanished as he let up on the brake. "Bye now."

"Good luck."

A family of eight strolled in front of Clancy's truck. He grumbled a few unheard curses, waited until the row was clear, then pulled out.

Cecil clutched his left arm, kneading it for a few seconds. My nose sought out his hand, hanging limply at his side.

"I'm ready to go home, too. Maybe we'll stop and get you a hamburger on the way?"

I barked my agreement. I would have preferred French fries, though.

A teenage couple walked by, their hands in each others' back pockets. In the boy's obsession with his mate, he failed to notice the trail of popcorn he was leaving behind. I vacuumed it up as we walked along.

"First, though," Cecil said, the pupils of his eyes reflecting the bright colors of the Ferris wheel, "I promised Bernadette a ride."

—o00o—

The glass of the unlit bulbs of the Ferris wheel sparkled a brilliant white in the late afternoon sun. Somewhere a cow bellowed. Pigs oinked in greedy protest. Geese, ever contrary, honked. The laughter of children on the Tilt-a-Whirl spilled through the air. Bells dinged at carnival games. Not far from us, the roller coaster went 'clunk-clunk-clunk' as it climbed on its tracks. Its nose dipped. Hands shot in the air. Screams ripped the atmosphere as it whooshed downward. I flattened my ears, the vibrations of its descent tingling against the pads of my feet.

We turned into a horse barn. Cecil patted the lump in his pocket. Bernadette stood halfway down the row with her friend Merle and a man I assumed was her husband Jasper. The men, when introduced, shook hands. Cecil led me inside a stall, heavy with the scent of hay and fresh manure. He unclipped my leash and bent close.

"I won't be long," he whispered to me. "An hour, at most."

His promise should have reassured me — Cecil was always a man of his word, honest to a fault — but instead it dropped like a lead shot through my gut. I'd had this feeling before. But when?

He stroked the fur along my backbone. "Wish me luck."

I swiped a paw on his pants leg. *Don't go!*

Once again, he didn't hear me. He stood.

Jasper locked the stall from the outside, and they went off. The shadows inside the barn grew long, until my little corner of the world was cloaked in darkness. I dozed off and on, the day's events streaming through my memory, playing over and over like a film on a loop. As memory melted into dreams, the past came back to me: that bleak winter at Estelle's, how my toes had been numb for months and my belly tight with hunger, how Ned Hanson had kicked me and later buried my mother in the manure pile. Then further back: to the day of Cam and Ray's funeral, and the day that they died. And somewhere in there: Hunter's arms draped around my neck as he cried softly into my fur while we waited for Lise to find us.

"Hunter, this way. We're late."

I scrambled to my feet, shook myself fully awake. The sides of the stall were high, but an old trunk and a half-used bale of hay had been left in the front corner adjacent to the sliding door. I hopped up on the bale, then the trunk, and stuck my head between the wide bars.

The center aisle was empty, the overhead suspended lights casting intermittent circles of yellow light on the packed sawdust. A wiry haired brown and white terrier slept on the lap of a young girl in tight white leggings and a dusty black blazer as she dozed in a folding canvas chair next to one of the stalls. Across the aisle, a chestnut pony nickered and bobbed its head at me. I woofed softly in reply. Further down, two older women seated on portable stools played a game of cards over a barrel.

In the stall behind me in the row outside, an old black horse snorted to get my attention. Nibbling at the top edge of the stall, he gazed down at me with rheumy eyes. Gray hairs confettied his long muzzle.

I sat, lifted a paw in greeting. He nickered softly, as if to say, 'Welcome to the neighborhood, kid.'

Didn't want to tell him I didn't plan on staying here long. As soon as Cecil came back, I was going home. There were still chores to do and if we had to do them by starlight, we would.

I turned around, ready to descend my little staircase and go back to sleep until Cecil came back for me. He had said it would only be an hour, but an inkling of worry had begun to gnaw at me. I wasn't sure how long an hour really was, but he'd made it seem like only a short time and it had to be more than an hour by now. It wasn't like him not to get home in time for evening chores.

The old black horse moved. Just past his sagging flank, the crown of a tawny-haired boy floated. Recognition tugged at my memory. He turned, gazed blankly at me with light blue eyes. Stopping, he raised himself up on tiptoes, so I could see his face more plainly. There was something familiar in his gaze, in the gentleness of his mouth, in the line of his nose. He blinked, reached out to stroke the ragged mane of the old horse.

"Hunter, c'mon!" another boy called.

Could it be …? I tried to remember what he looked like. It had been so long. No, it was some other Hunter. My Hunter was not that tall, his face had been rounder, his fingers shorter and chubbier. Besides, the Hunter I knew had moved far away. He hadn't been around here in many years.

As he hurried off to join his friend, I sat and watched everything, unable to sleep. The Ferris wheel twinkled above the barn roofs as it rotated slowly against the night sky. The crowd was beginning to dwindle. The girl across the aisle woke, brushed the little dog from her lap, and left as it bounced along beside her. Her figure flashed between light and darkness until she turned the corner.

Then other flashing lights came into view, bright red orbs twirling above a white van as it trundled between the rows of cars parked behind the barn. The sound of a siren burst, then went silent, then burst again. The two ladies at the end of the stalls snagged a passerby.

"What's going on? Some kid fall off one of those crazy rides?"

"Maybe someone got run over by a hog or a bull, Martha? Happens all the time."

"No, some old guy. Just keeled over."

"Heart attack?"

"That's my guess. They'd just gotten off the Ferris wheel when he collapsed over by the candy apple booth. The guy there did CPR until the ambulance came."

"Is he going to be okay?"

"Don't know. Never came to. Doesn't look promising, if'n you ask me."

"My, my. Tragic. Just tragic."

"Hope it wasn't anyone's father or husband."

"I'm sure we'll read about it in The Messenger tomorrow, if anything terrible happened."

"I hope not."

"Me, too. But the truth is, Florence, we all gotta go sometime. I'd rather drop dead at the county fair, a red pop and a bag of kettlecorn in my hands, than waste away in some old people's home all drugged up, with tubes snaking out of me and a urine bag hanging from my bed rail."

"Amen to that."

chapter 19

Cecil didn't come back that night. Or the next morning. The girl from across the aisle showed up early to brush her horse. The little dog wasn't with her. She was about to leave when I stood on my hind legs and gazed over the top of the stall with pleading eyes.

I really have to pee and even though this place reeks of urine, I'm not sure I'm supposed to do my business in here.

She extended her fingers, let me sniff them. "Do you have to go to the bathroom?"

Outside, yes.

"Okay."

She unhooked my leash, slid open the door, and took me over to a patch of grass next to a flagpole. *Ah, the relief.* When I was done, she retrieved a shovel from inside the barn and disposed of my waste, then put me back in the stall. Not that I wanted to go back in there, but at least I could tolerate it awhile longer now. A man wearing a black zip-up jacket and a badge on his chest walked by.

"Do you know whose dog this is?" she asked him.

He looked into my stall and shook his head. "Nope." He took a black box out of a pouch attached to his belt, flipped a switch on the side. Crackling noises came out of it. "You want me to radio to the

188

head office and see if anyone's missing one?"

"Sure, I guess. It's just that she's been here since last night and no one's been around this morning. I can take care of her for now, but I have to be in the ring by nine."

He put the black box to his ear, flipped another switch. "Hey, Charlie, has anyone reported a missing dog? ...What kind? Border Collie, I think."

Australian Shepherd, you idiot. I do not have a tail. And if you bothered to look more closely, you'd see that I carry my head upright, not down between my shoulders.

"No? You sure? ... All righty, then. Well, if anyone calls, there's one here in, uh, Stall 12, Horse Barn 3. Say, heard there was some excitement on the midway last night ..." He drifted toward the end of the stalls on his way out. "That right? Who was it? ... Really?" He stopped, looked back at me. I sank back down below the door and, after circling a few times, tucked myself next to the bale. "Do you know what kind of a dog he had with him?"

His boots pounded on the packed sawdust. I hunkered lower.

"Say," he said to the girl, "you mind keeping an eye on him?"

"Her, you mean?"

"Sure." He studied me for an uncomfortably long string of seconds. "I think I've figured out whose dog it is. Or was, actually."

The look he gave me was like a fist to my gut. They were talking about Cecil. And the news wasn't good.

"No problem. But like I said, only for a little bit. I have to bathe Isis and get ready for the ring. My mom will have a cow if I'm not there fifteen minutes ahead of time."

"That'll work just dandy. Thanks."

A minute later, the girl put a square Styrofoam container on the floor of my stall. In one side was a half-eaten burrito made of scrambled eggs and sausage. I inhaled it before she even had time to open a bottle of water and pour it in the other half. I licked my lips, wanting more.

"Sorry, that's all I got for now. Someone'll come back for you soon."

I hoped so. The boredom was killing me, not to mention the worry.

—o00o—

The someone that stared down at me was the last someone I wanted to see inside that stall with me. The stink of tobacco clung to Tucker's clothes. As he slid his hands down his thighs to grasp his knees, I could see the yellow cigarette stains on his fingertips and the way his lips were permanently pinched together. He wasn't old, but he was worn and used, inside and out.

He thrust out his hand. I retreated against the back wall. Bits of straw clung to my fur. My mouth was bone dry. Last night had been warm and the day was getting unbearably hot. The girl hadn't returned and so I'd been without water for over half the day. People had filed down the aisle endlessly, a few pausing at my stall to dribble baby talk to me, but all had moved on, mindless of my needs. At some point, I had awoken from a nap to find a handful of popcorn scattered in the mixture of dirt and sawdust. I ate it, but the kernels stuck in my dry throat and I ended up retching.

Again, Tucker reached for me. "C'mere, girl."

I curled my lip at him. *Don't touch me, you tapeworm.*

He snatched his hand back, sank to his haunches. "You're a lively one. Truth be told, I trust you about as far as I can throw you — and the thought of doing that has crossed my mind. Now, come a little closer and you and I will walk out of here. Don't you want to go home? Or maybe you want a dog biscuit first, huh? Puppy want a biscuit?"

Liar. I growled at him.

He twitched in fear. I could smell it in his sweat, hear it in his voice, see it in the way his fingers trembled as he reached up beside him to take hold of an old horse blanket hanging over the stall door. Slowly, he pulled the blanket between the metal bars. He draped it across his lap.

What exactly was he going to do with that thing? Sit down on it and stare at me until I befriended him? Not a chance in —

He crinkled a white paper bag beside him. "Maybe you want some barbecued ribs? Or would one of them breaded tenderloin sandwiches be to your liking? Why don't you come over and have a look, see what I got in here?" He pulled out a greasy golden potato wedge and waggled it next to his knee. "How 'bout some French fries?"

My mouth watered. I loved French fries. Possibly more than air. Loved the goldeny goodness, the crispy outside, the starchy inside, the warm coating of oil, but most of all … the salt. I ate them for the salt. Savored every crystal cube as it smarted on my tongue.

Once, when I was a puppy, I got my head stuck in a fast food bag, trying to lick the salt out of the bottom. I may have also once knocked the salt shaker off the table, trying to get it open. Trouble, the cat, had gotten blamed for that one, while I innocently emptied the entire contents of my water bowl. And there were all those times Hunter had shared his fries with me under the table.

Don't do it, Halo.

Tucker tossed a fry onto the ground, halfway between us. If I could be quick enough … I dove for it.

That was when he threw the blanket over my head.

Before I could wrangle my way out of it, he had the thing wrapped around my head. I flailed my snout left and right, biting at the blanket, hoping to puncture tender flesh with my teeth. But every time I thrashed he pulled the blanket tighter. I kicked and clawed, snapped at the darkness, yawped and wailed. The stiff, smelly cloth tightened around me. Through the muffled layers, his curses poured over me. "Goddamn mongrel. Jeezus, you nasty bitch, I'm gonna —"

Where's Cecil? Bernadette? Why didn't they come to get me?

Saliva foamed in my mouth. I gasped for air and inhaled a lungful of dust and horse hair. Panic set it.

"— think you're gonna bite me? No way in hell, you l'il sh—"

The blanket tangled around my legs, flipping me onto my side. He pressed his weight over me, held me down as I continued to struggle. My heart pounded, its rhythm so rapid it made one continuous sound. *ThumpThumpThumpThump* …

Fight! I told myself. *Don't let him take you!*

"— didn't like you the first time I saw you. Wolf eyes, that's what you —"

But I was getting tired. I needed to breathe. Needed … air.

Let him think you've given up. Let him trust that you have succumbed to his physical superiority. That he has outwitted you. That you submit. And then, when he's not looking, then bite him and escape.

Against my instinct, I willed myself to relax. I let my legs go limp, let the tension drain out of my muscles. His body was crushing my ribs, pushing what little air was in them out. I held my breath, hung onto it, until my lungs screamed at me to inhale again. When I exhaled a little puff of air so I could gulp in a breath, my ribs collapsed further, wringing the life out of me.

The sounds of the fair faded, giving way to the gentle pulse of blood in my ears. I thought of yesterday. Of the trial. The glow of pride in Cecil's face as the judge handed him the ribbon and the prize money. The touch of his hand as it grazed the top of my head.

Good girl, Halo.

Then Cam's voice, faint but clear. *That was a very good dog.*

Lise's words, overflowing with relief. *That was a very, very good girl.*

I am! I am a good dog, I said. But no one heard me.

And *that* was when I felt the sharp pin prick in my loin. The sting of icy poison being plunged into my veins.

192

The last thing I heard was Tucker Kratz's caustic laughter as I tumbled into a bottomless hole.

chapter 20

Tires vibrated over asphalt, jarring every joint in my body. Pins jangled, hinges rattled, and the constant clang of metal melded into a discordant percussion. Again and again, darkness was broken by a blaze of white light, followed by a thunderous hum as semi-trucks sped by. Every time the horse trailer I had been placed in was sucked into the vacuous void of their wake, the old trailer fishtailed several feet before being jerked back onto its trajectory.

Bile burned my throat, spilled over my tongue, and dribbled from my mouth until I was soaked in a growing puddle of it. Tight leather straps dug into the back of my head. Metal wires, woven into a stiff basket, encased my mouth. A muzzle. So, Tucker was afraid of me, was he? I had restrained myself from biting Ned Hanson. If given the chance, I wouldn't exercise the same self-control in regards to Tucker Kratz.

I tried to keep my eyes open, but the sleeping medicine Tucker had injected into my muscles was strong. So strong that I didn't know if a few hours or a few days had passed. I was too drained to gauge hunger or thirst, too numb to feel fear or anxiety. The only thing I could sense with any certainty, besides the constant jouncing of stiff rubber tires on a potholed road, was the cool surface of the rusty metal floor on which I lay.

Why was he doing this to me? I knew when I saw him that he had no intention of taking me home. I had recognized something surreptitious, something sinister behind his eyes. We dogs can tell the good people from the bad. Words mean nothing if actions belie them. It's all in the eyes, the tone of voice, the mannerisms. Dogs know these things in the same way we know hunger, thirst, and fatigue. We feel it, somewhere deep inside, in the pith of our souls, just as we feel joy or grief. We sense it in the same way we do danger. It is the ability to gather small, almost imperceptible cues, compile them instantaneously, and act without deliberation. It is a gift that has preserved our kind for millennia.

What had not been so immediately clear to me was the reason I had been abandoned in the stall at the fair. If there was a disconnect on my part, it was because, at first, there were pieces missing. Cecil and Bernadette had left with their friends Merle and Jasper. They had taken a ride on the Ferris wheel. Cecil's heart had failed him. The ambulance had taken him away. Bernadette, in her concern for Cecil, in her hysteria, perhaps even in her grief, had forgotten me until she sent her nephew to care for me. But I had no doubt that she knew nothing of his actions now. And had Cecil been all right, this past day would have gone very differently.

There was only one possibility. Cecil had not come back for me, because he was not here anymore. Not where I could see him, at least. Or anyone else, for that matter. He was on the Other Side, wherever that was. Where ghosts reside. That place where peace is omnipresent. Where time has no meaning. Where there is no want or need. There simply is ... what is.

I drifted on the verge, half aware, half alive, searching for Cam, for Cecil, for Bit. Hopeful. But I could not find them. They were not here.

It's not time, they told me in my dreams.

Yeah, I hear you, I said. *I wish you were wrong. I want to be where you are. You're not done.*

Done? Done with what?

No one answered. They couldn't hear me. No one ever did.

The whirr of the tires slowed to a rhythmic thudding. From the truck cab, the twang of country music floated. A pink glow of neon lights shone through the high window at one side of the trailer. The rear of the trailer was open up top — high enough for a standing horse to stick his head out, too high for a drugged up dog to see anything but sky. Through that opening, a traffic light winked, a luminous eye of green suspended in the endless night.

One of the truck doors slammed. The trailer shuddered. Boots scraped over gravel. A dog circled the trailer, snuffled, stopped. The 'ting' of a urine stream hitting the side of the trailer sounded. Then, "Get in." The door slammed again.

The boots. Stone crunching. The click of hard soles on asphalt. The tiny chime of bells against a glass door.

Somehow, I shifted from my stomach to my side. I breathed deeply, grateful for air. I watched the light change from green to yellow to red ... to green ... to green ... to green ...

—oO0o—

Morning light spilled gently into the trailer. A sparrow alighted on the ledge of the back door, chirped with misplaced cheer, and rustled her tiny wings. She hopped down onto the floor of the trailer and picked at scattered bits of hay seed before finally taking notice of me. With a burst of wings, she ascended.

Free, unlike me.

I had been awake for some time, although I hadn't moved. My fur stank of drool and vomit. My tongue stuck to the roof of my mouth. I moved it around, tried to work up some saliva, but couldn't. I needed a drink. My thirst was like an empty lake, needing filled.

"Hurry up," Tucker growled.

Canine feet crunched through dry grass. Urine splashed over dirt. A minute later, I smelled the pungent odor of feces.

Surely now Tucker would come inside the trailer, give me some water, let me pee? If I could pee at all, that is. I hadn't had water in over a day.

"Get in, Cerberus," Tucker grumbled. Nails clicked on metal, scrabbled over vinyl.

Boots thudded on the running board of the cab. Keys jingled. The door slammed. The engine whined, clunked, then rumbled to life.

My hope sank.

—o00o—

"You did what?"

My head shot up. I knew that voice, but whose …? A fog of funk clouded my head. I had regained control of my muscles, but my thoughts were still churning like cookie dough in a blender on slow.

"Good Lord Almighty, I can't believe that you … You thought *I* would want the dog?"

It was Bill Clancy. Tucker had driven me all night long and into the next day just to deliver me to Bill Clancy?

"You said —"

"I said I wished I had a dog like that, yes, but … How on earth did you leap from that innocent comment to stealing a man's dog and driving across two state lines to try to sell her to me?"

I was still in the trailer, although the muzzle had been removed. Beyond that, I couldn't tell where we were or what was going on besides Tucker and Clancy bartering for me. On wobbly legs, I stood. A rope had been tied to the ring of my collar. The far end of the rope was knotted around a metal loop on the front wall of the trailer.

197

"I know what these dogs go for." Tucker was starting to sound peevish, like this wasn't at all going like he'd planned. "She's worth three grand, but I'll take two since it's such short notice. I got some other buyers interested in my neck of the woods and another inquiry from a guy over in Illinois."

"Might as well call them. You won't get anything from me."

"Mr. Clancy, you deserve first dibs. Said yourself she was the best damn working dog you've ever seen, including your own. I'd keep her myself, but … my girlfriend's pregnant, you see, and my insurance won't cover —"

"I'm not paying you a dime. Now take her back."

"Can't. Cecil Penewit is dead."

"How can he be dead? I just saw him two days ago."

"Died of a heart attack while on the Ferris wheel. He was with my sweet ol' Aunt Bernie. Really sad how that happened all the sudden. No warning. Just *bam!* Keeled over dead. My aunt's all tore up. Couldn't even think about taking care of a dog right now. Penewit didn't have any relatives. So she gave the dog to me."

"First of all, I still have a hard time believing that, and —"

"Look it up. I'm telling the truth. The man died of a bad heart and left a dog behind. Somebody had to take it."

Clancy let a few moments of silence lapse while he took Tucker's story in. "Okay, say it is true. If she gave the dog to you, where are the papers?" He paused, waiting for an answer. "Yeah, I thought so. She has no idea you took off with the dog."

"She's trying to find the papers, Mr. Clancy. Penewit wasn't a very organized guy. His house was a mess. Practically a hoarder. Why, the living room was stacked to the ceiling with old newspapers, things he bought on sale, old bits of twine from hay bales, empty pop bottles and beer cans … Aunt Bernie's more than a little busy with funeral arrangements right now, too. You'll get the papers soon. I promise. I'll go look for them myself."

198

"And if the papers don't show up?"

"You could breed her. Get your money back."

"Without papers? How *dumb* are you? I'd have to give the pups away." Clancy scoffed.

"Put another dog's name on the papers."

"That'd be even dumber. Don't you know you have to DNA litters now?"

Tucker had no reply. He walked toward the trailer, grabbed the outer handle, and yanked it open. A wedge of daylight fell across the trailer floor. Outside, dust motes swirled in the summer haze. I squinted, drew against the back of the trailer, daring Tucker Kratz to come back there and stick his bare hand out. I'd make the ignorant bastard bleed. Shred him down to his sinews.

He turned his back to me. Pity there wasn't more slack on that rope. I'd have ripped a hole in his britches big enough to drive a Mack truck through.

Tucker moved aside as Clancy stepped up to the horse trailer. Behind him was his palatial trailer, taking up most of the view, but beyond that were more long, plain buildings, like the ones at the Adair County Fair. The smell of manure and hay lingered in the air. Gone were the green swelling hills of home. Here there was only flat farmland broken by dense stands of trees. Lying in the shade of Clancy's trailer was his dog, Brooks. But there was no sign of Tucker's dog, or any people. The place looked deserted.

I lowered my head below my shoulders, gazed at Clancy with soulful eyes, pleading. He'd made it clear he didn't want me, but I sure didn't want to stay with Tucker. The way things were going already, it was going to be far worse than things had been when I'd been in Ned Hanson's care. My ribs were still sore, the muscles of my right flank flaming where my captor had stabbed the needle into me.

Clancy inched closer until he was within arm's reach. He crouched down, elbows resting on his knees and his hands clasped together. He looked me over carefully.

"Appears to me this dog's had a rough couple of days, Kratz. Did you tie her to the bumper and drag her here?"

Tucker coughed a dry laugh. "Nothing a little scrubbing won't fix. B'sides, she doesn't seem to care for me much. Tried to feed her. Damn dog near bit my arm off. Seems to like you just fine, though."

Slowly, gently, Clancy held his hand out, palm down. I sniffed his fingers. The scent of Ivory soap, coffee thick with sugar, and ... dog treats. *Liver* dog treats.

Please, take me. Please!

I rolled over, presenting my underside to him. He raked his fingers over my chest and belly, scratching vigorously until he found that magical place that set my leg to thumping. A kind smile parted his lips. In that singular expression, I saw for myself a glimmer of hope, just like I'd seen when Cecil showed up at Estelle's and bailed me from that frozen hellhole of a kennel. He started to draw his hand back and I reached a paw out. He grasped my toes and gave them a light squeeze.

"Don't worry girl," he said softly. "Everything's gonna be aaallll right."

I believed him.

"Dumb fool didn't even stop to wonder if you might be spayed." Then raising his voice, "Will you take a thousand for her?"

Tucker inspected his fingernails a moment, then reached into his back pocket and tapped a cigarette out of its pack. "Fifteen hundred."

"Check?"

"Nope. Cash only."

"You think I keep that kind of money on me?" Clancy walked toward Tucker, leaving me alone in the bare trailer. Crawling from under Clancy's gooseneck, Brooks arched his back, then lapped at a bowl of water next to him. He wasn't even wearing a leash. Like being at home on the farm. My tongue scraped at dry lips.

"Today's Friday and the banks are already closed," Clancy went on. "I'm trialing the next two days. Can't get to the bank until Monday at the earliest — that is, if they'll even let me draw that much money out. I'm not exactly at my home branch."

A match flared in Tucker's hand. He lit his cigarette, took a couple puffs, flicked the match on the gravel road on which we were parked. A minute went by in which Tucker seemed to mull Clancy's proposition over. He walked over to the trailer and flung the door shut. It clanged with a heart-stabbing finality.

"Forget it," Tucker said. He went around the side of the trailer, toward the truck cab.

"Wait! Where are you taking her?"

"Not sure. Back home, maybe. Or maybe I'll head south, take her to that guy in Indiana."

"I thought you said he was in Illinois."

"Illinois, Indiana, same difference. Maybe I got more than one person interested."

The truck door slammed again, signaling another long ride holed up in a noisy, stinking trailer, baking in the summer sun. No food. No water.

No hope.

—o00o—

The heat pressed in on me. Wrapped itself around me like the suffocating horse blanket Tucker had thrown over my head. Threatened to boil the flesh from my bones. I'd felt heat on my skin before when I wandered too close to Cecil's little burn piles at home or when Lise had opened the oven door when I was a puppy and I'd rushed over to investigate the mouth-watering scent of cookies baking. But those encounters had been brief, the warmth touching me from the outside and only from one direction. This ... this was like being

201

dangled on a rotating spit above the fire.

I was boiling from the inside-out. My paws were hot. My belly was hot. My head was hot. The air itself was on fire. For a while, even as the trailer bumped down a washboard gravel road, I shifted on my feet, trying to distribute the heat as it scorched the tender pads of my feet. We jounced over a rut in the road and I was thrown onto my side. Too tired to get up, I lay there, my skull rattling, the heat of the trailer floor singeing my fur and slowly roasting my organs.

Every couple of hours, the truck would slow down, turn into a parking lot, and Tucker would get out to do his business in some comfortable, clean facility. Then he'd let his dog out. Invariably, it always made a point of pissing on the trailer tires. The stench of dog urine stung at my nostrils. Burned my eyes so badly my lids crusted shut. I stopped trying to open them. There was nothing to look at that I hadn't already been staring at for days.

I stopped hoping that he would let me out, too. Or give me food or water. Without a drink, I couldn't have eaten anything anyway. I'd stopped hungering. The only thing I wanted was water, a lake full of it, cool and clear. I'd stand up to my belly in it. No, my neck. And I'd just open my maw as I swam along and let the water fill me up. Renewal flowing through me. Water, the wellspring of energy. The source of all life.

I wanted water more than I wanted air. This hot, sticky, scorching air. Its flames incinerating my lungs, evaporating every drop of moisture in my withering body. I was becoming, quite literally, a sack of dried up bones. Soon, I'd turn to powder and blow away in a puff of wind.

I wanted to be in that place where Cam and Bit were. At peace. Never wanting for food or water or air. Never needing anything.

To just ... let go. To rest.

Forever.

chapter 21

Calloused fingers, moist with water, grazed my muzzle. I twitched my nose.

Yes. Water. Please.

The hand, gnarled at the knuckles, curved beneath my chin to stroke the underside of my jaw, the base of my throat, my neck. A cool drop of water splattered against my eyelid. I blinked.

Crap. I was still inside the trailer.

More water dripped on my head. Drops pattered on my fur, cooling me gently. Moistness seeped along the seams of the metal floor, pooling until a puddle had collected by my head. I parted my mouth, pushed my thick, clumsy tongue out between my teeth, and licked the rust-tainted water.

It was hard to swallow at first. It had been so long since I'd been able to. But little by little, the tiny amounts of water that streamed over the old dirty floor and gathered in a dented depression next to me were enough to invigorate me. If barely.

Rain crashed against the sides of the trailer, drumming relentlessly as it poured through the high open windows above me. For a moment, it was like we were water skiing as we sped down the highway, the trailer yanked behind the monster truck on its solid dually wheels. The jarring of the stiff trailer tires was gone. They had lost contact with the road. We were airborne.

Then the right hand tire hit hard, bouncing up off the road. The trailer tipped to one side heavily before the forward momentum of the truck jerked it upright.

With every action, there is an equal and opposite reaction, right?

The trailer swerved left. The hitch replied with a deathly clang, so loud it sounded like the bolt had snapped. I expected the whole contraption to flip sideways and send us tumbling in a jangled mess of metal wreckage down an embankment. The hitch held, but I was whipped back in the other direction. I slid across the damp floor, smacked the back of my head against the side.

A burst of white light obscured my vision momentarily. A hand pressed reassuringly against my back. I shut my eyes, afraid to look.

Halo? Come on, girl.

The soft rasp. The light touch. I knew whose hands and voice they were. But how ...?

I opened my eyes. Cecil was beside me. He pulled his hand back, tilted his head knowingly and winked. My heart melted at that one small gesture. Except for that time when he'd taken me to the place where humans buried their dead, he'd never said much to me. He never needed to. In each fleeting grin, pat on the head, or 'good girl', he'd defined our relationship. He had needed me as much as I'd needed him.

I felt several halting jerks as Tucker tapped on the brakes. Both vehicles shuddered as we eased to a full stop on the side of the highway.

Slowly, Cecil got to his feet. *You still have work to do*, he said to me. *I don't think I can*, I told him.

Sure you can. Just get up.

Lightning cracked so close that every atom in my body popped with electricity. Whiteness blinded me.

Let's go home, Halo.

I braved a look. Cecil peered out the back window. He was pale. Not just his face, but his shirt, his overalls, his boots. Like a faded photograph in a newspaper clipping.

Another bolt ripped through the charged air, cracking its fiery tendrils against a nearby tree. Through the small opening in back, I saw the sparks fly from a thick branch, then heard the crash as it fell to the ground. Thunder shook the world, its angry rumble dying away slowly.

I sat up, squinted into the watery darkness. A beam of headlights shone through the high window, then flashed by. My eyes adjusted. I blinked once, twice.

Cecil wasn't there anymore.

"Goddamn sonofabitch!" Tucker slammed the door and stomped through puddles. "Hold on, Vern … Aw shit, man. Tire's flat as squashed dog crap. I'm *so* screwed. Of all days …" He kicked at the tire, muttering curses in between apologies. "Okay, I'll tell you why I called. Here's the deal. You know this dog I was telling you about? Yeah, well, she's available. And I gotta get rid of her quick. I can be at your place in a couple of hours. Make that three — I need to unhitch the trailer and go back to the last exit to fetch a new tire. Anyway, I'll compromise and take nine fifty for her… What do you mean you …? No way. No freakin' way. I can't wait until then … No, I'm not bartering for her, either. What the hell would I need a ten-year old four-wheeler for? Cash only… Look, you said if my other contact backed out to let you know. Well, I'm doing that and now you're trying to finagle some flimsy deal with me? Whatever you're smoking right now it ain't Marlboros. I told you to stay away from those crackheads … Whatever, man! Crack, pot, magic toadstools, it's all the same."

A car raced by with a long honk. Water crashed in a thunderous wall against the trailer in its wake.

"Awww, fuck you!" Tucker slammed his fist into the side of the trailer.

The voice on the other end of the phone squawked.

"No, I wasn't talking to you, but I might as well have been. Just forget I called. And don't you dare *ever* ask me for any favors, you twit. You owe me about a dozen, as it is."

His phone let out a feeble beep as he pushed the end call button. Rain was still pouring steadily. Thunder rolled in the distance. Another car horn blared. Bolts and hinges groaned as Tucker stepped up on the trailer hitch. He pushed one of the side windows all the way open, reached down and unknotted the rope attached to the metal loop. It fell to the floor with a muffled thud. I jumped away from it, as if it might bite me like a coiled snake poised to strike.

What was this supposed to mean?

Muttering, Tucker marched back to the truck cab. A few seconds later, a dog's choker collar jingled as he walked around to the back and heaved the door open with a grunt of exasperation.

"Get the hell out of here," he ordered.

A shadow blocked my only route of escape. It was like no dog I had ever seen — if that's what it even was. A long legged, hulking mass of muscle stood silhouetted against a glow of headlights. Its sleek steel gray hide glistened with a sheen of rain. Massive paws anchored its bulk, dark toenails splayed in an oily puddle. Loose skin sagged from its gargantuan head, flews flapping as it ran a long tongue over jagged teeth. Bloodshot eyes disappeared into loose folds of skin. And the ears — outside of a terrier or two, they were the tiniest ears I had ever seen. Actually, they were more like nubs where his ears had once been. Made me wonder if he had lost them in a fight, because no dog could have ever been born with ears like that. And no dog could have been born *that* ugly.

A rumble of warning rose from deep within the beast's throat. On open ground, I could have outsprinted him in just a few strides. With a little more room perhaps, I could have evaded him with my agility. A dodge, a duck, a leap to the side, he would have barely touched me. But here, as weak as I was, closed in on three sides, no more than a few feet in either direction … my chances were looking slim. Dismal, actually.

I had been charged by rams red with fury, and attacked by a bull bent on reaching his heifers in another pasture. Those animals had horns, but they didn't have jaws meant for crushing smaller animals.

I backed up as far as I could. Dipped my head to show I didn't want a fight. But deep in my belly, I knew that that was what this monster had been bred for: to maim, to kill.

Frozen to death, cooked in a metal trailer, starved, kicked in the ribs. I'd survived all that only to meet my death this way. My flesh shredded, bones crushed, blood spurting and gushing in a gory display of machismo by this hellhound.

The headlights of a car coming in the other direction illuminated Tucker. He looked defeated. Like a drowned rat clawing his way out of the gutter, lying limply next to the curb.

The dog's lip lifted in a snarl, another growl vibrating his chest. I waited for him to lunge, to sink his giant teeth into my skin. Tucker yanked back on the leather handle of his chain leash. The dog obeyed, backing away just enough to give me an opening if I were brave enough — or stupid enough — to take it.

"I said get out," Tucker repeated.

The dog-monster growled again. Louder.

"Shut up, Cerberus." Tucker yanked him to his side.

I stayed where I was. They were only a few feet away. I didn't trust either of them.

Tucker pulled a full beer can from his jacket pocket and flailed it into the trailer. It ricocheted off the back wall and slammed me in the loin. A yelp split my throat.

Fueled by fear, I bolted. Ran without thinking or looking.

Ran for my life.

—o00o—

I took off without direction, the rope trailing behind me. My only thought was the need to get as far from them as fast as I could — and that meant in a straight line.

Rain fell heavily, smearing the world in streaks of white and red lights as cars and trucks zipped by. Two blazing orbs of light appeared in front of me, boring into the lenses of my eyes like lasers. I pulled up, almost stopped, unsure of which way to go. A horn blasted, piercing my eardrums. I dashed across the road and bounded into a grassy ditch. A few more strides and my feet sank in deep muck. I stumbled, rolled in a puddle underlain with sharp rocks, righted myself and ran on. Up a short incline. Onto another road.

A car swerved by me, its tires squealing on the slick pavement. I looked back to see it careen onto the shoulder, scud over packed gravel, then jerk back onto the highway. Just as I turned to go again, a wall of air shoved me backward as a double long semi roared by. Panicked, I stopped again, my front and back feet spanning a broken white line. Shivers of fright rattled me from skull to tailbone, even though the rain was warm.

I gulped in air, felt my heart hammering up high in my throat. I was just as afraid to turn back as I was to go forward. And then I saw another car barreling toward me.

Forward I leapt, into the darkness, unaware of how close the car was or whether there was another one coming. I saw a broad grassy strip, a line of woods ahead. A few strides more and I was across the road. The car whooshed by.

I didn't stop to look behind me. The danger was not past. For all I knew, Tucker and his dog could have dodged the cars, picked up my trail, and were bearing down.

So I ran. Crashed through the bramble, branches lashing at my face, thorns pricking my paws, the heavy rope banging against my legs, tripping me. Still, I ran. Through the night. Ran until my lungs threatened to explode. Across streams. Through woods thick with old growth. Through meadows of tall grass and across boggy ground. Ran until the rain stopped and the sun rose pink above a field dense with soybeans.

Until my muscles wouldn't allow me to go any further.

—o00o—

South. I kept heading south. Toward home.

Although for all I knew, home was hundreds, maybe even thousands, of miles away.

After a rest, I went on. More slowly this time, but still spurred by the fear that Tucker and his hellhound were on my trail. The knotted end of the rope caught on a forked branch on the ground, jerking me back. I got up, threw my weight forward as I tried to dislodge the branch, but it was solidly buried. One look told me the rope was too thick to chew through.

I sat awhile, pondering what to do, every sound in the woods setting off alarms in my head. Finally, I went to the end of the rope, faced the branch, and backed away. The collar, which had once been snug, slid over my head easily.

I was free.

chapter 22

I hadn't been able to see the world blur by as Tucker had driven to meet Clancy, but I was aware on which side the sun rose and set each day and I knew enough to go the other way. I stayed within sight of a busy highway, even though I wasn't sure it was the same one we had gone north on. All the while, I searched for hills that looked like those around the farm and kept my nose to the air, hoping to catch some familiar scent. I saw cows and more rarely sheep, but the land here was more flat than hilly. There were great swaths of woodland and even bigger spreads of land that the humans had built their cities on. There were no deep valleys and broad grassy hills, one after the other.

This wasn't home. It wasn't even close.

But I had to keep going.

The first few days were the hardest. I was bone tired. Being deprived of food and water the few days that Tucker kept me in the hot trailer had drained my body almost to the point of collapse. At first I was too afraid to go anywhere near a human dwelling, but I knew if I didn't then I would not survive. I *had* to survive, so I could go home and take care of the sheep. Without me, the senseless creatures were probably wandering around in the open every night, unprotected, afraid, being stalked by coyotes, their numbers dwindling day by day.

Water was easier to come by than food. The recent rain had left puddles everywhere. When those dried up, I drank from ditches. And so I never thirsted, even though the water was seldom clean. I stayed hidden and only approached the human dwellings when either there was no sign of their presence or it was well after nightfall. I couldn't take the chance that someone would abuse or neglect me again — or even confine me to the safety of their enclosed yard and keep me from ever getting home.

The humans kept their extra food in tall plastic or metal containers with lids, sometimes neatly wrapped in plastic bags. When the smell of food was evident, I easily toppled the containers, although sometimes the lids were tricky, and tore the bags open to gorge myself on chicken bones, buns, bits of hamburger, potato skins, paper cups with a milky substance in the bottom, and limp, cold French fries. Some days were a feast better than any I had ever had before. Other days, when I had to pick through the rancid offerings, it was barely sustenance. I learned early on to trust my nose and if something smelled bad my stomach would revolt.

The days were still warm, but the nights were becoming cooler. Usually, I slept in the woods, away from the houses and roads, but the woods held their own dangers. One night, I burrowed myself a nest at the base of a tree where I slept soundly, only to awaken to two dogs staring at me, their hackles raised. One was lanky, with short black hair and droopy ears, while the other was small, but muscular, mostly white in color with a brindle patch over one eye and a stub like mine for a tail. The smaller one snarled and snapped her jaws, while the bigger one just stood and growled. They could have jumped me then, torn me to bits, but all they really wanted was for me to get out of their territory and move on.

Many days into my ordeal, I saw an old metal barrel at the end of a short path into the woods. The path looked like it had been formed by tire tracks, but no vehicle had come this way in a long time. There were other objects lying about, mostly tires, but also rusted bicycles, the metal framework of an old mattress, bits of cardboard, a very old TV with the front glass smashed out, and plastic jugs filled with nasty smelling liquids.

It had rained all day and the barrel was a dry place in which I could rest. I had no sooner poked my nose into the opening than a skunk whipped her rear end around and sprayed me with her foul scent. My eyes burned. I had killed a groundhog or two in my time, but I knew not to mess with a skunk. So I ran — the smell clinging to me like a billboard announcing my arrival a mile ahead of me. Wherever I went, it shouted, 'Here I am!' I rolled in dirt, waded in every pond I could find, but still the smell surrounded me. And just as I thought the stink was fading, a little rain, a roll in dewy grass, even the dampness in the air would stir it up from the roots of my hair.

On another occasion, I was lured by the smell of food coming from one of the metal containers behind a barn. I waited and watched for a long time to make sure there were no people around, even though there were no vehicles to indicate they might be there. I slunk around the corner of the barn, padded up to the container, and sniffed all around it. This one had no lid, but there were good things inside. I placed my front paws on its rim and, standing on my back two feet, I pulled it toward me. As it began to tip, I leapt aside. It wasn't trash that spilled out first, but a barn cat.

Back arched high, she yowled that otherworldly yowl and swatted with her claws, slicing the leather of my nose. I yelped, spun back the way I had come from, and ran. To my right, a screen door banged shut. An old woman stood on the porch of the house, a shotgun gripped in her crooked hands. She cocked it, raised the barrel, and took aim.

Out in the open, I had no place to hide. I ran faster. The shot exploded with a bang. A shell whizzed over my head, buried itself in the clothesline pole directly in front of me. The pole's edge burst into splinters. She primed the shotgun again as I raced over the lawn. Ahead lay a fallow field. I had ventured too far from the woods. The next shot went wide, plunging into the dirt behind me. I ran across that endless field while she continued to lob her ammunition at me. I ran until my tongue hung low, and my lungs screamed for air, and my muscles could go no more.

By the time I stopped to rest, I had no idea where the highway was. I couldn't retrace my scent and go back. She would be there waiting with her gun. She would kill me.

And so I waited until morning, no food in my belly that night. At dawn I rose, skirted as far around the farm as I could where the crazy lady with the gun had tried to kill me, and followed my scent until the highway came back within sight.

For several more days I followed that highway — cars and trucks buzzing in the distance, its length lit up at night like a ribbon of red and white taillights — until at last I came to a place where the hills were taller and more abundant. A place that was looking more and more like home.

Trotting up and down the hills was tiring. Opportunities for food were fewer than they had been. But I was getting close, I knew it. And so I pressed on, even when I sorely wanted to lie down and sleep, even when the prospect of food beckoned from a cluster of human dwellings.

I had grown accustomed to a certain pace, fast enough to carry me many miles over the course of a day, slow enough to keep from tiring too easily and to stop occasionally to gauge my direction. I climbed a very steep hill, more determined than ever. But when I topped it, my heart sank.

There, in the distance, was the biggest creek I had ever seen. A river, Lise once called it when we went on a long car ride to visit her mother and then friends in Ohio. It cleaved the land in two. A barrier

213

to my path home.

I sat on the top of that wooded hill for a very long time, thinking of all I had endured and how far I had come, thinking that if only I could get across that great expanse of water, then home must not be far away. But no matter which way I turned it in my mind, I couldn't see how it was possible.

Because the only way across was the highway bridge — and that road had more cars on it than I'd ever in my life seen.

—o00o—

I went as close as I dared. The rumble of semis stirred an abject fear deep in my gut. They could not easily stop, they could not easily swerve. It seemed they could only go forward, far faster than my four legs could manage, bearing a tremendous weight at dangerous speeds. Any animal in their path was in the way. Dead.

During my solo journey, I had learned a bit of the patterns of humans in their vehicles. They were most active during the day, less so at night. The quietest hours on the road were the small hours before dawn, when twilight melted into daylight. Humans were just beginning to stir then, but most were not yet travelling.

That following night, I stirred often to gaze at the sky, trying to judge whether the time was right. Clouds blotted the sky. There was no smell of rain on the air, but the clouds made it impossible to gauge the time. When I next awoke, the highway was already buzzing with traffic. I was too late.

For a brief time I considered trying to swim across, but when I went to the top of a small ridge that overlooked the river, all I could see was brown swirling water and no sign of the river's bottom. The distance to the far bank was so vast that the cars driving along the road there were only tiny dots. A small, swift boat zipped downriver, while two, long flat boats bearing piles of black dust slogged upriver. No, I would tire and drown before I reached the other side.

And so I waited another day. The rain started overnight and continued on well into morning. Another day went by.

I awoke deep into the night. This time, however, the sky was clear and scattered with stars and a moon so bright it was like a floodlight.

It was time.

—o00o—

The land sloped down toward the highway, trees giving way to those great swaths of grass that humans were so fond of mowing. This area, however, hadn't been mowed for some time, and I was glad for that, so I could move through it less obviously. A possum ambled down the hillside in front of me, taking her time as she raked her claws through the gravelly dirt, searching for grubs and worms. She was no danger to me; still, I avoided her, as I had avoided all creatures for many days now.

How many days *had* it been? My species is not good at keeping track. After a few, the days all blend together. We tend to mark the passage of time by events — and my crossing this bridge was sure to be an event I would not soon forget.

Bathed in the silvery blue glow of moonlight, I could see everything so clearly. That was comforting and terrifying at once. The bridge was a monstrous thing, the biggest structure I had ever laid eyes on. Metal arms linked together stretched across the river, supporting a length of road so long and arched so high I couldn't see to the other side. Cars still sped along, but they were far fewer than in daylight hours. It would be impossible to get across without having to share the road with at least a few of them. If I kept to the side, on that narrow strip between the solid white line and the low concrete wall, perhaps I could make it across.

Then again, perhaps I was stupid to try. But how else was I going to make it home?

I sat for an eternity, watching the headlights appear in the distance, cross before me, and then go across the bridge. If there was any other way ... Well, fact was, there wasn't.

A stiff wind roared in my ears, making it hard to hear. I studied the road, waited until another truck went by. Just as I set my foot on the pavement, two more cars crested the bridge, coming my way. I scurried back and hid in the tall grass. When they were gone, I tried again. This time, I couldn't see any cars at all.

The road rose up like a small hill. I ran as fast as I could to the place where the road left the land and soared above the water. My heart beating wildly inside my ribs, I stayed tucked tight against the wall. Above the howl of the wind, I could just barely hear the gurgle and sloshing of the turbid water below.

Faster, faster, I raced. This wasn't a time for caution. It was a time for reckless speed, for muscles to ache for oxygen, for lungs to pull in air in great, heaving gulps. Stride after stride, my legs churned. In my travels, I had grown quick and strong and in this moment it served me well. At the farm, my work was usually done in short bursts of speed, but now I was even leaner and more hard muscled.

Halfway there! I crested the pinnacle, saw the land on the far side — and not one, but two cars headed straight for me. Their lights were blinding. I slowed, put my head down, and hugged the side wall. The first sped by furthest from me, but as the second passed, a blast of air shoved me into the concrete. I closed my eyes. The smell of rubber and gasoline invaded my nose. The road vibrated under my paws. The bridge itself shook.

When the shaking finally stopped, I started again, still running, but more wary. The road dipped downward. My stride gained speed. It was hard to distinguish the wind from the rumble of an oncoming vehicle. I resisted looking back. Too much time lost.

Almost to the other side, I eased my pace. On my side of the road were buildings, lights illuminating a parking area outside of them. How had I not noticed that before? If I had, I would have gone down the other side. I was about to stay my course when I saw people milling about outside one of the buildings. No, I should go to the opposite side, avoid them. No sense taking chances. Not when I'd come this far, crossed the bridge.

I passed a glance over my shoulder and cut across the road. But I had misjudged the distance remaining. Before I reached safety, a vehicle came flying over the bridge behind me. I didn't hear it. And it … didn't see me.

There was a burst of light, a blast of air, and then an explosion inside my chest. I felt myself lifted up, flung high, slammed onto the road, and then I skidded across the rock hard surface before landing on the gravel strewn edge.

Ahead of me, brakes screeched on pavement, igniting the smell of rubber. Then a car door slammed, feet pounded.

Two faces hovered over me.

"Oh my God! I didn't see it," a woman said. "I swear I didn't see it."

"It's okay, honey. It's okay. Go get the blanket out of the trunk. We'll put her in the car, then go over to that gas station. They can tell us where the closest vet is."

The man put his hands on me, stroked my head.

If I could have run away then, I would have. This time, though, I wasn't going anywhere.

I couldn't move.

chapter 23

I was stretched out on a towel reeking of something astringent, my head resting upright against a cool surface. I'd been sleeping for a long time and it was a wonderful thing to do. I wanted to keep sleeping, but my senses were sharpening. Unfamiliar sounds stirred me to the verge of alertness. I was aware of things happening around me: people talking, other dogs barking, a cat growling, the ping of metal instruments, and water running. It took some time before I recognized the smell: disinfectant.

The vet's!

That was the last place I wanted to be. Being at the vet's meant needles jabbing at your skin, fingers probing in delicate places, thermometers in your —

How can I get out of here?

I pried my eyes open. Images blurred together. I had to focus for several minutes, my head lolling uncontrollably, before objects sharpened. I felt oddly weak, just as I had after Tucker had given me that shot.

In front of me were thin metal bars in a woven pattern. The door to my cage was set on solid hinges, with a trigger-type of latch on tightly coiled springs. No amount of biting at the wires would free me — I didn't need to break my teeth on it to know that. These cages were meant to be inescapable prisons, any entrance or exit controlled only by the dexterity of human hands.

Proof that these people meant to keep me hostage, too, just like Ned and Tucker.

A long needle had been inserted into a vein on one of my front legs. Tape held it in place and from the bottom of the layers of tape a clear tube emerged. The tube snaked out through the bars, leading to a plastic bag that dangled from a hook near the top of the door. I nibbled at the edges of the tape, but every small movement I made only brought a fresh stab of pain, so I left it alone for the time being.

Stretching a stiff neck, I looked outside my cube of a prison. I could tell by the sounds that more animals were caged on either side of me and some above. There was a small bank of cages to the left. Mostly cats with their ears flattened, looking totally pissed off. I shuddered. I had yet to meet a cat I liked. Why humans kept them around was a mystery to me.

In one of the cages that I could see, though, were four small puppies. They huddled against one another, fright evident in their limpid eyes. Their coats were dull, their ribs gaunt, and their bellies distended. They were sick and underfed. I wondered if that was how I had looked when Ned Hanson was supposed to be taking care of me? I wanted to lick the puppies, bring them food, snuggle against them until they were well. I wanted to care for them like I had wanted — needed — someone to care for me.

Further down the narrow room and to the right was a row of kennels. The angle made it hard for me to see inside, but occasionally a black Labrador Retriever would come to the kennel door and look out. He thumped his tail against the sides of the kennel and bounced on his feet in greeting every time a human passed. Was he insane? He should be hiding at the back end, not inviting people to take him out and poke at him.

219

A young woman with a high ponytail and wearing pink scrubs came toward me. I straightened my legs to push myself against the back of the cage, but the moment I did that an unexpected tightness flared over my left hip. Baffled, I glanced toward my rump. My coat was shaved from my loin, forward to my flank, then down to the bulk of my thigh. A long scar puckered over pink skin, stitches crisscrossing a jagged line.

"You're awake." The woman slipped her fingers between the bars and wiggled them.

I inhaled her scent, but hung back. I would not be as gullible as the Lab. My trust had to be earned. I guarded it closely. Relying on myself had preserved me ever since Tucker Kratz shooed me onto the highway from that rusty trailer on a rain-drenched night.

"Don't worry, girl." She smiled, but her eyes were sad. "I won't hurt you."

Yeah, I've heard that before. It earned me a kick in the ribs once, a drug-induced haze another time.

She disappeared for a minute, then returned with a handheld rectangular device. Flipping the latch on my kennel up, she reached inside. If I'd had the strength to scoot away, or even the presence of mind to bite her, I would have. But it was as if every thought in my head was swimming through pond muck. I couldn't think quickly, couldn't act quickly; I was at her mercy.

She waved the device over my withers. It beeped softly. She turned it over, squinting at the display.

"Ah, you do belong to someone, then. Well, that's good news, isn't it? We'll just make a couple of calls and you should be back home in no time."

Home. The word echoed in my head. *Home. Home. Home.* The best word that humans ever spoke.

Please, please, please send me home.

I was tired of wandering alone, tired of not knowing when my next meal would be or how long it would be before the nights turned unbearably cold and the water froze everywhere.

I wanted to go home, sleep beneath Cecil's kitchen table, wake to the smell of Bernadette cooking bacon on the stove, put the sheep out every morning so they could eat their fill in the green hilly pastures and then bring them in every night so they would be safe from the coyotes.

Before she even drew her hands out, a high-pitched scream tore from a back room. They were torturing a dog back there, I could tell. The woman appeared unconcerned.

"Poor thing. You're shivering." She ran a hand over my neck, stroking lightly. "Are you cold or just scared?"

I gazed into her kind brown eyes. She seemed like a good person, but ... I tensed as her hand drifted toward the stitches.

A tiny growl escaped my throat. Narrowing her eyes, she pulled her hand back slowly and shut the door.

"Hmmm, not sure about me yet, are you? That's all right. I'd be pretty out of sorts, too, if a car rolled me on the highway, fractured my pelvis and femur, and I ended up here with pins in my leg, wondering what the heck was going on. Well, if you had to get hit, you're lucky it was by someone with morals enough to bring you to a veterinarian." She took a pen out of her breast pocket, glanced again at the display on the device, and jotted something down on the clipboard hanging on my cage. "The way these microchip listings go, if your owner has been looking for you, we'll get a contact number pretty quick. Good luck, girl."

The Lab thumped his tail against the concrete block wall as she walked by. She stopped and pressed the flats of her palms against the links. He licked them, his big pink tongue making slurping noises.

She laughed. "You're such a good boy, Henry. You get to go home soon. How do you like that?"

I rested my head between my paws, eyeing the tape on my leg and the tube that connected me to the bag of fluid.

I wanted to go home, too. More than anything.

The problem was that I wasn't sure where home was anymore.

—o00o—

I didn't see the woman with the ponytail the rest of that day. Others came by to check on me, cleaned my wound, changed the bag when it emptied of fluid, and gave me fresh water and small portions of canned food to eat. The food had a bitter taste to it, and I suspected there was some drug in it that kept me groggy, but I ate it anyway. I was hungry, very hungry.

The humans made a point of talking to me. I wasn't interested in their lies. They talked of 'home', trying to lull me into giving my trust so they could keep me on hand for whatever wicked purpose they had waiting. I refrained from biting any of them, although the opportunities were abundant. I needed the sustenance they gave me, needed to grow stronger, needed to wait for the chance to bolt to freedom and find my own way home.

As the day wore on, all the people in their scrubs left except one, a younger man with wiry red hair, who busied himself taking the kennel dogs out on leash and feeding the puppies. A man in a suit came and took the gullible Lab, who was beside himself with joy at the reunion. The red haired man locked all the doors and left after that.

Then came the night. The puppies whined incessantly, the cats yowled like they were in mortal agony, and every dog there, except me, joined in a chorus of howls. While I shared their misery, I didn't have the energy to sing with them. My body was busy mending. Rest was important if I were ever going to get better, so I could move the sheep when I went home.

Maybe someday, Cecil and I would trial again. Not that it mattered whether we won or not. I just wanted to work for him. To show the world how tightly interwoven our relationship was. Because working is what I was born to do. It was my purpose and in fulfilling my purpose, I made my human content. I needed Cecil because *he* needed me.

Yet, I wasn't sure if I had merely dreamt of Cecil while in the trailer — or if that, too, had been a ghost.

I preferred to believe I was just crazy. That I had never seen any ghosts at all. Ever. Because Cecil had to be alive. There *had* to be someone for me to go home to, a reason that I had survived.

—o00o—

A hand curled around the door frame and flicked a switch on the wall. Lights flickered and hummed, until their full brightness flooded the room. Immediately, all the animals, except me, scampered to their feet, toenails tapping on metal and concrete. The Chihuahua next to me whimpered annoyingly, begging to go out.

Craning my neck toward my bowl, I drank my fill. That was when I realized I needed to pee. As in I really, really, *really* needed to pee. Now!

I braced my front legs, tried to push myself up, but my legs slid out from under me. My ribs smacked down on the bottom of my cage. Not to be thwarted, I tried again. The needle pulled at my skin. I clamped my teeth on the tubing and jerked it free. Clear, sugary fluid dripped onto the floor of my cage. The needle, still in my leg, burned. A tiny drop of blood spotted through the tape.

"Whoa, whoa!" The ponytailed woman rushed to my cage and opened it. She pressed her thumb to a spot just above the needle and carefully pulled it free, then slipped it into her pocket. "Looks like you're awake today. I suppose you want to go outside, huh?"

Outside? Yes, I woofed softly. I didn't want to sound too enthusiastic. It was important that I remain aloof.

223

I attempted to pull my back legs under me so I could stand, but my left one seemed fused straight. I couldn't bend it.

"Hold on a minute, girl." Her hand pressed firmly down on my ribs so I couldn't stand, she called toward the door for someone. A few moments later, a round-bodied woman shuffled in. Together, they lifted me from the cage and set me down. Then the other woman wrapped a towel under my belly like a sling.

Thus began the most humiliating day of my life. I couldn't walk on my own. I had very limited control of my back legs. If I tried to stand, I wobbled. I would have fallen if they were not there to steady me. When I tried to walk, I pitched to the right and my body threatened to fold into an embarrassing heap of bones and skin. Again, they held me up.

Step by step, we worked our way to the short hallway and out the side door. The scents of outdoors hit me like a drug of giddiness. I squatted and peed a lake, relief washing through me as my bladder drained onto the gravel. I didn't care that it splashed on my barely bent legs, or that I had actually dribbled a few steps before making it outside. I had awoken thirsty and full of piss. Not to mention feisty enough to rip the tube from my leg. I was feeling more like me.

This place, reeking of disinfectant and full of fretting animals, may not have been home, but I was warm and dry and fed. I had been hurt, and they were taking care of me.

Because I was too tired from my brief jaunt to walk back, they carried me to the cage, each supporting one half of my body. After I was laid inside and my water bowl refilled and my food dish heaped with a mixture of dry kibble and canned food, I may have nuzzled the hand of the ponytailed woman. I can't remember. There were a lot of drugs in my system.

Still, I wasn't too proud to show my gratitude.

Later that morning, they took me out again. This time I was able to bend my legs ever so slightly and support myself long enough to do my business.

Before returning me to my cage, Ponytail bent down, held my head between her hands, and kissed me on the nose. Her breath smelled like bubble gum. Like Rusty. "Guess what? Your owner is coming to get you tomorrow. She was so happy someone found you."

She?

chapter 24

The clacking of her bracelets alerted me to her arrival. Bernadette appeared in the doorway, wearing a long flowing blouse with swirly red and yellow flowers. Ponytail and the round helper lady stood just behind her, tears of happiness swimming in their eyes. Bernadette had on the same bright coral lipstick and gobs of eye makeup that she always wore, but there was an underlying sadness in the lines of her face. She pulled a tissue from her purse to dab away the tears threatening to smear her mascara.

Finally, someone I could trust.

"Oh, Halo," she blubbered, her voice choked with emotion, "I thought you were gone, too."

Well, I hadn't left of my own accord.

A-roo-roo-roo, I said, which meant, 'I'm glad to see you, too'.

"Usually, for a dog with injuries this severe," Ponytail said, "we'd keep her another day or two to monitor her condition, but it's pretty clear she needs to be in familiar surroundings. She wasn't too keen on us handling her. Can't say I blame her. It looks like she's been through a lot lately."

"More than I'd like to admit. I feel so bad. I trusted someone to look after her when ..." Bernadette bunched the tissue in her hands.

"Anyway, she ended up getting loose pretty far from home, evidently. How did she wind up here?"

"She tried to cross the bridge on 275, east of Newport. It was just before dawn. A car hit her. A couple of Good Samaritans brought her in. Luckily for Halo, she didn't suffer any internal injuries. A few bruised ribs. The leg was broken in multiple places, though. We had to rebuild her hip joint, too. But veterinary science has come a long way in a couple of decades. She's almost like new. It could have been much worse."

"Poor thing. It looks painful. Will she be okay after it heals?"

"For the most part, yes. She'll be able to get around well enough. But she'll probably always have a limp and some pain in that hip. Arthritis will be a problem for her. Stairs might be a challenge as she gets older. Anything requiring her to run, jump, move quickly — I'd advise against it. Short walks would be best, when she's ready for it. For now, a ten foot trip out the door to potty is about as far as she can go."

I wagged my nub, overjoyed to see a familiar face. If I could have, I would have spun in circles and then jumped into her arms. Instead, I was relegated to being lifted carefully out of my cage and set on the floor in front of her. I wanted so badly to race around like a puppy on a sunshiny day, my heart bursting with happiness, but the dull fog of drugs was giving way to an ache in my left hip that was almost unbearable. It hurt just lying there, let along trying to stand without falling over. So I stood with my back oddly hunched, hoping my legs wouldn't slide out from under me, gazing up at Bernadette pleadingly.

"Do you want to go home, Halo?"

I did, I did, but ... I was beginning to understand now, although I didn't want to believe it. There was a good reason Bernadette had been the one to come get me. It *had* been Cecil's ghost I'd seen in Tucker's horse trailer.

In that moment, my heart broke into a million tiny pieces.

227

The joy that had seized me when Bernadette first walked in was suddenly replaced by a gaping emptiness. It wasn't that I didn't love Bernie — my life, Cecil's life, they had both changed for the better when she became a part of it. It was that I couldn't imagine life without Cecil. Who would I rise with in the early morning hours, to sit beneath the table at his feet, before going out to do our chores? Who had been taking care of the sheep in my absence? In his?

The home I'd known the past six years was a new unknown. I didn't like change, didn't like getting to know new routines.

Mostly though, I missed the Old Man.

All that hoping, all that fighting so hard to get back to the farm … It wasn't about going home to a place. It was about going home to be with him.

"All right, then," Ponytail said cheerily. "I'm going to go up front and get a copy of the bill for you. If you need to pay in installments, that's no problem. We understand. Meanwhile, Susan here can show you how to help Halo go outside and fill you in on her follow-up care. As soon as that's all taken care of, you're good to go, Mrs. Penewit."

"Oh, no." Bernadette waved a hand at her. "I'm not … I wasn't Cecil's wife. He … he died last month."

So, it had been him in the ambulance at the fair. Why had I not sensed it then?

"Ah, I just assumed … I'm sorry," Ponytail said.

"It was very unexpected. I'm his good friend, Bernadette Kratz. He didn't have any close family. I'm just helping straighten out his estate."

"That's good of you. Not many people would do that for a friend."

"We were close." She looked down. "Really close."

Ponytail removed my clipboard and gave Bernadette a sympathetic smile before starting toward the door.

"Thank you for taking such good care of her, Dr. Chapman."

Ponytail nodded politely, then inspected the clipboard. "Tell you what, Ms. Kratz, we'll waive the surgery charge. Take Halo home. If you have any problems, just call us, okay?"

—o00o—

It was a long, *long* way home. Bernadette stopped several times and let me out twice. Although it was very difficult for her to get me in and out of the car by herself, she managed. Of course, I suffered for her clumsiness, but I didn't blame her for bumping my leg against the car door to send daggers of pain up my spine, or nearly dropping me to the ground that second time. She was doing her best, just like I was.

Unable to sit up, I didn't see the miles go by. I just stared at a cloud-choked sky through the back window as pale gray light yielded to darkness. I slept a good part of the time, thanks to the drugs they had given me before I left that took away the sharpest edge of the pain.

When I was awake, I thought about Cecil. About how he had saved my life. Given me purpose. I had believed my life with Lise and Cam was perfect. That my world revolved around Hunter's giggles and Lise's belly rubs and the time spent trailing after Cam on Ray's farm. Then that all changed, for the worst, until Cecil plucked me from that frozen kennel and let me sleep in his kitchen. After that, he'd taught me to control the sheep by insisting that I be patient, that I trust him enough to listen to his commands. And when I'd earned *his* trust, he had let me make my own decisions when he was not quick enough to assess the situation.

I was valued. I was needed. And I knew that I was loved, even though Cecil had never spoken the words.

I was a dog. Words were not always needed, although I so often wished I could speak them.

I had so many questions I wanted to ask. Who would care for me now that Cecil was gone? Would Bernadette, despite the fact that I made her sneeze? The farm was not hers. I had been to her home only once. It was a small, but cozy rental house two blocks from the library in Faderville. Smaller, even, than Cecil's little farmhouse. There were crocheted afghans and framed jigsaw puzzles and silk plants everywhere, as if every square inch needed to be filled with color. In nearly every drawer containing cloth items, she had stuffed sachets scented with lavender and cloves. The closets smelled of cedar and mothballs, the kitchen of pumpkin and nutmeg potpourri, and the living room of the peppermint candies she kept in a dish by the front door.

Cecil's house had smelled of the dirt that fell from the treads of his boots, of the hay that clung to his overalls at feeding time, of black coffee and burnt toast. Simple things. I had smelled them in my dreams when I was trying to find home. I could smell them now ...

—o0Oo—

"Halo, honey. We're home."

I blinked, stretched my legs, and yawned. The car door gaped open. Cool air surrounded me, tickling my whiskers, awakening my senses. Bernadette stood just outside the car, her plump, short body washed in the harsh glare of the barnyard floodlight.

She looked over her shoulder. "Merle, you're gonna have to help me this time."

Merle wedged herself between Bernadette and the door to look at me. "My, my. Sure has been through the ringer, hasn't she? Can she stand? Walk yet?"

"Barely, but the vet told me she'd gradually get better, although she'll probably never be able to work livestock again. Shame. She was so good at it."

Together, they pulled the blanket on which I lay toward them.

Merle grunted as she took hold of my back end.

"Careful now," Bernadette cautioned. "She has a pin in that back leg — and a new hip."

"Like you. Soon, anyway." They lowered me to the ground and made sure my legs were solid underneath me before letting go. "When are you scheduled?"

Bernadette rubbed at her lower back with both hands. "Later next month. I'm not looking forward to it, but I don't know that I can last much longer like this. It's getting harder and harder to do simple things."

"How are you going to manage?"

"I'll be staying with my daughter near Bowling Green. Soon as I'm well enough to go home, there's in-home care that'll help me out. Paula wanted me to just move in with her, but they've got four kids and barely have room as it is. No, I told her, I'll do fine on my own once the doctors say it's okay. Besides, all my friends are here. And the library."

While I did my business, they chatted about Bernadette's grandchildren. Then we walked slooowly toward the front porch. I stopped at the first step. They might as well have expected me to climb to the top of one of the catalpa trees. There were only four steps total, but I was not up to going up even one right now. I looked at Bernadette, waiting for her help.

With a series of grunts and puffs, they helped me up and onto the porch. As winded as they both were from that simple task, I reckoned I was on my own as far as making it around on the flat. Abruptly, the conversation turned back to me.

"So," Merle began with a drawn out sigh, "what are you going to do with the dog?"

"I haven't quite figured that out yet … but I have an idea."

chapter 25

Cecil had never owned much. Just as he had a tenuous attachment to words, he was the same with physical objects. If a thing didn't serve some practical purpose, it had no place in his home. There were only two exceptions to this: Sarah's picture and the trophies on the closet shelf. Still, even though the farmhouse had always been uncluttered, the stark bareness of it when I walked in with Bernadette and Merle that first day home was a shock I wasn't quite prepared for.

You wouldn't think that dogs would have an attachment to things, either, but we do. You see, we are creatures of habit. It's not that we covet things. A dog could care less whether the sheets are designer brand or secondhand. It's that their presence is the landscape of our surroundings. Removing physical objects from a home is like clearing the trees from a forest. Without Cecil's things in this house, it was no longer Cecil's house. It was just *a* house.

Somehow seeing the place stripped of its furnishings — save the couch where Bernadette occasionally slept and the little dinette table and its two vinyl padded chairs — it was like walking into some other dimension. A shell of a dwelling, haunted by memories so fresh they still stirred the senses.

Even though Cecil's scent had faded, I could still feel his

presence: in the impression of his body on the kitchen chair seat, in the tarnish on the doorknob he had turned every morning, in the gouge mark on the counter when he missed the cutting board with the butcher knife and nearly took off the tip of his thumb. It was as if he could walk in the door at any moment. Except ... I was slowly beginning to realize that wasn't going to happen. Ever.

Too much had changed. The toaster where Cecil had toasted his white bread every morning, the coffee maker that percolated and steamed the air with its sharp aroma, my rug under the kitchen table ... all gone. Stiffly, I gimped my way through the house, checking all the rooms. The bedroom had been stripped of all its furniture, save the bed, which was nothing but a metal frame and a lumpy old mattress. Doors gaping open, the closets had been emptied of their clothes and linens. The rugs had been removed, the handful of pictures taken down from the walls. A short wall of boxes, scribbled with black marker, lined the hallway.

"So when are they kicking you out of here?" Merle looked inside one of the boxes.

"Not anytime soon." Opening and closing three different cupboards doors before she found what she wanted, Bernadette set a box of teabags on the counter and a container of sugar. "Blackberry Pomegranate okay? It's all I have left here."

"Sure, that's fine."

With my rug from underneath the table gone, I had nowhere soft to lie. So I carefully lowered myself next to the register at the edge of the living room, where I could see into the kitchen. The metal grate was still warm from the last time the furnace had kicked on. Cecil would have chased me out of the room. I wasn't supposed to be in here, but then ... Cecil wasn't around to tell me so.

"Say, I think the cups are in that next box, if you wouldn't mind checking. And if they're not, they're in the one underneath. I've just been so scatterbrained dealing with all of this, I can't remember where

I've put what lately."

The teacups tinkled as Merle grabbed two and brought them to the counter. Bernadette filled the tea kettle and put it on the stove. They sat across from each other, the old chairs creaking as they shifted, trying to come up with words to fill the dreadful silence.

Tapping a spoon on the table, Merle looked around. "No family at all? None?"

"He was an only child. Had a couple of cousins who passed years ago and from what I gather, his more distant cousins lived out in California and Oregon. Fortunately, he'd recently written up a will with provisions for auctioning off the place and his belongings and giving the proceeds to charity once his funeral arrangements and debts were paid. And as far as debts, they didn't amount to much. He inherited this place from his parents. Paid cash for every vehicle or piece of farm machinery he ever owned." She twisted a ring on her left hand, her eyes growing damp. A diamond sparkled in a gold pronged setting, surrounded by a corona of alternating sapphire and emerald stones. "Even this."

Merle patted Bernadette's fingers. "I'm so sorry, Bernie. My heart just about broke when you told me he'd proposed on the Ferris wheel and not five minutes later ..." She squeezed her hand tighter. "Just doesn't seem fair when a good man like Cecil is taken from us without warning like that."

Bernadette looked down at her lap. "I think he knew."

"Knew what?"

"That he wasn't well. I heard from Darla Willoughby a few days later that he'd been to the heart specialist over in Elizabethtown a couple times lately. Her sister works there and — well, it was probably violating some patient confidentiality for her to say so — but she said the doc there was trying to talk him into having some kind of procedure."

"Procedure? What do you mean by that? Like an angiogram? An

EKG?" Merle covered her mouth with her hand. "A bypass? Kenny Mills had a triple bypass. The surgeon said he was one Quarter Pounder away from kicking the bucket."

"I don't know. She wouldn't say."

"He didn't tell you about this?"

"No, you know how Cecil was. He didn't talk much about himself. I wish he had, but then … I thought we had years left to get to know each other."

The tea kettle shrieked, and Bernadette poured the water into the cups and set them on the table. She didn't sit down right away. Instead, she went into the hallway, moved two boxes aside, and lifted a little wooden box from one of them. She came back into the kitchen and took a yellowed newspaper clipping out of the box.

"What's that?" Merle pushed her glasses further up onto the bridge of her birdlike nose.

"I found this when I was cleaning out that hall closet. You know how I told you Cecil and Sarah had been married and never had children?" She hurried on without waiting for a reply. "Well, that wasn't entirely true. Here." She pushed the clipping across the table and waited for Merle to read it.

"A little boy?" A frown tugged at Merle's mouth, distorting her wrinkled lips even further. "And only a week old."

"His wife Sarah was forty-three when she had him. He was born with Down syndrome. Just like Rusty down at the library. Unfortunately, Cecil and Sarah's little one had other complications."

Merle didn't seem comfortable talking about the death of an infant. For a while she busied herself dunking her teabag and then squeezing it before she set it on a paper towel. "You didn't say — what charities is his money going to?"

"Some will go to the library, to help pay for a new building and to continue the literacy program. The largest portion will go to the cancer society. His wife died of uterine cancer. The remainder will go to the local animal shelter."

They both glanced at me. I shut my eyes, pretending to sleep.

"Well," Merle said, taking a final sip and then getting up to place the cup in the sink, "I have to be at my son's house early in the morning to watch little Max. Call me if you need any more help. Will you be here until the auction in two weeks?"

"No, I've done about all I can do here. I'm heading back to my place day after tomorrow."

As much as I adored Bernadette, I didn't like the idea of staying at her place — not that the house was too small for me. I didn't need a lot of room indoors. But Bernadette had no sheep. Besides, the patch of grass she called her backyard was barely big enough to park her car in. The garage took up most of the space and it was full of the remnants of her life.

"I'll see you Friday at lunch then." Merle took her coat from the peg on the wall and went to the back door. Just as she went to pull it open, the phone rang. They glanced at each other with a startled look.

"I'll get it." Shrugging, Bernadette heaved herself up from the chair. "Might be Paula, making sure I made it back okay."

The phone was on the wall next to the hallway. It was the only phone I'd ever seen that had a curly cord attached to it. Bernadette once told Cecil they hadn't made those for decades, but he dismissed her by saying it still worked. She waited until she'd caught her breath before lifting the receiver from its cradle.

"Hello? … Yes, hello Sheriff Dunphy. I'm just fine. How are you this evening? … Yes, I have her right here… Oh, she looks pretty ragged, God bless her heart, but she could've been much worse. She fell into good hands, thank heavens… Yes, I have someone coming day after tomorrow I think she'll be glad to see… Is he, now? Well, that's troubling to hear. The boy has serious issues. Running from the law isn't going to help that any. He needs more than a slap on the wrist… Oh, you bet your life I will when the time comes. I don't care if he's family or not… Thanks for all your help, sheriff… Mm-hmm, will do."

The moment she hung up, Merle was right in front of her. "So they finally found Tucker, did they?"

"I wish. He was holed up with one of his many girlfriends over in Owensboro just yesterday, but the rascal got away before they got there. They think he might be headed down to Tennessee to one of his old army buddies."

"So when they do catch him, what'll they charge him with?"

"Theft, extortion … *and* turns out he was part of a gambling ring. It's true what they say about the apple. I tried to get him on the right track, went to all that trouble of getting him fixed up with a good job, and he goes and does a stupid thing like this. What in the world was he thinking?"

"Hard telling. But you did the right thing, Bernie." Merle gave her friend a hug. "Don't you dare lose a wink of sleep over it. It's exactly what Cecil would have wanted you to do."

"I know. Just a terrible shame that nephew of mine didn't turn out better. I wish I could have made a difference in his life, that's all."

"You've made a difference in the lives of a *lot* of young people, Bernie. Not your fault Tucker couldn't see what a blessing your help was. Say, how did the state police figure out he had Halo after all?"

"Bill Clancy turned him in. You know how Tucker told me someone had let Halo out of the stall at the fair before he ever got there? Well, turns out he'd taken her after all. After that, he headed up to Michigan, to Saline, where Clancy was slated to trial again the next weekend. The birdbrain tried to sell him a spayed dog as breeding material for a premium price, so Clancy knew something wasn't right. Tucker told him I'd given the dog to him after Cecil died. After Clancy turned him down, Tucker headed back south. The trailer blew a tire somewhere up in Ohio. Near Lima, I think. He'd noticed a state trooper tailing him earlier, so he evidently became a little paranoid and abandoned the trailer. The best we can figure is that Halo either got away from him or he let her go. She must have traveled hundreds of miles on nothing more than instinct. Amazing, isn't it?"

"I'll say. Well, thank the good Lord there are fine people like Mr. Clancy in this world. Not to forget the people who took her to the vet." Merle reached into her pocket and jangled her car keys. "Bye now."

"See you Friday."

"You sure you'll be okay here by yourself?"

"I'll be fine. It'll only be another day or two. I'm almost done. Besides, nothing ever happens here anyway. I think it's a little on the dull side, but it's what Cecil loved about the place — the solitude, the peacefulness, the ..." Lower lip quivering, her words fell away. She whipped out her embroidered handkerchief, lifted up her leopard print glasses, and mopped at her eyes.

"I'm so sorry, Bernie." Merle flung her arms around her friend.

They clung to each other awhile, Merle rubbing Bernadette's back, and Bernadette releasing her grief on her friend's thin-boned shoulder.

"It feels wrong leaving you alone here," Merle said as they drew apart. "I'll come back in the morning."

Bernadette straightened her shirt. "That's nice of you, but being here ... well, it makes me feel closer to him. Sometimes I almost feel like he's sitting right there" — she gestured at the dinette chair next to the window — "looking out into the barnyard, planning out his day while I cook up the eggs and bacon."

My ears perked at the word 'bacon'. It took me a moment to realize she wasn't referring to making any at that moment.

Bernadette wiped her nose, and then stuffed the handkerchief back in her pocket. "Odd, but I even find myself talking to him and waiting for him to answer. Even though he doesn't, I get the feeling that he hears me."

He does, Bernadette. He does.

I got up from my warm spot, limped to her, and shoved my nose under her hand.

"You know what I'm talking about, don't you, Halo?"

More than you know.

chapter 26

Where are the sheep?

I paced up and down the fence line, worrying myself to a frazzle. It wasn't long before my limp got so bad that I had to stop. Shivering as I stood on three legs, I scanned the pastures, the barnyard, the open barn door ... Open door? Some idiot had left the door wide open! I snorted in fury. Ice encased my breath in a vaporous white cloud before me.

"Halo? Halo?" One hand pressed against her hipbone, Bernadette hobbled around the corner of the house. She motioned to me, as if she couldn't make it the last fifty feet, and pulled her housecoat tight around her. "Come back in, girl. It's chilly out here."

Frost sparkled on the tree limbs and crunched beneath my feet. It was cold, but I wasn't going back inside until I found the sheep. No matter how biting the ache in my hip. I turned away from her, started trotting toward the gate. It was open, too. The outrage! How could Bernadette be so incompetent? I hadn't expected her to know everything, but how could she have been dumb enough to leave both the barn door and the pasture gate open?

"Halo, come here."

I ignored her and circled the pasture, pausing at each corner to look into the distance, study the hills, searching for them. She was to blame for this. Cecil would have expected his sheep to be cared for, to be protected, *not* to be wandering loose. How could she have let this happen?

"Halo!" She stomped her foot, her chubby arms flapping at her sides like an old hen. "Halo, come *here!*"

Just as she entered through the gate, I ducked past her and headed for the barnyard. She screeched at me, but the words didn't register. Someone had removed the feeders and emptied the troughs. If the sheep were loose, how did she expect to lure them back? With nothing to come back to, they would stay in the hills as long as there was grass to eat. If they felt threatened, they would bolt for the woods and then we'd never find them. If it snowed, if the winter was long, they could starve. If the spring was damp and chilly, they could get sick and die. I couldn't let that happen.

Maybe they were penned up in the barn? Bernadette couldn't get around easily and she had no dog to help her in the fields. Keeping them in the barn might have been the easiest thing for her. As I turned toward the door, a bolt of pain ripped down my spine. Stumbling, I let out a yelp. But I kept going. I had to find the sheep. Had to know they were safe.

The door to the barn stood open. I hopped inside, holding my bad leg up off the ground. A curtain of darkness fell across my vision. I stood on three legs, squinting into the dim light, inhaling the goodness of hay.

I heard the truth before I saw it. Silence. Emptiness. Nothing but bare framework, remnants of hay bales, and vacant pens.

They were gone.

The door boomed shut. I looked behind me just as Bernadette flicked on the overhead light. I barked at her. Twice. Three times.

What did you do with them? Where are they? BRING THEM BACK!!!

She stood in a wedge of lamplight, its harsh light casting eerie shadows on her drawn, round face. For a moment, Bernadette looked like a blanched ghost, but there was a fullness and a solidness to her form that denied the notion. She appeared as worn and depleted as I felt, as if these last few weeks had taken just as much of a toll on her as on me.

"I'm sorry, Halo." With a huff, she leaned her shoulder against a roughly hewn post for support. "The sheep were sold off a few days after Cecil's funeral. The neighbors down the road came and took care of them until then. Honey, I know you think it's your job to look after them. Cecil was always so proud of you. You have no idea how much having you around meant to him. Working with you was what he looked forward to most every day. Heck, he always made sure you were fed before he'd sit down to breakfast with me." She turned to rest her back against the post. The light played off a tear as it slid down her cheek, bare of its usual layers of makeup. Her bouffant hairdo was a flattened mess, its tight red curls all loose and out of place. "Because of you, Halo, he opened his heart to love again. Because of a dog, for a few months, I got to know and fall in love with the best darn fellow in Adair County. It wasn't nearly long enough, but by God I wouldn't trade a moment of it for anything."

Too tired to stand any longer, I crumpled to the dusty floor. I'd understood enough of what she said to know that the sheep had been taken somewhere else. I also understood that she missed Cecil as much as I did. But *she* hadn't lost her job or her home. She couldn't possibly know what it was like for me. I had nothing left. Nothing but her — and it wasn't clear to me how long that was going to last.

"Come on in to the house with me, honey, while I get ready." Wiping the dust from her housecoat, she stepped away from the post. "Time you and I went for a ride."

Ride? I wasn't really in the mood. Besides, there had been a few car rides in my life that didn't end so well.

The door groaned on its casters as she heaved it open. Daylight spilled in. In the corner closest to the door, Cecil's old shotgun was propped. I could only recall him using it briefly when I first came to the farm. It was early morning and buzzards were circling ominously above the barn. There had been a coyote raid the night before. The sheep had worked a gap loose in some fencing. Two lambs and a ewe had been killed in the pen attached to the barn, the only outside place the sheep had access to at night. For a week, Cecil stalked the property just after nightfall and again before dawn, the shotgun loaded and clutched under his arm. But the coyotes didn't reappear. He never fired a shot.

Outside, a light fog hovered above the earth. Bernadette tilted her head toward her car. "You and I need to go talk to Cecil. He'd probably appreciate knowing you're okay."

Well, I was certainly confused now, but I suppose it was worth finding out exactly how we were going to do that.

—o00o—

I knew the place long before we got there. The odor was unmistakable. With every breath I inhaled, sadness seeped deeper and deeper into my soul, until I was so burdened with the weight of it that I could barely will myself to move off the seat when Bernadette opened the car door.

"He's over this way," she said.

I waited for her to reach in and clip a leash to my collar. Her back was already to me and she was several feet away before I realized she hadn't even brought one. I eased myself from the seat to the floor of the car. The short ride had stiffened my joints so much that I dreaded stepping out.

Bernadette tossed me a sad look before continuing on down the single lane asphalt road. Okay, so she wasn't going to wait. I never thought I'd see the day when the sixty-plus year old redhead with a

243

distinct limp and a waistband the size of a bathtub would outpace me, but sure enough she was. My mouth clenched to hold back any unintentional cries of pain that might eek out, I stepped down gingerly and landed on three feet. I paused a moment before hopping after her. Every ten paces or so, I had to stop and rest.

Even though the noonday sun had burned off the frost-fog, there was still a sharp chill in the air that slipped beneath my fur to chill my skin. By the time I reached Bernadette's side, though, the short walk had warmed my joints and muscles, making them feel slightly more fluid, if not more tired.

We were standing before the stone where Cecil had asked his first wife, Sarah, for permission to ask for Bernadette's hand. Except this time there were two stones side by side. The same size, same color, same shape. And beside them, the even smaller one. The only thing different was the markings on the front of each one.

"This is a cemetery, Halo," she said in a husky voice. "It's where they lay dead folk to rest. So God can know it's time to take them up to heaven."

Why was she talking to me like I didn't know this already? Oh yeah, because people think dogs *don't* know any better, that we can't figure this stuff out on our own.

Bernadette blotted at the mascara running from the corner of her eye. Then she blew her nose into the handkerchief. Loudly. Like a goose on its way to Canada.

I walked a few feet from her to distance myself from her blubbery noises. For a full minute, I stood there waiting for her to say something else or go back to the car. Finally, a wave of fatigue washed over me and pulled me down to the ground. The winter-dead grass was soft but cool on my belly.

"Oh, Halo!" She waved her hands at me, the floral handkerchief flapping in one like a banner in the breeze. "You're lying on his grave."

Yes, I know.

I laid my head down, closed my eyes, breathed in the air that was *him*, submicroscopic molecules of the carbon and oxygen that had once been Cecil Penewit. Let it flow into my lungs, mingle with my blood, fuse with my bones and muscles. I fully expected a blanket of sorrow to wrap around me so tightly that I would suffocate within seconds. But nothing like that happened. Instead, the memories came rushing back, one after the other, so quickly that I flinched at the brightness of the visions flashing through my mind. Grungy overalls, black coffee, toast, rug, table, crook, barn, trough, sheep, Sarah's picture, the hall closet, the Y-chute at the trial, Clancy and Brooks, riding in the truck to the feed store, walking through the hills at Cecil's side, counting the lambs on a cold spring morning …

Bernadette's snuffles escalated to mournful sobs. I opened my eyes to see her rocking from side to side, her arms crossed tight against her breast. Black streaks ran down her cheeks. Her mouth gaped open with each heart-wrenching wail, its duration broken only by her need to gather another lungful of air.

It shocked me to see the effervescent Bernadette so full of grief that she couldn't even find words. Dogs know sadness, too, but we cannot speak of our feelings or shed copious tears. We are reduced to moping, to low ebbs of energy, to loss of appetite, and on rare occasions, a bout of forlorn howling — at least until some human interrupts our mourning and tells us to hush.

Truth be told, I wasn't sure whether to go to her so she could take comfort in petting me, or to just remain where I was until all the blubberiness had drained out of her like a sponge wrung free of dishwater. Surely, she couldn't go on crying like that forever?

And then I saw Cecil — no, Cecil's *ghost* — enfold her in his arms and hold her tight. She stopped rocking. Her keening fell away to a sickly sniffle. She leaned her head forward ever so slightly, as if to lay it on his shoulder.

245

"The world doesn't seem right without you in it, Cecil," she mumbled. "The children at the library miss you and Halo. *I* miss you. I wish, more than anything, that I could bring you back."

He's right here, I barked. I got to my feet and limped toward her, my eyes still on Cecil as he gazed lovingly at her.

She covered her mouth with her handkerchief as her sniveling gave way to a bubble of laughter.

Startled by the unexpected sound, my eyes shifted to her face for a fraction of a second. She tried to wipe away the smile dancing over her glossy lips, but it wouldn't be banished. When I looked again to where Cecil had been standing, he was gone.

"I know, I know, sweetie. You're probably worried about me." She folded up her handkerchief and tucked it back in the hip pocket of her stretchy slacks, and then pulled her knitted sweater down over her bulging middle. "Let's go back to the farm, okay?"

A pair of aging cripples, we dragged our broken bodies back to the car. Bernadette's breathing regained a regular rhythm. The sadness had vanished from her face.

With considerable effort, I pulled myself up into the car, grateful to lie down after even just that short walk. It was the experience, the well of emotions, that was more draining than the effort. After shutting the back door, Bernadette slid her bulk into the front seat and put the key in the ignition. She didn't turn it right away, though.

I sensed her gaze and looked up to see her watching me in the rearview mirror.

"For weeks now, I've been walking around in a blue funk. There were days I woke up and it was hard to justify breathing, even. It was like someone stole all the joy out of my life that night. Zapped it, like that." She snapped her fingers in the air. "Felt like the walking dead. Like the thing I looked forward to most, spending the rest of my life with Cecil, suddenly it wasn't there anymore. The only thing that kept me going was my grandkids — and still I had a hard time smiling for

246

them.

"The night before the vet's office called, I sat at the tiny little dinette, staring at a glass of Jack Daniels and a bottle of sleeping pills, wondering how many it would take to do the trick for an old cow like me. And I told myself, 'Bernadette, give it one more day. One more day.' Then … then they called about you. Gave me something to fill the hours, driving up there to get you. Still, I couldn't shed that feeling that life would never be as good again." Her keychain clinked as she twisted the key in the ignition. "But for some reason, I feel a whole lot better now."

Cecil is the reason, I tried to tell her, my thoughts coming out as a pathetic whimper. *He wants you to know everything's okay. That he's fine — and he'll wait for you. You'll be together again. You will.*

As usual, she couldn't hear me. No one ever did.

Story of my life.

chapter 27

Bernadette lay face up on the sofa, her mouth wide open as she emitted a snore as loud as the engine of Cecil's old John Deere on a winter morning. Her blanket had fallen to the floor in the early hours of morning after much tossing and turning. She wore a flannel nightgown, dotted with a busy flower pattern, this one of red and white roses. A single fuzzy pink slipper peeked from beneath the edge of her nightgown.

Rolling over onto my side, I stared at that slipper for the longest time and thought just how well suited we were to each other now, Bernadette and me. I was a little wishful that this would be my job for the remainder of my days, sleeping on a bed of folded blankets beside her, but she had made it clear that was not to be, that she couldn't take care of me.

I wondered what was going to become of me, then. Where would I go? Who would I live with? Other than companionship, I had nothing to offer. I wasn't a very old dog ... but I wasn't young, either. With my bum leg, I couldn't gather sheep from the field or move cows through the loading chutes. I couldn't bring down a groundhog or chase the squirrels from the bird feeder. I could barely get down the stairs. I couldn't even have retrieved a ball. Old before my time, that's what I was.

Bernadette's hand dangled down by my nose. I snuffled it, couldn't resist licking her fingers, trying to gently wake her. It was well past dawn. I had to pee.

"Oh my word!" She struggled to push herself upright, then swung her legs to the floor. "It's a quarter to nine. She'll be here any minute."

Shuffling into the bathroom, she splashed water on her face, scrubbed it with a wash towel, and proceeded to do a truncated ritual of her usually lengthy morning routine. I stood in the doorway, staring intently at her with a message that said: *I need to go out. Now, please.*

She was only half-dressed, standing there bare-faced in her nylons and underwear, before she finally remembered. Slipping her housecoat on, she ushered me out the door.

Warmer this morning, the sun was already high in the sky, its strong light igniting the amber and garnet in the trees on the hills. I stood on the front porch, not at all eager to take those four steps down and then back up again. I walked to the top of the steps, looked out over the farm, took it all in: the faded red barn, the steep-sided creek down the lane, the leaning mailbox out by the road, the muddy corner of the pasture where the sheep would wait for their morning hay in winter, the majestic tulip tree where the squirrels used to drop nuts to the ground to taunt me …

There's one now!

A perky gray squirrel rubbed its tiny claws together, darted around the base of the tree, and then came toward me in starts and stops. I took the first step faster than I should have. A sharp reminder of my incapacity stabbed through my leg. When it finally faded, I went more slowly. On open ground, I was better. I could at least manage a brisk walk, or shuffle, rather, but I kept the pace leisurely, my head pointed toward the barn so I could keep the squirrel in my peripheral vision. The little rodent flicked its tail smugly. I paused as I neared it, pretended to look away, but all the sudden it dashed across the lawn and up the tree. Disappointment whooshed out of me in a single breath.

Dang it. So close. This could have been the day. All this time I'd been trying to beat the thing across the lawn before it went back up the tree, when maybe I should have taken a lesson from the local barn cats and stalked it instead, lulling it into a false sense of security before springing on the thing and eviscerating it.

Trotting over to the tree, I stared up into the branches. The thieving rodent was nowhere to be seen. I squatted at the base of the tree, letting my puddle of urine soak the ground as a reminder that this was my territory. Just as I turned to go back to the house, a silver minivan turned at the mailbox and drove up the lane. I stayed where I was. If it was someone I didn't want to see, some stranger — which it likely was — then I had time to take off. Had I been, well, less of a wreck, I would have stood my ground and barked my head off, telling them in no uncertain terms to *go away*. In my current condition, however, I was a sorry excuse for a guard dog.

The van curved around the loop at the top of the driveway, stopping before the front porch. No one, except someone who hadn't been here before, came in the front door. A woman got out — I could tell from the build of her hips and the way she walked — pulled her gloves off, and stuffed them in her pocket as she climbed the stairs. She was wearing a felt hat, the brim turned up in front, her hair bunched up in a bun at the back of her neck. I couldn't see her face from where I stood, but her presence stirred a flutter in my belly.

She knocked on the door. Only a few knocks, soft and polite, as if she expected Bernadette to be right there waiting to open it. After a few moments, she knocked in the same manner again. When that brought no response, she pulled her sleeve back from her wrist to check her watch, then knocked more loudly, six times.

Yes, dogs can count. Not in great numbers, but enough for simple things. How else could my mother Bit have kept track of all of us and known when I was missing? How else would I have known when a lamb had strayed?

The woman stepped over to the picture window and peered inside. She had turned to go down the steps when Bernadette threw open the door.

"Come on in! So glad you could come. I'm Bernadette." She circled her arm in a welcoming motion. "Sorry I'm such a mess, honey. Overslept, I'm afraid. I've got tea if you'd like some."

The woman put her hand in Bernadette's and shook it. "Hi, I'm Lise McHugh."

I'd taken several steps forward before I realized what I was doing. Lise? Here? A mess of emotions muddled my head. At the same time that I wanted to be angry with her for leaving me with Estelle and never coming back to get me, I also wanted to run to her and smother her in kisses.

"Who else would come all the way out here this early in the morning?" Bernadette shut the door behind Lise as they went inside."

Only yesterday, the thought had crossed my mind that it wouldn't be so bad living with Bernadette in her tiny house, if she could manage it somehow. The loss of Cecil had been as big a blow to her as it had been to me. That reticent old-timer, set in his ways, a workaholic, had wormed himself under our skins. He was a man who loved sparingly, but deeply, who gave all his attention and loyalty to his farm, his dog, and lately his sweetheart, Bernadette. When she came into our lives, it was like the missing piece of the jigsaw puzzle had finally been found. Those weekly trips to the library had been an exciting respite from the monotony of daily chores. I welcomed the hugs of the children, their stutters and lisps as they stumbled over the words in the books, their small triumphs as Cecil read with them, and then their smiles of delight as Bernadette praised their efforts and improvement.

There had been an ebb and flow to daily life that approached perfection. Bernadette and I could have kept each other company. We could have provided therapy for one another if she had taken me on short walks. Surely it was important that she remain mobile in her ageing years? And yet, she had seemed reluctant to keep me as part of her life, something which baffled me. Yes, she had her family, but what was life without a dog at your side? How could such an existence be complete?

Now here was Lise, waltzing back onto the stage as if I might not care that she had abandoned me when *I* needed her most. Who the hell did she think she was?

I started toward the house, trotting with a purpose. I didn't bother to hide the hitch in my stride. Let her look out here and see what I'd been through. Let her mire in guilt.

I was a dog. A living thing. A loyal companion. A guardian. A soulmate.

I could not be tossed away like a dirty rag or a piece of burnt toast.

Bypassing the front porch, I swung around to the back door. There was only one short step up onto the patio there. I hauled my lame hind end up and stared at the door. I didn't have to wait long.

"There you are," Bernadette beamed. "Come in, little honeybunch. I have a surprise for you."

Surprise? I wouldn't call it that. Maybe an unexpected development or a wrench tossed into a set of gears, but I wouldn't class it as some sort of pleasant intrusion on life's daily rituals — not that we had any of those yet, but we would. It was just a matter of time. Bernadette would come around. She'd have her surgery and realize how much she needed me to help her get better.

In the short time that I had spent plotting the demise of the squirrel, she had finished dressing, although her hair was slightly out of place and her makeup scant, relatively speaking. Her cardigan slanted to one side. She'd missed a button.

"Well, what are you waiting for? Someone's here to see you."

I snorted as I brushed past her. I took one disinterested look at Lise, who stood by the sink with a mug of tea cupped in both hands. Then I lay down under the table in my usual spot and closed my eyes. Bernadette had moved my blanket bed there. She was training up well. Another six months and she'd be baking homemade dog biscuits for me. I could cotton to a life of leisurely retirement. Days spent warming myself on the living room floor in a ray of sunshine, afternoons at the library while children swarmed me, evenings stretched out, bathed in the glow of the TV. It would take some getting used to, but —

"Halo?" Lise set the cup on the counter and knelt down, turning her head sideways to look under the table at me. "Hey, girl. How're you doing?"

I opened one eye, closed it.

"Remember me, Halo?" she said.

I do, but I don't see the point in you being here. You let Ned Hanson take me away and never came back. Just go away.

"I'm sorry I wasn't able to come back for you after Cam died. Sooo sorry. Things were … complicated."

I rolled over, away from her, onto my good hip. Bernadette had forgotten to give me my pill this morning. It was getting worse.

Lise scooted a chair out and sat. Her foot was by my head. The soles of her shoes smelled vaguely like hay and … earth. I inhaled deeply, slid my chin a little closer to her foot.

"I just don't think she feels like herself," Bernadette said. "They said the break was pretty bad and it's a wonder —" She spun around, her eyes scanning the mostly empty cabinets. She opened one, then another, then a third before finding the right one. "My age is catching up with me. I forgot her pain pill this morning."

After fumbling with the cap, she tapped one into her palm and came toward me. I scooted further under the table.

"Ohhh, the last time I gave her one of these, she spit it out three times. I know she hates them. I just wish she'd understand it was for her own good."

This was one of the many times I wished I could explain to her that I *did* understand. I just didn't like gagging on them, or the bitter taste they left in my mouth.

"Do you mind if I have a look?" Lise asked. "I learned a few tricks over the years."

"Go right ahead — although you won't find much in there."

Lise slid her chair back. The refrigerator door opened. She looked high and low, moved a few jars around, slid a drawer out. "Aha, here we go. I used to use bologna, but this is even better."

A plastic wrapper crinkled. My head shot up. I knew that smell. Was she —?

Lise pulled a piece of raw bacon from its packaging. The first drawer she opened contained the silverware. She cut the bacon into thirds.

"Would you like me to cook that?" Bernadette's penciled brows folded in concern.

"No need to." Lise took the pill from her, then motioned for her to have a seat. "Dogs like their meat raw just as well as cooked." She winked at Bernadette, then knelt down next to the table. "Now watch."

Lise dangled a piece of bacon in front of me. Saliva soaked my mouth. I licked away the drool that threatened to drip from my quivering lips. Who was I to resist this offering of peace? Careful not to snap, I took the bacon. I really, really tried to savor it, to let its smoky goodness melt on my tongue, but instinct overcame me. I swallowed it whole.

Extending her palm, she offered another piece. This one was carefully wrapped around that nasty pill. I could see the nubby little white end poking out. Still, it was wrapped in *bacon*, the food of gods. I slurped it up and swallowed it whole. The lump inside caught in my throat for a second. I worked my tongue in and out, feeling the urge to retch, but before I could expel it, Lise pushed another piece of bacon between my teeth. I devoured it, and the pill slid down smoothly, greased by the coating of bacon fat in my throat.

Lise patted me gently on the head. "Good, was it?"

Pure heaven.

Her hand curved under my muzzle, scratched the soft place at the base of my throat. I leaned into her touch, stretched my neck. A tiny moan of delight escaped me. I flopped over onto my side, lifted my front and rear left legs as far as I could, given my condition. Her nails scrubbed at my tummy.

Flinching as she caught a closer look at my stitches, she sucked air between her teeth. "Poor girl. She's been through so much. If I had known ..." She smoothed the fur over my ribs. They were still tender, but her touch was light. "Was she happy with Cecil?"

"Oh, yes! Worshipped the ground the old coot walked on. That dog was never more than five feet from him if she didn't need to be. They had their little routine every day. Up at dawn, outside for chores until noon, errands in the afternoon, then more chores after supper. You'd have thought they'd get tired of doing that day in and day out, but no, it was like something they *had* to do. He took that dog everywhere he could. Did I tell you they came to the library every week for a reading program? I almost couldn't get Cecil to come at first. Turned out he had dyslexia. He was embarrassed about it, but it was something that actually helped him connect to the kids. And Halo here ... she was so tolerant of Rusty — he's a little boy with Down syndrome."

"That's good to hear. I'm happy that she had a good life overall, even though there were some bumpy parts here and there." She had been smoothing down my fur the whole time Bernadette was talking, but suddenly her hand paused, hovering over the place where my heart was. Her touch amplified my heartbeat. "Anyway, thanks for hanging on to her until I could get here."

Bernadette plucked at the cameo on her gold necklace. "Lise, maybe it's none of my business — and you just straight up say if that's so — but why did you ever give her up? You don't seem like the kind of person who would've done something so drastic without a really good reason."

Pulling her hands into her lap, Lise sat back. A few moments passed before she answered. "It's okay to ask, really. Truth is, it was the lowest point of my life. Like the whole universe was crashing in on me and I couldn't catch a break. When I left Faderville to move in with my mom, I was pregnant. Cam and I had been trying for so long that knowing I was carrying his baby again, even after losing him so young and so suddenly ... I *should* have felt blessed, but I also felt incredibly sad that he would never know his own child. Then, there were the financial issues to deal with. Cam had accrued a huge amount of debt after a failed business venture. I never knew just how big those debts were until I was going over things with the lawyer after his funeral. It was a mess just getting straightened out exactly what I was or wasn't responsible for. I had no choice but to sell our home. In the middle of all that, my dad passed away and my mom's health issues got even worse. She had a mini stroke. For a while, she needed constant care. I couldn't imagine leaving her in someone else's hands. Here I was, seven months pregnant, and caring for a bedridden elderly person."

She kneaded at her kneecaps. "Then there were Hunter's heart problems to deal with. I was so worried about him. I took him to every specialist within an eight-hour drive. They all told me the same thing: not to worry. But it was all I did. He'd also become withdrawn. He was functional, but non-communicative. I took him to a counselor for a few months, but then the insurance money ran out and I just couldn't afford it with all the legal fees and medical bills that were piling up."

"How is he now?"

"Better, thanks. Still very quiet though. He manages well academically at school – he just keeps to himself. He's had a few fainting spells, but nothing more serious. We lived just outside of Covington until my mom … she had another stroke. That one left her completely incapacitated: paralyzed on one side, unable to speak. She couldn't even use the bathroom or feed herself. I knew then that I couldn't care for her anymore. It was more than I could handle. My sister and I found her a good nursing home after checking out nearly two dozen. I know I shouldn't have, but I felt guilty about leaving her at Whispering Pines."

"Sweetheart," — Bernadette put a hand on Lise's shoulder — "you did everything you could. You have two children and a life to get on with. I always tell my oldest, Paula, that if I ever become a vegetable with tubes and machines keeping me alive, I don't want her loitering at my bedside out of guilt. Your mother, is she …?"

"She died, yes. Two months ago. It was hard, but not unexpected. That's when I decided to come back to Faderville. My mom's condo sold last year, so I have the money from that and I'm looking for someplace to live. I thought maybe if we could have a dog again, it would help Hunter. He loves animals more than anything."

Lise rose and pulled her gloves from her pocket. "I should probably go now. I start my new job Tuesday, so I have to do as much house hunting as I can before then. My friend Grace is watching Hunter and Cammie for a few hours and I have a couple of houses to go see. Hunter likes spending time with his sister, but they can get on each others' nerves after awhile."

At the sound of Hunter's name, I emerged from beneath the table. Had it been him that I'd seen at the fairgrounds after all? Did he remember me?

I approached Lise and nosed the gloves she held bunched in one hand at her side.

Please, I want to see Hunter.

"Are you going to keep her?" Lise said, then quickly added, "I mean, I know you said you had some major surgery planned soon. I was just wondering if you had someone lined up to take care of Halo?"

I looked from Lise to Bernadette. Fingers outspread, she turned her hand so the morning light played off the facets of the jewels in the ring that Cecil had given her. Finally, she gathered up the teacups and set them in the sink. "Are you asking if you can take the dog?"

Suddenly, Lise looked very uncomfortable. Shaking her head, she tugged her gloves on. "Never mind. That was thoughtless of me. Halo probably means a lot to you." She turned toward the door. "I'll just go —"

"Wait." Bernadette stopped her with a hand on her arm. "Sit down a minute. Please."

Lise complied.

"I'm old. I'm falling apart. Well, more physically than mentally, but the point is I'm going to be out of commission for a few weeks. I'm actually allergic to dogs, too. Downing all that antihistamine is giving me brain-fog and making me want to nap five times a day. Anyway, what's important to me is that Halo be well cared for."

A flicker of hope lit in Lise's eyes. "Okay, okay. I can do that. The kids will love having her visit. When do you think you'll be back on your feet?"

"Visit?" Bernadette shook her head. "I'm not just talking about a visit, Lise dear. I'm talking about Halo becoming a *permanent* part of your family."

"Permanent? You mean you'd ...? I don't know what to say."

Bernadette patted her arm. "Say yes. I can hang on to her while you find yourself a place. A little dog hair for a few more days won't kill me. There are plenty of properties up for sale around here lately and the prices are good for buying. Have you taken a look at the old

McCloskey place down on Birch Hollow? Nice big yard. They kept it in good shape, too. Shouldn't need a lot of fixing up."

"It was on the listings the realtor gave me. I'll ask her if we can see it on short notice. Meanwhile, are you going to be here awhile longer? I'd like to bring the kids by to meet her first. Hunter probably remembers her, but Cammie … She was bitten by a dog when she was three. It was a small dog, a Lhasa Apso, but she's been scared of dogs ever since."

"Don't you worry. Halo's a charmer." Bernadette's lip quivered the tiniest bit. "When would you like to come back with the kids?"

"Would eight o'clock be okay? I know it'll be after dark, but I've got a lot to do today."

"That'll work just fine. I don't have anything to do but catch up on my Hawaii Five-O episodes."

"Okay, I'll be back then." Lise bent down, took my head in her hands, and kissed me on top of the head, just like Ponytail had done. "Halo, if all goes well, you'll be coming home with us."

A little bubble of happiness welled up inside me. I couldn't help myself: I licked her face.

chapter 28

There was a time when I would have jumped on the couch to watch all day out the picture window at Lise's house for Cam to come home. Right now though, I felt old. Older than I was. My left hip ached fiercely, my neck and spine were so stiff I could barely stoop to drink from my water bowl, my joints did not want to bend, nor my legs bear the weight of my body. So I lay under the table, wishing Bernadette would give me another pill so I could drift off to sleep until Lise arrived with the children.

If I'd had the energy to go to her, stare at her, run back to the cabinet where she put the pill bottle — which incidentally was not the one she'd put it in before — then I might have had my needs met. Instead, I had to suffer in silence, waiting for the hours to pass, for Lise to come, for Bernadette to remember how often she was supposed to give me those pills.

After Lise left, she mopped the kitchen floor, which meant I had to move to the living room. Then she took a nap, ate lunch, washed dishes, took a second nap, talked on the phone to Merle, packed a few more things in boxes, took another nap ...

I was only vaguely aware of her activities after that. I felt like sleeping all day myself. Mostly that's what I did — until the pain woke me up. Twice she opened the back door to let me out, but I was too tired to bother. The third time I didn't get up, she came to me and pressed two fingers to the leather of my nose.

"My, you're hot! I'm going to call Dr. Chapman, see what she says. Or better yet, maybe Doc Samuels. He's more of a large animal vet, but I think he's the one Cecil used to use for the sheep. Dogs can't be much different. I'd take your temperature, but I don't know whether to stick the thermometer under your tongue or in your ear."

Neither, I wanted to tell her, but of course … well, you know how it goes.

—o0Oo—

Cold metal pressed against my chest. Fingers probed me everywhere. My eyes flew open when something poked in my anus. I stiffened.

"There now," Bernadette said, one hand firmly pressing down on my shoulder, the other snugly around my muzzle. "Doc's almost done."

I was lying on the cool linoleum floor, Bernadette squatting before me and old Doc Samuels kneeling toward my flank. Cecil had been old, but he was probably just entering grade school when Doc Samuels graduated college. The man had more wrinkles than a box of raisins.

"Running a fever, all right," Samuels said. I looked at him out of the corner of my eye. He used to help Cecil medicate the sheep whenever one was sick, although sometimes the purpose of his visits was not always so hopeful.

Lambs, it's said, are born with one foot in the grave. Peaceable creatures, driven primarily by fear of their predators, they are of an unusually delicate constitution. One day they're bucking and leaping through the clover and the next a damp wind sends a sickness into their lungs that can't be dislodged with any dosage of shots or pills. By

261

the third day they are on their sides, wheezing, feverish and listless. Before that day's done, they're dead.

So you see, I was even less thrilled to see the vet making a house call than I would have been to see him at his office. The home visits were the serious ones. The prognosis was often grim. I'd stood beside Cecil as we buried more than one limp, tiny lamb or aged ewe.

Doc Samuels flicked his finger against a syringe three times, then depressed his thumb. Milky liquid squirted out the end of the needle.

"Hold her now," he said. Memories of Tucker injecting me with the sleeping potion rushed back.

No!

I thrashed against Bernadette's hold. She pitched her weight into me. I struggled to breathe. I tried to open my mouth to bite, but her hold on my muzzle was so firm I couldn't even turn my head, much less sink my teeth into her hand. She was surprisingly strong. Or maybe I was surprisingly weak?

The needle pricked my flesh. I flinched. Liquid burned as it seeped into the muscles of my flank.

"Will that help with the pain?" Bernadette asked.

"That? No. That was just the antibiotic." He rummaged through his bag of evil instruments, pulled out another vial, and drew its clear contents into a new syringe. "This one should help her sleep through the night. She's developed a little post-surgery infection somewhere in her system. It happens. It's a good thing you called when you did, though. The earlier we catch these things, the better. If she's not looking more spry by morning, bring her to my office."

Not the vet's office, no. I strained to lift my head to see what Doc Samuels was doing back there, but Bernadette still had a death grip on me.

Lise and the kids are coming tonight, I want to be —

Another needle jabbed me behind my shoulder blades.

"That should do the trick. Remember, call me if you need

anything. I'll leave the pills on the counter. Start them in the morning, but like I said, if she doesn't look right, bring her in."

"Thank you, Doc. I appreciate you coming out so late."

I pried an eye open. The two of them stood by the back door. When had Bernadette let go of me? I hadn't even heard them walk away. Through the curtains, I could see it was dark outside already. Where was Lise?

"No worries. Just part of the job. Keep her quiet for a couple of days. Oh, give her one pill four times a day."

"Will do. Bye now."

The back door opened and shut. Cool air wafted in.

Why couldn't I get up? Why was I so tired? When were Lise and the kids coming?

I fought to keep my eyes open. I had to watch the door, so when they got here I could be on my feet to greet them.

My eyelids drifted shut. Sleep called. Just a short nap, maybe. Only a few minutes …

—o00o—

Mroaaarrr, mroarrr, mroarrr.

I woke up to blinding daylight, the hum of the vacuum cleaner, and the overpowering smell of Pine-Sol. Bernadette was cleaning. Again.

"You're awake!" She clopped across the tile floor to me. Her sensible Dr. Scholl's clogs had been replaced today by a pair of black leather boots with a low heel. Her gray slacks, an unusually subdued hue for her, even had the smell of 'new'. I recognized the canary yellow blouse with the frilly collar, though. She brushed two fingers over my nose and cheerily declared, "Fever's down. Let me get you something."

A few moments later, the delectable aroma of bacon tickled my olfactory senses. I lifted my head. A bit stiff, but I didn't feel like I was wading through a mud pit anymore.

"Glad you're feeling more like yourself, today. Lise was so concerned when I called her yesterday. She even came by late last night to see you."

When was this? You mean I had slept through the whole thing? Had the kids been with her?

"She wanted to wait until you were up on your feet. We'll see how the day goes. I was hoping to be back at my own house by tomorrow, but moving you right now doesn't seem practical."

She helped me to my feet and we took the slow walk to outside. My left rear leg was getting stronger, but I was woozy and still very groggy. It was hard to walk straight. More than once on the way back to the house, I veered to my right and bumped into Bernadette's leg. Inside, she showed me to a dog bed.

"Lise brought it by last night. Memory foam, so you're more comfortable. Evidently, when she talked to the kids about getting a dog it was pretty unanimous. Well, I think the little one took some convincing, but it looks like you're finally going home, Halo. You have your own family. They just need to find themselves a place to live."

Did she say what I think she said?

Home. Family. I rolled the words around in my mind. They had such a beautiful ring to them. A hummy, soothing sound that conjured visions of lazy mornings with children in fuzzy slippers, spoons pinging as they dunked for cereal and slurped the last of the sugary milk from their bowls; the tromp of feet as they grabbed their backpacks and ran to catch the bus; long naps on the rug warmed by the sun's rays; a full basket of toys behind the recliner, the cottony guts removed from each overstuffed squirrel or obnoxiously squeaky duck; brisk walks with Lise on fall days, leaves whisking across the road; afternoons watching out the window, waiting for the bus to bring the children home so I could greet them each time as if they'd been gone for months; long games of ball; winter days romping through snowdrifts; evenings spent by the TV, while buttery hands lobbed kernels of popcorn at me; nights stretched out beside the bed of my boy, vigilant to every sound.

My heart swelled with joy. I could fill that role. The family dog. No longer the working dog. I could get used to the idleness, the simplicity, the outpouring of love.

That was when I noticed Bernadette, pressing my pills into tight rolls of bacon as she sniffed back tears. I went to her, leaned my still bruised shoulder against her leg, and gazed up at her. For a minute, she went on preparing my pill sandwiches, her plump fingers tucking the bitter pink and white capsules into the fatty strips, then turning them end over end, one after another. She dashed the back of her wrist under her nose with one hand, while the other drifted down to her side. I licked it clean, which brought a smile to her face.

I didn't like the thought of leaving her, even if she did already have her children and grandchildren. We could have been a family, the two of us.

She fed me the pills — four of them, had the vet told her that many? — and then washed and dried her hands. I emptied the kibble bowl she set before me and drank my fill of water. Bernadette said nothing, just went about wiping down counters and scrubbing the sink, like she was trying to fill up the time.

My belly full, nature called, so I went to the back door and stared at it. Bernadette hobbled into the living room to fold up her blanket and rearrange the pillows. She flicked on the TV and punched at the remote control until a show came on with people seated on a stage, wailing and yelling with pointed fingers at one another while a man with silver hair pulled a paper from an envelope and pronounced, "Our results show ... Billy John, you are *not* the father."

Bernadette stood transfixed in the doorway. "Well, I could've told you that. That baby doesn't have his chin or its mother's."

If she didn't open the door soon I was going to empty a river of urine right there. I whined once. Then more loudly. One hand on her bad hip, Bernadette shuffled back into the kitchen and pushed the door open.

"Hurry up, then. They could be here any minute." She glanced at her watch. "Did she say 9:00 or 9:30? I can't remember now." She brushed her hand at me. "Well, go on. I've got some tidying up to do."

My gait a little looser now, I trotted across the yard to the area where I usually did my business. Even though the leaves had begun to fall from the trees, it was warmer than it had been in many days. The ground was damp from a late night rain and the smells of the farm were particularly strong. I put my nose to the air, inhaling the memory of hay bales and baby lambs.

Soon I found myself standing in the opening of the barn. As I stood there, letting my eyes adjust to the shadows, a tiny mew emanated from somewhere within. I wandered between the empty pens, looking everywhere until I heard the sound again. It came from up high, where a small black and white kitten sat atop one of the cross rafters, its eyes wide with fright.

We locked eyes, taking each other in. As I watched it hunker down, I folded to the ground. A yawn gripped me. My eyelids drifted shut. I shook myself awake, feeling the pull of sleep. It was the pills, I knew. Not only did they dull my pain, but they made me tired. This was as good a place for a nap as any. As soon as I heard Lise's van, I promised myself, I'd go back to the house.

I glanced up at the rafters. A skinny black tail flicked above me. Golden-green eyes glared distrustfully down. If that kitten was going to go anywhere, it would have to get past me first. Closing my eyes, I kept my ears open, listening, as I dreamed of the life that lay ahead with Lise and Hunter and the little girl I hadn't yet met and wondered how Bernadette would manage without a dog.

—o0Oo—

The slam of a car door registered vaguely in the recesses of my awareness. It wasn't until I heard greetings exchanged and the bang of the front door that I realized Lise and the children had arrived. Bernadette had forgotten me once again.

After a good shake, I scanned the rafters. I was still very sleepy, but I didn't want to miss Lise again. The kitten was nowhere in sight. I left the barn and made my way toward the house. Before circling around back, where I expected Bernadette to let me in, I paused to look through the front window. A tall young boy, just entering the awkwardness of adolescence, stood at Lise's side, his bangs hanging down over his eyes, his hands shoved deep in his pockets. In Lise's arms was a little girl with a flowing crown of long blonde hair. She clung to her mother, head tucked against Lise's shoulder. As I stepped closer to the porch to get a better look, the little girl turned her head in my direction. Her eyes widened, not unlike the kitten's. She dug her fingers into her mother's back and whimpered.

So that was Cammie — the daughter Cam had never known? I scurried to hide behind the scraggly yew bush between the edge of the front porch and the corner of the house.

"It seems someone is having second thoughts today," Lise said to Bernadette as she stroked her daughter's head. "I'm sorry. I thought this was going to go more smoothly."

"Oh …" Bernadette's voice sank with disappointment. "Maybe she just needs time to get to know Halo? Tell you what, why don't I check in the kitchen? I just might have a fudge pop or two stashed in the back of the freezer."

Cammie tugged at her lip, her head twisting around to watch Bernadette disappear into the kitchen. I darted around to the back to wait at the door there, the pins in my leg sending little bolts of pain into my hip with each halting stride. I was slow. Couldn't make myself move any faster.

Bernadette's voice carried through the closed doors and windows as she rattled on about houses in the area, neighborhoods, and schools. Lise answered politely, but the children remained silent.

I scratched at the door to let Bernadette know I was there. She cracked it open.

"Stay there a few minutes," she said in a hushed voice. "We don't want to overwhelm Cammie. I'm going to tell her how good you were at the library."

I woofed impatiently. *Let me show her*, I meant to say, but all I could do was give that huff, indecipherable to human ears. She wagged a finger at me and clicked the door shut.

The minutes stretched out. It was hard to stay awake. I contemplated swinging around to the front door and barking until she let me in, but thought better of it. I didn't want to scare Cammie again.

I stared at the door knob for a long while. Nothing happened. Clouds scuttled across the sun, driven by a sharp wind. Bare branches clacked. From somewhere, the kitten mewed softly, persistently. I swiveled my head around, scanning among the trees. For a while I saw nothing, but the sound plagued me, scratched at my nerves. Curiosity seized me. I searched some more, until I saw a little blob of fur, high up in the catalpa tree on the far side of the lawn. Scrawny back legs swung from a horizontal branch, as the kitten gripped a lean bough with its front claws.

I took off across the yard, my speed hindered as I dragged my bad leg along. The wind gained force, until it was a gentle roar in my ears and I could no longer hear the sounds from the house. I limped to a halt at the base of the tree and barked several times, hoping to convince the kitten to do anything but let go. Cats could fall long distances and land safely, but this one was small and fragile.

It took a few minutes, but somehow the kitten scrabbled around the side of the bough until it was straddling it. I wasn't sure whether I should wait where I was until Lise or Bernadette came out to discover the problem, or go back to the house and alert them. Cold pellets of sleet stabbed at my face. Blinking as miniature balls of ice bounced off me, I glanced at the back door, a good distance away from where I was.

That was when I saw the lanky, scruff-faced man skulking along the side of the house with a long tubular object clutched to his chest and a bottle swinging from his other hand.

Alarms clanged inside my head. I knew the loping stride, the bony shoulders, the sharp nose and jutting chin.

My hackles bristled.

chapter 29

Tucker Kratz yanked the back door open and barged in, slamming it firmly behind him. The glass in the window rattled in its pane.

A growl rumbled low in my throat. I ran straight for the back door, evening out my stride for speed despite the knife of pain that threatened to flay me open from spine to hock. I flew over the patio ledge and skidded to a halt at the door on the slick surface. Something told me not to bark. If Tucker knew I was there, if he had found the shotgun from the barn, then all he had to do was point it at me and pull the trigger.

No, I had to stay quiet, get inside. But how?

Bernadette shrieked.

"God *damn* you, Aunt Bernie!" Tucker hollered. "You's the one what told 'em where I was, wasn't you?" His words were slurred. There was a poutiness to his tone, like that of a little boy who hadn't gotten his way and was about to burst into tears. "Why'd you do that?"

"Tucker, now, put that thing down," she urged. Although she kept her voice low and even, there was a tremor to it. "Don't make matters any worse than they already are."

"Worse? Tell me how they can get worse. God Aw-mighty,

270

woman! If'n they catch up with me, I'm already goin' to the big house. Does it matter if I get fifteen years or thirty? Naw, I'm gonna settle some scores before that comes around — and you're the first."

Carefully, I raised myself up on my hind legs to peek through the window of the back door. Tucker cocked the shotgun and lurched toward Bernadette. She stumbled backward into the hallway. Her back hit the wall with a thud. She slid down, her legs splaying wide. Tucker guffawed at her, then grabbed his whiskey bottle off the counter with his free hand and chugged.

I could see Lise and Hunter standing at the threshold between the living room and hallway. Cammie was out of view, but I knew she was in there somewhere, too.

Gathering her legs beneath her, Bernadette tried to stand, but Tucker slammed the butt of the shotgun down on the table. Bernadette flinched.

"Don't move!" Tucker sat, leaning back on two legs of the chair, his index finger stroking the trigger.

As he stared Bernadette down, Lise drew Hunter slowly to her and cast the slightest glance over her shoulder, toward the front door. I couldn't see it from where I was, but I knew that's where Cammie had to be.

"Now Tucker," — Bernadette tilted her head as she tried to plead with him — "if —"

"Shuuuut! Up!" Tucker flung the bottle across the kitchen. It crashed against the cupboard next to the sink, close to the back door. I ducked. Slivers of glass exploded everywhere, a few of them clinking against the window pane I had just been watching through.

"Money. Is that what you want?" Bernadette said.

"What kind of money we talkin' about, huh?"

"What do you need?"

While he was busy thinking — which, knowing him, could take awhile — I left the back porch and raced around to the front, stepping softly as I crept up the steps to stand before the door.

"— would be enough to get me to —" He snorted a laugh. "Aw shit, man, I can't tell you that. Let's jus' say I need a *lot* of cash. Loads of it. But I can't have you raisin' suppish ... puspish ... Damn it! I mean sus-pi-cions at the bank. Maybe I ought to just stay here with these two while you go fetch me some moola? What d'ya say?"

Careful not to make a sound, I stood on my back feet to look through the picture window. My injured leg quivered with the strain. Lise and Hunter stood with their backs to me. Beyond them, I could see Bernadette's legs sticking out in the hallway and past her Tucker's gangly legs stretched out before him, his boots speckled with mud, a hole nearly worn through the sole of one. In his left hand, he gripped the shotgun loosely. His face was hidden from my view.

I still couldn't see Cammie. My guess was that Tucker hadn't seen her either.

"That'd be fine, Tucker," Bernadette said. "I just need a little help getting up."

He lowered the barrel at her and leaned forward. I shifted over to stay out of his line of sight.

"Not yet," he said. "I need to think about this a minute. You were a little too quick there. Gotta be some catch."

"There's no catch," Lise said. "She gets you the money. You go free."

"And who the hell are you, again?" he said. "Naw, never mind. It don't matter. But maybe ... maybe you got money, too. What if I kept the boy and sent each of you one at a time? Now that could be lucrative."

Right and left I looked. Then I saw it — the closet door was cracked open. Two small, wide eyes gazed back at me. Cammie's lip was trembling. Tears streaked down her cheeks, but she didn't make a sound, not even a snivel.

Tucker pulled his feet back and stood. I lowered myself to the ground. If I didn't stop him, this could end very badly. I tucked myself in the corner of the porch, so he wouldn't see me. I had to think of something. Meanwhile, he rambled on about all the bad breaks he'd gotten in life and how he'd been set up every step of the way.

In quick succession, Tucker opened and slammed three cupboards. "Where do you keep the whiskey around here?"

I contemplated returning to the barn and barking up a storm to lure him outside. Maybe running to a neighbor's house and trying to lead them back. Either way that meant leaving all the people I loved with Tucker Kratz. I couldn't. Not now.

And then I heard a creak from the floorboards just inside the house. I cocked my head, stepped back, ready to leap behind the bushes and make a run for it if shells started to fly.

The front doorknob turned slowly. Someone tugged on the door from behind. A tiny hand slid around the edge.

Cammie popped her head into the opening. She motioned me inside.

As I brushed past her leg, Tucker started warbling a Keith Urban song. Murdering it, actually.

Slowly, Cammie closed the door, but the hinges were old and rusty. They let out a long groan. Cammie froze in terror. Tucker stopped singing.

"What the fuck!?" he roared.

The little girl glanced at me, then dashed into the closet, pulling the door shut as far as she could without clicking the latch into place.

I squeezed behind the sofa. There was barely enough room between it and the wall for me to breathe, but I pushed toward the other end. Halfway, a board in the framework of the sofa dug into my shoulder. As I slid further, the sharp edge of the wood caught against fresh stitches. Skin tore open. The wet warmth of blood seeped beneath my fur, oozed down my hindquarter.

"Tucker," Bernadette said, flailing a hand at him from the place where she sat, "you can't just —"

Just as I stretched my neck forward to get a better view, Tucker raised the butt end of the shotgun up above her head and slammed it down. Bernadette crashed sideways, her head hitting the floor first. The scent of iron filled my nose: blood. And not mine.

Leveling the shotgun, Tucker shoved Hunter aside. Lise caught her son, steadying them both against the doorway.

Jaw twitching, Tucker's eyes zeroed in on the closet door as he lifted the barrel, took aim —

"Nooo!!!" Hunter shouted.

Tucker whipped around. Lise yanked Hunter back, trying to drag him into the hallway. But he had grown bigger. He was too strong. He ripped himself from her arms, hands thrust before him, even as the barrel of the shotgun swung toward him.

Now! Cam's voice said from somewhere faraway. *Do it now, Halo!*

I launched myself from my hiding spot, mouth wide, my head turned sideways. My teeth sank into Tucker's flesh, pinching the tendon low on his calf, just above his heel. His leg jerked forward, but I gripped tighter. Held on.

The shotgun blasted.

A crash. A scream.

Then … silence.

chapter 30

The ambulance turned at the mailbox and rolled down Sweet Potato Ridge Road, its sirens mute. A minute later, it disappeared around the bend beyond the next hill.

Patches of blue sky shone between pewter clouds. A beam of sunshine spilled down to brush the land with golden light. The snowy limbs of sycamore trees shone brilliant against the darker tangles of locust, oak and ash, their branches long bare of leaves.

Looking over it all — the wooded hills, the grassy slopes, the places where sky met earth — filled me with great sadness. I was going to hate leaving this place.

I stretched out my front legs and lay down. My feet dangled over the edge of the porch, just above the first step.

Gentle fingers scratched at my neck. I leaned into them.

"I missed you, Halo."

I nosed Hunter's wrist. He turned his hand over. It smelled of fried chicken. I licked his palm, the trace of grease smooth on my tongue. Scooting closer, he curled his arms around me.

I missed you, too.

"I know this sounds funny, but … when that man aimed at the closet, I thought I heard Dad's voice. Like he was right next to me. He told me to stop him. So I did." He kissed the top of my head. His voice caught, grew softer. "Thanks for saving me … again."

The door creaked behind us, then banged shut. Small feet padded over the weathered planks. Cammie settled down on the other side of me.

Hunter lifted his head and inhaled. "Do you smell skunk?"

"Nope," Cammie said. Tentatively, she held her hand out. "She's our dog now? Really?"

I sniffed at her knuckles and sneezed. Giggling, she stroked my side. She was careful not to touch my stitches. The wound had pulled apart slightly when I caught myself on the nail, but Lise had taken care to clean it up and make sure the bleeding had stopped.

"Yep, all ours." The stiff material of Hunter's coat crinkled as he jerked sideways. "You aren't going to run away screaming every time she looks at you, are you? She won't bite *you*, you know."

She shook her head, looking offended. Then she pulled her shoulders back and lifted her small chin as if mustering her courage. "I'm *not* scared of her."

"Good." He pointed a finger at her. "Because she only bites bad guys."

Cammie smiled. "She got him good, didn't she?"

"Yeah, real good."

Voices drifted from the rear of the house. Shoes scuffed over limestone rock. Both children looked to the right as Lise and the sheriff rounded the corner of the house.

"Thank you for getting here so fast, Sheriff Dunphy." Lise wrapped her arms tight around herself to ward off the cold.

The sheriff reached out, his fingers brushing her upper arm. "Not often something as exciting as this happens around here, ma'am. I'm impressed you were able to detain him. Whatever gave you the idea to tie him up with the electrical cord from the vacuum?"

"A lot of MacGyver as a kid. Besides, he tripped over it when his feet got tangled in it. When the light fixture fell on his head, he was pretty stunned, so I just grabbed the cord and wound it around his ankles and wrists. It helped that he shot such a big hole in the ceiling and all that plaster dust fell in his eyes."

"We can thank the dog his aim was off." Sheriff Dunphy's gaze rested on me a moment, then swept over the old house: the flaking gingerbread framing the front porch, the gutter pulling loose from the eaves, the overgrown bushes. And then to the property beyond: the carefully tended fence rows, the freshly painted barn. "Beautiful setting. Place sure could use a little sprucing up, but overall it's in good shape. It'll make some family a wonderful home, I hope."

Lise's face took on a faraway look.

Sheriff Dunphy waved a hand in front of her. "Is everything okay, Mrs. McHugh? Do you want me to call the EMTs back?"

"What?" Lise stared at him blankly for a moment until his words registered, then shook her head. "No, I'm fine. And please, call me Lise. I was just wondering about Bernadette. They're taking her to the hospital, you said?"

"Yes, the one in Somerset. Just a precaution. Looks like a minor concussion. She might need a few stitches, too. Nothing serious."

"Thank goodness. I was so worried when he hit her. I think I swallowed my heart."

"Things could have been much worse." His gaze shot to Hunter. "Son, in a way that was incredibly foolish of you. Charging at a man with a loaded gun ... You could've been killed." His eyes softened as he approached the boy. He stooped down before him. "But in my twenty years in the department, it was also the bravest thing I've ever heard of. Your sister's alive and safe because you took action." He offered his hand. "Well done, young man. I'll make sure Cynthia Wunderly down at The Messenger sends someone out to take your picture for the Sunday paper."

Hunter took his hand. "Thanks, sir."

Lise's mouth fell open.

"Something the matter?" The sheriff started toward her.

"It's just that ..." She blinked several times. "That was the first thing he's said to anyone outside the family since ... well, for years."

"Oh, I have the feeling he'll be telling this story a lot from now on." Sheriff Dunphy tugged his hat down closer to his dark eyebrows, and then drew a business card from inside his jacket and handed it to her. "I think the boys are just about done inside. If you need anything, anything at all, call me." He turned back around and patted me on the head. "That's some dog you have there. I have the feeling you won't ever have to worry about your family as long as she's around."

A commotion arose from the rear of the house.

Two deputies escorted Tucker to a second Adair County police car. Tucker strained against the cuffs, cussing and spitting at the men. One opened the back door, while the other pushed him inside.

Before the door swung shut, Tucker shouted, "You tell Aunt Bernie I'm gonna get her for this! She better —"

The deputy slammed the door on him. He exchanged a look with his partner.

"He'll be lucky to get out in fifty years," the other one said.

"Yeah, if he ever does." They laughed.

Sheriff Dunphy nodded at Lise. "If you'll excuse me ..."

"Sheriff," Lise said, "can you answer a question for me before you go?"

"Certainly."

"How much does a place like this usually go for?"

His mouth twisted in thought. "Hmm, if I recall, it's just over eighty acres, twenty or so in timber ... House is on the small side." He tapped his chin with a forefinger. "This end of the county, maybe two hundred grand, but developers have been scouting the place. Likely, they're looking to divide it up into acre lots — that or some industrial corporation has their sights on it. If they get in on the bidding, it could go for two or three times that."

"Is there any way to make a pre-emptive bid?"

"Might be. But you'd have to approach the estate executor about that."

"And who's that?"

"Bernadette Kratz." With a wink, he pinched the brim of his hat between his thumb and forefinger. "Good day ... Lise. By the way, the name's Brad." He was about to get in his car when he stopped and came back to her. "I was just wondering ... Have you ever been to Adam's Rib, down in the square? It's a new place. Folks say the barbecue sandwiches are really good."

"No, I haven't. Why do you ask?"

"Just wondering." He glanced at the kids, then at his car. "I'm, uh, not supposed to ask women out while I'm on duty, but ... you have my card there. That one has my cell number on back. Call me sometime."

Tilting her head, she cocked an eyebrow at him. "Do you write your private number on the back of all your cards?"

He motioned toward the house. "No, actually, you're the first. I did that just before I came outside here. Almost didn't get up the nerve for it. Anyway, hope I get a chance to talk to you again."

Without waiting for an answer, he marched back to his car. As he grabbed the door handle, Lise called out, "Brad?"

He looked over his shoulder at her.

"Day after tomorrow all right? For a call, I mean. I've got so much to do before then."

"That'd be good." He smiled broadly. "Real good."

He got in his car and the two vehicles started off down the lane. Mouth flapping, Tucker Kratz pounded his forehead on the window.

"Mommy?" Cammie jumped down from the porch and skipped to Lise. "Can we live here?"

"I don't know, pumpkin." Lise picked her up and hugged her

daughter tight. She held her other arm wide, inviting Hunter into the embrace. He joined them. "That's a lot of money. I'm *still* paying off my school loans. Physical therapy school wasn't cheap, but at least I get paid more than a teacher's salary now."

"Please, Mom?" Hunter cast a pleading look up at her.

She ruffled his sandy hair. "We'll see."

The little girl tugged at her mom's sweater. "If we stay here, can I have a kitty?"

"Why on earth would you ask that? You've never wanted a cat before."

Cammie's tiny finger pointed at the barn door. The black and white kitten stood in the opening, its tail flicking side to side as it mewed softly. It trotted across the open yard, skidded to a halt at the base of the steps, then struggled to climb them as if they were a mountain.

I scooted back, considered bolting, but if I so much as flinched, the devil creature would probably fling a paw out and eviscerate me with those razor sharp claws. Rear feet kicking, it pulled itself over the last step.

The kitten arched its back and headbutted me. I eased back and prepared to launch myself from the porch in a single, energy-packed leap, but the thing just kept rubbing my cheek and neck with its head. Then it began to ... rumble?

Bouncing happily to us, Cammie scooped the kitten up and tucked it inside her coat. "Aw, Mom, he's purring. And he *loves* Halo!"

Yeah, but Halo doesn't love him back.

I might, maybe, possibly, learn to tolerate him. Given enough time.

—o00o—

"That Sheriff Dunphy is sweet on you, darlin'."

Lise poured Bernadette a cup of apple juice and placed it on her bedside table. "What makes you think that?"

Footsteps rang down the hallway, came closer, and then passed by. I lay low, my snout tucked in the warm space between Bernadette's arm and her ribs. She'd pulled some strings with the hospital staff to get me into her room that morning, lauding my recent hero status and reminding them that I was practically a local celebrity already, due to my work at the literacy center. She pressed a button on a control in her opposite hand. The bed made a strange whirring sound, and then started to fold upwards, so she could sit up. I inched toward the edge, looking down at the floor.

"Stay here, Halo," Bernadette said. She let out a series of sneezes and blew her nose on a tissue. "I'm not leaving yet. Apparently it takes two hours to fill out release paperwork. I'm starting to think they've forgotten about me. That or they don't want me to leave. Or maybe …" — she clutched both hands over her heart — "Lise, oh my. You don't think they found something else wrong with me, do you?"

"Relax, Bernadette. They're short on staff today. They told me about it when I said I was here to pick you up." Lise offered the juice to her. "But you didn't answer my question. Why do you think Brad has a thing for me?"

"Hmm, on a first name basis already, are you?" She guzzled her drink, eyeing Lise with interest. "Maybe because he came by this morning and asked a few questions about you."

"Like what?"

"Like if you were serious about staying around here."

"And you said …?"

"I told him he'd have to ask you." Bernadette pushed herself up from her pillows and dangled her feet over the side of the bed. Pulling off her fuzzy socks, she gestured at a corner of the room. "Say, can you hand me my shoes there? I was going to stay comfy until they discharged me, but I'm about ready to just waltz right out of here. I can't believe they made me stay all night for observation. Just a little ol' bump on the noggin. A goose egg." Her hand drifted to the gauze taped from the middle of her forehead to her temple. She winced as she grazed it.

"Concussions can be serious. They were only being cautious." Lise showed her a pair of red suede mukluks with gray fur on the sides and little pink roses stitched over the toes. "Merle wasn't sure which boots you meant when she packed them. Will these do?"

"Oh my. Those are slippers, not boots. And they clash with my outfit. But, I suppose if we slip out of here quietly, not too many people will notice." She slid them on over swollen ankles. As Lise helped her down from the bed and she limped to the bathroom, I could see how badly her hip hurt her. Mine was feeling a little better every day, but I was sure it would slow me down over time, too.

Lise busied herself packing Bernadette's things away in her overnight bag. The nurse finally came in, pushing a wheelchair.

"Hospital policy, I'm afraid," the nurse said.

Wrapping her arms around me, Lise gently lowered me to the floor. "I'm sure she won't mind."

The nurse bent down, ran her hand over my spine. "Is this the dog?"

"It is."

"She's an angel. Lucky for you she was there when you needed her. She's yours, I take it?"

The bathroom door popped open and the nurse stood up to help Bernadette to the wheelchair.

Bernadette ran her fingers over the chrome spokes as she settled in for the ride. "My, my, my. Sure would love to have one of these fancy chariots to wheel myself around in, maybe even a motorized one, but I don't think it'd fit through the doors in my little cracker box house." The nurse flipped the foot rests down for her, then spread a blanket across her lap. "Can you hoof it out of here, honey? Everyone's been absolutely lovely, but I'm aching to get back to familiar surroundings." Then aside to Lise, "Plus, the menu leaves a little to be desired. If you don't mind me making a call, I'll spring for a deluxe from Romeo's Pizzeria."

"Sounds great." Lise snapped my leash on and gathered up the last of Bernadette's things. "I'll loan you my cell when we get to the car. I'm pretty sure Hunter has dialed that number half a dozen times since we rolled into town."

We fell into step beside the nurse as she wheeled Bernadette down the corridor. Bernadette craned her neck to gaze into every doorway, waving and shouting to the other patients, "I'm going home. Get well! Come visit me at the library." If she'd meant to slip out unnoticed, she was doing a poor job of it.

When we got to the outer lobby, Lise and I fetched the car. I took my place in the back seat, my nose prints generously displayed on the window behind the front passenger seat. Once Bernadette was in the car and the call made to the pizza place, Lise glanced at Bernadette several times before speaking.

"Thanks, for everything. For going to get Halo after the vet up north called you. For taking care of her. For calling me … I don't know how I'll ever repay you."

"Sweetheart." Bernadette laid a hand on her forearm. "There are some things in life you don't keep score over. This is one of them. There's plenty of folks, like me, who are nice just because, well, because we understand that everyone needs a little help now and then."

Lise turned the key and pulled the shifter into 'drive'. We rolled slowly through the parking lot, easing over each speed bump. "Yeah, um … I've been thinking. Provided the paperwork all clears with the bank for the farm — and by the way, I still don't think it's enough — then I was —"

"It's more than enough. I've already talked to my cousin Garrett's son. He's a contractor. He said there'd even be enough left over for a

283

few computers and reading program software for the children with the money that's been set aside for the library. They're going to name the new wing 'The Cecil Penewit Center'." Turning her head aside, she pretended to look down the street as the car came to the parking lot exit.

"Good, I felt like I was taking advantage of the situation."

Bernadette sniffed. I couldn't tell whether it was her allergies or because she was getting emotional. "Well, you're not. But what were you going to say?"

The turn signal clicked a dozen times before Lise pulled out into the nearly empty street. "I have enough extra money to add on to the house. I was thinking a couple of bigger bedrooms and an office, maybe. I start my job as head of the new physical therapy place downtown next week and what with my hours and all, it occurred to me that —"

"I don't mean to rush you, but I'm not getting any younger."

"I was wondering if you'd move in with us once the addition is complete? I know you have grandkids of your own, but I need someone to look after Hunter and Cammie until I can get off work every day."

Slowly, Bernadette turned her head back. She looked very serious, maybe even a little sad. "My grandkids are all either grown or live far away." Then, a smile spread across her face. "I can't think of anything I'd rather do than watch your two young ones grow up."

Lise breathed a sigh of relief. "Good, because I was afraid you'd say no. Life has been so crazy lately. I never know what's going to happen next."

"I felt like that when I was your age. And then I kind of figured that things usually turn out just like they're supposed to. You gotta believe" — she turned her eyes heavenward — "that someone's looking out for you. Takes a lot of weight off your shoulders."

"Sure felt like that yesterday, didn't it?"

"Mm-hmm, sure did. But yesterday, it was Halo looking out for us."

"Cam was right about her. He said she was 'the one', that she was very special."

"I'd say he knew what he was talking about then."

Lise gazed at me in the rearview mirror. Her eyes crinkled. "You know, if she could talk, I'm sure she'd have a lot to tell us."

You don't know the half of it.

chapter 31

I hadn't seen Cam or Cecil's ghosts for years now. I'd like to think they were still here, watching over us all, but that they'd just run out of important things to say. Things we needed to hear.

Lise still flipped through the old photo album on days when she was alone in the house, which wasn't often, given how full the place was. She'd always pause on that picture of young Cam in his fancy cowboy hat, showing his prize steer, and say how much Hunter looked like him. Her wedding picture with Cam and another with the two of them and Hunter as a four-year old hung in the hallway at the very end, near the children's rooms. There was also one of Brad and his first wife — she'd died of pneumonia a few years before he met Lise. When the addition was done and she was debating which pictures to put up, Brad had insisted she include some of Cam. He and Lise were engaged by then, but he told her it was important to remember the people we once loved. Not to lament that they were gone, but to carry forward with all the wonderful ways their love affected us.

I couldn't have said it better myself.

Brad and Lise had their own child now. Emily was a precocious second-grader at Faderville Elementary. Like her big brother Hunter, she loved learning about animals. There was barely room on her bed for her to sleep, what with all the stuffed animals piled around her. How she emulated her big brother, followed him around during chores before he left for college. Every other day, she asked either Lise or Bernadette when he was coming home.

He was home now. Summer break. He spent most days riding around in a pickup truck with old Doc Samuels, doing farm calls, because he was going to be a veterinarian when he finished school, maybe even take over Doc Samuels' practice someday.

Today, though, Hunter had taken off from work. He was lying on the kitchen floor, squeezing my paw lightly every time I winced. His touch helped. At least until the next knife of pain stabbed deep in my belly, twisting my insides, turning them inside out. Every time that happened, my vision went all blurry. Shapes blended, went dark. Sounds came to me muffled, as if I were listening underwater.

We'd just celebrated my fifteenth birthday a few days ago. They took my picture. Sang to me. Then Bernadette served me a plate of bacon bits and scrambled eggs. Swallowing was difficult. I gagged halfway through, unable to keep them down.

It had gotten harder and harder to hang on. Not so much like I was being pushed toward death, but more like I was being pulled toward some other place. A better place. Although I found it hard to believe there was anything better than the life I'd lived. That may seem an odd thing to say, considering all I'd been through. But it was Ned Hanson's cruelty that made me appreciate Cecil's kindness even more. And Tucker Kratz's selfishness only served to highlight Bernadette's caring nature and the love of Lise and her family.

If only Ned and Tucker understood how powerful love like that was …

Hunter ran his hand down my foreleg. Spoke to me. The words sounded tinny, faraway. Something about sheep and playing ball, maybe.

He'd grown so tall, so strong. He was still quiet. Not in a shy way, but thoughtful, soft-spoken, contemplative. Animals were so easily calmed by his presence. He only had to glance at them, extend his hand and murmur a few words, and they were won over.

Lise still fretted about him, though. And for good reason. Twice since they'd come back to Faderville to live, he'd collapsed and been taken to the hospital. Last year, his heart had stopped completely. They revived him at the hospital and when he came home following his surgery, there was something different about him. Something very … tranquil.

You'd think dying like that would have made him afraid that it would happen again, but if anything he seemed less so.

"I've seen it, Halo," he had told me. "The Other Side." His eyes lit up, as if he were dreaming of visiting a faraway galaxy. At the time, we were sitting alone together on a hill overlooking the small flock of sheep that Lise kept. He plucked a yellow-faced dandelion from beside him and twirled it between his thumb and forefinger. "Dad was there. Grandpa Ray, too."

Lying back in the grass, he squinted into the sunlight. "They told me to go back."

And that was all he ever said about it.

—o0Oo—

The family was gathered in Hunter's bedroom, watching over me. I'd slept here ever since the new addition was completed, even when Hunter was away at school. In fact, I'd been allowed in any room I wanted to go in, but when it was time to go to sleep, I always chose this one. Because my place was beside Hunter. And when he wasn't here, I was waiting for him.

Brad stood just outside the doorway, rubbing Lise's shoulders. Cammie and Emily sat on the edge of the bed, holding each other tight, tears streaming down their cheeks. Tinker, no longer a kitten, was curled up in Emily's lap, looking unconcerned and all-important, as cats always do.

Behind them, Bernadette gripped the handles of her walker. "Poor girl. She must be in so much pain. I can't imagine … Well, I can, in a way."

"Honey." Lise came to Hunter, knelt beside him. "The meds don't seem to be working anymore. Do you want me to call Doc Samuels?"

For a while, he acted like he didn't hear her. He just kept on stroking my paw, his eyes on my face. Finally, "I don't think you need to."

She glanced over her shoulder at Brad. He shook his head, then motioned her out of the room.

"Come on, girls." Lise rose, held her arms out. "Let's leave them alone."

Bernadette hobbled out of the room behind them. Just as they got to the door, Cammie turned around and rushed back to me.

As she scooched down to kiss me, a single tear dripped onto my nose and slid down my muzzle. Her whispered breath tickled my whiskers. "Say 'hi' to my daddy when you see him. Tell him I love him, even though I never got to meet him."

I will. Soon.

She disappeared as a thickening fog swirled around her.

My breathing grew fainter. The whiteness of the fog grew brighter. Like sunlight glinting off snow.

I could barely keep my eyes open. I saw Hunter's arms reach out, curve around me. By the way the room moved around us, I knew he was lifting me up, even though I couldn't feel it.

I couldn't even feel the pain anymore.

But I felt the warmth flowing from his chest and arms through my body, like a tide washing over me, filling me.

The pictures in the hallway bounced past. The back door swung open. High, cottony clouds streaked across a glass-blue sky, dotted with a flock of grackles, their iridescent blues and greens flashing in the midday sun.

He laid me in the shade of a catalpa tree. From high up in the branches, I heard the faint chatter of squirrels. I had stopped stalking them years ago, although they had never stopped mocking me. I no longer cared. That was the glory of growing old. Small things that used to drive you crazy just didn't matter anymore.

Only love mattered.

Hunter sat beside me, pulled me gently to him, and lifted my head into his lap, so I could see the hills, green as the greenest green that ever was, one last time before I closed my eyes again.

And there on the hills, the sheep were all scattered about. Eating, as always.

epilogue

I see him!

My heart is ten sizes too big for my chest. It thumps so loudly that for a few moments I can't even hear him call my name.

Squatting down halfway across the bridge, Hunter throws his arms wide. He looks older than I remember. Maybe in his thirties, possibly early forties. His shoulders are broader and his chin and cheeks are covered with light scruff, like he's been too busy to shave for a couple of days.

I run to him. Great, bounding strides, the tall grass whipping across my forelegs as I leap high. My body is light as air. Gems of light sparkle in the dawn sun's corona, throwing spears of gold across the sky. Bands of fiery orange and pink streak above the horizon.

I near the banks of the river. The water, deep and wide, is so clear I can see all the way to the bottom. At the edge, I glimpse my reflection. Gone are the traces of gray around my muzzle, the cloudiness in my eyes. Ripples distort my image and I look up. He's still there. This is real.

Shaking his head, Hunter smiles faintly.

Curious, I remain where I am. "What is it?"

"There are dogs here?"

"In heaven? Of course there are. Did you ever doubt it?"

"I guess I just never thought about it. But I'm glad." Rising, he shoves his hands in his pockets, the same way he always did. A white mist curls around his legs, making it look as though he's standing on a cloud above me. "You doing okay?"

"Great!" I move onto the bridge, take one step, and then another. My toenails click on the planks as I climb the arch of the structure, bands of yellow and red and violet stretching onward beneath me.

"Halo," a deep voice calls from behind me, "come here."

"Dad?" Hunter says.

I stop, look back.

Cam waves at his son. But he doesn't approach him. He's wearing worn jeans and a white T-shirt beneath an untucked blue plaid shirt, like he's ready to go to work on the farm. Bit lies next to him, her body stretched out to warm in the morning sun.

"It's not your time," Cam says to Hunter.

"I just needed to know —"

More firmly, "You have to go back."

"Why?" The joy fades from Hunter's face. "You tell me that every time. Why can't I be here, with you?"

"Because you still have work to do. They're relying on you."

"Who is? What work? I don't understand." Creases of frustration form on Hunter's forehead. He clenches his fists at his sides.

"You will. You just have to trust me."

"But ... I'm not afraid to die." Hunter's voice grows quieter, less insistent. "I've been ready my whole life."

"I know *you* are." On the hill behind Cam, the leaves of the great oak rustle in the lightest of breezes. "But maybe heaven's not ready for you."

A spark of reluctant understanding flickers in Hunter's pupils. There's no arguing the point, he knows. More than once, I'd flirted with death, too, only to find out that it wasn't yet my time.

Hunter starts back over the bridge, away from me. The joy that had seized me a minute ago dampens.

I take a few more steps. "Hunter?"

He looks at me. "Yes?"

"When someone dies, they never stop loving you. Tell everyone that. Tell them we're waiting at the bridge, that we'll see each other again."

Several moments pass as he looks down at his feet. Then he raises his eyes. "It's so hard to wait."

If only I could make him understand that a year there is only a day here.

His eyes glisten with tears. He fights to hold them back. "It hurts not to have you with me anymore."

I understand all too well. When Cam died, my life turned upside down. When Bit was poisoned, I wanted to die, too. And when Cecil departed, a dull ache filled my chest. But always, *always* there had been someone else to love, to comfort, to discover new joys with. Sometimes, it just took awhile to figure out who.

"The hurt is trying to tell you something," I say.

"Tell me what?"

"That you still have love to share."

He glances toward the great oak, then out at the slowly flowing river. "Will the hurt go away then? I mean, if I find somebody … another dog, even?"

"Mostly. But the love … the love only grows bigger each time you spread it around. And when you come here for good — when it's time — you get to experience all that love all over again."

He says nothing at first. I wonder if he doesn't believe me. Then he nods. "I suppose that's worth waiting for then, huh?"

"It is." I smile at him. And yes, dogs do smile.

"Goodbye, Halo." He waves at me. "But not forever, right?"

"The only 'forever' is in this place. And here … there are

no goodbyes."

author's note

Halo is many dogs — a compilation of all those I have ever raised or trustingly sent off to new homes. She is the shy dog who we thought had run away, only to discover her a day later, shivering and tucked in a hole she had burrowed beneath our sidewalk, afraid to come out for fear of being reprimanded for her excavations. She is the brave and protective dog who came to my rescue when another dog bit me in a rage and wouldn't let go, the same one who wouldn't leave my bedside for two days as I recovered from my stitching up. She is the busy, thinking dog who was returned to us after being left alone in a room by herself at a young age for hours and who alleviated her boredom by ripping out drywall and starting on the electrical wires. She is the dog who was abandoned in an outdoor kennel as winter approached and visited by concerned neighbors only once a day when the owner suddenly moved to another town to care for her elderly mother without making long term plans for the animals she had collected over the years.

I cannot imagine my life without dogs in it. They have been my protectors, my uncomplaining companions, and my much under-rewarded therapists. In my youth, I was the kid who gained the trust of the neighborhood strays, much to my parents' dismay. Through patient observation, I knew when to bend down, when to offer a treat, when to extend my hand, and when not to.

Dogs give us their trust when we earn it, when we have proven we mean no harm, that we truly want to be friends. Dogs also know things about us that we do not. They sense our fears, our pains, our

295

contentment, and our joys.

They do all this without ever saying a word. They watch. They listen. They perceive what is never spoken aloud. They are always there for us, asking so little in return. We should all have more true friends like that.

When you're lucky enough to find your 'heart dog', the one whose soul is connected to your own, you realize you don't ever want to be without them. The sad fact is, however, that dogs don't live as long as we do. And so when we must say goodbye, we do so with profound sadness, knowing we're laying a piece of our hearts in the grave alongside them. Then, because we find it so hard to live without the fierce loyalty of a dog, their selflessness, and their unbridled joy for everyday things, we bring another into our lives and the cycle is repeated yet again.

The story is often told of a place called the Rainbow Bridge, where all our beloved pets wait for us until we pass over to the Other Side to join them. Whether or not such a place exists, I don't know. Nobody has ever produced proof of it. But knowing and believing are two different matters.

There are some things I do believe, however. Dogs have souls, I'm sure of it. I can see it when I look in their eyes.

acknowledgments

Heartfelt thanks go out to the members of Team Say No More, who helped bring this story to its final stages: Sarah Woodbury, Rebecca Lochlann, and Julie Conner. Special thanks to Linda Mahoney for lending her stock dog training expertise on this novel. Your wisdom, honesty and encouragement have been invaluable.

about the author

N. Gemini Sasson holds a M.S. in Biology from Wright State University where she ran cross country on athletic scholarship. She has worked as an aquatic toxicologist, an environmental engineer, a teacher and a cross country coach. A longtime breeder of Australian Shepherds, her articles on bobtail genetics have been translated into seven languages. She lives in rural Ohio with her husband, two nearly grown children and an ever-changing number of animals.

Long after writing about Robert the Bruce and Queen Isabella, Sasson learned she is a descendant of both historical figures.

If you enjoyed this book, please spread the word by sharing it on Facebook or leaving a review at your favorite online retailer or book lovers' site.

For more details about N. Gemini Sasson and her books, go to:
www.ngeminisasson.com

Or become a 'fan' at:
www.facebook.com/NGeminiSasson

You can also sign up to learn about new releases via e-mail at:
http://eepurl.com/vSA6z

Made in the USA
Columbia, SC
14 October 2020